SHAKESPEA

REX RIC

This is the first book I've written, and it's dedicated to my dad, a TV broadcaster who died pursuing the evidence proving the conspiracies in this book.

Dad if you're looking down from somewhere, I hope you enjoy it. At its heart, this tale of royal and literary conspiracy, love, murder, lost treasure, secret societies, deceit, desire and danger is your story.

It's also for N. She was my inspiration, as once I hope I was hers.

If you enjoy books by people like Dan Brown, John Grisham, Ken Follett, Bernard Cornwell, and you want a page turner with serious food for thought... I'm pretty sure you'll enjoy reading *Shakespeare's Truth*! Drop me a line and tell me what you think.

RRx
www.rexrichards.com

Copyright © 2008
Published by Thrilling Books

ISBN 978 0 956234 00 1

Manufactured in the United Kingdom
Printed and bound by CPI Cox & Wyman
Reading, RG1 8EX

Prologue

"To be or not to be, that is the question."

Hamlet

The Tower of London, 1554

The guard fixed his gaze on the flickering torch at the end of the stone passageway and started to count to ten. Before he reached six, another scream erupted from the cell behind him.

He restarted his count. This time he reached three. Fresh howls of pain ripped through the air and he tried to not to imagine what was going on behind the bleak door.

Inside the cell, the woman lay exhausted on the straw bed, the smell of stale sweat heavy in the air. The pain was so fierce she was barely aware of the three women surrounding her in the fragile candlelight. One of the women grasped her hand whispering instructions, another knelt in front of her splayed legs and the third muttered prayers.

She could feel the baby wanting to escape from the prison of her womb. She screamed again as she followed the midwife's instructions and pushed. As the baby was coaxed out into the world, she saw it for the first time. Its eyes were tightly closed against the rude interruption. She too closed her eyes, the emotions that flooded through her left her terrified.

Elizabeth wanted desperately to see her son and to hold him in her arms, but she knew that would never be.

As the child burst into life and screamed its presence to the world, she felt as if a needle had been slid into her heart. She was the daughter of King Henry VIII to the executed Ann Boleyn, and was currently held prisoner in the Tower of London by her treacherous half-sister Mary who had stolen the throne in her place.

Elizabeth believed her destiny was to be Queen Elizabeth of England, head of the House of Tudor. If she could survive the Tower, her chance to become Queen could come. But if the Church ever discovered she had given birth in a prison cell and that the father was already married and a commoner, she would never leave these walls alive, let alone take the throne.

For the sake of England, Elizabeth knew her baby would have to be a secret never to be admitted to anyone, not even to herself.

Act 1: Scene One

*"Out, out brief candle! life's but a walking
shadow, a poor player that struts and frets
his time upon the stage and then is heard
no more."*

Macbeth

18th December 2009, 5.00 am

Sunbeams slid through the bare branches of the trees of Hyde Park and settled on the cold stone of a small, delicate statue of Peter Pan. The stone figure had been carved to look full of life and youth and seemed exuberant, ready to leap off its plinth and fly through the air to welcome in the cold dawn.

Sitting on the harsh concrete, with his back propped up against the base of the statue, was an English prince. He was stripped to the waist. His arms hung loosely at his side, and it was with a huge effort the young man lifted his head up, forcing himself to try to take in the beauty of the morning. The sun rose, cutting through the branches of the wizened oak trees and into his eyes. The scent of damp grass was tainted with a faint sourness. Blood.

He tilted his head and look down. Matted blood highlighted the horrific cuts in his chest, a dozen or so deep slashes made by a cruel hand armed with a lethal blade. Blood dripped rhythmically onto the concrete floor around the statue, a slow tattoo beating out the last moments of his life. The cuts formed two words. He tried to think, what could they mean? But constant waves of pain made it impossible to hold any thoughts for more than a few fractured seconds. He gave up on the words, knowing he was dying, and tried to think back on his brief life, had he done what was expected of him?

What were the thoughts he wanted to treasure? His mother, dressed in white, the joy in her eyes all those years ago... flashing multicoloured lights and his kid brother's wild dancing at last night's party... that text from his girlfriend, her funny tan lines after that first holiday in Belize at the Bella Maya Resort in Placencia... his father's voice last week as he tried to persuade him to come up with the family for a stag hunt at Balmoral...

But then another image surfaced in his mind. The face of his attacker. There had been such burning hatred in the man's eyes as the knife had bitten into his skin.

After it was finally over the man had leant in close, hot breath brushing his cheek. "You have no right to be here. No right to your life. I'm taking it all away from you. And when you die, a new destiny will be born."

As the sun rose, the city of London emerged from its sleep and stretched into life; unaware that the future king of England, His Royal Highness Prince William, had died alone.

Act 1: Scene Two

"Now is the winter of our discontent."

Richard III

Jonny, the Head of Client Services, was in full flow and his regulation shaved bald head bobbed up and down inside his regulation black shirt.

"Car parking is an exciting business. It's full of challenges, rewards and passion. How about this?" As he spoke he lifted his hands in front of his face as if forming the words in the air. "We don't just like what we do. We love what we do. We're passionate about car parks."

Dan watched his boss, trying not to laugh. The remorseless marketing double talk pinned the three clients from Heathrow Airport Car Parking Services into their chairs. Jonny had used the same basic pitch last week to Cadbury on the launch of their new range of organic premiere milk chocolate and the week before to the glorified burger bar TGI Friday's. Next week's meetings with Victoria's Secret and the Ministry of Trade would no doubt unveil the same miraculous conclusion.

Although there were aspects of his job Dan loved, such as being asked to dream up ground breaking ideas for advertising campaigns, he hated all the hot air and spin. But, he was good at it, and it was a fair living.

They were sitting in a glass walled meeting room. On the other side of the office a goggle eyed lump was gawping at him. It was the star of the show, a catfish called Eric who lived in the huge aquarium at the centre of the busy marketing agency Big Fish Branding. Dan felt a peculiar affinity with Eric. They were both foreigners trying to adapt to the English way of life. In Dan's case, he was an American working as a creative director in London; in Eric's case he had been scooped out of an African river before ending up in London via three months on a ship and a pet shop.

As Jonny talked, Dan's mind wandered from the meeting, contemplating instead why Eric was flapping about in such a listless manner. He guessed that having Deep Dish Doughnuts as a client and an account team always dropping crumbs into Eric's tank might be part of the problem. Dan's reflection stared back at him from the meeting room windows and he wondered whether he was in better or worse condition than Eric. His dark hair, grey eyes and high cheekbones looked good from a distance. Yet up close it was a different matter. His pale skin and black rings under his eyes signalled too many hours working late at the computer. It had been a demanding few months.

"I've got it," continued Jonny. "We need a positioning statement for the car parks, something positive so that people can see that you're not just converting that meadow at Terminal 2 into a car park for no reason. It's there to provide a better service to your customers who want the convenience of a nine minute bus ride to the terminal and cost effective parking solutions. How about this for a strap line?" He held up his arms as if visualising a biblical scene in front of the clients. "Space to grow." He paused for dramatic effect. "More spaces for parking, and with some of the meadow preserved, plants can still grow."

"But the central p-part of our business projections is to optimise the land use. Err... we... we don't see the need to keep any of the meadows. Each space we don't exploit costs us significant r-revenues." The perspiring rotund face of the senior client Derek leaned forward across the faux Formica table. His profile cut into the beam from the projector and created shadows on top of the PowerPoint presentation that looked like a hippo sitting on a toilet. Derek's tie strayed dangerously close to his glass of sparkling water and came to rest on the plate of melting chocolate biscuits.

Marnie the Kiwi girl was the other member of the Big Fish branding team in the room. Derek, in his usual cold bullying way, pointed at her. "You've been v-very quiet, what do you think the key issue is for us here?" Dan could see Marnie jump, there was no way that she would know anything about this presentation. She was even fresher off the boat than him in London and had only been drafted in to the meeting to make up numbers. Her face turned crimson.

"Aaaah well, I er..." she mumbled.

Dan cut in. "Funny you should ask. Marnie was saying only yesterday it would be great PR if you could preserve some of the meadows in the new parking lots. The green lobby would love you. Who knows, they might even park their electric cars there when they're going on holiday." Dan leaned forward and clicked the mouse button on the Apple laptop, launching a hypnotic animation and the next part of the presentation:

Additional Revenues from Airport Car Parking Perceptions of Profit.

"Letting people park up is just the start," said Dan. "We want to talk about what happens next, when people are in the airport and on the plane. We've put together an in-depth proposal on how you can increase income with extra services and keep a section of the meadow to satisfy the environmentalists."

Jonny winked slyly at him and took over. "We're talking mobile dry cleaning services. How handy would that be when you've parked your car? We're talking advertising revenues inside car parks. We're talking about weevils. A colony inside a section of meadow we'll preserve, right in the middle of the world's first ecologically sound, carbon neutral, solar powered, pro-green and highly profitable car park."

Jonny was interrupted by a delicate knock on the door and Heidi the office manager came in bearing cups of coffee, pain au chocolat and doughnuts. It was all going terribly well and everyone took a ten minute break. Dan stood up to stretch his legs, and leaving the clients chatting headed back to his desk to check his email.

Heathrow Airport wasn't Dan's only regular client. On average he had to deal with about eight or ten, all of whom thought they were the most important people in his life. Every spare moment to catch up was essential. There were three new emails from Heathrow, all making last minute additions to the meeting agenda. Predictably the clients had forgotten all about them. Dan raced over his other emails, clicking on one from his mom in San Diego. She was asking what he wanted for Christmas, which was still a couple of weeks away, so off his radar. He dashed off a reply to her, explaining that yes, everything was okay and yes, he could look after himself in London. After all he was in his mid-thirties. Then another email caught his eye.

Subject: Destiny Sent: 18 December 2009 09:46:21
To: Dan Knight (CD)
(dan@bigfishbranding.co.uk)

Dan Knight of San Diego – your destiny waits.

http://www.nextkingofengland.com

His finger hovered over the delete button, but something stopped him. The email didn't look like ordinary spam. This was different. The sender knew his name. That wasn't unusual in itself, but the fact they also knew his home town seemed strange. Dan read the email address; it was a *No reply*. He knew the virus paranoid IT director Marco would hate the idea, but Dan decided to break the rules. He clicked through to the website. It linked to the video website YouTube and a window popped up on his screen. There was a low quality blurry image of a street late at night. To Dan it looked like security camera footage. The date stamp showed it was from last night. The video showed trees, streetlights and a couple of parked cars. A black cab passed by. Dan kept watching and after perhaps a minute, a man with his arm flopped over the shoulder of his girlfriend flickered over the screen. Then a limousine drove past. Another thirty seconds passed and another man appeared on the screen. He was tall, reasonably young and well dressed. He walked with his back to camera but just for a split second he turned and looked up at the camera. Dan had to stop himself gasping out loud.

The image that flashed in the camera lens was blurry but he was sure that just for the briefest moment he was looking at his own face. The video still had another six minutes to run but Dan's mind was spinning.

It wasn't him. He had been at home all night.

Suddenly strong hands grabbed him from behind and span him round in his chair.

"Those weevils are waiting," said Jonny, "don't disappoint them. Get back to the meeting."

Act 1: Scene Three

"The evil that men do lives after them."

Julius Caesar

"You're a fucking disgrace to this family. What sort of attitude do you call that? Call yourself a Fletcher? Consider yourself my worthy daughter? You're a fool." The old man's thin, long face had been thrust forward, his whole body twisted in rage.

It had been months ago but the words echoed in her mind.

Fiona was in the main lecture auditorium at University College London when the unwelcome memory had surfaced. Today was a big day for her, an introductory lecture to a new course that she had designed. She had hoped that a few minutes of quiet contemplation before her students arrived would focus her mind on the upcoming lecture. Instead she found herself huddled in the deafening silence, paralysed by the ghosts of the past.

It had been early September and she had been at her parent's house for the weekend. Throughout the visit her father had followed her and her mother everywhere, talking incessantly but vaguely about his new research. Every hour or two, Fiona had asked him to sit with her and talk through what he had uncovered. Every time he had refused, telling her it wasn't a safe enough place to reveal his secrets.

Then on the Sunday afternoon, as she was wheeling her Triumph Bonneville motorbike out from the garage to head back to London, he had appeared in front of her. It was then, just as she was leaving, that he insisted she listen to his discoveries. She told him she didn't have the time, she was late.

His response was to explode with anger. "How dare you treat my work like that? You would be nothing without me. Do you hear me? Nothing. How can you claim Shakespeare's of no interest? Who the hell do you think you are? Why don't you go back to London, to your pathetic ignorant runts, your chattering classes students? You're not wanted here. And look at the way you dress, Fiona. It's a disgrace," he had screamed. "You're no daughter of mine, why can't you be more like your brother? You don't see him coming up here in dirty jeans looking like a ghastly hippy."

"You don't see him here at all," she muttered.

"What was that? Don't you answer me back girl. Don't you damn dare talk back to me."

Three of his front teeth were missing and he hadn't shaven properly for days. Tufts of wiry grey hair were massing under his chin and the veins stood out on his neck. In hindsight Fiona knew that was the moment she should have realised how bad things were. But as it was, on that day, she had wanted nothing more than to escape.

Yet within minutes of being on the road through the beautiful Cotswold countryside, she had pulled over and burst into tears. She beat her thighs with her gloved fists and threw her helmet onto the grass verge in frustration. She was overwhelmed with a sense of guilt at leaving her mother on her own, but the desire to run away and get back to her own life had won out.

But just one week later, when Fiona was back in London, something had changed in her father's brain. His fragile hold on reality had finally shattered, he had lost control and as a result her mother had nearly died. Months later, Fiona was still plagued by guilt. She knew her father's violence had been a result of his illness, but all the books in the world about psychosis and schizophrenia couldn't stop her hating him for what he had done and herself for not being there.

Fiona's mobile phone buzzed in her bag, dragging her back to reality. There was a message from her best friend Nicky, a mature student at the University.

```
Good luck honey! Coffee later? Nx
```

There was a sudden commotion as the main doors to the auditorium were pushed open and her students flooded in. She made her way up to the lectern and waited for the students to settle down. On the lectern was a heavy medieval book she had chosen for this introductory lecture, and her laptop. She carefully opened the book at the page she had marked. The musty pages offered a familiar comfort.

She composed herself for a moment, looking out over the crowd. She leant forward into the microphone. "Hello everyone, my name is Fiona." She paused, waiting for the students to fall silent. "Welcome to this introductory lecture titled, 'Secret Histories, the Science of Secrecy'. I'd like to thank you guys for showing up and hope you'll get enough of a buzz out of my lecture to sign up to this history module. To kick things off I'm going to read you a quote." She leant over and began to read. "Suppose that a famous weaver of magnificent cloth always presented to the world designs that people recognised as his own. Then, suppose if you were to examine in more detail the very weave of the cloth, and in truth saw it revealed a different design, from a different weaver."

She closed the book and looked up. "Now I doubt anyone here can tell me who said that, but you might have an idea what they were talking about?" As she expected there was total silence. She continued. "That quote was from a guy called Sir Francis Bacon. To those of you who don't know, Sir Francis Bacon was nothing to do with an English breakfast." There was a snigger from the crowd. "He was known to his friends as the 'jewelled mind', because of his intellect. He's been dead for quite some time now; he lived at the same time as Queen Elizabeth the first, so over 400 years ago. As well as being a spy and politician, he was a world expert at the art and science of secrecy, developing many new techniques, some of which we'll be checking out. That quote is from a book he wrote explaining something fundamental about how secret communications work." She walked over to her laptop and pressed play on the video player. "If you can get your heads around this next bit you'll understand what the course is all about."

A giant screen behind Fiona flashed into life showing a montage of images from the modern world: mobile phones, fax machines, television, postmen, radio, satellites. She talked over the top of it.

"Imagine life in the sixteenth century. There was no television, no internet or computers, cars, trains, planes, faxes, post offices or even a police service. You couldn't pick up the phone and you certainly couldn't send an e-mail. If you had information that was important, the only way to get it anywhere was with someone on a horse, unless you wanted to walk. Think how long it would have taken to get from one end of the country to the other on a horse. Hundreds of years ago, it was as difficult and time consuming to get from London to Manchester as flying round the world is today. Mind you, in those days most of them thought the earth was flat."

"You what? You mean it isn't?" The voice came from the audience, followed by a burst of laughter. Fiona followed the sound, spotting a smart looking British Pakistani boy sat amongst a group of similar students who had enough hair gel between them to be classified as an industrial accident. Fiona suspected he was the leader of the group.

"So what's your name?" Fiona asked.

"Mohammed. Mo to my mates."

"Okay Mo. Let's imagine you're in Elizabethan times. You've got some secret information you need to get to somebody, the problem is that he's a week's journey away by horse. How would you hide the information so it didn't get intercepted on the way?"

"You could shove it up the horse's arse?" Everyone laughed.

"Nice idea Mo, but I'm not sure you would ever get

it back, let alone be able to read it. No, think a bit more laterally. In the ideal world, the courier doesn't even know they are carrying secrets in the first place." A look of confusion flashed over Mo's face, but Fiona could see one of his crew smiling. He was a stocky youth in a Bolton Wanderers football shirt. She turned to him. "Yes. You. Go on, what do you think?"

"I'm thinking, like that guy said in that book, if you can hide the stuff inside something else, like another message that look innocent, no-one gonna know it there in the first place."

Fiona was impressed. "Yes, spot on. That's exactly what we're going to learn about; ciphers, the technique of hiding a message within another message. This wasn't just something that aristocrats used to send their mistresses sordid love notes. It's been a vital tool used by governments and royalty for hundreds of years. Who's heard of the Enigma machines?" This time there were more nods. "Enigma was a German cipher machine that the Nazis used in World War Two to tell their U-boat submarines where our naval fleet was operating. Ciphers and codes at one point controlled the future of the world. If we hadn't been able to crack those codes, Hitler would probably have won the Second World War and we would all be goose stepping down Oxford Street. Internet security works essentially the same way, but that's the tip of the iceberg. There are hidden codes and meanings in almost everything from the designs on banknotes, great works of art, barcodes and..."

Fiona stopped abruptly. There was a commotion at

the back of the room. A student had run in and was talking excitedly to the students on the back benches. A Mexican wave of chatter cascaded through the students. Fiona called the newcomer down to the front. "What's going on? Why'd you interrupt my class?" The student who arrived was red-faced and perspiring, her eyes wild with excitement. "Haven't you heard?" The girl's voice was shrill, almost a scream. "No, of course. I'm sorry, I'm sure you haven't. It's Prince William. He's dead. It's on the internet. A video. It's horrible. It's like a horror movie. If it's true, if he's dead, then he must have been murdered."

Act 1: Scene Four

*"Now cracks a noble heart. Good night
sweet Prince, and flights of angels sing
thee to thy rest."*

Hamlet

The two men faced the row of oversized steel drawers that covered the wall of the cold room. The constant hum of industrial refrigeration units was broken by occasional clicks from harsh strip lighting and the frigid air had an acidic aroma that lingered in the memory of the room's visitors for days afterwards.

Inspector Brian Sawyer, a squat and heavyset man with curly black receding hair and small dark eyes, leant forward and pulled at one of handles on the wall. The drawer slid open easily, revealing the form of a body covered in a white sheet. Waves of chemically refrigerated air flowed into the room. Sawyer rolled back the sleeve of his dull brown suit and pulled the sheet back to reveal the cold naked body of Prince William.

The two men looked down at the corpse. Neither spoke. The taller man was middle aged, blond haired and blue-eyed with a naturally warm expression. He was dressed immaculately in an understated navy blue suit. On seeing the body he staggered forward, catching the metal tray with one hand to steady himself. He dragged his eyes away from the face and sighed deeply.

"I can positively identify the deceased as His Royal

Highness. Now I trust with that unpleasant formality out of the way you will allow me to take possession of the body and make arrangements?"

Inspector Sawyer looked over at his companion. He didn't quite know what to make of the Major. He was the head of Royal Security at Buckingham Palace and by all accounts a *very* close friend of the Royal Family. Inspector Sawyer had been told by his bosses, in voices reedy with panic, that this man had total authority in this case. He, a mere Inspector in Special Branch of the London Metropolitan Police, was simply there to do this man's bidding. This annoyed the hell out of Sawyer.

"Major Barnes-Jones this is a murder investigation. We're going to perform an autopsy."

The Major had seemed lost in thought as he stared at the body, but snapped upright as Sawyer spoke. "There will be no police autopsy. This is the body of the man who should have become King of England. For God's sake do you have no respect?" The flash of anger on the Major's face disappeared. "Now that I have made a positive identification of the body, from this point forward this investigation is to be under the jurisdiction of Royal Security."

Sawyer looked down at the body with a sense of wonder. Despite all of his security and protection, the most privileged and important young man in the country lay dead in front of him. He couldn't begin to imagine the fallout.

The murder of the heir to the throne was going to be the most scandalous event in living memory, perhaps outweighing the death of his mother in the public conscience. The Inspector felt that he had only just recovered from the ordeal of the London 7/7 terror bombings, but here it was starting all over again – sixteen hour days, constant stress and the inevitable arguments with his wife.

Sawyer's eyes flicked over the Prince's body, making a mental note of the visible wounds. The face had been left untouched. Instead the attacker had concentrated on the torso. Deep gouges ran across the whole of the rib cage and stomach. Black blood had congealed at the edges of the wounds adding a macabre outline to the cuts, making them stand out against the pale skin.

At first glance the cuts had seemed random. But once he had seen past the dried blood which covered the Prince's chest, Sawyer realised there was nothing random about it.

The cuts formed crude words.

SHALL DISSOLVE

"Shall dissolve? You can see that too?"

"Yes." The Major had been watching Inspector Sawyer closely, trying to work out exactly what sort of man he was dealing with. He trusted his instincts, they had saved his life on more than one occasion. At first glance the police officer portrayed the image of being nothing more than a gorilla in a cheap suit. Having spent time with him, the Major was sure Sawyer was a capable, professional and experienced man. "Have you had any time to speculate as to what it may mean?"

"If you mean why did the nut who did this decide to use the Prince's chest as his notepad? No, I haven't had time to speculate. Not that I would ever speculate. In fact at this point, as this is under the Official Secrets Act and your authority is denying me any opportunity to officially examine the body, it's not going to be easy to speculate." Sawyer could feel his anger starting to come out and forced himself to calm. "In any case there was the matter this morning of taking down that video."

"Yes. Thank you for your actions. Scotland Yard's internet security team is to be complimented on acting so promptly and with such efficiency."

"I'll pass that on."

"This is no longer a police investigation. I need your assurance that no copies of the video exist."

"None of us have one," replied Sawyer honestly. "Can I ask you a question, Major?"

"If it's relevant."

"How did you let this happen? How did Prince William end up on this slab?"

"Inspector Sawyer, you'll be advised in due course of the role that the police will play. Now, we must go up to your office and sign over ownership of the Prince. The Royal household is taking this matter extremely personally and it is my duty to begin to seek resolution as soon as possible."

Act 1 : Scene Five

"Something wicked this way comes."

Macbeth

A crash reverberated through the building and Dan woke up, startled, staring into the semi darkness. He glanced at his alarm clock. The green figures showed 5 am. He groaned.

When he had first arrived in London and looked at the map, Shepherd's Bush had seemed to make sense as somewhere to live. The Georgian style building had appealed with its stucco fronted exterior, retro art deco interior and polished wooden floors. However, that was before he had realised that away from upmarket areas like Chelsea and Mayfair, London was a sea of police sirens at night. Directly below him in a flat designed for two people lived six Australians. Three or four nights a week he was convinced that his floor was about to disintegrate into dust as the vibrations from the jackhammer sound system started up once again and the Australian party animals set about destroying their cage. This was in stark contrast to the Manhattan flat he had left. It had been higher up, in a more exclusive area and much quieter. Perhaps if he hadn't been in such a rush to get over here and get away from his old life, he might have done some more research. He sighed. This place was a crushing reality check compared to his old haven overlooking the East River. Had he been right to leave? Why did he always feel the need to head off into the sunset and never settle anywhere?

As he lay awake in the darkness, his mind turned back to the brief flash of what could have been his face in the video he had been emailed. He had wanted to go back to it, but work had been so insane he hadn't had time to draw breath. Jonny had insisted on sending out the proposal to the clients that night, resulting in the team working until midnight. He'd got back home exhausted.

But now he was awake, the video started praying on his mind. Dan rolled out of bed, slipped on a pair of shorts and a T-shirt and staggered through to the living room. He sat down in front of his laptop and turned it on. While the system booted up, he looked out of the small metal framed windows and tried to admire the view of Shepherd's Bush Road. His eyes flicked along the motley collection of newsagents, Halal butchers and expensive convenience stores crowding the busy street. At this hour their ugliness was masked by the fluorescent glow from the street lights. The computer finally booted into life. Dan opened the e-mail.

> Subject: Destiny Sent: 18 December 2009
> 09:46:21
> To: Dan Knight (CD)
> (dan@bigfishbranding.co.uk)
>
> Dan Knight of San Diego – your destiny waits.
>
> http://www.nextkingofengland.com

Dan could feel pricks of sweat breaking out under his arms as he clicked on the link. The email software launched his Firefox web browser and he felt his pulse rising as the software searched for the video. He hunched forward in anticipation, but an error message flashed onto the screen, informing him that the page no longer existed. He slumped back, feeling a mixture of relief and anticlimax.

He stood up and started to walk over to the kitchen to get some water. As he moved across the room, he focused on something pushed under the front door. He frowned and walked over to have a closer look. He stooped down. It looked like some sort of thin black tube. The object was metal and had a thick glass end, like a lens. He put out a hand to touch it.

It shot backwards, disappearing under the door.

In the same instant there was a deafening crash and the door's lock splintered in the frame as a huge weight forced it inwards at tremendous speed. The door crunched into Dan's forehead, throwing him backwards onto the floor. Before he could react, three figures dressed in black and wearing balaclavas glided into the room. The largest of the invaders instantly landed a savage kick in Dan's ribs.

The breath was blasted from Dan's body and he collapsed onto his knees. Blood oozed into his eyes from the wound on his forehead, his vision blurred as an intense pain shot through his head. He thought he was going to vomit. He tried to get to his feet, flailing his arms around for support. Another precise kick, this time across his head. Dan collapsed back onto the floor as the man who had delivered the two kicks grabbed his arm and twisted it behind his back.

"Finish it," the man said.

Dan opened his mouth to scream but a white cloth was clamped over his face. He could feel resistance melting away as a chemical vapour flooded into his nose and throat. His mind was slipping into darkness. Within a few seconds he was unconscious.

Act 2: Scene One

"Cry 'havoc,' and let slip the dogs of war."

Julius Caesar

19th December

It wasn't until lunchtime the day after the rumour had broken that Fiona and her friend Nicky were finally able to see the video for themselves. Together with eight of Fiona's students, they had gathered in a bedroom in the halls of residence. The small room smelt of stale bodies. The computer was being operated by a nervous first-year student. He was perched on a stool in front of his desk, hemmed in by the crowd.

"Look, take it easy you lot. I'm starting to get sick of this. You're absolutely the last bunch, okay? I'm starting to feel like some kind of bloody rubbernecker. I've only still got it because I haven't left the web page. Everyone else who closed down their browser will have lost it. Someone's done a sweet number getting rid of it. I can't copy it, there are some really sweet codecs flashed in that make all the usual download tools useless, but I've taken screenshots and I'm going to Facebook those. But this whole thing is freaking me out. Do you think the government might come after me if I do that?"

At last the student stopped complaining, fumbled with the computer mouse and the video started playing.

Fiona's first impression was of a montage of clips, taken from security cameras all pointing at the same tree lined street. In each shot there was either a vehicle going past or somebody walking. It was dark and there wasn't much to see. Then the picture suddenly changed. It was still late at night but now the camera was no longer in the street, instead it was pointing at a small statue.

"Shit, I recognise that. It's the Peter Pan statue in Hyde Park! Shit, my mum lives near there in Notting Hill," cried one of the students. As the group watched, the picture suddenly shook then settled.

"I reckon that's one of the cameras being positioned somewhere," babbled their host. "It zooms in and out. It changes in a minute to another camera. It's a hand held one, like a mobile, a small wireless unit probably. I'm guessing one or two megapixel resolution."

"Shut up Martin, you tool," said one of the other boys. "This isn't an episode of 24. Jack Bauer isn't about to roll out from under the bed and whack you off. Just let us watch the thing."

For a minute or so nothing happened. The camera just pointed at the statue. Then from the corner of the screen, a shape slowly emerged into view. It was a man, dressed in a dark red robe, a hood covering his face. The man was moving slowly. He was dragging something heavy. A small distinctive design was printed on the front of the robe. Fiona's heart jumped. She recognised it immediately. Then her hand flew to her mouth as the figure's burden came into view. It was the lifeless body of a young man, naked from the waist up. The man in the robe grabbed the limp body by the shoulders and heaved it into a sitting position against the Peter Pan statue.

The view switched to the hand held camera, the image was distorted and blurred as it swung wildly about. Abruptly, the image cut so the face of the young man could be clearly seen. The cramped room erupted with screams. It was Prince William.

The camera froze briefly on the Prince's face, then jumped and cut back to the other view which was now focused on the chest. It was red, covered with flowing blood running down his arms and torso, before dripping onto the ground. Fiona saw a pattern of cuts underneath the blood.

"Oh my God!" shouted one of the girls. "It says... what does it say... Shall something?"

"Jesus, you're right! What was it? I missed it?" said another girl.

"It says 'shall dissolve' I think," said the boy using the computer.

"What does it mean?"

"Crap knows. I've Googled it, but there are thousands of possibles."

Fiona gasped. She had seen the words before. A very long time ago.

The camera jumped back once again to the Prince's face. There was no movement. Suddenly, as they watched, his eyes flicked opened and the room erupted in more screams. He was still alive! She felt a body moving close to her. It was Nicky. Fiona instinctively reached out and hugged her crying friend.

Act 2: Scene Two

"And thus I clothe my naked villany,
with odd old ends stol'n out of holy writ,
And seem a saint, when most I play the
devil."

Richard III

Inspector Sawyer leaned back in his office chair in Scotland Yard and started jotting down notes, recalling as much of the content of the video as he could before the details faded. He wondered what the Major was going to do about it. Explain it away somehow or come out in the open and admit Prince William had been murdered? For the hundredth time he wished he hadn't listened to the bigwigs upstairs and had been smart enough to keep an illegal copy of the video.

The Inspector's mobile had been ringing constantly since the video had been removed from the internet. Several journalists from the more sensationalist papers had heard rumours or seen the video and Sawyer's *'no comment'* reply was starting to wear thin, even to him. The Major was too busy to speak to him directly and a Brigadier Peters was acting as official liaison between the Major's Royal Security teams and Scotland Yard.

Sawyer's mobile phone beeped as a new text arrived. He glanced at the display and immediately thrust the small phone into his pocket, ignoring the journalist's message. He stood up and walked out into the busy main office. The harsh lights, ringing phones and the bustle of the station flooded over him. He checked his watch. He still had ten minutes before he needed to give his team their weekly briefing in the main incident room. Everyone knew something extraordinary had happened, but nobody knew quite what. Sawyer was still unsure what he was going to say in the briefing. He could feel his mobile vibrating again. He sighed, pulling the damn thing from his pocket. It was Brigadier Peters.

"Can you keep it brief Brigadier?"

"I'm advising you that the Royal Press Office has decided to go public on the death of the Prince. The news embargo will be lifted at 6 pm." The clipped military tones on the other end of the line showed no signs of wanting to be anything but brief.

"What about the video? Is there going to be any mention of that? What's the official cause of death? Shouldn't you be consulting with Scotland Yard on the best strategy for releasing the news?"

"Calm yourself, Inspector. The two police officers who discovered the body have been interviewed and we're satisfied they will not compromise the cover story. However, I need your assurance that there is nobody else there that knows about the video or has any other information."

"I am calm." Sawyer could feel his voice rising. "I told the Major the officers had the sense to call it in as an unidentified body. When you say that you've come up with a cover story, what exactly do you mean?"

"The second point that I would like to raise is in relation to the online dissemination of the video. This situation is not entirely under control."

"What do you mean? My men performed miracles getting that video offline."

"I'm afraid it's a little more complicated than that. International websites have been publishing rumours. It's become the bloggers' hot topic of the day. You may have managed to prevent the video from redistribution on YouTube, but screenshots of His Royal Highness are appearing everywhere. I myself have received two e-mails with the same image, a close-up of the face accompanied by a lurid description of the video. The blogosphere is getting obsessed with this phrase 'shall dissolve'. It's in danger of getting out of control."

"I get the picture. We'll get on it."

"We feel your assurances that you could control the material online were extremely naive. As a result, we have had to develop an emergency strategy." Brigadier Peters' voice had taken on an acid edge.

"Look, I'm an old-fashioned policeman. I don't know the details of all this techno stuff." Sawyer cursed to himself. Why was he apologising to this prick?

"No matter. From this point forward you need no longer concern yourself with this issue. Our technology teams have assumed control of the online threat."

"So you've cut us out of that too?"

"Now back to the strategy. There will be a statement tonight from the Royal Household announcing the tragic death of His Royal Highness. The existence of the video will not yet be commented on. We will make it plain to any news organisation that raises the issue that it is not to be mentioned out of sensitivity to the family.

We will explain later that the video is clearly a malicious fake."

"What are you going to say?"

"The official position we will be taking is that the Prince was a victim in a catastrophic road accident. We will say that he was returning from a public function with his bodyguard when he was hit by an out of control speeding driver in the vicinity of Hyde Park. He died almost instantly."

"An RTA? Are you crazy? That's going to create even more questions. This isn't a bloody soap opera."

"Given the circumstances, there are very few ways in which a young man can die accidentally in London that would lead to the police being involved, roads being closed and a major park being cordoned off." The Brigadier paused briefly. "The most important aspect of the situation is to minimise any possible public aggravation. The one impossible course of action would be to publicly state the Prince was brutally murdered and mutilated. I am sure you can see the veracity of that."

"You want to minimise public aggravation with something as weak as that?"

"Yes, and that leads us on quite conveniently to the final part of our discussion. It is absolutely essential to give the appearance to the public that the culprit will soon be brought to justice. As a result, the role of the London Metropolitan Police has been reassigned. Your team at Special Branch will be leading an investigation to apprehend the, as yet unknown, hit and run driver. You are not now or at any point to comment in any way on the video. The Prince died in an accident. Public safety depends upon this perception. Do I make myself understood?" The phone fell silent. "Inspector, are you still there? It is essential that you comply."

"I understand," said Sawyer. "The Palace doesn't want the world to know that the future King of England was murdered. Yet you expect people to believe that a fake video of him dying from someone cutting words into his chest, around the same time he was supposed to be hit by a car, is just a fucking coincidence?"

"Congratulations, Inspector. You appear to have hit the nail on the head. I am sure you will see there is a certain poetic irony to the situation. Of course this won't be the first time that the Palace has had to adapt a story of a Royal death in a road accident."

"You're talking about the boy's mother."

"The video will be explained, if required, as the work of a sick minded individual looking to dramatise a sad occurrence for his own perverted pleasure. Please cancel your briefing and inform your team that new orders are to be posted. Develop a brief for this investigation and send it over to me for approval."

"So do you have a fall guy lined up for us? How do we go about looking for someone for a crime that didn't happen?"

"Put plans in place as you would do normally to find a hit-and-run driver. We'll provide you with all the evidence you need to create a convincing story. I'm sure you'll flush out some interesting characters and as is usual I believe, plenty of people will come forward with bogus stories saying that they are the guilty party."

"That's just great. Meanwhile you continue with the real investigation into the murder? And leave us out in the cold." Sawyer replied bitterly.

"This is a private matter. From this point forward, it is to be handled internally by the Royal Family. This has been cleared as a course of action by all relevant parties, including the Prime Minister. Believe it or not, Inspector, the British Royal Family does have quite a history of resolving such matters without external help. You may have noticed that we do have access to military and security personnel and involve the police purely at our own discretion. Much as we appreciate your efforts to date, they are no longer required." There was a click and the line went dead.

Act 2: Scene three

*"O! it is excellent to have a giant's
strength. But it is tyrannous to use it like a
giant."*

Measure for Measure

The first thing he was aware of was a constant rumbling noise, occasional hissing, and a stench of oil. Dan opened his eyes. Slowly, as his eyes got used to the low light, he could start to take in his surroundings. He was in a long thin room, about twelve feet wide, a small rectangular window high above let in meagre shafts of light. The room was almost unbearably hot. Two huge pipes ran the length of one wall. They were bolted down at intervals. It was obvious they were the source of the noise and the stifling heat.

He was sitting in an old wooden chair. He tried to lift his hands but it was impossible. He strained his neck to look down and saw that his wrists and feet were tied to the chair. He tried leaning forwards but a wave of nausea shot through him.

As the feeling of sickness began to subside, it was replaced by a sensation of rising panic. His mind kept returning to the email and video link; it was the only connection he could make, but it made no sense. If only he had had time to watch it.

"Calm down. You've got to stay calm. It's just a mistake. Everything will be alright," Dan mumbled to himself, trying to keep a lid on the panic.

As his eyes became accustomed to the low light he became aware that there was someone else in the room with him. He could distinguish the outline of a body tied up and slumped in a chair at the far end, near another door.

"Hello." Dan's voice was cracked and dry. "Hello. Can you hear me? Who are you? Hey! Can you hear me?" There was no response. "Hey!" He shouted louder.

The exertion made him feel dizzy and he stopped to draw breath. As he steadied himself, the figure opposite slowly began to raise its head. Strip lights on the ceiling flickered into life. With a flash, the whole room filled with a brilliant white light and at the same time a deafening orchestral crescendo crashed in from speakers.

Dan snapped his head back in astonishment, sending a fresh bolt of pain through his body. It only took him a few seconds for the familiar tune to register - *God Save The Queen*.

Looking over at his companion Dan was shocked to see an elderly lady, dressed in country clothes: jodhpurs, Wellington boots and a heavy green coat. Silver tape had been placed over her mouth. Dan stared at her. He looked on in incredulity as he realised that sitting, bound to a chair, looking exhausted and older than he would have expected was Queen Elizabeth II of England.

As suddenly as it had started, the music cut off and the door behind Dan opened. He could see the Queen staring hard at whoever had entered the room. Three men came into Dan's view, walking past him and positioning themselves behind the Queen. They stood facing Dan, dressed in black belted robes with blood red hoods covering the top halves of their faces. On their robes a badge could clearly be seen, a red rose set in a golden cross.

They were all armed with guns and one of the kidnappers had an ornate dagger hanging from his belt. Dan could see enough of their faces to realise that they were clean-shaven and of white European origin. The largest of the three men was directly behind the Queen. The man then slowly raised his grey pistol, pointing it directly at the Queen's head.

"Who are you? What do you want with us?" Dan's voice was on the edge of total panic.

The man's response was to move the gun closer to the Queen.

Her head shook with rage. She was doing her best to talk, but all that could be heard were distorted mumbles from behind the tape. The man pushed the gun against her temple.

"Quiet, old bitch," he spat. "You're not recognised here."

He then lowered the gun and turned his attention to Dan. "You. American. Find Shakespeare's Truth. Follow your destiny or you both die."

Dan tried to control the panic but failed. "Help!" he screamed. "Help us!"

One of the men strode over to Dan and punched him hard in the side of the head. Coloured lights flashed before his eyes.

The tallest of the three men was smiling. "Keep your mouth shut and listen boy, otherwise she'll suffer and you'll take the blame." He swung the pistol around and cracked the Queen lightly on the side of the head. "You have been chosen to deliver us Shakespeare's Truth. It is your destiny." The man spoke with conviction. "If you do not wish to see this charlatan Queen, this thief of nobility die and then yourself blamed and killed, you will find it."

"What the... destiny? This is connected to that email isn't it? That's what it said. The video. I didn't see it. I don't know what it shows."

"The message was there, cut into the royal whelp before he died."

"The royal whelp? You mean somebody else? You've killed somebody else? You murdered a member of the Royal Family?"

The man holding the gun stepped around the Queen and walked forward and down the room, steel toecaps clicking on the worn oak floor. He was now directly in front of Dan. He was a big man, bulky but not fat and he towered over his captive. His hot breath stank of whisky.

"Yes, we killed her grandson, the pretty blond boy. He's dead and this sham queen will die too unless you accept your destiny."

Dan was stunned. "You killed Prince William?"

The man lazily raised the pistol, pointing it directly at Dan's head and smiled. "Remember, when death comes, nothing is left. You've disappeared into nothing, like the true English race." Dan could feel himself panicking as the barrel approached his forehead. "When death is about to claim you, you'll wonder why you didn't spend more of your life following your true destiny." The man lowered the gun and moved closer, whispering. "If you go to the police, the army, your Embassy or any of the authorities, we will know. We will find you and skin you and feed you screaming to the pigs, but only after you have watched her die. We left the mark on William's chest when he died. This was the sign left by the fra rosi crosse that points the way. Accept your destiny. Tell me you're ready to find Shakespeare's Truth or I'll kill her right now in front of you. She'll die here and now and so will you." The man suddenly stood up, swinging the gun round so that it was pointing at the Queen. He gripped his gun with both hands and roared out, "'Yea all which it Inherit, shall dissolve.'"

"What? Is that Shakespeare?" Dan spoke out loud, for a moment he was utterly disorientated. His mind raced, where had he heard that before? Was it from the play *The Tempest*?

Dan could see the man's arms shaking as his fingers tightened on the trigger. Then there was the explosive crash of a high calibre weapon being fired. The man with the gun looked down at his chest in surprise. A gaping hole had appeared in it. A red rose of blood was already staining the robe around the wound. From above, shards of window glass came falling to the floor. The man collapsed to his knees, knocking Dan's chair over and crumpling on top of him.

"Get behind her! They won't risk hitting her. Get her

out of here!" one of the two remaining men screamed. Gunfire once again exploded into the room. Plaster puffed on the walls, as bullets sprayed in from the window. One of the kidnappers produced an Uzi from under his robes, crouched on one knee and raised the gun before returning fire up towards the window. The noise of the rattling machine gun was thunderous.

Dan was lying sideways on the floor, unable to move under the weight of the dead kidnapper. The remaining two men cut the ropes holding the Queen and one of them started to drag her down the room, heading towards the back door. Two more shots came in. One bullet glanced off the wall, the other splintered the door missing the kidnapper by a fraction. The shooting from the window stopped as the Queen and her captor disappeared.

The remaining man ran over to his dead companion. He bent down and picked up the dead man's pistol and straightened up, staring at Dan. For a moment he stood motionless, seemingly unsure what to do. Then suddenly he bent down and pushed the gun into Dan's cheek.

"You cannot escape from your destiny," the man hissed. There was a boom from behind Dan as the door was kicked in. The kidnapper rose, lifting his gun, screaming and shooting. The noise was astonishingly loud in the confined space. His wild shots were returned with accuracy. The man jerked backwards, a bullet blowing off the top of his head. Dan closed his eyes, his whole body was shaking as blood and brain rained down on him. For a few seconds all he could hear was a ringing sound in his ears.

He opened his eyes as he heard a voice speaking above him. "She's gone. Room clear, requesting clean up team. Blue team look for a trace on exits two and three." The voice crouched down beside him, and Dan saw a tall blond haired soldier in his late forties. He was holding a large pistol. The man's icy blue eyes studied him with interest.

"Who the hell are you?" said the Major.

Act 3: Scene One

*"All the world's a stage, And all the men
and women merely players: They have their
exits and their entrances."*

As You Like It

20th December

O n the north bank of the River Thames,
sandwiched between Sir Christopher Wren's
monumental St Paul's Cathedral and the
imposing square mass of the new Ministry of Defence,
stands a majestic gothic chateau. Whitehall Court looks
as if it has been lifted from the pages of a Victorian
romance and dropped into the centre of London.
Although its position suggests it should be a
government building, Whitehall Court is in fact an
apartment block commanding the most central position
of any residential building in London.

Dan was in one of the building's penthouse flats. He
hadn't slept. Last night, the Major had escorted him here
for questioning and recuperation. The apartment was
beautiful, smooth oak floors, clean white walls, tasteful
art and furniture and stunning views of the sweep of the
river. Apparently it was owned by the Crown and
normally used for visiting diplomats. A faint aroma
from the fresh flowers filled the air, the only sound was

a faint creaking as Dan shifted his position on the huge antique Chesterfield sofa.

He looked out as the red sun rose behind the giant London Eye, casting a crimson glow onto the River Thames. For a few minutes the view was flawless, no clouds, nothing to take away from the majesty of the arriving day. He opened the window, and a deep rumble echoed into the flat. Far below another train rolled into Charing Cross station. Hundreds of people were making their way across Hungerford Bridge towards Trafalgar Square and Covent Garden, ready to take their position behind desks, shop tills and everything else that made up the life blood of a great city.

Dan was trying to focus his mind, but the kidnapper's threats and the image of the Queen kept flashing into his mind. He sighed and checked his watch. 8:05 am. He had arrived with the Major just as Big Ben had struck midnight. They had sat in silence for a short while, both gazing out at the darkness of the city, the multi-coloured lights creating ribbons of red and blue reflections on the river. The Major had made him sign the Official Secrets Act. He had then taken Dan's fingerprints and run them through a portable biometric identity system and waited for the CIA and NSA to confirm who Dan was. Then for the next two hours the Major had interviewed him. Throughout the interrogation, Dan's mind replayed the kidnapper's threat: *no police, no army, nobody from the authorities. Say nothing.*

"I'm sorry," Dan had said. "I don't know why I was kidnapped. It must have been a mistake. We've been over this ten times already. It all went by so quick. I just figured they were crazy people. I didn't take it in."

"It's true that innocent people get caught up in extraordinary events," said the Major, "or that they can't see the connection themselves. But it's strange. There's no connection I can see between you and Prince William or the Queen and this terrorist group. From an analytical point of view it's unlikely, but just about possible, it ended up being a mistake on their part."

"Yes, that's right. It has to be a mistake. There's no reason for them to want me for anything. I'm an American, I'm just over here to work." Dan tried to encourage the Major.

"You're not listening. It may have turned out to be a mistake, but there will be an initial reason as to why they took you. It's just that we're not seeing it."

Dan tried to think of something the Major might buy into. "Maybe they were using me for PR? Maybe they thought they could grab someone off the street, show them the Queen and then send them off to the media with the story?"

The Major leaned back on his chair, looking at Dan. "Publicity is the life blood of terrorist organisations, they live on creating fear far more than their actual actions. A story from a beaten and frightened victim, telling the papers of a secret kidnapping of the Queen. Yes it makes more sense than anything else so far." He paused, seemingly contemplating Dan's idea.

"And as I am an American, it has more poignancy. It would have been a lead story Stateside as well as over here."

"How so?"

"CNN would love it. They would get global coverage on their story instantly. It would be much bigger than if it was a Brit being involved."

"True enough." The Major seemed to be taking Dan's idea more seriously.

"I just don't know what else to say," said Dan. "Who are they anyway? Do you think they're some sort of religious group, in those crazy robes?"

"When the terrorist whispered in your ear, what did he say?"

Dan's heart jumped. What had the Major heard? "I don't know. He was just rambling, making random threats, saying he was going to kill the Queen."

The Major's face hardened and his tone became abrupt. "We've got two ways of playing this Dan. The first way, the standard way, would be to arrest you for suspected treason against the Crown and to keep you locked up whilst the investigation develops. I'm not saying you'd be in the Tower of London in thumb-screws and on the rack, but not far off. If this was a Secret Service operation you would have already been arrested, pumped full of sodium pentathol and thrown into a secure interrogation room. The truth is that the fastest and easiest way to get the information that I want would be to subject you to severe and rather barbarous interrogation techniques. To be honest, that's an approach that I am still seriously considering." His words hung in the air.

"The second way?" A weak smile appeared on Dan's lips.

"The second way is to give you the benefit of the doubt. It's up to you. If you tell me everything, and I mean *everything* that you can think of, I can then decide which route to take."

"You were watching from up above. You must have heard everything that was said anyway. You already know as much as me, or more." Dan started to worry. Was the Major testing him?

"No. We arrived in our observation position only a few seconds earlier. I had to take immediate action. Her Majesty's life was in danger. Our other units had not secured the perimeter before the fire fight, there simply wasn't time. We lost the terrorists when they exited the building."

"But you heard the man scream out that Shakespeare quote?"

"Yes. Did you recognise it?"

"I think it's from *The Tempest*. I studied English at college and it rang a bell."

"Correct," said the Major, surprised at a stranger's knowledge of Shakespeare. "Dan, do you have any idea why he used that quote? Was anything said before that would make any sense of it?"

"No. Nothing."

"And you didn't recognise it from anywhere else?"

"Anywhere else? What do you mean? The play?"

The Major's face had changed, the soft smile had returned. "You've signed the Official Secrets Act. What I am about to tell you must remain confidential. Two words from that quote have featured somewhere else. There was a video released on the internet. It was neutralized, but hundreds or thousands of people saw it. You should watch it. Maybe it will jog your memory on something you've missed." The Major spun his laptop around to face Dan and launched a file.

Dan recognised the video immediately.

"That's the Prince's car," said the Major pointing at a limousine as it drove past. "They included some film, CCTV of the street the Prince drove down in Mayfair before the next section, which is I am afraid quite horrific." Dan watched in relief as the Major fast forwarded past the part of the video where Dan had seen his own face.

"If it's CCTV, can't you trace it?" said Dan, regretting instantly that he had drawn attention to the footage he was in.

"The CCTV source was easy to isolate of course, but it's available to the whole of the London Met, the City Council and a dozen other sources via online streaming. There are about four thousand different IP addresses that accessed this footage on the night in question. It would take months to trace each one, but we'll persevere in any case."

The Major clicked the controls and started the video on normal speed as the camera switched to the scene in the park. Dan watched in stunned silence as the gruesome drama played out.

"Major Barnes-Jones, I don't know what to say, it's so horrible it's unreal, like some sort of... I don't know. How did it happen? Surely the Prince was under guard?"

"It was the driver. He must have been working

undercover for years, building up trust in the organisation. He killed the bodyguards, switched cars and from that point on the Prince had no hope. As we have already established these people are professionals."

"And now they have the Queen. Incredible."

"Not so incredible. She was kidnapped from the Scottish estate at Balmoral while the family was on a hunting trip. An estate of millions of acres in size is impossible to police and the Queen regularly takes a Land Rover out on her own against my wishes, but what could I do when Her Majesty insists?"

"But you found her quickly enough?"

"That was our one piece of luck. She had a tracking tag in a piece of jewellery, the one precaution she did allow me, but the signal died last night. If it was up to me, they would have trackers implanted under their skin, but the Duke of Edinburgh won't hear of it." He smiled grimly. "I think that policy may be updated now."

"What do you make of the words cut on William's chest? The same as the man shouted?"

"Right now we just don't know." The Major paused and seemed to be making a decision. "I won't arrest you, we'll agree on a compromise solution. I want you to stay here in this flat, it's secure and monitored. Some team members will go over to your flat in Shepherd's Bush and sweep it for surveillance devices, improve security and then you can go back there when advised. You'll be under surveillance at my discretion. I want you to report in to me directly, for the next five days while we make a threat assessment. Then after that period, I'll give you a final decision. Oh and my men will bring you new clothes, your laptop and some other essentials to keep you going. You can't return to work, so we'll drop you some cash."

"That's great, thanks so much."

"It's not entirely selfless on my part. Resources are somewhat stretched while the machinery grinds into action and I have higher priorities than babysitting you. My advice to you might sound counter intuitive, but it's sound from a psychological point of view. You need to do something relaxing and different. Maybe take in the sights, get some air. Let the events mull over in your mind. See if anything comes up. If it does, let me know immediately."

Act 3: Scene Two

"This was the unkindest cut of all."

Julius Caesar

His mobile's insistent ring woke him. For a moment, Dan had no idea where he was.

"And where the hell have you been?" Jonny's tone was laced with anger. "Come on mate, out with it. Nobody's particularly pleased here. In fact I would go so far as to say that our friends at the airport were positively pissed off. Never mind those darling little weevils that are going to be horrifically crushed by the wheels of industry unless our car park proposal gets sorted. Actually never mind the weevils getting crunched, you do realise we're in the middle of a fucking economic credit crunch? You can't just piss off for the day and not even bother calling in."

"I'm really sorry, Jonny. I know it's incredibly un-professional but I was pretty badly mugged. I spent yesterday in hospital and only got out this morning." Dan was surprised by how easily the lie flew from his mouth.

"Shit, mate," Jonny's voice was now full of interest. "What the bloody hell happened? I hope it wasn't one of our rivals or some dodgy branding agency trying to crock my favourite creative director?"

"Very amusing but no actually, I really have no idea who it was."

"Now be serious, mate. How are you? Lose an eye?

A few teeth? I hope you weren't too horribly beaten. Our resident bit of New Zealand totty might be a bit upset if you've lost your looks. She's a big fan of yours now after you rescued her in the meeting you know. I hope that you didn't lose your laptop. That's company property, mate."

"Your concern's very touching, I feel underwhelmed, Jonny. I've got a bump on my head that would make the Elephant Man blush and some pretty choice cuts and bruises over the rest of me. I'm in a fair amount of pain too."

"I'll pass the word around. I assume you won't be in the office today, not that you get much done on a Friday, but we'll see you after the weekend."

"I'll try. But realistically, I'm not sure."

"Really?" Jonny's tone was less sympathetic. "When do you think you will make it? Tuesday? That fat perv from airport parking is back in at the end of next week."

"I'm not sure. I feel pretty bad. The week after?"

"You got mugged, you haven't got fucking leprosy."

"I'm in a lot of pain and I can't really concentrate. Can I call you next week?"

"Sure. We'll speak later." The phone went dead.

Dan thought about sleeping and was making his way to the bedroom when the doorbell rang. He approached the heavy oak door and cautiously glanced through the eyehole. All he could see was the empty hallway. He half opened the door and peered out. A black suitcase had been placed at the foot of his door but the black and white marble corridor was empty. For a moment he froze, unsure what to do. It was not until he saw the small gold crest on it marked 'Royal Security' that he decided to pick it up.

Closing the door he returned to living room and opened the suitcase. It was exactly as the Major had promised - clean clothes, his laptop, post, and on top of it all, an envelope.

Dan ripped open the envelope to find a bundle of twenty pound notes and a booklet of tickets. He estimated that there was about two hundred pounds in cash, together with free passes to some of London's most popular attractions. He flicked it open. It included Westminster Abbey, Buckingham Palace, the London Eye. There was some sort of note explaining this was standard hospitality for foreign dignitaries using the apartment.

He plugged in his laptop and searched for a wireless network. He could see a router plugged into the wall and soon found the security key stamped on the side. He was quickly online. On reflex he checked his work email but when a flood of unread angry messages started downloading, he closed it down.

He went onto Google and starting typing in words that were carved on Prince William's chest, 'shall dissolve'. A confusing mass of nonsense came up, ranging from cookery tips to song lyrics and blogs. Next he went online and searched for the quote from *The Tempest* the kidnapper had screamed at him, *'Yea all which it Inherit, Shall dissolve.'* As he suspected, dozens of websites talking about *The Tempest* and William Shakespeare appeared, IMDB movie reviews, Wikipedia pages, tourist pages, books for sale, play productions.

The only interesting page was a link listing statues and monuments dedicated to Shakespeare around London. Pictures of Westminster Abbey and the British Library came up on the screen. But when he clicked on it, it turned out to be a tourist site, trying to sell tickets for a commission. Exasperated he closed the laptop and stared out of the window.

It was a clear day and he thought back to the Major's suggestion that he should get out and clear his head. Although Dan had been living in London for six months, all he had really done was work. He had seen nothing of the city outside of the office, a few local bars, and the shops around his apartment. He stuck the booklet of free tickets in his back pocket and decided to get outside.

Dan made his way down the Victorian marble corridor, flanked by stained-glass windows and then into an ancient lift. In the entrance an even more ancient porter stood eyeing Dan suspiciously through ancient thick glass lenses. The revolving door opened onto the busy Whitehall street, Dan felt the cold sharp air hit his face.

To his right was Trafalgar Square. To his left was Parliament Square, Big Ben, Downing Street and the river. He started walking in that direction. The street was crammed with a mixture of tourists, Christmas shoppers and business people in slick suits streaming in and out of the many government buildings. Christmas lights festooned the lampposts, glinting quietly in the full winter sunlight. He looked at their faces as they flowed by; a mix of stress, impatience, happiness and resignation. What would he give to go back to being in blissful ignorance, back to his old life of yesterday! A businessman in a bland uniform of a pinstripe suit strode past, staring into the middle distance. Dan wished he could just grab the guy, shout at him, tell him all this was his problem, his dead prince, his missing Queen and then he could just go home, get into bed, hide under the sheets and wait for it all to go away.

He sighed. That wasn't an option right now, tempting as it sounded. He decided to head left and in just a couple of minutes he reached Parliament Square and the grandeur of Big Ben. As Dan was standing, staring upwards, the clock struck half past the hour, the clock's huge bells rolling out across the city. He walked past the Houses of Parliament, where intricately designed walls radiated ancient authority and power. Statues of former leaders glowered down at him. He stopped for a minute to admire the craftsmanship, and ferocious ugliness, of Oliver Cromwell.

The titanic, gothic columns of Westminster Abbey reached into a perfect blue sky. It was an incredible sight, particularly to someone like him who had grown up in an area where the oldest building was about the same age as his grandparents. Dan stopped in front of the yawning stone entrance. Something was tugging at his memory. He snapped his fingers. Of course! There was a website that mentioned Westminster Abbey in connection with Shakespeare. He pulled out the book of tickets. As he thought, the top one was for Westminster Abbey. He ripped the ticket out and joined the small queue of tourists at the entrance.

Act 3: Scene Three

"Something is rotten in the state of Denmark."

Hamlet

Fiona had woken up early that morning. In the moment of waking, between sleep and consciousness, the stream of vivid images from the online video played out in her mind and before she even opened her eyes she had known what she had to do. She had jumped out of bed, gone into her living room and hunted around on the shelves. There was a book she needed to take with her today.

She had not visited Westminster Abbey since she was a child. Yet even after so many years, nothing had changed. As she picked her way up the stone steps, visions of her father flooded back. Their last visit together had been decades ago, when she was just a proud little girl skipping alongside her father, the famous history professor. She had loved their day trips to London. They had been everywhere, but Westminster Abbey and the Tower of London were the most fun.

"Now then Fee-Fee, my little code cracker," he used to say, "let's see what we can find today shall we?" She had felt involved with him and special. "Do you know how many ciphers there are in public monuments in London?" he had joked. "Dozens. And most are still hidden! Now let's see if we can find one!"

The official story that the Prince had been killed by a

drunk driver left her confused and angry. At first she had expected the story to change; after all she was not the only person to see the video. Yet, as the day wore on, all the news channels ran the same story. No one challenged the official explanation. Instead, the same library footage of the dead Prince was broadcast over and over again.

The channels showed films of him playing polo, his time as a student at university, then following in his mother's footsteps and helping with charitable causes in Africa. He was always smiling, blond hair glinting in the sun.

Dan reached the front of the queue. He guessed this was about as quiet as it got. He was an hour or so ahead of the main tourist groups of the day and at this time of year most people were at home preparing for Christmas.

As he handed in his free pass, he asked the pale young woman at the ticket desk what the connection with Shakespeare and the Abbey was.

"Shakspur? Is statue." The accent was Polish. She looked bored out of her mind as she waved her hand in the direction of the main building.

Dan walked inside. The Abbey was nothing like he had imagined. His immediate impression was more of a sculpture gallery than a church. High vaulted stone ceilings soared above his head, intricate coloured beams of light streamed through stained glass windows. He was surrounded by statues commemorating the great and good of English history. There were monuments honouring members of the aristocracy, scientists and other luminaries, but it was the Royal tombs that dominated.

He began to stroll aimlessly, keeping an eye out for a Shakespeare statue, shoes echoing on the stone floor. He was aware of the ethereal sounds of a distant choir and the subtlest scent of flowers.

After several minutes of wandering around, Dan stumbled upon the tombs of Queen Elizabeth I and Mary Queen of Scots. He assumed one day Queen Elizabeth II would be entombed here, but what about Prince William? Was this to be his final resting place? He was chilled by the thought that someone somewhere was already preparing the Prince's funeral. He stopped walking and leaned against the wall. Surrounded by stone royalty, he began to get the eerie feeling they were judging him. He breathed deeply, forcing himself to stay calm. Suddenly the ancient church was folding in on him and he was filled with the urge to just run like hell, get out of there.

He breathed deeply and told himself all he needed was a change of scene, perhaps a coffee and then back out and into the fresh air. Dan started to follow signs to the café at the far end of the building. He stopped in his tracks in front of an enormous circular window shaped like a flower. Sunlight streamed through it in azure slabs of light, highlighting an area of the Abbey that was very different to the rest. It had a sense of space, with less monuments and statues crowding the space.

The sculptures here seemed less haughty and morbid ... some were carved with a more free and expressive hand, offering a flourishing and welcome sense of relief in the imperious church. He looked more closely. There were names here he knew, names of poets, playwrights and authors from his childhood: the Bronte sisters, Byron, CS Lewis and William Blake. According to a quick skim of the map, he was standing in Poets' Corner, an area dedicated to the memories of great writers. He saw the tomb of Charles Dickens and underneath a deep blue window, was the simple tomb of the medieval poet Geoffrey Chaucer.

But the dominant feature was a square marble arch about ten feet high. In the middle of the arch stood a full sized statue of a man. William Shakespeare. The Bard was standing in the arch with crossed legs, leaning on his elbow, which rested on top of a tall pile of books. Below the books, Shakespeare's finger pointed to a scroll of parchment. Into the base of the statue the images of three young men's faces had been carved into the anaemic stone. Shakespeare himself was staring straight out into the Abbey.

In an instant, all of Dan's ideas of leaving the Abbey vanished. With the kidnapper's words ringing in his ears, he walked towards the statue.

Act 3: Scene Four

*"All that glisters is not gold.
Often have you heard that told."*

The Merchant of Venice

Fiona had to hold back from pushing past a family of tourists at Queen Elizabeth's tomb. There was always a bottleneck at this point in the Abbey. It was a tiny room and visitors were forced to double back around the sculpture of the Queen that lay on top of her tomb, as if asleep.

Fiona hated looking at Queen Elizabeth. She loved her as a historical figure, especially the combination of her incredible success coupled with the sadness of dying childless and unmarried. However, she had always felt hackles go up on the back of her neck when she looked at the Queen's death mask. It had a sense of resignation and defeat as if after all the great victories, Elizabeth knew she had left her kingdom to an uncertain future. Fiona brushed past it and headed to Poets' Corner and the Shakespeare monument.

Dan was staring intently at the carved parchment on the monument. A quote from one of Shakespeare's plays had been inscribed into the stone and Dan had to lean in to make out the words. The type was small and had, at some point in the past, been painted over. He started to read it through.

THE CLOUD CUPT TOW'RS. THE GORGEOUS PALACES
THE SOLEMN TEMPLES. THE GREAT GLOBE ITSELF
YEA ALL WHICH IT INHERIT,
SHALL DISSOLVE;
AND LIKE THE BASELESS FABRICK OF A VISION
LEAVE NOT A WRECK BEHIND.

Shall dissolve! There it was, right in front of him, and
the quote his kidnapper had screamed too. This was
something to do with Shakespeare's Truth. It had to be.
But what? He had absolutely no idea. Dan leant in to
take a close look at the carved inscription. The more he
looked, the more confused he became. The layout of the
quote was incredibly amateurish. He didn't understand.
Why would an expensive monument so brilliantly
carved have such bad typography? Looking closer he
noticed something genuinely peculiar. One of the words
that Dan had thought said 'FABRICK' didn't say that at
all. On closer examination the 'a' in the word was
actually an 'n'. It didn't say 'FABRICK', it said 'FNBRICK'.

As Fiona approached the Shakespeare monument
she noticed a tall man crouched in front of it. Although
his clothes looked expensive and trendy, his hair was
dishevelled, and there was a large purple bruise on the
side of his forehead. Fiona removed her notebook from
her shoulder bag, and ignoring the stranger, began her
search.

She knew the words 'shall dissolve' featured on the
monument, but it was the cloaked man in the video that
had convinced her to come down here. She had seen a
badge on his cloak, a red rose inside a cross. It was the
unmistakable icon of an ancient secret society known as
the Rosicrucians. She had been stunned, she thought

they had faded away into history, but here was some kind of modern variant, alive and killing.

Fiona had done some research on the Rosicrucians before. Back in history they were known as experts at cryptography, and she knew the Shakespeare monument was funded and built by Alexander Pope and Sir Christopher Wren, both Rosicrucians, in the eighteenth century. She had a faint idea there was some kind of modern Rosicrucian movement today that was open to the public, a philosophical study group.

For some unknown reason, some modern Rosicrucians had brought attention to the Shakespeare monument in Westminster Abbey, and murdered the heir to the throne at the same time. It was utterly baffling.

Fiona examined the statue, looking for clues, beginning at the base, close to Shakespeare's feet. She quickly located the letters TT, carved into the statue base. Fiona knew these initials were a reference to thirty three, or $33°$, a highly significant number to Rosicrucians and Freemasons alike. Then she saw, on Shakespeare's casually crossed stocking covered legs, engravings of roses and crowns. Could that be important? Fiona wasn't convinced; the roses could also have referred to the Tudor dynasty of which Queen Elizabeth I was the last. But it was unusual to find roses and crowns together - crowns usually suggested a royal controversy.

Fiona was suddenly aware that amongst the crowns and the roses, was a new image. A tiny familiar face had been engraved into the stone. She had seen it before on a seventeenth century oil painting – it was a copy of an official portrait of Sir Francis Bacon.

Fiona smiled, this was getting really interesting. She used Bacon in her lectures mainly because he was one of the greatest cipher experts in history, but there was more to it than that. Amongst his many achievements, the accepted view was that he had founded the Rosicrucian movement in the sixteenth century.

Excited, she turned her attention to the parchment and the quote. The figure of Shakespeare had been carved so his fingertip rested on just one word - 'Temples'. Fiona knew the word temple did not mean a place of worship to Rosicrucians, it meant a secret meeting place. Underneath the scroll were the carved heads of three crowned Princes in the classical style, youthful, powerful, and imperious. They seemed out of place. Her eyes lingered on their cold, white stone faces as she wondered why they had been included in the sculpture. Then it came to her. The middle of the three faces was another portrait of Sir Francis Bacon. She had seen it looking out at her dozens of times from books. It was a copy of an original work by the sixteenth century painter Hilyard, a master of miniatures and one of Queen Elizabeth's favourite portrait artists. The particular miniature of Bacon copied here would have been familiar to the Queen. The original was inside her prayer book.

Fiona felt someone nudge her shoulder. The strange man was right next to her, staring at the carved parchment containing the quote, apparently unaware of her presence.

"Excuse me," said Fiona. "Would you mind stepping to one side, I'd like to have a closer look here if you don't mind?" The man looked at her for an instant, his face blank. Then he turned his attention back to the quotation.

Dan had been trying to ignore the woman. She had barged past him when she first arrived and then set about examining the statue in some detail. He had glanced over at her, her eyes instantly catching his attention. They were huge and oval shaped, brown, accentuated by her long dark hair, pulled back and tied with a scrunched up satin band, loose locks flowing aimlessly over her shoulder. Dan thought she was pretty, despite the fact she was dressed like his aunt.

"I'm sorry, I asked you to move so I could have a look and you don't seem to have heard me." Fiona started to get annoyed.

Dan sighed. "Look, I don't see why you can't either squash up or wait a couple of minutes."

"Listen, it's extremely important to me to be able to look at this. I need to study this quotation, if you don't mind."

Dan stood up straight and looked at the girl more closely. "I don't really know what I'm doing here, but I've seen that quotation somewhere else recently, and I'm studying it too."

Even though he was a bit intimidating, Fiona found herself wanting to carry on talking. "Don't think I'm being crazy or anything, but can I ask you, did you see it on an online video?"

"I saw it. It was kinda a... ummm... home movie you might say."

"Now look, don't think I'm off my rocker or anything, but in the video, was there anyone, how can I put this, unexpected in it?" Fiona felt her pulse quicken.

"When I say home movie, it was more of a snuff movie to be honest. It had someone, Prince William in it. And he was, well there's no easy way to put this, but it was showing his death."

"Yes I know," Fiona said in a rush. "I've seen it too, along with some of my students, it was awful."

"Students? Are you like an English teacher or something? By the way, my name's Dan. I'm really sorry about what happened to your Prince, and sorry about the egg on my head too, I don't normally look I've done five rounds with Mike Tyson and fallen asleep in a wind tunnel. It's all connected to this, but you don't need to know the details."

Fiona smiled. "Well, today I can believe anything. Yes, it's the most awful news. My name's Fiona, and no, I'm not an English teacher, I'm a university lecturer, but I won't take that as an insult."

"No, of course not, teachers do a damn fine job. Apart from my old history teacher."

"I specialise in Elizabethan... history."

"There are exceptions to every rule, even ones as illogically formed as mine. Professor Fiona, it's a pleasure to meet you." Dan reached out his hand. Fiona hesitated for a second before shaking it.

"So Dan, did you see the words cut into his chest?"

"Yes I did."

"I assume you've noticed the same two words are here on this statue. That's why I came down here."

"You must be well read. 'Shall dissolve' could have

meant anything."

"Yes, whoever cut them onto the Prince didn't want the whole world here."

"Fiona, let me ask you a question about this thing, right? I'm not a world expert or anything, I loved English classes at college and majored in it, so I know a lot of the spelling is pretty messed up in Olde English and all that, but check this word here out, that can't be right can it? Not even Shakespeare would have spelt the word 'fabrick' with an n would he?" Fiona followed Dan's finger, leaning in closer to examine the statue.

"And another thing," Dan continued, "the layout is really weird. Maybe I'm being anal, but I work in design so I get paid to see these things. Look, our favourite two words, 'shall dissolve' here. See how they are on their own on a line? It doesn't make design sense. What does it mean?"

Fiona looked at him in surprise. The misspelling and anomalies in layout were classic signs of a cipher. "Why are you so interested?"

"I've got my reasons. What were you going to do if you found anything out?"

Fiona leant forward to look at the quotation. "I hadn't thought it through. Go to the police I suppose."

Dan was startled. He had been warned by the gunmen to keep well away from the police. And here he was, with someone who was talking about involving them. Images of the Queen tied up in that room and the gunfight flashed into his mind, and he fought to control a wave of panic. It was too much of a risk. He turned and walked away.

Act 3: Scene Five

"There is nothing either good or bad,
But thinking makes it so."

Hamlet

Stretching in front of Buckingham Palace was a parade ground, sealed from the public by high iron gates. Behind this glowered the grey Palace. It was a vast, flat-fronted Georgian mansion with dozens of windows, epic carved balconies and towering columns that framed the monolithic front doors. Every day, thousands of tourists made their way to and from Buckingham Palace, where, for a price, they were let inside the majestic building to wander around a few carefully chosen rooms to get a flavour of life inside the Royal Court.

The most popular tourist event at the Palace was the daily Changing of the Guard. Huge crowds gathered outside the black and gold gates, jostling for position, children raised high on shoulders, all eager to catch a glimpse of the Queen's crimson soldiers, with their noisy and exuberant preening. These were the costumed pride of the Queen's military machine, a daily reminder of past glories.

But the death of Prince William had changed the routine. The crowds still came but they had lost their eagerness. Instead, they filed past a vast and growing mound of flowers to pay their respects. The scent of the thousands of roses, lilies and other fast wilting blooms subtly filled the air, trickling down into St James Park and towards Trafalgar Square.

As the day wore on, more and more people arrived and waited for something to happen. Amongst the crowds were TV camera crews, journalists, families, tourists, people from every corner of the world. Yet, no one emerged from the Palace. The Royal Family remained in Scotland and were not due to return for several days, but still the crowd waited.

Unseen, below the crowd's patient feet, the heart of Buckingham Palace continued to beat. Sixty feet down under the streets was a self sufficient military bunker designed to keep the Royal Family out of harm's way in the event of disaster. It was built in the 1960s but over the years it had acquired a network of rooms with their own power supplies, food and water, technology and a frightening arsenal of high tech weaponry.

The Major was in the central incident room. He was surrounded by a team of ten handpicked soldiers. They sat around a heavy and broad circular oak table littered with ashtrays, empty coffee cups, and beer cans. The team had not slept for over 24 hours but were still alert. They were all experienced soldiers, recruited over the years from the British Special Forces. The Major knew each man personally. They were all English and they all had an intense loyalty to their country and the Royal Family.

The chairs on which the men sprawled were ultra-modern, leather and stylish. In contrast the oak table was an antique, its surface pitted and deeply polished. On one of the walls of the underground room a bank of monitors played video footage of the leaders of a number of extreme religious and political parties. Some of the faces were European, most were African, Middle Eastern and Asian. A bulky air-conditioned computer squatted next to the only door, connecting Royal Security to MI5, Interpol, the CIA, FBI and other global intelligence organisations.

The soldiers were debating the importance of Dan.

"Listen boys, ultimately he's a civvy who happened to get in the wrong place at the wrong time." The Major was speaking calmly. "Whatever the kidnappers' intentions, he's oblivious to them. The American seems convinced that it was all a case of mistaken identity. CIA and MI5 buy that too."

Vaughan, a brute of a man, tall, huge shoulders, flat face, nose broken and disfigured, blond hair shaved back, spoke first. "What do you think boss?"

"I can't see any logical reason why he would have been kidnapped. However, we have to operate on the assumption that the kidnappers had a reason for getting Mr Knight involved, even if it was just to create a media frenzy."

"But he's back on the streets now boss; why wouldn't he just bugger off, run back home to the States or at least claim diplomatic immunity? Is he fucking with us?"

"No. It's possible he will leave, but not right now. He feels partly responsible for the Queen not being rescued," the Major paused, "which he is. Although he's scared, it's my instinct after talking to him, he'll try and help if he can, at least for a while. I put the frighteners on him and he agreed to stay in the secure Whitehall Court flat."

"What do we know about this Dan Knight bloke?" said Vaughan.

"He's got no military training, in fact precisely the opposite. He's over here to work at a London marketing agency; came over on his own on a contract. He used to live in New York doing a similar job. Unmarried, low level of debt, no major political or religious affiliations. Seems to move around somewhere different every two years on average. Good credit profile, owns a holiday flat in Belize. One night in prison as a teenager for crashing into a police car in an unlicensed vehicle whilst drunk."

"One night?"

The Major smiled. "The vehicle in question was a shopping trolley. Knight scored extremely high in art, design, that kind of thing. He studied English at university, he is thoroughly conversant with literary staples such as Shakespeare, Dickens, Bronte, Wordsworth, Blake, etc. Spent his career in marketing. So, a bit of a book worm, an academic. The details are in his file."

"So he's a creative type, probably a nonce too," said Vaughan, a tight grin spread on his face as he spoke. "Most of 'em are, right?" Vaughan laughed at his own joke. "He sure isn't a tough guy. He looked pretty messed up when we scraped him off the floor."

A new voice broke into the conversation. "I think we should bring him in, bust his chops, knock him about a bit to see if he's hiding anything, then just flush him away and forget him. Old school style."

Jackson had been the only black student in his year at Eton, there on a sports scholarship, and learned from an early age that if he wanted anything from life, then he would need to fight. That had suited him fine. He had broken all school athletics records before being seduced for a few wayward years into the gangster lifestyle. Afterwards, he had refocused and won an Olympic silver medal in karate. It was not until he returned to the UK that he committed himself to the British Army, eventually joining the SAS.

"That's not going to happen," snapped the Major. "You sound like that plod Sawyer, that's the sort of approach he would take. We need to give this guy some room. He doesn't know what he's doing, or why he's involved. He certainly has no additional useful information. But it's possible the kidnappers might get in contact with him again, even if it's only to kill him."

"The kidnappers won't be back. He's a muthafuckin' waste of muthafuckin' space. If he had any value at all, they would have taken him with them. But they didn't. They just dumped him. Right? Now if for some reason they decided taking him with them was too difficult, why didn't they just kill him? It would have been a piece of piss." The other soldiers nodded at Jackson's military logic. "It was a fuck-up getting him involved, plain and simple. But they had an initial reason. I buy into the idea of them grabbing some bloke who would go running to the press."

"Jacko's got a point boss," chipped in Vaughan. "Don't forget that video was obviously supposed to create a huge public panic."

Jackson jabbed his finger at the Major. "Something else has been bothering me. Why grab someone in a flat? Why not just grab someone on the street?"

"So what do you reckon Jacko?" said Vaughan.

"They grabbed the twat because he's a fucking loudmouth American marketing professional, someone skilled in the art of shooting his mouth off to the media. Someone who knows TV, radio, the internet and the press. The perfect fucking patsy to dump in a scene like that."

"Jacko's right boss." said Vaughan. "Knight would have gone cackling to the media on both sides of the pond and squealed like a pig with a spear up its jacksie."

"Fact is," said Jackson, "they know we're involved. There's no way they'll risk getting in contact with him again, even if for some fucked up reason they wanted to. Don't tell me he's the only fucking lead we got. Please."

The Major let the debate run its course before speaking. "Of course I've thought that through. The chances of Dan Knight being significant or useful to them from this point onwards are minute. However, much as I enjoy your rather colourful monologues, Sergeant Jackson, we're still going to maintain covert surveillance on him for now. It's unlikely anything will come out of it, but those are your orders."

"Okay boss," said Vaughan. "We'll keep a weather eye on the wimp and see what happens. But assuming the answer is nothing, we're still stuck with the big question: What are these terrorists up to?"

"If I knew that, Sergeant Vaughan," said the Major,

"we would be a damn sight closer to finding out why they murdered the heir to the throne and what they want with our Queen."

Act 3: Scene Six

"My words fly up, my thoughts remain below: Words without thoughts never to heaven go."

Hamlet

A s the caffeine from the coffee filtered into Dan's system he could feel his mind relax and his mood improve. He breathed in the aroma and looked around at the Westminster Abbey café. It was a large open room with a high ceiling and ancient windows offering a narrow view onto a wide grass courtyard beyond the walls. Dan could see the sharp winter sun against the walls, the light highlighting the ancient stonework. If he hadn't known how cold it was outside, he could easily have been fooled into thinking it was a glorious summer's day. As he gazed across the room, Fiona appeared on the far side of the café.

She paused when she saw Dan. After a nervous smile of recognition she bought some water and sat down at the opposite end of the room.

Dan watched as Fiona produced a small notebook, a second slim book with a black cover from her bag and started scribbling notes. He started to wonder, had he overreacted walking away? The only person he knew who might be able to help was this frumpily dressed yet striking girl sitting at the other end of the café.

He was going to have to try and patch things up. He picked up his coffee and walked over to her, forcing a smile onto his face.

"Hey there Fiona, mind if I join you?" He indicated a chair opposite her and sat down.

"It looks like you already have, doesn't it?"

Dan's cheeks coloured. "Yeah, look, I'm just saying sorry. Back there, in the Abbey, you said you'd seen the video. Do you mind if we talk more about that?"

"I was about to chat about it, but you walked off."

"I know, I was rude. I'm not trying to make excuses, but all I can say is I've got a huge amount on my mind."

"Well you're not the only one, you know."

"You're right. Do you think we could start over? Pretend I hadn't been a jerk?"

"I'll accept your half baked apology."

"I can bake it a bit more if you like."

"You'll probably end up burning it to a crisp. Let's just leave it."

"Thanks, I appreciate that. So, what are you up to here? You're obviously some kind of expert, with your books and everything?"

"Yes, I suppose I am. I've been here before. As soon as I saw the video I knew I had to come and have another look. I'm sure there's a cipher in the quotation carved on the monument."

"Wait up – a cipher?"

"I'm not explaining myself very well, am I?" Fiona allowed herself a tiny smile. "My area of expertise in history is cryptography." Dan still looked blank. "Secrecy, spying, codes, that kind of thing. When I was a kid, my father used to take me around places like this, looking at public monuments, old books, all sorts of things. We would look for hidden ciphers in them. It was fun. It turned into a hobby and then into a job."

Dan noticed Fiona was wearing very little makeup and the small amount she was wearing had been applied by an inexperienced hand. Her cheeks had a powdery look, her eyeliner was smudged and she was wearing what could be politely described as comfortable shoes. "That sounds like a geeky childhood, running around old churches and things. I bet you were a tomboy. You've probably got a scar somewhere from falling out of a tree."

"I suppose it was pretty weird, but you know what it's like when you're a kid – you just think whatever you're doing is normal even if it looks funny to other people."

"True enough. So tell me Professor Fiona, what's a cipher?"

Fiona shifted in her chair, flicking her wayward hair back over her shoulders. "Ciphers are essentially codes that you apply to text to reveal hidden information. Imagine being around when Shakespeare was alive. If you wanted to send a private letter, there was always a very real chance it would get intercepted. People got round that by sending messages that seemed innocuous but included hidden, valuable information that was only revealed when a cipher was used."

"What has this got to do with Prince William's murder and a statue of Shakespeare?"

"It all goes back to the video. Do you remember the guy in the weird clothes? A kind of cloak? Well, he was wearing a badge. It was only on the screen for a few seconds, but I saw it was the symbol for the Rosicrucians."

"The who? Rosey what?"

"The Rosicrucians. An ancient secret society. Really quite important back in history. They were especially powerful in the time of Queen Elizabeth the first."

"So you came here to try and find a connection between the Rosicrucians and the statue?"

"Yes."

"Fiona do the words 'rosy cross' mean anything to you?" asked Dan.

"You mean *fra rosi crosse*?"

"Yes, that's it."

"Where have you heard that? That's was how the Rosicrucians used to label themselves. It means the brotherhood of the rose in cross."

Dan ignored her question. "Tell me, what sort of people were they, these Rosicrucians? Scholars, soldiers, bakers?"

"Definitely scholars and soldiers. They were hugely imperialistic. They believed England was the natural leader of the world. They had a vision of a new world order called 'The New Atlantis', based on a book written by their founder and leader Sir Francis Bacon."

"Sir Francis Bacon. So he was some sort of power crazed lunatic? The Doctor Evil of the Seventeenth Century?"

"No no, not at all. God, that's really annoying to hear someone say that. One of my favourite ways of summing him up to my students is to quote the writer and poet Alexander Pope, who incidentally commissioned Shakespeare's monument here in the Abbey. Pope said Lord Bacon was the greatest genius that England, or perhaps any country, had ever produced. Bacon was a confidante of Queen Elizabeth, a spy, and a hugely influential philosopher and scientist of the day. I believe he pretty much formalised science as a form of study."

"But that was all hundreds of years ago. What has any of that got to do with Prince William?"

"I know, it seems crazy. But I'm sure the Rosicrucians are behind his murder. And for some reason, they've subtly drawn attention to this statue."

"You think there's some sort of a cipher on the statue?"

"Yes, I'm sure of it."

Dan started to get excited. Was that what Shakespeare's Truth was? A hidden cipher on Shakespeare's monument? "So was Shakespeare a Rosicrucian?"

"No. He lived around the same time as Bacon but the two men couldn't have been more different. Shakespeare was far too common to be invited into a secret society like that."

"So, let's assume you're right and there's a cipher in the statue. How do we figure it out?"

"Ciphers are an art form as much as a science, there are quite literally hundreds of different types, some simple, some incredibly complex. Bacon's own ciphers usually used a mix of mathematics and clues like spelling mistakes, layout, weird use of words, things like that, often in combination with something visual."

"When I started talking about the spelling mistakes

and strange layouts in the inscription it set off alarm bells in you head?"

"Exactly!"

"So what do we do?"

Fiona glanced at Dan. He had leaned in closer too, his chin rested on his hand as he listened. "I've already made some headway."

"I can see you've been writing something down in your notebook. And you've got another book. Why?"

Fiona picked up the slim book and showed Dan the cover.

"*The Tempest*? You brought the play? Why?"

"I wanted to check the quote in the play against the quote on the monument."

"Why?"

"Is that your favourite question? 'Why?' Have you never done any research? First rule, always check your sources." She lifted up her notepad. "I've compared the original against the one on the monument."

Original

The cloud-capped towers,
The gorgeous palaces,
The solemn temples,
The great globe itself,
Yea, all which it inherit, shall dissolve,
And, like this insubstantial pageant faded,
Leave not a rack behind.

Monument

The <u>Cloud cupt Tow rs</u>, The Gorgeous Palaces
The Solemn Temples, The Great Globe itself
Yea all which it Inherit,
Shall dissolve;
And like the baseless Fnbrick of a Vision
Leave not a <u>wreck</u> behind

Dan studied the quotes. "That's mad. There are loads of differences between the two."

"I know."

"Why?" He checked himself. "I won't keep asking why. But come on! An official monument for the most famous playwright in the world, and they can't even get the quote right? It makes no sense."

"Unless you assume it's deliberate, and a way to hide some other information in the form of a cipher. You spotting the misspelling of 'fnbrick' for 'fabrick' convinced me. Making a mistake with a quote is one thing, but something so clumsy? It has to be a cipher."

"So how do we go about finding this cipher? I still don't quite know what one is." Dan pulled his chair around the table to get a better look.

"Don't worry, it makes more sense when you see one. As I say to my students; with ciphers, the starting point is always the grid. Because every cipher is a hidden message, what we need to do is isolate the hidden message from the rest of the words in the quotation. The way to do that is to lay the quotation out in a grid, letter by letter. The cipher is then applied and hey presto, the hidden message pops out."

"Sounds logical, if confusing. How the hell do you do it?"

"Okay, the first question is, how big is the grid."

Dan glanced at the pad and then back at Fiona. "Let me get this straight. We need to create a grid of letters out of this quote. However, we don't know how big the grid should be and we don't know which word to start the grid with?"

"That's about the size of it." Fiona smiled as she spoke, starting to relish the challenge. Dan lifted his hands to his face and rubbed his eyes. A dull pain emerged from the wound on his forehead.

"What about starting with the word temple," said Dan, "after all it's the word old Will is pointing to."

"Not a bad guess for an amateur. But too obvious. Temple is a reference to the Rosicrucian origins of the monument. All Rosicrucians would have belonged to a temple." Fiona replaced the pen on the table. "No, I think there's a much simpler signal we've already been given, 'shall dissolve', the words cut into the Prince's chest."

"Of course."

"'Shall dissolve' is thirteen letters." Fiona huddled over the paper, sketched out a grid and began to add the letters from the inscription. Dan found himself examining her hands as she carefully formed each letter. Her fingers wrapped around the pen, almost holding it too tight. When she had finished she raised her head and examined her work.

S	H	A	L	L	D	?	S	S	O	L	V	E
A	N	D	L	I	K	E	T	H	E	B	A	S
E	L	L	E	S	F	N	B	R	?	C	K	O
F	A	V	?	S	?	O	N	L	E	A	V	E
N	O	T	A	W	R	E	C	K	?	E	H	?
N	D	T	H	E	C	L	O	U	D	C	U	P
T	T	O	W	R	S	T	H	E	G	O	R	G
E	O	U	S	P	A	L	A	C	E	S	T	H
E	S	O	L	E	M	N	T	E	M	P	L	E
S	T	H	E	G	R	E	A	T	G	L	O	B
E	I	T	S	E	L	F	Y	E	A	A	L	L
W	H	I	C	H	I	T	I	N	H	E	R	I
T	S	H	A	L	L	D	?	S	S	O	L	V

"Okay," she said, "there's our grid. Now what we need to do is find the cipher."

"I'm still not really clear what a cipher is."

"Think of it like a stencil, a pattern that highlights letters on the grid. Those letters are then grouped. Then they reveal an anagram and there's your secret message."

"We're looking for a visual pattern? That sits on top of the grid?"

"Yes. There will be clues in the grid too. You know the misspelling you saw on the carving in the word 'fabrick', where the 'a' was substituted for 'n' to create 'fnbrick'?"

"How could I fnget?"

"Look, are you taking this seriously?"

"More than you know. But you do sound a bit like my university English lecturer. Don't be offended. She was my fantasy older woman when I was a kid."

Fiona smiled. "Maybe that's because I am a lecturer,

cheeky. Anyway, that misspelling is obviously central to the cipher. Plus I also think it's pretty likely the word 'tow'rs' is important too, another difference between the original quote and this one. Then finally there is the word wreck instead of rack. That must be important too."

Dan stood up from his chair. "I agree, but something else is more important. Can we take a five minute break? I need to get another cup of coffee. I'm wrecked, or should I say racked."

Fiona looked on in astonishment. "We've only just started."

"I really need to have my head together on this, so I think another coffee could do the business. Do you want anything?"

"No. Nothing for me."

Dan threaded his way through the now busy café back towards the food counter. Fiona watched him walk away and then turned back to her notepad. Her first thought was to look at vertical and diagonal lines running across the grid, but quickly gave up. Perhaps the reference to 'TT' at the bottom of the statue was relevant? Fiona had been sure it was a Masonic reference to 33°. She tried every third letter but with no luck.

She was starting to get stuck. Maybe a coffee or perhaps a herbal tea wasn't such a bad idea. Fiona looked up from the table. She caught sight of Dan's tall frame as he emerged from behind an overweight woman pushing a pram through the sea of pine tables and metal chairs. He held a cup of coffee in one hand

and a small white china plate in the other. On the plate was a slice of carrot cake and a plastic fork. He sat down heavily in the chair.

"Boy, do I need this. Come on, at least you can share this with me?" He pushed the plate towards her. Fiona surprised herself as she picked up the fork from the plate. She smiled at Dan and then cut off the small pointed end of the cake. Balancing the moist cake on the end of the fork she lifted it to her mouth.

"You can have more than that. Go on, because if you don't, believe me, I will."

"No, this is fine."

"You've got a crumb on your chin." Dan took a sip of his coffee. "Want a taste?"

Fiona shook her head.

"Anyway, Fiona, while I was over there, I had an idea."

"Go ahead."

"Check this out." Dan was smiling. "What about a cross? That's the sign of the Rosicrucians, isn't it? You said it was a rose within a cross. And we are in a church."

"Good. Let's see what letters we get off the grid if we make a cross with our misspelt 'n' at its centre." She traced a cross with her finger and wrote down the letters that came out of it.

lenfboelt

She stared hard at the letters but couldn't see a meaningful anagram in it, not even when she tried Latin and Greek. "No, it's not right. There has to be something else we're missing. Tell me your impressions of the statue."

"From a design point of view, you've got the figure of Shakespeare himself, the quotation, the pillar with the heads on, and of course the arch it all sits inside."

"The arch. What did you notice about that?"

"I didn't see much like it anywhere else. There are plenty of other statues and flowery inscriptions, but not too many arches. From a purely design standpoint it's a pretty strong shape. Iconic. What are you thinking?"

"It could be too simple, but the best ciphers often are. If we just imagine a large arch in the middle of the grid that mimics the shape of the one Shakespeare is standing in…" Fiona quickly leaned over the note pad. "Now if we also assume that the 'n' in 'fnbrick' is significant."

She started writing down letters.

eiahwsleesfnbriccaecosplae

She stopped. "I don't know Dan. That feels too random. I'm sure we could find an anagram in there if we looked, but I was expecting something neater and more concise."

"What next?"

"I'm starting to feel there's a reason no-one has ever found this cipher; it's too well hidden, if it's here at all."

"What? Now you're saying there might be nothing there?" Dan sat back in his seat and rubbed his eyes. "God, what a fool I am. I was starting to believe we were going to crack it. As if it would be so easy." He stood up. "Fiona, thanks for everything. But I really need to go."

As he started to walk away he heard Fiona's voice. "Sit down. I didn't say I'd given up." He turned back and looked at her. "That last arch I drew was just using the 'n' in 'fnbrick' but what if we use the words 'wreck' and tow'rs to dictate the size of the arch..." She drew as she spoke, the strokes of the pen quick and certain over the top of the grid.

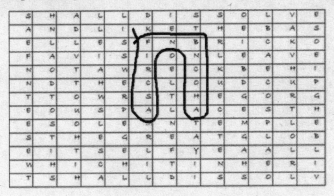

She wrote down the letters the new arch threw out.

ascrifnbncoha

Fiona saw it immediately. "Dan look, it's a name." She wrote it down.

francis bacon h

"What about the h?"

"Easy, just ignore it."

"Ignore it?"

"H was used silently in Elizabethan English. The arch shape is a perfect anagram of Francis Bacon."

Act 4: Scene One

"Why then the worlds mine oyster,
Which I with sword will open."

The Merry Wives of Windsor

D an had returned to Whitehall Court ecstatic at the discovery, convinced that he had stumbled upon part, or possibly all, of Shakespeare's Truth. Fiona and he had agreed to meet up on Sunday to talk about it again. He'd even managed to suggest she didn't talk to the police. Yet as the day wore on and he found himself trapped in the almost too perfect apartment, he began to have doubts. What had they actually found? A name of someone who died a long time ago? The leader of the Rosicrucians? What did it really do apart from just confirm the Rosicrucians built the Shakespeare monument and signed it in secret?

But the consequences for failure were too great. The thought of his own life and the life of the Queen of England depending on him making sense of some obscure threat from an arcane secret society made him feel physically sick.

He turned on his laptop and went online. He typed 'Queen Elizabeth II' into Google and hundreds of thousands of results came back: birth, family tree, important events, family, wealth, ceremonies. As he read, it slowly dawned on him just how little he actually knew about the Royal Family. There were so many sides to them, the power, the fame, the money, their role over time, the different dynasties, the charity work, the size of the family. It was impossible to get a handle on it all.

After a while he felt swamped and decided to try search for the video. No matter what combination of search strings he tried, all he came up with was dead links. There were some screenshots and hundreds of obscure forums discussing the incident at length. Each thread had a different theory, each more bizarre than the last. None were even close to the truth and none even hinted at the disappearance of the Queen.

Dan noticed that most of the links fed back to the BBC website. It gave the official version of the Prince's death. He read a quote from the officer in charge of the investigation, an Inspector Sawyer, which talked of the search for the hit-and-run driver and a call for information from the public. As Dan read he found himself laughing out loud. He wondered if the police even knew they were being sent on a wild goose chase. It made him realise Fiona hadn't even questioned the authenticity of the video.

It was getting late when Dan walked to the kitchen to make a coffee. He filled the kettle with water and turned it on and fished around in the immaculate cupboards until he found some expensive looking filter coffee marked *By Royal Appointment* and a cafetiere. He stared glassily at the kettle, his mind numb as he waited for it to boil.

Armed with his new coffee, Dan felt curious to see how the news had been reported back home. He located some of the better known American news blogs and read CNN's coverage. After just a few minutes the message was clear – William's murder was a worldwide event. He sat back on the sofa, staring out of the window again at the view of the River Thames. The sheer scale and importance of the situation he had found himself in was not just terrifying, it was utterly exhausting.

His mind went back to his old life in New York, to the months before he had left to come over here. He had getting itchy feet again, and his then girlfriend hadn't been too happy. What was that phrase she used? Ah yes, he remembered, that was it. She'd called him an 'emotional cripple, unable to commit.' He half smiled, she had had a tongue like a razor blade, that girl. She'd made him even keener to get on the road quickly and come and experience London. But why had he thought of her suddenly? A thought popped into his brain. At first he found it shocking, but the more he thought about it, the more appealing it seemed.

He had run away then. Why not just run away now?

Act 4: Scene Two

*"Cowards die many time before their
deaths. The valiant never taste of death but
once."*

Julius Caesar

21st December

The next morning, from his vantage point high up on the roof of the Ministry of Defence, it was easy for Sergeant Theodore Jackson to track Dan Knight as he left Whitehall Court. His figure was clearly silhouetted in the scope of his military grade, laser focused, infrared binoculars. Jackson had spent an uncomfortable night on the roof, doing surveillance on the entrance to Dan's apartment building. It was a very boring detail, plenty of time for his mind to wander. Dangerous as Mogadishu city in Somalia was, it was a lot more fun than this.

Jackson had been the first to arrive at the kidnap scene with the Major. The initial moments of the operation had been filled with confusion, but Jackson had clearly seen the terrorist pointing a gun at Dan before swivelling to target the Queen. His view was that the terrorists had been using Dan for PR purposes, but it had gone wrong. As he was mulling it over for the fiftieth time, his earpiece crackled into life.

"Unit two, this is HQ. Sit rep on target. Over." It was

the Major.

"Roger HQ. Eleven hundred hours." He saw the doors of Whitehall Court open. Dan appeared. "Target in sight. Just leaving the building. It looks like he's taking a right down Horse Guards Parade, likely to be heading over to the bridge to cross onto the Southbank and the London Eye. Over."

"Roger that."

"The target spent the night in Whitehall Court. He didn't make any calls, nothing of interest on the video from flat. He went online, we tracked his activity. He spent a few hours reading up about the Royal Family and His Highness' death. The server log is available for your analysis. No email or mobile activity. Over."

"Roger that. What is your assessment? Over."

"Low risk, he's in a busy, tourist area, bodies in the zone. Over."

"Roger that. Get back to HQ immediately. There's been a development and I want all eyes on it. We've got some positive information from MI5 on the identity of the kidnappers. An expert criminal profiler is coming in to brief us at fourteen hundred hours."

"Roger and out."

Dan had woken up with conflicting thoughts in his mind. Should he stay and fight, or just run? He had always enjoyed city life. He felt safe in the busy streets, anonymous but involved. London and New York were similar cities in many ways. In both you could walk for hours without having to speak to another living soul, yet all the time be surrounded by thousands of people. He decided to take a walk along the riverside. He threaded his way past the tourists, and made his way back to the front of Whitehall Court, crossed over the busy Victoria Embankment main road and started heading to the gleaming and jagged Hungerford Bridge that crossed over to the south side of the River Thames.

His rambling journey was stopped by a work of art. It was a three dimensional representation of the Battle of Britain. A long narrow monument that appeared out of nowhere on the pavement, a startling and complex brass edifice about the length of a Spitfire fighter plane from World War II.

Along one side were carved hundreds of names of pilots who had lost their lives. The other side was dominated by carvings of St Paul's Cathedral, fighter aircraft, explosions, fire, death, firemen, women working in a munitions factory, burning buildings. At the very centre of the piece determined young pilots leapt out, literally bursting out from the front of the sculpture. They were heading to their imaginary planes as an air raid siren announced another attack from the German Luftwaffe. It was an extraordinary and modern piece, but the style of it reminded Dan of an old black and white war movie. He could almost hear the sirens and the bombs exploding around him. He looked at the carved faces of the pilots and a sense of their bravery swept over him.

He had been seriously considering packing his bags and running away. Yet faced with the sacrifice of these young pilots from all those years ago, he was humbled. All of them faced death every day, all would have lost friends and seen others burned and mutilated in front of their eyes. Their entire country and culture as well as their individual lives had been under threat, but they hadn't flinched for one moment. They had stared a fantastically determined and technically superior enemy in the eye and faced them down. Against the odds, they had triumphed.

Dan turned to face the grey river. A cold breeze blew off the water and he shivered. In front of him stood the London Eye, the world's largest Ferris wheel. It towered above the nearby buildings, dozens of glass cylindrical capsules hanging from the pure white steel frame. In each of the capsules he could see groups of people, silhouettes in the low light. The Eye's slow rotation made it seem stationery, but as he crossed Hungerford Bridge to the South Bank its movement became clearer.

There was a coffee shop next to the ticket office and Dan sat down, staring up at the towering wheel above him, wondering what to do. The idea of running away was fading. What would it achieve? Where would he go that would be safe? His gaze moved down to look at the queue in front of the London Eye and the crowds coming down the exit ramp. They all had smiles on their faces and he envied their carefree mood.

He felt exhausted and stood up to buy a coffee. He shoved his hands in his coat pockets looking for change and came across the booklet of tickets from Royal Security. He pulled it out and saw, underneath a half ripped ticket for the Tower of London, one for the London Eye.

He looked up, startled by a booming laugh from a middle aged African man whose children were jumping around, talking about all the sights they had seen from the top of the Eye. Dan looked at the family, and down at the ticket. He shrugged his shoulders. Why not? He joined the queue.

The line of people waiting was short and moving quickly. It took about five minutes for Dan to reach its head. He could see a capsule approaching and edged himself forward. The Eye never stopped moving. As each capsule reached the boarding platform its doors slid open and people quickly shuffled in, then the doors shut and the capsule moved on in its endless journey.

"On your own? Or with a group?" The attendant looked at Dan as he spoke.

"I'm on my own."

"Hey, a fellow American. Want to come in with our group bud?" Dan turned round to see a cluster of four guys. Two of the group were large middle-aged men, sweatshirts, similar glasses and baseball caps making them appear almost, but not quite, identical twins. The other men were younger, better dressed. They seemed disinterested in Dan, both already with cameras eagerly poised.

"Sure, why not?" said Dan.

As the capsule rotated into place the group of five stepped through the sliding door. Inside, there was a long slender bench and curved glass walls giving a vast view of London. The movement of the wheel was almost imperceptible but almost before he realised it, the capsule had slipped away from the platform and started its climb skywards. Within a few minutes he was gazing down on the rooftops of Buckingham Palace and

St James Park, and smiled as he saw the window of the apartment he was staying in at Whitehall Court. It looked tiny from up here and he realised he'd left the light on.

Dan glanced across to the other passengers, "Thanks for letting me bust into your group, guys."

"Hey it's no problem." The voice belonged to one of the almost identical twins, a big man with florid cheeks and a mop of unruly grey hair under a Chicago Bears' cap set off by a moustache sitting on top of grey stubble.

The group ignored Dan. Instead they jostled for position, snapping pictures of Big Ben, St Paul's Cathedral and the London skyline as the capsule rotated.

"You'd better turn off the flash," said Dan. "You'll just get pictures with light flashes against the glass and a black background."

"Neat idea, bud."

Dan smiled. He hadn't heard anyone use that phrase for years. "So where are you guys from?"

"Boston." The man was standing behind Dan, looking over his shoulder towards St Paul's Cathedral and Tower Bridge.

"Boston? Sweet town. Very European. You sound a bit more west coast to me," said Dan, "maybe over to Cali."

Suddenly Dan felt a huge arm snake round his neck. It jerked tight on his throat and he felt a cold metal object push into his back.

"That's because I'm from Kent, you cunt." The voice had changed. The odd American accent was gone to be replaced by a harsh London growl. "We've been watching you, Danny boy. What do you think you're playing at, son? How do you think you're going to find Shakespeare's Truth taking a ride on the London Eye? Think you'll see it from up here? Winking at you like a happy cat's arse?" Dan's eyes bulged in panic and pain as the grip on his throat tightened. He could see the reflection of the men in the glass.

"Wait, wait, I have. I've found it, the secret." He felt the grip on his throat lessen. "It's true, I found a name on Shakespeare's monument in Westminster Abbey, Sir Francis Bacon. That's Shakespeare's Truth isn't it? That's what you meant?" The grip on his throat relaxed and he breathed in relief, but then suddenly the arm tightened again and he was pushed forward, his head cracking against the glass window.

"You've discovered the father's name. That's not the truth we seek, you idiot."

"What else is there? What do you want me to do? I don't know what you want!"

"You were right, Luther." It was a new voice in the group. "You can see it in his eyes, he wanted to run away, to avoid his destiny. Look at his face. There's no strength, just cowardice and fear." Dan looked in the glass, he could see the man's reflection. He was grinning, his teeth bared in a snarl, his voice tense.

"I agree, but Damascus says he is the one we seek. He cannot be questioned."

"I would never question the leader, but you can still see the fear in his eyes. Look at him, Luther, he's weak. We should just kill him."

"No wait, you don't understand," said Dan, fighting to speak, "I don't know why you want me? Luther? That's your name? Who is Damascus? You're Rosicrucians aren't you? Is he your leader? Tell me what you want from me!"

Luther slightly loosened his grip on Dan as he reached into his pocket for something with his free arm.

"We want the proof of the fra rosi crosse, Shakespeare's Truth. You've found the father's name and now you need to take the great step beyond that. If you test our patience any more, if you are so blind you don't see your destiny, your own death and hers will come. And neither will be quick or painless." Luther brought his hand in front of Dan's face. His opened his fist. Inside was a severed human finger.

At one end was a long nail, unmistakably that of a woman, the red nail varnish contrasting against the wrinkled skin. Luther brought the finger closer to Dan's head, holding him tighter as he struggled. He traced the nail in a small arch on Dan's cheek, then with a sharp movement Luther thrust the end of the finger up into Dan's nose. Pain shot through Dan's head. The men burst out laughing. Dan could see his face in the glass. He looked pathetic and frightened.

"She'll lose a lot more than a finger soon, Danny boy. Maybe we'll move onto her eyes and send you those. Fancy telling your mates the Queen's got her eye on you? If you have any mates, that is. I fancy you're a bit of a Danny no-mates."

Dan's breath was coming in rasps. The capsule was now nearing the end of its journey, he was only minutes away from getting out of there. Luther unhooked his arm from around Dan's neck. Dan span around to see a snub-nosed matt black revolver pointed at him.

"Ladies and gentlemen, we'll shortly be landing, we hope you've enjoyed your flight on the British Airways London Eye. If you'd like to look towards the East corner in approximately one minute we'll be taking a photograph of your group." The metallic voice echoed through the capsule.

Luther smiled, the severed finger nowhere to be seen. "Not very thoughtful, boy. The Queen gives you the finger and you don't give her anything in return. How about it? Got something for the old bird?" Luther grabbed Dan's left hand and yanked his little finger backwards. A jolt of pain shot through Dan's arm and he screamed as he felt the finger snap out of its socket.

"There, we're a bit more even now. Next time it'll be an eye for an eye, bible style. Find Shakespeare's Truth. Save your life and hers."

Dan found himself being manoeuvred by the men so he was in the centre of the group. Pain washed over him. He could hardly stand. As the doors of the capsule slid open he felt the gun barrel pushed into his back.

"Now be a good boy, unless you want your spine to be splattered all over London." The group walked out past the waiting queue of people. No-one paid him any attention apart from one small boy who stared at him open-mouthed.

Once out of the Eye and free of the crowds, Luther leant over and whispered in Dan's ear. "Don't think you can run to the police or those Royal Security soldier wankers. We know who you talk to, boy. Go anywhere near your Embassy, the cops or the soldiers and you'll die. Run away and we'll find you, tear your eyes out and piss in the holes. I'll chop off your meat and two veg and choke you with your balls. I'll gag you on your own entrails and drown you in your own cowardly piss."

"So I'm on my own? I can't talk to anyone else?"

"Bloody hell Danny boy, are you dumb as well as daft? If you need help, you find it. Just be bloody careful about it. Any soldiers, anyone who can come after us – and the Queen gets stuffed and you drown in the old cow's fetid blue blood." Luther leant forward and whispered into his ear. "When you find it, we'll find you, don't you worry about that." He stood up, his voice suddenly jovial and normal. "Now then Danny boy, I'm nipping off to the boozer with the boys, but there's something else I want to talk to you about first."

Act 4: Scene Three

*"We few, we happy few, we band of
brothers. For he that sheds his blood with
me shall be my brother"*

Henry V

The Major sat at one end of the oval table in the Royal Security incident room flanked by Jackson and Vaughan and the rest of the soldiers in the task force. A much milder looking man in a conservative blue suit sat opposite the Major. He seemed uncomfortable, his briefcase clutched protectively on his knees.

"Good news," said the Major. "Two breakthroughs. First of all, we have a positive ID on one of the dead kidnappers. He's been identified as the same man in the video featuring the Prince." The Major produced a police photo of a round faced skinhead with florid red cheeks.

"Nick Grey, known as Manchester Nick. A history of mental illness with form for GBH and attempted murder. Passed capable of living in society by our glorious Care in the Community social workers seven years ago, promptly half killed a teenage girl. Sado-masochist. Compulsive obsessive, cruel and socially inept. Came out of Brixton slammer about nine months ago, apparently a reformed man. Married an East European prostitute two months later. Disappeared on her when she got pregnant."

Vaughan laughed. "Another passport shag eh. Where's the lowlife been since then?"

"He dropped off the map. His profile marks him out as a classic vulnerable, the perfect target for radicalisation. That leads me onto the second breakthrough. The identity of the kidnappers. Doctor Dawkins?"

The newcomer to the group stood up, placing his briefcase on the table in front of him. The soldiers shifted in their seats, turning towards him. He cleared his throat and began to speak in a soft Scottish accent.

"Gentlemen, my name is Doctor Peter Dawkins. I am from MI5 and my role is to give advice in regards to the psychological profiling and psychographic analysis of potential... suspects." Dawkins stumbled on the word, as if searching for the correct phrase. His eyes flicked around the room. "In essence, the likelihood is ninety seven percent that the terrorists are a religious and political secret society."

"What about the other three percent?" asked the Major.

"There is of course the possibility that it is a contemporary political movement like the ETA separatists in Spain or the IRA in the Republic of Ireland, but that is highly unlikely bearing in mind the ritualised nature of the killing and the lack of stated demands."

"Do you have any particular suspects?"

"There is a shortlist, Major." Dawkins opened his briefcase and slid out two photographs. One was a digital image captured from a video. It showed the kidnapper, identified by the Major as Manchester Nick, dragging the Prince's body. The other was a close up photograph of the robe he had been wearing when the Major had killed him.

"There is a small design that is consistent across the images. An icon of a red rose within a cross. I assume you've already seen this on the video. It's the sign of an ancient secret order called the Rosicrucians. They were formed around the time of Queen Elizabeth back in the sixteenth century."

Jackson leant forward in his chair and spoke directly to Dawkins. "So they want us to work out who they are? They're sending us clues like that sick fuck in Somalia." Two of the other soldiers around the table laughed.

Dawkins looked confused by the comment, his eyes shifting to Jackson for explanation. "Sorry Doc," said Jackson, "me and some of the boys were out on covert ops for a couple of months in Somalia, there was a particularly unpleasant warlord who had a fondness for burning out people's eyeballs with cigars. He'd leave the bodies around so we'd know it was him. Fuck knows why, and anyway it wasn't anything that couldn't be sorted out with an axe."

"We're not here to talk about how you earn your pocket money soldier. Dawkins, please continue."

"Thank you Major. However, your Sergeant does make an interesting point. The Rosicrucians have made it clear to us they want their identity discovered. We've got a profile on them here," he tapped his briefcase, "but it's all flimsy evidence, seeing as our only research is from seventeenth and eighteenth century documents. The reality of it is that, like many other ancient and secret orders, the Rosicrucians became much more mainstream over time, peaceful and non-threatening, more obsessed with their own dogmas and rituals. However, it appears that an extremist and highly aggressive and secretive faction also exists, who we need to concern ourselves with now. This splinter group has twisted their philosophies into justification for murder."

"So most of them are peaceful and happy-go-lucky, but there's a minority of psychos on the rampage, going around radicalising vulnerable people like our dopey skinhead and murdering people. You sure they're not really muslims?" said Vaughan, causing laughter from the soldiers.

Dawkins seemed embarrassed. "For the sake of this conversation, I'd like to restrict ourselves to these radical Rosicrucians from this point forward."

"Yeah sure, we don't need to go on a hippy hunt," laughed Vaughan.

"You spoke of a shortlist?" interrupted the Major.

"I was referring to a shortlist of groups that could lead us to them. As a secret group they had strong affiliations with the Freemasons and the Church of England. Investigating these is a rather delicate process. That said we do have another, more innovative theory on how to trace our terrorists."

The Major looked surprised. "Really? Excellent. Let's hear it."

"The CIA found the connection. The founder of the main Rosicrucian movement was Sir Francis Bacon, the Elizabethan philosopher and statesman. One of Bacon's big ideas was that in the unforeseen future England would become the 'New Atlantis,' a golden, all powerful country that ruled the world."

"He predicted the British Empire?" said Jackson.

"No, this was different. Bacon's 'New Atlantis' was a book detailing a whole new societal structure, a blueprint for the ultimate government and state he documented in a book, his vision of a perfect England. Now it appears this book became like a bible to our extreme Rosicrucians. After Bacon died his reputation grew within the group, taking on mythic and mystical proportions. They made Bacon their God." Dawkins paused and opened his briefcase again. He pulled out photocopies of an ancient handwritten document, on which a couple of paragraphs had been highlighted. He passed the papers around the table. "About a hundred years after Sir Francis Bacon died, the cult of Baconism was at its height within the Rosicrucians. One of the most prominent leaders at that time was allegedly Sir Christopher Wren, the architect who designed Saint Paul's Cathedral. We found mention of a document written by Wren hinting at a great treasure bequeathed by Bacon that he, Wren, had access to. Wren gave the Rosicrucian leaders two words, 'shall dissolve', as a sign. The claim was that this treasure was something that could change the country, something so valuable it needed to be hidden until the time was right."

"The time was right for what?" said Jackson.

"To create the New Atlantis of course. For England to take its rightful place as leader of the world."

"So, let me get this straight," said the Major. "After hundreds of years, an aggressive splinter group of the

Rosicrucians has chosen this moment to emerge from hiding and take lethal action against us. The phrase 'shall dissolve' is a clue that leads them to some kind of treasure they believe will help them bring about this new improved version of England, this New Atlantis. We know that 'shall dissolve' is from the Shakespeare play *The Tempest*, but that quote is used in any number of places. Films, TV shows, statues, books, never mind the play itself. What is its significance?"

"Right now, I'm not so sure it matters."

"Why on earth not?" The Major looked surprised. "They carved it on the body of Prince William. It must be important."

"The fact that they are flaunting these words on the body of a murder victim suggests that whatever this treasure is, they already have it, and they merely wish to signal that fact. Their plan is clearly in motion, and it is logical to assume they would only take those steps if this treasure, whatever it is, was already secured."

"We don't know they have this treasure for sure," said the Major. "Maybe they're still looking for it."

"It's possible, but why be so public unless they are in a position of power already?"

Jackson spoke up. "It could be simply to throw us off track. These fuckers seem to enjoy trying to fuck with us."

"A diversionary tactic? It makes a kind of sense." The Major nodded reluctantly.

Dawkins sighed. "To be blunt, we know almost nothing about what that phrase really means, or what their plan is. I'd rather focus our time now on what we do know. We have a strong lead on how to find them, and we also think we know how much time we have."

"You can work out where the freaks are?" said Vaughan. "We've drawn a blank so far. They dissolved into thin fucking air."

Dawkins smiled. "I may be able to help. Sir Francis Bacon's birthplace is documented as being in London. More precisely it was at York House on the Strand."

"York House? Isn't that the medieval mansion alongside the river near the Savoy Hotel?"

"Yes Major. It became the spiritual heartland for many Rosicrucians, a kind of private church. His nursery, where he was brought up as a young child has become a shrine. It's immensely important to them. We're sure they will still be using the building as an essential part of their rituals."

"If we track who goes into that building, we find a link to the Rosicrucians?" asked Vaughan.

"Oh yes, indeed that is the case." Dawkins voice picked up and a smile appeared. "Half of the building is privately owned, but the other half is used as an art gallery. It is also hired out to private groups, book clubs and the like. We've been through the visitors for the last few years and one regular group that stands out is the Atlantean Society, a group of mainly retired academics and researchers who meet to discuss Sir Francis Bacon. They seem like a group of harmless enthusiasts. The fact that the Atlantean Society are regular visitors to York House would make them an excellent cover for the Rosicrucians to gain access to the building."

The Major stood up and began to pace about the

room. "It's clever. If the Rosicrucians would ever overlook anything, then this could be it." He turned to his team. "The first step will be to investigate Nick Grey's background and associates. We also need to interview the members of this Atlantean society and monitor York House. Vaughan, I'm giving you field control over Alpha unit. You've got a list of Nick Grey's known associates. I want them hit hard and fast. Who's seen him, where, when."

"It's not a very long list, just four people."

"In that case you can get to them quickly. Just do me a favour. Don't kill anyone and don't get fingered. There's a good chap?"

"Right boss, I'll do my best."

"Jackson, I want you to put together a tactical team. You're running Beta unit. I want immediate interviews of everyone in this Atlantean group. It's got to be done quietly and effectively. I'm going to have a look at making some discreet high level enquiries into the Church and the Freemasons." The Major snapped his fingers. "Wait a minute. The Freemasons. Dawkins. Do you remember all that bad publicity about them, when was it, about eight or so years ago?"

"Yes of course, I believe the publication of a book detailing their secrets may have been responsible."

"I seem to remember one of their leaders leaving in very controversial circumstances. Does that ring a bell with anyone?"

"Oh yes indeed, Major." Dawkins smiled. "It was high profile at MI5, there's a lot of casework available. Surveillance, a wire tap at the time. Sebastian Moseley I believe his name was. It's an interesting theory."

"A disgruntled former leader, sets up his own radical faction? It's possible. Can you detail some resource into him and getting me the files? I'll work it this end."

"Of course, Major."

The Major smiled. "Looks like we have some proper direction at last."

"Major Barnes-Jones, I'm afraid there is another issue we need to consider. Because the Rosicrucians haven't demanded any kind of ransom, we believe they are working to a ritualised timetable."

"Meaning?"

"I suspect it's no coincidence that all this has happened at this time of year. They believe that when New Atlantis arrives it will be on January the first, and it will be heralded by a great sacrifice as a symbol of the new era. Legends state New Year's Day was the day when the Three Kings visited Mary, Joseph and Jesus. On that day, the Kings received Jesus' blessing and were given a thousand years of heavenly wisdom to take back to their own people. It's extremely likely that whatever they are planning will culminate on New Year's Eve."

"You mentioned the freaks have a sacrifice?" said Vaughan.

"Yes indeed they do." Dawkins' voice faltered. "And we believe they already have their victim lined up. The Queen."

Act 4: Scene Four

"When sorrows come, they come not single spies, But in battalions."

Hamlet

Fiona absentmindedly ran her finger around the rim of her wine glass as the news report on the TV continued. Her living room was hot, the heaters on full blast, keeping the winter chill at bay. The news pictures showed the Royals on the balcony at Buckingham Palace. Mountains of flowers grew in front of the gates and thousands of people stood huddled in the sickly light.

The news presenter's words sounded hollow. "The public got what they were waiting for today, as for the first time since the tragic events of last week, the Royal Family publicly expressed their grief with an appearance at Buckingham Palace. As difficult as it must have been, the Prince's father, his Royal Highness Prince Charles, and his second son Harry, appeared in front of the crowds. Prince Charles spoke of his deep respect for the public's expression of their grief for the loss of his son. He then appealed to the press and public to allow the other members of the family, principally his mother, some privacy over the next few weeks. But some commentators have said there was a note of insincerity to the Prince's speech, as if he was holding something back. Many people have begun to question the lack of support from the Queen. She has failed to appear in public since the killing and it is thought that she is simply too upset for a public demonstration of grief. This is not the first time that the Queen has come in for major criticism at her apparent coldness towards the death of a member of the Royal Family. Of course, when William's mother Princess Diana died, her apparent lack of emotion or involvement outraged many people. That story was brought to life quite wonderfully in the movie *The Queen*."

Fiona's thoughts drifted away from the TV as she contemplated her half full glass of wine. Her attention snapped back when the commentary turned to the subject of the Prince's funeral.

"The big news today is that the funeral will take place in the second week of January, next year. This is an unusually long time to wait, nearly a month. We can only assume this is to give Her Majesty time to recover. This is Jeremy Breen at Buckingham Palace, now back to Natasha." The camera switched back to the studio, where the news anchor briskly began the next story.

"Will you turn it off, please Fiona? I can't bear it any more. It's just been William's death constantly for days." Fiona's friend Nicky Dudley leaned forward from the cream coloured sofa they were sharing to grab some crisps from the wooden bowl on Fiona's coffee table. Nicky took a sip from her wine glass and stared at Fiona. Her blue eyes flashed from her narrow but pretty face which was framed by short cropped jet black hair. "Since we saw that video, I just feel so sure they're lying about that business of a road accident. When it happened last week everyone I spoke to thought the

Prince had been murdered. Then yesterday when I tried to talk about it they just wanted to believe that rubbish on the TV. That girl Jamie in the physics department called me a conspiracy nut and asked me if I was into crop circles and sat at home reading Dan Brown books on the toilet, the bitch. It's a joke."

Fiona looked at Nicky and smiled weakly. They had clicked on the first day they met. Although they hadn't know each other for long, it hadn't taken Fiona long to realise they couldn't have been more different. Nicky was outgoing and confident around new people, often flirting outrageously and nearly always getting her own way with men. She, on the other hand, avoided the limelight whenever possible. Fiona thought they complimented each other, together making one whole person.

"Yes, I know what you mean," said Fiona, "I've thought about that video a lot recently."

"Anyway, why are we moping? We should be out enjoying ourselves." Nicky smiled mischievously.

"I hope you don't mean like last week. That Student Union bar was full of eighteen year olds. I felt like their mother."

"Oh that's not what they thought of you. You're their fantasy, the older woman. What about that rugby looking type with the blond hair?"

"Nicky! How dare you. I might be the fantasy of some drunken posh public schoolboy who wanders around with his collar turned up talking about his daddy's yacht, but believe me, he's not my dream."

"Yes, I know. You go for the bespectacled academic types who want to go on camping holidays and wear stripy cardigans. The sort of geek who thinks Paris is a city as opposed to a heroine of modern culture."

"Very funny." Fiona felt slightly annoyed. "Well I met someone actually. Yesterday."

"Oh really, do tell."

"Well, for a start he's gorgeous."

"Are you sure he's not gay?"

"He's a creative type, very arty, very well dressed. Looks like he takes care of himself."

"How old?"

"No idea, I would guess mid to late thirties? A bit older than us."

"Where I come from everyone is married by the age of twenty two or propping up a free council flat with a couple of kids. He's definitely gay."

"No! Anyway, it doesn't matter. Nothing will come of it. He's this American guy I met whilst I was at Westminster Abbey."

"Really? American? Was he flashing his dollar bill at you? You know how strong the dollar is against the floppy English pound these days? Oh my God, you have to tell me more. You met him in a church? Was he a choirboy? Did you ruffle his cassock?"

"Nicks! We're meeting tomorrow for breakfast."

"Breakfast? Um, honey, isn't that normally the sort of thing you do after, you've, you know… shagged his brains out?"

"Nicky you're a scandal! It's not like that. We got talking about the video."

Nicky sat upright, swinging her head to look at Fiona. "He's seen it too?" Nicky's voice had an edge of suspicion. "Did you explain your ideas to him and more importantly did he think we're crazy conspiracy freaks?"

"No. In fact, after a bit of a wobble we got on quite well. That's really the reason I asked you over."

"What, to talk about men?"

"Nicky, stop it. I really need to talk. We've made an amazing discovery but I don't know what it means."

"Honey! Open that other bottle and tell me more."

Act 4: Scene Five

*"Let us assay our plot, which if it speed,
Is wicked meaning in a lawful deed."*

All's Well That Ends Well

The soldiers looked at Dawkins in shock.

"New Years Eve. Not much time," said the Major.

"That's the understatement of the fucking century." Jackson looked angry. "They're sneaky fuckers, these Rosicrucians. The fuckers are probably laughing at us."

"We've got a plan of action now thanks to Doctor Dawkins. I'm chasing up this Freemason leader, Moseley. You have your orders..." The Major's mobile rang. He dug his hand into his pocket, glanced at the screen and took the call. "RS HQ, Barnes-Jones."

"Major Barnes-Jones, it's Dan Knight."

"What's wrong?"

"I've had enough."

"What do you mean? We agreed that you would spend a couple of days taking it easy." The Major heard the stress in Dan's voice and tried to calm him down.

"I just don't see how I can help you."

"Dan listen. We're taking you off surveillance. Get back to your normal life. We've been making excellent progress here and the investigation is in full swing."

"It was just a mistake I got involved in the first place. You believe me, don't you?"

"Yes, we know that. We're on your side here. You

don't have to feel pressured in any way, just stay around in case we need you."

"No, I can't."

The Major's tone hardened. "Listen here, Knight. This is a national emergency. You do not have the right to walk away. I'm issuing you a direct order. You will not risk placing Queen Elizabeth's life in any more danger by your lack of co-operation. Do you hear me?"

"No, I'm sorry Major, you can't order me around. I'm an American citizen. I thought about running away from this last night and now, after today, I've decided that's exactly what I am going to do. I'm out of it now. I'll go back to the apartment, but I'm just getting my gear then I'll be out of there in the morning. I'm heading back to my apartment in west London. I'm exhausted, I've had enough. Find your Queen on your own. Goodbye."

Act 4: Scene Six

"Some rise by sin And some by virtue fall"

Measure for Measure

L uther stood up from the bench where Dan sat with his head in his hands. "Good boy. I think that went pretty well. You should have been an actor. Maybe you could have taken the lead in a Shakespearian play, eh?" Luther lightly slapped Dan on the cheek with the flat of his hand. "Now don't forget lad, you don't go near that Major or his lot again, alright? If you talk to him, we'll know and then it's good night sweetheart for you and the old dear. I'll choke you on your own intestines, alright?"

"I get it. You'll kill me if I talk to the Major. You'll kill me if I talk to the police. You'll kill me if I go anywhere near the American Embassy. You'll kill me if I don't find this Shakespeare's Truth. And if I do find it, then what? You'll kill me?"

"Then my boy, you might just live to die a natural death, sitting in front of the fire gobbing on to disinterested grandchildren about how you once managed to save your rotten neck by following your destiny." Dan looked up and nodded. Luther laughed. "Good lad! No soldiers. No police. If fact, nobody that wears a uniform at all, not even a lollipop lady."Luther's breath was cloudy in the cold air. "Just one more thing. You have until New Year to solve your little riddle. Ten days. Then it's all over." He grabbed Dan's swollen hand and squeezed it in a mock handshake. Pain rushed up Dan's arm, and he collapsed onto the ground. When he looked up, the Rosicrucian was gone.

Back in Fiona's flat, Nicky and Fiona were still deep in conversation.

"So honey, this boy you met, is he on your side with everything?" asked Nicky.

"Yes, he actually helped me find the cipher. He had some good ideas."

"Why is he so interested?"

"I don't really know. It's a good question."

"You never know, maybe he's just interested in you. I think you should trust your instincts on this one. Give him a chance."

"But it did seem a bit weird as well. Why *is* he so interested? It's a bit scary. Maybe I should back off? Go to the police?"

"Come on honey, don't be crazy. Keep the police out of it. They'd be more likely to lock you up than anything else. Give the boy a break. It's scary, but exciting too, right? I'm sure he has his reasons. I think you should help him every way you can, and see how it develops. Come on, life's for living. I can chip in too, if you need it."

Fiona leaned forward and poured herself another glass of wine.

"You know what? I do really love our girly chats, but you've never really told me about how you're into all this history stuff. You look more like you should be putting on parties or working in PR, not studying for a history doctorate."

"So you'll help this boy out? Give the poor lad a seeing to in the sack at the very least?"

"Nicks! Okay, yes, yes, whatever. Now answer the question. Why aren't you in PR and parties?"

"Not that you're stereotyping, honey."

"Well, we are pretty different."

"No, fair enough. I've told you already my dad died last year."

"Yes, I'm sorry to bring it up. Was that tactless?"

"It's fine, really. I've just about had enough to drink to talk about it. Anyway it was his fault I got into history. Me and my sister never got to read Harry Potter when we were kids, we were watching videos of the lives of kings and queens of England on DVD. We were total losers in the school playground, a couple of right geeks. Of course, that was before I discovered boys and started going to the gym." Nicky laughed nervously.

Fiona looked over at her friend and saw a tear on her cheek. "Oh Nicky, I'm really sorry."

"I can't help it sometimes." Nicky wiped her cheek and leaned forward to pick up her glass of wine. "My dad's big thing was the Romans. He was only a teacher at the local school. It was nothing special, not like your dad, the famous Elwood Fletcher." Fiona drew her legs up to her chest defensively, wrapping her arms around her knees. "Tell me Fiona, how many books has he got published?"

"Two or three."

"Two or three hundred more like. Anyway, my dad and a few other friends were obsessed with Roman history. He even compiled some god-forsaken family tree trying to go all the way back to Caesar. He would spend weeks writing up programme ideas for the BBC, all of which were rejected. I wasn't really interested in it at first, but my sister Manda was fascinated. They would spend hours together discussing ideas. I felt left out. I just wanted dad to spend hours with me. So I pretended I was interested. But over time I grew to love it."

"Yeah, I know that feeling. Me and my brother were the same. I used to think my father didn't love me as much as him. So I threw myself into father's ideas. It was a way to be close to him. Looking back on it now, I just needed the attention. In the end, my father and brother fell out, but in my case it turned into a career."

"Yes, that was me and my sister too. I used to sit around feeling like an idiot. Knowledge was important to my dad. It was all that he had to offer. Just look at me now, doing a PhD on the influence of Roman gods on the development of Christian theology."

Fiona giggled. "Yes, we're a right couple of nerds." The mood was broken by the ring of a mobile. Fiona sprung to her feet and scurried into the kitchen to find her phone.

"Dan! That's a surprise."

"I'm so sorry to disturb you. Can I come over?"

"I thought we had arranged to meet tomorrow? I've actually got someone over here at the moment. We're in the middle of something. But it's…"

"Forget it. See you tomorrow." Before Fiona could reply the phone went dead.

Standing in the cold night on the bank of the River

Thames, waves of nausea swept though Dan's body. He didn't even know why he had rung her. He slowly began to retrace his steps back to the London Eye. A uniformed attendant appeared out of the haze; an acne ridden teenager, his ill-fitting polyester suit hanging loosely from his skinny frame. He looked suspiciously at Dan.

"Dude, are you alright? You're so pale dude."

"I need a hospital." Dan staggered as he spoke and the attendant's arm shot out to steady him.

"Woah, steady on dude, it's cool, man. We've got a paramedic here. Chill, I'll get you help." The teenager released him and swung around, sprinting back towards the ticket office. But as Dan collapsed onto the cold London pavement, a new emotion burrowed though the pain. He was surprised to find it was anger.

Act 5: Scene One

*"This above all: to thine own self be true
and it must follow as the night the day, thou
canst not be false to any man."*

Hamlet

22nd December

The café in the British Library was separated from the library by huge windows. It was early and the building was still quiet. From where Dan sat he could see each person as they walked in.

The café was festooned with Christmas decorations, each a character from a different Christmas book. An aroma of coffee and hot chocolate floated through the air, mixing with something Dan guessed was the smell of several hundred thousand ancient books in one space.

His eyes were drawn to the cartoon image of Scrooge from *A Christmas Carol* by Dickens. It was three days until Christmas and Dan could not have felt less festive. Only last week he had made plans to fly home. Now he needed to phone his mom and make excuses for not being there.

The visit to the hospital had been almost as traumatic as his run-in with Luther. The accident and emergency department had been crowded with festive revellers whose drunken antics had ended in disaster. He had sat, in pain, for two hours as the queue of invalids dissolved. When it was finally his turn to see a surprisingly young and unsurprisingly stressed Doctor, the treatment had been quick and painful. His broken finger had been x-rayed, set back in place and then strapped. A splint had been placed between the two fingers to stop any movement. Now, even with the painkillers, a dull pain throbbed through his hand.

Dan had arrived early for his meeting with Fiona. He passed the time rehearsing his story in his mind. It was going to be difficult. He had to tell her enough of the truth to make sure she was committed to helping him without frightening her off, but not burden her with too much.

The clock on the wall showed Fiona was twenty minutes late when she arrived. She looked different. Her clothes seemed more stylish and her hair was loose, the chestnut strands flowing over her shoulders.

"Sorry I'm late," she said. "The buses were rubbish. No tube. Sunday timetable..." Her voice trailed off.

"Let me guess what you're thinking." Dan raised his hands in a mock gesture of surrender. "You're wondering if I've been in a fight with a truck and spent the night on the sidewalk drinking lighter fluid and then managed to slam my fingers in the front door when I finally dragged my sorry ass home, right?"

Fiona smiled and sat down. "To be honest, I was wondering what I was doing here. We hardly know each other, and here you are looking like some sort of designer tramp."

"That's fair enough. For all I know, you could be an axe murderer!"

"And you could be a kitten drowner."

"Miaow! The truth behind my battle scars isn't very glam. I'm really sorry about last night too. I shouldn't have been hassling you on the phone."

"Well, I was surprised. You sounded… confused."

"I had a pretty messed up evening." For a moment Dan was tempted to tell Fiona everything. It would have felt wonderful. "Fiona, I've got to say, going through that with you at Westminster Abbey was pretty special for me, I was in the middle of something. I really felt like I'd screwed the pooch, but you made a difference. I know we don't really know each other but the way you popped into my life was just amazing."

"I'm hoping that's a compliment, although I'm not sure about screwing any pooches."

Dan looked down at his coffee and stirred it, staring at the brown liquid as it whirled round the green ceramic mug. "This sounds a bit nuts but I know a lot more about this whole business with Prince William and I need someone to share with."

"What? What else do you know?" Fiona's voice rose.

"Basically, as I'm sure you can imagine, there's a big security team, a military unit controlled by the Royal Family investigating Prince William's death."

"What, investigating the stupid idea that it was a hit-and-run?"

"No, that's just a cover story for the press. They're investigating the truth."

"The video. The Rosicrucians."

"Yes."

Fiona thumped the table with her fist. "I knew it. All

that stuff on the news, it's all lies! Well I've got some news for you too. I was having dinner with my best friend last night, Nicky, and she's totally on our side. I told her about our discovery and she says she's happy to help. She's a very clever girl. She's studying to get her history doctorate at the university."

Fiona had known of the secret for only twenty four hours and already she had told someone else? Could he really trust her? He realised he had no choice. "This girl Nicky. Do you trust her?"

"Of course. We're best friends." Fiona paused then made up her mind. "I'll text you her number. Maybe you should call her yourself?" Fiona looked up Nicky's number on her phone and forwarded it to Dan.

"Have you told anyone else about this?"

"No, I was waiting until I had spoken to you. I wanted to go to the police but Nicky thought we should wait until I saw you. She thought it could cause a lot of trouble, and she said you and I should decide what to do together."

"She's a clever girl. And she's right. The police genuinely believe in the hit-and-run. Telling them about a cipher on a statue and ranting about the video will only get us in trouble and confuse everything."

"How come you're so involved anyway? Are you some sort of spy?"

Dan burst out laughing. "Oh Jesus. Fiona, that's so funny."

Fiona's tone sharpened. "That's very rude. What am I supposed to think?" She folded her arms and looked away.

"I'm sorry, it's just that laughs are in short supply these days. No, I'm exactly who you think I am. I fell into this whole thing by accident."

"How?" Fiona was still feeling angry.

"Well – the simplest way of explaining it is, um, how can I put this, the Rosicrucians killed Prince William, and then they grabbed me because I work in the media. They held me at gunpoint and wanted me to go to the press. But I was rescued."

"So you were grabbed off the street by the Rosicrucians? Randomly? Then rescued? Who by?"

"A military unit controlled by the Royal Family, who know the video is real."

"So why do the police think it's a car accident?"

"The military are controlling them, and all of the media. They think the truth would create panic. Plus, there's more to it, there's someone else involved too."

Fiona leant forward. "Who?"

This was the moment Dan had been rehearsing. Everything depended on how Fiona reacted. "This is just between you and I. You can't tell Nicky." Fiona nodded. "The Rosicrucians didn't just kill William. They also kidnapped the Queen."

"The Queen!" Fiona thought her heart was about to jump out of her chest and she shot up in her chair, almost falling backwards off it. She looked around nervously, two people at another table, a bearded Jewish man in a black jumper and a student were staring at her from the other end of the café. She whispered to Dan. "What happened? How did they get her?"

Dan shrugged. "She was up on their Scottish estate, out in her Land Rover. It was probably a helluva lot easier than you'd think."

Fiona felt herself calming down. She glanced over, the two men had gone back to their conversation. "The Rosicrucians have the Queen and this army unit is trying to find her? But why are you still involved?"

"I got involved by accident, but now I'm committed to do whatever I can to help."

"We need to tell these soldiers about the cipher we found. Today."

"No!" Dan almost shouted. He checked himself and took a deep breath. "We can't. Not yet anyway. We need to get more useful information, something more compelling. It was an amazing accident I met you and we found the cipher, but we'll need something more concrete to take to the soldiers. They'll just laugh at what we have now. We'll only get one shot with them, it needs to right. And there's not much time." He looked at her. Was it obvious he was lying?

"Not much time?"

"The soldiers believe the Queen will be killed on New Year's Day unless they find her."

"Oh my God, that's just over a week! It's the 22nd today." Fiona felt her heart hammering again. What had she stumbled into?

"I know. I feel involved. I'll do whatever I can in the meantime to help."

"Oh, me too." Fiona's mind whirled. To think that she might help save the Queen was an astounding feeling. But it was more than just doing her best for

Queen and country… it was easily the most exciting thing that had ever happened to her, and she was starting to love the thrill of it all.

An unwelcome but useful thought flickered into her mind. "My original idea for today was to do some background research, something we could have shown the police. But things have changed. There is something I can do to help us get the evidence we need for the soldiers, Dan."

"What is it?"

"It's not a what, it's a who." She took a deep breath. "My father. You know I talked about him when we were going around Westminster Abbey yesterday."

"Sure, I remember. He got you into all this."

"Well it's a bit more complicated than that. He's a walking encyclopaedia when it comes to the history of ciphers, Elizabethan mysteries and secret societies. In fact, he's probably forgotten more than I'll ever know."

"This is great! When can we go and see him?"

"It's not that simple. We don't really get on. We had a falling out and I haven't seen him for three months. He's seriously ill." Fiona stopped.

"You okay?"

"Not completely, to be honest," she replied, forcing a smile, "it's just a bit painful. He's a paranoid schizophrenic with complications including mild dementia. He's very unpredictable and gets terrible mood swings. He's not the man he was. "

"I'm so sorry."

"He's in a hospital up near mum, Shakespeare's home town of Stratford-upon-Avon in fact. A bit ironic considering everything. I'm not sure how much you know about schizophrenia, but he has delusions, including hearing voices. They give him instructions. It's very scary when he gets like that."

"Sounds very difficult for you to cope with."

"It is, but a lot of the more extreme behaviour is controlled by the drugs. The knowledge is still there, locked away in his head. When he was in his forties and fifties he used to be on the lecture circuit in the USA. He's got shelves full of books he's written, mainly biographies of Elizabethan figures. You don't just lose all that knowledge."

"Do you think he could help us?"

"I'm sure of it. We'll go and see him, but it's going to be quite hard for me."

"I can imagine, seeing a parent or anyone you care about when they are sick is always difficult."

"There's more to it than that. The reason I haven't seen him since September is that after things had been getting gradually worse at home I had a huge argument with him and left. I knew it was just his disease making him behave that way but I just couldn't deal with it at the time. After I left, he tried to kill my mother by locking her in the barn, his office, and setting it on fire. I got up there just in time. My father was arrested and locked up in a secure hospital. Mum was okay. She was quite badly burnt, but thankfully was out of hospital after a few weeks."

"And you haven't seen him since?"

Fiona shook her head and then the tears came. Dan jumped up and held his arms open. Fiona paused, staring at him as the silver lines of tears crossed her checks. Then she rose and embraced him. Dan could feel her sobbing into his chest, her body was soft and warm, and he was overcome with a feeling of selfishness mixed with desperation and hope. He had pulled her into the middle of the storm his life had become. All he could hope for was that she didn't get too badly hurt.

Act 5: Scene Two

"Tis time to fear when tyrants seem to kiss."

Pericles

S ergeant Jackson hated wearing suits. They made him think of sad, weak chinned accountants; the types of impotent little white turds who would in another era have been gassing jews, gays and gypsies in a Nazi concentration camp. Yet here he was, in a blue pinstriped suit about to try and get some info out of some old fogey without scaring the silly old buffer to death.

It was a quiet street full of Georgian stucco-fronted houses with immaculately trimmed hedges and alarm systems, hemmed in by looming blocks of grey council flats full of illegal immigrants subletting without the local council knowing and desperate single mothers with out of control kids. He had stationed a second officer at the back of the house to monitor the rear exit and another two soldiers sat in a warm car parked a few yards down the street comparing girlfriends.

The Sergeant glanced about one final time before striding up to the front door. It took him a few seconds to locate the bell, hidden away at the side of the door, obscured by overhanging ivy. He pressed the button and waited. It was nearly a minute before the door was opened slightly to reveal an ancient eye looking out.

Jackson was in no mood for games. It had already

been a long day. Without waiting for an invitation he pushed hard on the door. The frail body belonging to the eye had no chance as the heavy door swung open. Jackson stepped quickly through into the hallway, eyebrows raised at the porcelain flying ducks on the embossed maroon wallpaper.

"William Milner?"

The old man nodded a reply. Milner was dressed in a grey cardigan and a tired grey suit hanging off a withered skeletal frame. Jackson thought the pensioner's face looked like a wrinkled onion. A shock of white hair was greased down on the crown of Milner's head. Behind, the hallway extended into a kitchen and Jackson noticed a second person, an equally old woman. She peered out of the gloom, her eyes fixed on the intruder.

Jackson produced a fake ID from the inside pocket of his suit and as he thrust it forward the old man shrank back against the hall wall.

"I'm secret service. We're investigating a murder." Jackson let the words linger in the air, enjoying the stark fear he saw in the man's eyes. "We know you're a member of the Atlantean Society. We know you spend time at York House and we know why. We're interested in finding a man called Nick Grey. He is a Rosicrucian. We suspect he has infiltrated your group. Do you know him? He's tall, young, skinhead, scar on his face."

The old man seemed to regain his composure and his body straightened as he lifted himself from the wall. "Sir," he spoke clearly, "I am not sure where you have retrieved this rather insidious information, but I suspect you are mistaken. I can assure you that the Rosicrucians are merely a self-help group, and one we are rather disinterested in."

Jackson's shoulders slumped. This was the ninth member of the Atlantean Society they had tracked down in the last eighteen hours and all of them had been the same. The third person he had interviewed had been even more of a disaster. Jackson had become frustrated with stuttering answers and vague responses, so Jackson had pushed the old duffer hard in the chest. The old boy had proceeded to have a heart attack. Jackson still felt annoyed at the hour he had wasted trying to sort out the mess.

The wife came out of the shadows. She was a tiny woman, shrunken by old age, a walnut in a dress. Her steps were slow but a pride burned in her eyes.

"Billy, what's all this about?" she said, her gaze fixed on Jackson. "What's this man talking about, what have you done?"

"I've done nothing, Edith, I've not even heard of this criminal he's talking about."

Jackson drew his gun from an inside jacket pocket. It was a stumpy black Sig Sauer P226 pistol. The gun fired 9 mm parabellum cartridges, which Jackson knew were perfect for blowing a man's head apart at close range. He pushed the gun against the old man's cheek.

"I didn't say he was a criminal. Now let's make this nice and simple. You tell me what you know about Nick Grey or that shitty fucking wallpaper's about to get some brain coloured stripes." Jackson smacked the butt of the pistol against the old man's head. A wrinkled hand shot to his face, fingers that came away spotted in blood.

The old man looked at his wife and then back to Jackson. "Fine, I'll tell you. There have been a couple of new members join the group recently. They were different from the rest of us. They were youngsters, in their forties. We haven't had new members in twenty years, so it was a bit of a shock. They came along to a couple of meetings. Then we didn't hear from them again."

"Go on."

"Then one evening I got a call from Alfred."

"Alfred Potts?" interrupted his wife. "I've told you to stay away from that man, he's nothing but trouble."

"Ignore her. Keep talking old man."

"Alfred said he'd seen the two men going into the Temple in York House. It's not unusual for members to do this. You see you can request keys for the meeting room from the Atlantean society treasurer Mr Wilmslow. Members will often meet privately to discuss matters of interest."

"Get to the point, old man."

"The thing is that you have to have been a member for three years to get a set of keys, even then Mr Wilmslow is a bit of a dragon. He used to be a librarian at the British Library. He's a stickler for everything being shipshape and Bristol fashion. We couldn't believe how easily these new people had the keys. We called up Mr Wilmslow, but his wife said he was retiring from the society and didn't want to talk about it. We were shocked. So Alfred and I decided to find out what was going on." The old man looked up and smiled nervously at Jackson. Jackson pulled the gun away and put it in his pocket. The old man began to talk faster and more confidently. "It was all a bit of a game at first. We dressed in dark clothes and kept watch on York House. It was all very Sherlock Homes. However, it soon lost its novelty and we were about to give up when one night we hit the jackpot. Men turned up, out of the blue, and they let themselves into meeting rooms. Alfred had brought his keys along with him, so we let ourselves in after them."

"What do you mean, Billy, what is all this?"

His wife was starting to sound shrill and Jackson found himself getting even more annoyed. "You can have a domestic about it later old lady. Just keep talking, old man."

"Alfred and I heard them talking, as we approached the main room. We walked in through the open doors and they didn't see us at first. A man was standing up in front of a group of three or four younger looking chaps. He was crying and screaming for repentance of his sins, for his time in prison. I heard his name. Now I think back I am sure it was Grey. I am also sure he had a scar on his face. I never forget a face."

"Keep going."

"It was then that they saw us. They stopped and a chap came over and explained that this was a different group. I recognised him as one of our mysterious new members. He said the meeting had nothing to do with the Atlanteans. They were just using the room with Mr Wilmslow's blessing, nothing to do with us."

"These new members, tell me more about them."

"I can't reveal information about members of the society without talking to the chairman."

Jackson sighed and put his hand in his jacket pocket, allowing the gun to slide into view. The old man took a deep breath before he told Jackson everything he knew.

Act 5: Scene Three

*"Witch: When shall we three meet again In
thunder, lightning, or in rain? Second
Witch: When the hurly-burly's done, When
the battle's lost and won."*

Macbeth

The motorway meandered through the English countryside like a sluggish grey river. Dan was always shocked by just how busy the English motorway system had become. American freeways, though in places equally busy, were on the whole much quieter. You could drive for hundreds of miles without passing another car, an endless horizon stretching away on every side.

"Take this exit, Dan," said Fiona.

Dan eased the Jaguar XKR off the inside lane of the M40 and into a slip-road, a green and white signpost indicating Stratford-upon-Avon. He stole a glance at his passenger. Fiona was hunched up in her seat, legs pulled up to her chest and staring blankly out of the window. Dan's iPod was plugged into the Jaguars hi-fi and *Hot Fuss* by The Killers was playing in the background. Dan and Fiona had nearly come to blows over the choice of music and the album was one of the few that they had both agreed on. Dan had suggested Sufjan Stevens, Fiona had wanted Lily Allen. He had been insulted that she even thought it might be on his iPod, but after listening to The Killers for the second time he was bored.

"Driving this thing is a real trip, Fiona. Are you sure you don't want to have a go?" Dan was doing his best to keep Fiona's spirits up, the closer they got to the hospital the more withdrawn she seemed.

"No thanks, I don't really do cars, I'm more of a bike person."

"I prefer four wheels."

"You've obviously never been on a classy machine like a Triumph then. Bikes are much more fun. Cars are just to get from A to B. That Ford would have been fine. I don't know why you insisted on this monster."

"Hey, I'm having the week from hell and I don't get out of London much, so I thought the very least I could do is get a top dollar rental. Anyway, Miss Fletcher, why don't you tell me a bit more about yourself?" Dan said, trying to keep her distracted.

"What do you want to know?"

"Oh you know, brothers, sisters, that kind of thing. Where did you grow up?"

"The place we're going to after the hospital is where I grew up. One older brother, but he may as well be from another planet thanks to my father. We talk maybe once a year, he lives in Edinburgh. I have no idea what he's even doing these days. What about you?"

"Originally I am from an egg." Dan looked across at Fiona. She smiled slightly. "I was born in the mid-west. It was all very agricultural. We started to move around a lot when pop got a job in the Air Force. We never really stayed anywhere for too long. I spent time in Denver, Hawaii, even Germany. We always seemed to end up in some bleak Air Force house or barren little town with me feeling like an alien. It's hard being the new boy at school every year. I suppose it was a bit sad really. Any time I made some good buddies we split somewhere else. Pop finally quit the Force and went into engineering and technology. We ended up settling in San Diego, as good a place as any I suppose. I've got one older sister, Tam. She lives in Manhattan."

"It sounds like a very mobile life."

"That's one way of looking at it."

"I suppose you must find it hard to settle down anywhere, even now? Is that why you've found yourself in England? Another place to drift through?"

He looked sharply at her. "I'm not sure I'm quite that disconnected. I'll settle soon enough." His voice trailed off, he started to think he was sounding apologetic. He was shocked. She had hit on his most personal fear, that his life had no real meaning or direction.

Fiona coloured slightly. "I didn't mean to pry." She paused and cleared her throat. "So, um, have you always worked in design and things?"

Dan smiled, happy to be back on firmer ground. "Pretty much, rightly or wrongly, it's always been my passion, my escape, something to dive into when reality is a bit much. I'm lucky enough to be good enough to make a living at it, and at the weekends I'll be trying to write some music, poetry, short stories, or even painting. Just trying to create something unique that chimes with my view of life."

"What, painting the walls?"

"Ha ha. No, you know what I mean but I'm no

Picasso. Unless we're talking abstract faces, although mine are more accident than design."

Dan navigated his way around a huge three lane roundabout. "How come your pop is in hospital in Stratford-upon-Avon?"

"It's a matter of geography. My Mum only lives about a half an hour drive away from the hospital in the Slaughters."

"What?"

"Upper and Lower Slaughter. It's the name of two upmarket Cotswold villages."

"So you could say you grew up in a slaughterhouse."

"Oh my, I've never heard that joke before."

"Are you sure your mom doesn't mind me crashing there as well?"

Fiona giggled. "Believe me, it'll be fine. My mum will probably try and marry us off by the end of the evening. It's one of her little obsessions. She jokes that she could write a book on how I make every relationship fail."

The traffic on the road became heavier as the Jaguar approached Stratford-upon-Avon. The green fields slipped away and were replaced by an ever increasing number of houses. Soon the main road become crisscrossed with smaller streets, roundabouts sprung out of nowhere and row upon row of 1930s houses appeared at the side of the road, drab and flat in the grey afternoon.

"There's one thing that's confusing me." Dan pulled to a halt at a set of traffic lights.

"What?"

"Was Sir Francis Bacon the founder or leader of the Rosicrucians?"

"Both. The legend is that he founded the order and wrote the philosophy they follow."

"So he really is at the centre of all this. What about Shakespeare? Your pop was doing some research?"

"I knew he'd been busy on something for months before his mind finally went. He'd been pretty secretive about the whole thing. But that last weekend I was up there he wanted to talk to me about Shakespeare. He went on and on all weekend, but kept refusing to show me his findings until I was about to head back to London. By then I just wanted to get away and didn't want to listen."

Dan glanced at her, he sensed she was closing up. "I can tell you what I know about Shakespeare if that helps."

"Go ahead."

"Alright, I know two things about the bard. Zero and zip. What about you?"

Fiona shrugged. "I know just the basics. Shakespeare's plays have been translated into every major language on earth, tons of movies. Personally I find the sonnets even more beautiful than some of the plays. 'Shall I compare thee to a summer's day?' Lovely! I know he is credited with inventing about two thousand words and he used about thirty thousand in total in his plays. That's pretty amazing when you consider there are only about eight thousand different words in the bible and Charles Dickens used more like seven thousand."

"Oh, so you don't know any detail then?"

"Ha ha." The road ahead was still busy and yet another set of traffic lights were visible in the distance. "Just keep straight on at these traffic lights." The Jag slowed and then sped across the junction, the car's powerful engine reacted instantly to Dan's slight press of the accelerator. "He was born in 1564, died in 1616."

"Shakespeare?"

"Yes. He worked as an actor. He was pretty good by all accounts and was successful for quite some time. He performed for both Queen Elizabeth the First and King James. Shakespeare did marry Anne Hathaway, but he dumped her after his son died at age eleven. His two daughters both lived to get married and have their own children in Stratford but I'm not sure that they used his name. I don't think he was a very good parent at all."

"So there might be direct descendants of William Shakespeare running around somewhere in Stratford today?" Dan smiled. "How bizarre, they probably don't even know who their great-great-great-great grand pappy was."

"What about you? You said you knew something about the plays if not Shakespeare himself?"

"Sure, I did study three or four when I was majoring in English. *Macbeth, Hamlet, Romeo and Juliet.* I always found his work fascinating. I guess the thing for me was the thought and imagination. There's so much depth, you could study just one for years. I guess if you really look at them, you can see they encapsulate every truth about human nature."

The car was continually stopping and starting as a

never ending series of traffic lights appeared. Dan looked at Fiona, she was leaning back in her seat staring at the grey houses as they stuttered by. He pushed himself back in his seat and lifted his right hand in the air, waving it dramatically. Then, in a deep, mocking English accent he said, "To be or not to be, that is the question. Whether 'tis nobler in the mind to suffer the slings and arrows of outrageous fortune or... errrr... have some fish and chips instead?" Fiona laughed so Dan carried on. "O Romeo, Romeo! Wherefore art thou Romeo? But, soft! What light through yonder window breaks? It is the east, and Juliet is the sun. And lo, she hath put ye kettle on and is making ye tea. Good job, I'm blooming spitting feathers mate, know what I mean darlin'?"

"You sound like Dick van Dyke in *Bednobs and Broomsticks* or whatever it was!"

"What's the plan anyway? Go and see your pop, then head on over to your mom's house? Would you like to try and grab a drink or something to eat before we go into the hospital?"

"I can't eat anything, I feel sick. God, I can't believe I'm doing this. Slow down here, then turn left in front of that newsagent. Then straight down that road and right at the T-junction."

Dan followed her directions, the car moving quickly now they were away from the traffic of the main road. He manoeuvred the car down a narrow street with rows of cars parked on either side.

"Look, there's the hospital." Fiona pointed at an utterly characterless set of squat red buildings nestled on the horizon. "Can you see it? Up the hill on the left?" The hospital reminded Dan of a set of giant Lego blocks he had once bought as a Christmas present for a friend's child. He couldn't remember which child or even where he had bought the present. His life before this last week was starting to feel like a dream.

Neither spoke as they arrived at the hospital. Dan swung the car though the entrance, following the signs for the visitor's car park. He parked up and looked over at her.

"Are you ready for this Fiona?"

"I'm going to have to face him sometime, so it might as well be today."

"How do you want to play it? Do you know what you're going to say to him?"

"Say to him? God, I don't know. See how he is? Ask him if he can help with the connection between Bacon and Shakespeare?"

"What about telling him about the Rosicrucians?"

"Oh Jesus Dan, I don't know. Stop going on about it." Before he could reply she was out of the car and striding towards the hospital entrance. Dan followed.

There was a garden outside the entrance and in the middle was a bench. An old man sat on it, dressed in red and white striped pyjamas, though they hardly concealed his emancipated frame. The skin on his face was tight and pale. One hand hung loosely at his side, a half-smoked cigarette dripping ash. The other was held up to his ear, his head bobbing back and forth to the silent sounds of an invisible radio. A large smile was glued to his face.

As Dan and Fiona approached the hospital the large glass doors slid open automatically and a faint odour of disinfectant seeped out. Inside was a long grey corridor. Patients and staff trudged up and down it. Above them hung a cluster of signs indicating that they should walk forward to reach Macbeth Ward, Cotswold Ward and Vale Ward. Fiona paused, her hand instinctively reaching out to stop Dan.

She stared at the signs. "Mum told me he's in Vale Ward. It's a secure unit." The couple weaved their way through the hospital looking for Vale Ward. Eventually a sign painted on the wall announced that they had found it.

"Oh God. Dan, I don't know if I can do this." Dan looked at Fiona and saw the fear behind her eyes. She reminded him of a little girl, lost and vulnerable.

"You don't have to."

"No, we've got to. I've got to." Fiona took hold of Dan's hand and then rang the bell.

Nothing happened at first. They heard a distant buzz and then a shuffle of movement, chairs scraping, raised voices. Then the door opened.

A short, dumpy and extraordinarily plain woman in a nurse's uniform appeared in the doorway. A broad smile flashed across her face, exposing nicotine stained teeth.

"You must be Fiona!" The nurse had a deep Welsh accent. "Come in, come in my loves. I'm Helen. I'm the senior nurse." Helen looked at Dan, her eyes flicked up and down. "And you're a family member?" "Um no, he's with me," said Fiona.

"But only for the night," said Dan. Helen burst out laughing.

"No, I meant..."

"Not to worry, my loves, I wish I had offers like that. Anyway Elwood is in his room. We told him you were coming about an hour ago, but don't be shocked if he's forgotten."

They walked into the ward. "God, what is that smell?" Fiona whispered.

Dan recognised it immediately. It was the smell of the old and ill. It reminded him of his childhood, the reason they had ended up in San Diego. That's where his grandparents had lived. The memories of visiting his mum's father as he died of cancer... a shudder ran through him and he grabbed Fiona's hand, squeezing hard.

Helen guided them through the entrance hall and into the ward. Dan tried not to stare at the collection of shrunken and despondent old people littering the sofas and chairs, staring numbly at a huge old TV hanging off a garish yellow wall. They had walked into a large open room, cheap abstract modern art was nailed all along one wall, festooned with haphazard Christmas decorations. The tinny sound of Christmas carols could be heard from a cheap hi-fi in the kitchen. Dan looked over and caught sight of three plump nurses chattering over a large packet of chocolate biscuits and cups of tea.

They walked past the open area and into a second corridor. Down one end, Helen halted in front of a closed door with a small square window containing a pane of frosted glass. "This is your father's room. Give me a shout if you need anything my loves. Oh yes, one final word. He's on some tranquilisers at the moment. We had a bit of a scene this morning but he should be hunky dory now." As she turned to leave, she stopped, her lilting accent taking on a softer tone. "We all love your dad here you know."

Fiona stared at the retreating nurse in surprise. They loved her father?

"Are you ready Fiona?"

She looked up at Dan and nodded. He pushed open the door and they walked in.

Dan hadn't known what to expect, but he was still shocked by the pale thin old man in front of him. Professor Elwood Fletcher had a hooked nose, thunderous black shaggy eyebrows, dark brown piercing eyes and grey thinning hair. He had been freshly shaven and the skin on his face clung tightly to him, like a skull covered in pale linen. He lay in a large bed that dominated the small room, a single bare light bulb above him bathing him in artificial light.

"Father? Is that you?" It seemed impossible to Fiona that this old, thin and weak man was really her father. Only a few months had passed since the fire. On that night he had been tall, strong and full of energy, screaming in rage, his hair wild, red-faced and roaring. Fiona stepped hesitatingly towards the bed, her hand raised in front of her body. "Father? Can you hear me? It's Fiona."

Suddenly the old figure came to life. A smile crept onto his face, growing until it revealed grey teeth that hung from the top gum of the skeletal face.

"Fee-Fee!" The words rasped from the old man, just the few words seeming a big effort. "Hello my little code cracker. How are you? Would you and your husband like a drink?" Fiona let out a huge sigh, relief that her father had recognised her.

Elwood held up his thin hand and she stooped to grab it, leaning in close and kissing the cold dry skin.

"Fiona, do tell me, is this your husband? Roger, isn't it? How are you old chap?" Elwood leaned forward slightly in his bed, offering the hand Fiona had kissed. Dan took the old man's outstretched hand and shook it gently. He felt long, uncut nails digging into the palm of his hand. "Can I get you youngsters a drink? G and T for you? How is life my dear?"

"I'm fine father. Same as usual I guess. Still living in London. How are you?"

"Oh I'm fine my dear, they look after me well. I'm only here for a few days while we sort things out at home with your mother. How is life, Fee-Fee?"

"I'm fine daddy. Still lecturing. I did a session before the Christmas break to get me warmed up."

The old man's eyes lit up. "Lecturing again eh? I trust you still stick with the great subjects? Secrecy? Ciphers? Bacon still cooking your goose is he?" Elwood tried to laugh at his own joke but his chuckle disintegrated into a fit of coughs, each one wracking his weak frame. Dan wanted to help, but as he moved forward Elwood waved him back.

Fiona waited until the coughing subsided before answering, "Yes daddy, still teaching the same old things. This is my friend Dan. We're working together on a project that we thought might interest you."

"So you need my help do you?" said Elwood.

"Have you seen the news recently?"

Elwood looked confused. "The news? What do you mean? Has something happened? Have they found it?"

"I'm taking about Prince William, daddy. His death. You haven't heard about that?"

"A Prince has died? Was it natural? Or was he killed. You, young man, you can tell me."

"He was killed," answered Dan, "he died badly." Dan paused, looking at Fiona, she nodded slightly. "He had a Shakespeare quote cut into his chest." Dan was surprised when Elwood burst into fits of laughter. The laughs soon turned into coughs. Dan and Fiona waited uncomfortably for the old man to regain his composure.

"I suppose it was inevitable." Elwood said eventually, spittle hanging off his chin.

"What do you mean sir, inevitable?"

Elwood narrowed his eyes. "They told me this would happen."

Fiona felt her pulse quicken. "They?"

Elwood smiled. "The voices." He swung his head to stare at Dan. "So. You're an American. You're married to my daughter. I'm really not sure I approve but I suppose yours really is the modern empire, is it not? Don't you have a white man with a black father who ran off to Africa running your country now or something fascinating to debate like that? What did you say your name was again? Roger?"

"No, it's Dan."

Elwood turned his attention to Fiona. "Sit down next

to me Fee-Fee." Fiona pulled over a chair and sat down next to his bedside. Dan moved to stand behind her.

Elwood leaned forward in his bed and moved his head close to Fiona. "I've got a terrible idea I've done something wrong," he whispered. "I don't know what it is, but something may have happened to your mother." Pushing himself even further forward, his voice now barely audible, "I don't know why I'm here?"

"Yes daddy, something did happen. A few months ago. But it's not important now. I need to ask you something else. I... we need your help. It's about Shakespeare."

Elwood suddenly sat back, his back slumping against the pillow, his eyes drifting toward the door. "I expect they'll be in with my pills soon. I knew you wanted my help. Just like they want me to take their dratted pills. The voices have left me since I've been here. You only ever call me daddy when you want something." He swung his eyes to stare at Fiona. "I seem to remember that the last time I saw you I wanted your help. I wanted to talk about Shakespeare but you weren't interested in my work. That hurt me a lot you know. I have always valued your input. You always brought a fresh voice." His voice rose. "I also believe, correct me if I'm wrong, but you have up until this date chosen to spurn my research into Shakespeare. I wanted to talk to you about the biggest discovery I had made in my career, but you simply drove away."

"That's not fair." Fiona felt crushed.

Suddenly Elwood smiled. "I have to say Fee-Fee, I really don't see you much these days do I? Where are you living? London is it? Would you like a drink? G and T is it?"

"Yes, we both live in London," Dan said. "Now as we were saying, Prince William is dead."

"And what precisely do you expect me to say about that, young man? That I'm sorry?"

"There's much more to it than that, daddy. There was a quote from Shakespeare cut into his chest."

"Yes, yes, you said. You don't have to repeat things to me you know. Well, knowing you, as I do, I'm sure there's more to this sorry tale than you are letting on. Out with it."

"There were two words cut on the Prince's chest, I realised they were on the monument in Westminster Abbey. Me and Dan examined the statue and discovered a cipher that revealed a name."

"What name?"

"Francis Bacon," replied Dan. Elwood burst out laughing. His whole body retched and jerked as the humour turned to coughing again.

"So you found Sir Francis Bacon's name inside the Shakespeare monument?" said Elwood eventually. "Well, well, well, my little code cracker, you've done really well this time. That one slipped by me I have to confess. And you now require my help. You only ever called me daddy when you wanted something."

Elwood's eyes began to close and his head slumped back on his pillows. Dan and Fiona looked at each other unsure of what to do next. Fiona noticed her father's breathing had become deep and relaxed. She leaned forward and gripped his hand.

"Daddy?" Elwood's eyes flickered open. "Stay with us daddy, we need your help. This is really important."

The old man's cracked lips formed into a faint smile as he spoke. "Sorry Fee-Fee, it's these wretched pills. How I loathe them. Not to worry, I'll be home in a day or two I expect. So what is it that you want?"

Fiona felt so relieved she sprang forward, kissing her father on his forehead. "Thank you daddy. What we were wondering is, why do you think Sir Francis Bacon's name is on the Shakespeare monument?"

"I assume that you are familiar with the plays of William Shakespeare." Elwood spoke, looking at Dan.

"Yes, sir."

"Good. Now tell me, my boy, what is the first thing you notice about his plays?"

"The language. The words. Oh, and the ideas, there has never been anything like it."

"Yes, you are correct but there's much more to it than that." Elwood's voice was beginning to take on a lecturing tone, a new level of energy appearing. He sat up in bed, levering himself awkwardly into place. "Shakespeare's plays are dazzling in their complexity and beauty. They are intensely poetic, political and philosophical. They cover thousands of years of history from the time of Julius Caesar and Anthony and Cleopatra right through to what was then the modern day. Plays such as a *Midsummer Night's Dream* and *The Tempest* show a deep knowledge of myth and legend. *Hamlet*, *Macbeth* and others show a detailed and complete knowledge of royal life and issues within the royal courts of Europe. Now tell me, where do you think he got all these ideas from?"

Dan had no idea. "His imagination?"

"Don't be ridiculous. Some of Shakespeare's plays borrow historical elements and storylines from some of the oldest and greatest tales ever written. He took his inspiration from stories first fashioned in ancient Greece, Rome, Egypt, Denmark, Italy and others. He didn't just make up the love story between Anthony and Cleopatra, he researched it from a documented legend and presented it in a new and more wonderful way." The old man had suddenly become very animated, his arms swinging in his bed as he spoke. "Doesn't that strike you as strange?"

"I guess he read a lot?"

"You don't have to pretend to be entirely stupid just to humour an old man. Do you think there were handy translations of Roman legends lying around a tiny market town like Stratford? Shakespeare was an actor, don't forget. He wasn't a scholar. Books were expensive, not something you could pick up at your local market. They needed to be ordered from specialist merchants and then imported from Europe. Even if Shakespeare had managed to get hold of all these rare books, he would have needed a working knowledge of Latin, Greek, ancient Greek, not forgetting a whole host of regional dialects from around the world. He would have needed to translate the texts before he could even begin to analyse their meaning. For a normal scholar this would have been a life's work. But for an actor it was impossible. Take just one country that he features, say Italy. There were several variations of dialect in the

Italian of the sixteenth century, did you know that?" Dan shook his head, feeling like a schoolboy. "No, of course not, how could you? But Shakespeare would have needed to understand them all. He would have needed to have spoken maybe fifteen languages. Now, surely this is beginning to strike you as unusual? Come on, as you Americans say, do the math!"

Fiona tried to restrain herself but a small giggle emerged. Dan shot her a look. She felt sorry for Dan but had forgotten just how eloquent her father could be.

"Yes, you're right. I guess he was an amazing man," fumbled Dan.

"And what about the subject matter? The detail and the beauty. The intrigue, the mystery that exposed so many hidden worlds. *Hamlet* for example and the royal courts of Denmark." Elwood paused and in the silence Dan could hear a distant radio in the hospital playing a disco version of *Jingle Bells*.

Elwood was now sitting bolt upright in his bed, the energy that emerged in his voice making his body seem stronger. "Don't you think it's strange that Stratford isn't mentioned once in any of the plays?" Elwood looked at Dan but didn't wait for a reply. "Think, man, you know the truth. As it says in *Hamlet; 'This above all: to thine own self be true, and it must follow, as the night the day, thou canst not then be false to any man.'* How on earth could a person like Shakespeare from a small town in the middle of England, with no education, possibly have such a degree of knowledge and expertise of a royal court in another country? Shakespeare never even left England, he had no knowledge of places like Venice,

Rome, even Scotland. This was an actor, who spent the last decades of his life as a corn trader and theatre manager, who came into money mysteriously. How on earth could this man be able to write with such authority about the lives of the nobility in Italy in the *Merchant of Venice*? As he said, '*Nature hath framed strange fellows in her time.*' Can you see it yet? '*The quality of mercy is not strained, it droppeth as the gentle rain from heaven upon the place beneath. It is twice blest: it blesseth him that gives and him that takes.*' Does that sound like the words of a corn salesman?"

Elwood slumped back on his pillow, this outburst leaving him physically tired. Dan moved to the side of his bed where a pitcher of water and two white plastic cups had been placed. He poured a cup of water and handed it to Elwood. The water was warm but the old professor thanked Dan and drained the cup, his Adam's apple jerking up and down in his throat.

"You must realise," said Elwood to Dan, "that these conclusions are based on serious and valid research. I have failed to discover even the slightest bit of evidence that William Shakespeare had even a single day's schooling. There is nothing to associate him with anything featured in his plays or sonnets. There are no letters that exist from him. The only piece of writing that can be positively identified as having been written by him is a crude signature on a mortgage. For a man who called knowledge '*the wing wherewith we fly to heaven*', is it not strange that his daughters also had no schooling and they couldn't even write their own names?"

"Wait a minute, this is all getting a bit mad," said

Dan. "You're making it sound like Shakespeare didn't write his own plays?"

"Mad?" Elwood repeated the word slowly.

"Oh, nothing, it was just a figure of speech. What I meant is, it seems shocking. It's just like... it's like saying Winston Churchill was never a Prime Minister of England, or JFK was never President, or George Bush didn't invade Iraq. Everybody's heard of Shakespeare, it's logical to assume that he wrote the plays?"

"Exactly. Everyone has heard of the plays. But did you know that some of the plays were originally presented anonymously? The first time that all of Shakespeare's plays were seen together, in one place, with an author's name attached, was seven years after his death. Yet even then twelve new plays suddenly appeared from nowhere?" Elwood looked at Dan. "It was only then that he began to develop the reputation as a great English playwright. This would explain why the monument in Westminster Abbey wasn't erected until over a hundred years after his death. But even then it was done privately with Rosicrucian money. But if you're not convinced, then how do you explain that there are no records of Shakespeare receiving any payments for the plays?"

Elwood stopped speaking. Dan felt drained. The verbal barrage had him beaten. He tried to reply but gave up, turning to Fiona. She just looked back, her face blank, then Elwood spoke again.

"I have one last question. One that has puzzled me for many years."

"What is it?" asked Dan, recovering his voice.

"Why did this man, this Shakespeare, die of arsenic poisoning?"

The words hung in the air and neither Dan nor Fiona knew what to say. When Fiona finally broke the silence, she had moved to sit on the bed next to her father.

"Is that what you wanted to talk to me about daddy? Your research was about Shakespeare not writing his own plays?"

"Yes. But you didn't want to listen." Elwood looked drained. He had changed back to a frail old man, the passion and fire gone.

Dan's mind raced. He had hoped that the meeting with Fiona's father would help him find Shakespeare's Truth, but instead it had left him more confused. He felt strangely sorry for the old man. "Sir, forgive me for asking. But if Shakespeare didn't write the plays, then who did?"

A broad smile spread across Elwood's wrinkled features. "At last! A decent question from the American. However, you already know the answer."

Suddenly, Fiona sprang forward, words spilling from her in a shout. "Francis Bacon! It's Francis Bacon. It has to be! Of course, it makes such perfect sense. He was an intellectual, widely travelled, would have spent half of his life in the library, the other half in the royal courts of Europe, his mother was a linguist who taught him languages. If Shakespeare didn't write his plays, he's the perfect candidate to be the true author."

Elwood was now lying in his bed, his eyelids heavy as sleep edged into his body.

"That's right, my clever little code cracker," he

replied, "Bacon was the Bard. Somebody whose own words in *Anthony and Cleopatra*: '*A rarer spirit never did steer humanity,*' might also be applied to himself? That's why you found his name in the monument, hidden there by his Rosicrucian soldiers." Elwood's eyes closed, his words slowing as sleep arrived. "'*Things must be as they may,*' that's from *Henry the Fifth....* '*To sleep, perchance to dream, ay, there's the rub*'... that's from ..."

Dan and Fiona watched in silence as the old man drifted away into a deep sleep. As they left Fiona stooped over her father, kissing him on the check. It seemed to stir the old professor and as the couple moved to leave the room he spoke, his words drifting like gossamer threads through the air.

"From *Twelfth Night. 'Some are born great, some achieve greatness, and some have greatness thrust upon them.'*"

Act 5: Scene Four

"If music be the food of love, play on."

Twelfth Night

The sun was low in the sky as Dan guided the Jaguar through the Cotswold country lanes. The thin winding roads felt claustrophobic. Overbearing hedges closed in on both sides, occasionally allowing brief glimpses of a low red sun drifting down over sweeping meadows and rolling hills. They had retraced their steps to the car after seeing Elwood and suffered the rush hour traffic before breaking free of the city and into the final leg of the journey to Fiona's mother's house.

Fiona had been silent since they left the hospital. Now she twisted in her seat and spoke to Dan. "I just don't understand. When we went in there he was so weak, but calm. Then, I saw the devil inside him. Just for a moment, but it was there. And when he talked about hearing voices, it scared me."

"Yeah, there were a couple of very intense moments there for sure. But when it started to pour out, I felt like I was being hypnotised. It was like listening to one of those TV evangelists you catch on cable. I half expected him to ask me for a credit card number."

"Don't try and make jokes about it, please. Can we just get to my mother's house?"

Dan turned his attention back to the road, feeling stupid. It had suddenly become busy as a queue of cars appeared in front. He could see the long snake of traffic was held up by a tractor dragging a plough of some kind.

"Do you mind if I put some music on?"

"Actually I do."

Fiona found the silence numbing. The meeting with her father had left her feeling vulnerable. Part of her had hoped that when she arrived at the hospital she would find the father she had remembered from her childhood. A quiet, bookish and often mischievous man. Instead she was confronted by the train wreck of his life.

She was beginning to regret getting involved. Surely these soldiers Dan talked about were best placed to help the Queen? "It's about another eight miles before the turn off, let me know when you see a sign for Lower Slaughter, I'll show you where to go from there. It'll be a turn on the left." She closed her eyes and leaned back in the seat.

Dan glanced at her. He wished he could talk about what had happened but knew the timing was wrong. He started to run through everything Elwood had said, more questions coming into his mind. He was so preoccupied in his thoughts that he didn't see, sitting in his rear view mirror, the black BMW that had been trailing them since London.

It took about fifteen minutes for them to arrive at the house. Gravel crunched under the wide low profile tyres as Dan swung through a gap in high ancient hedges into a large driveway. Brambles, holly, roses and elder wound through the hedge's branches, creating a barrier more impenetrable than a steel fence.

Fiona's mother was waiting on the drive as the car slowed to a stop. She stood in front of a long sand coloured Cotswold stone farmhouse, arms folded across her chest. The roof was a traditional thatch, its ends professionally finished into flat and solid edges. Dan thought it looked just like an English cottage should. It was the kind of cottage that executives in Hollywood would have the world believe that all English families owned. A wild looking herb garden and orchard stretched away behind the house towards a steep hill.

"Fiona, this place looks like something out of an advert for organic jam, where they try to convince you it's home-made from an ancient recipe as opposed to a huge factory in Ohio. Look at those windows, are they lead lined? And those ancient beams running up the side of the house. What a place to live."

"You should try it as a kid. Nobody to talk to, nothing to do, not unless you think getting the coal in, feeding the chickens and chopping wood is fun. It's no wonder I turned into a bookworm." Fiona pointed out of the car window. "Over there, that's where it happened." On the far side of a patch of unkempt grass sat a small barn. It was about the size of a double garage and stood separate from the main building. As Dan looked he noticed that two windows in the red brick and timbered wall had been burnt. The wooden frames were charred and the glass was broken and smudged black by smoke. The roof was badly damaged, one corner was completely missing. "It looks like some of the roof has burned away. Don't things get wet inside?"

"It's my father's study. Mum hates it. Everything in

there could fall through a hole in the floor to hell as far as she is concerned. Neither of us has been in there since it happened." Fiona climbed out of the car. "Mum! How are you?"

Fiona's obvious closeness to her mother was something that Dan had never felt with his own mom. As the two embraced Dan was amazed by how similar they looked. Fiona's mother was wearing Wellington boots, grey corduroy trousers, a heavy white woollen jumper and green waterproof coat. Her long grey hair was dishevelled and tumbled over her face. Dan got the impression that the fringe was almost a mask, hiding her from other people's gaze.

Stepping forward and extending his hand Dan smiled. "Good evening, Mrs Fletcher. My name is Dan. It's really wonderful of you to let me stay here." Fiona's mother accepted Dan's hand and shook it softly. Her hand felt odd and looking down Dan could see a mass of silver scar tissue. Dan withdrew his hand, perhaps too quickly. He realised the damage must have been from the fire.

"Oh that's fine, it's a pleasure to meet one of Fiona's special friends. Call me Imogen."

"Mum! Dan and I are work colleagues, nothing more. We're working on a project together."

"It must have been a pretty important project if it meant you going to see your father. Come inside, tell me about it. Let's have a cup of tea and some fruit cake."

Imogen and Fiona walked to the house, arms linked, whilst Dan heaved out the bags from the boot of the Jaguar. By the time he made his way into the kitchen

Imogen already had the kettle boiling and was making three cups of tea. Fiona stood quietly chatting to her mother, leaning one arm against the marble work surface. The kitchen was larger than Dan had expected and was dominated by a low ceiling with warped beams stretched across it. There was a delicious heavy warmth in the room, heat was pouring out of a large green Aga cooker which smelt faintly of burning oil. The smell reminded Dan of the room with the Queen and he was transported in his mind back to that day, the sound of the gunfire...

"Sit down, please." Imogen pointed to a large pine table surrounded by six matching chairs, each with a hand embroidered cushion.

"Thanks." Dan was snapped out of the memory.

"I suppose I ought to ask how he was?" Imogen spoke as she poured out three cups of tea and set three slices of cake. "It made me feel very odd, you going to see him. Sometimes I wish he would just disappear off the face of the planet, but then I remember he's still my husband. Until death us do part, and all that." As she spoke Dan felt something brush his leg causing him to flinch. He looked down to see a huge ginger cat. The cat stopped and looked up at him with a demanding expression, expecting what? Food? Attention? Dan put his hand down to stroke it, but it slid under the table at his touch.

"Oh mum, it was so strange. I can't tell you how scared I was before I went in there, but he looked so thin and weak. When did he get like that?"

"It's been a long few months." Imogen brushed her

hair away from her face. "I don't go so much now. I last went three weeks ago, it was awful."

"Oh mum, I'm so sorry, I should have gone before, I..."

"Hush, Fiona. I understand, but I had to go, it was my duty. You'll know what I mean when you're married and have your own family."

"So what happened when you were there last?" Fiona asked. Imogen glanced over at Dan.

"I'm sure your friend doesn't want to hear me being a moaning minny."

"Don't worry about me Mrs Fletcher. I'm quite happy with my fruit cake. Which is delicious."

Imogen turned to face Fiona. "A few weeks ago, the nurses told me he had been shouting, screaming all day and all night, no words or anything that made sense. Just screaming and screaming. Whatever medication he was on hadn't worked. I think they were trying something new. But the last time I went in to see him, he grabbed my hand and began shouting at me. He called me such awful things – saying I was evil, saying he wanted to kill me. Telling me the voices wanted me out of the way."

"Oh mum, why didn't you tell me? Why do I only ever hear about these things when it's too late?"

Imogen turned to Dan. "So Dan," she said, as if it was suddenly the most important thing in the world, "tell me all about your life in London. How are you finding living over here in England?"

"I don't mean to interrupt your chat." Dan could see Fiona was annoyed.

"Nonsense. You must tell me everything. Start with where you were born." The conversation weaved uncontrollably with Dan talking about his job, flat, childhood in American, taste in music, family. After about fifteen minutes Fiona interrupted and suggested her mother should show Dan to his room.

Dan was surprised to see just how large the spare bed was and once Imogen had left him he lay down and closed his eyes, just for a minute. He couldn't remember being so tired.

What felt like a few seconds later, he was woken by a hand shaking his shoulder. He opened his eyes and was greeted by Fiona's smiling face.

"Ahh, you look so sweet lying there. I could hardly bear to disturb you, but it's time for supper."

"How long have I been asleep?"

"About three hours."

Dan groaned. "You're kidding. I'm so sorry."

"No probs."

"I've just been having the weirdest dream. I was at the top of this huge building, a massive skyscraper, and these people were going to blow it up and I was stuck on the roof."

"Oh, so no obvious symbolism at all then."

"It was a great dream for me."

"How do you work that out?"

"This is the first one in a week where I haven't been in that room." Dan stopped.

"What room?"

Dan lifted himself up into a sitting position and rubbed his face. He turned to look at Fiona. "Hey, Miss

Fiona Fletcher! You're wearing a skirt and a very nice skirt at that. Wow, I can actually see your legs!"

"I will have you know that I can look feminine when the mood takes me." Fiona turned away and started back down the narrow stairs. "Food's nearly ready. Hurry and sort yourself out. I don't want to keep mum waiting. Just be wary of her homemade wine."

"Her what?"

"Homemade wine. It's her latest hobby. Blame me for encouraging her. Anything to keep her mind away from father."

It had been a long time since Dan had had any real home cooking, it made a change from microwave meals and take away. After supper he and Fiona sat around an open log fire, chilling out on a huge deep red rug, their backs leaning against a green sofa. Imogen had excused herself and gone to bed.

It was dark and late. The only light was from the fire and the gentle heat made them both drowsy. Above the fire sat a mantelpiece and hung above the clutter of open letters, nick-knacks and antique ornaments was a long piece of dirty grey string with thirty or so Christmas cards hanging on it.

"No Christmas tree?"

"Mum's on her own this year, no grandchildren to spoil or anything, so I guess she just hasn't bothered."

"It must be really tough on her. I wonder how many of those cards have trite comments in them, you know the sort of thing - 'So sorry to hear about Elwood, hope you are bearing up.'"

"You sound like you've had experience with this

kind of thing too."

"When my grandmother died mom got so sick of people saying they were sorry. It drove her crazy. After a while she almost started shouting back at them, telling them that when someone has been sick for such a long time it's just sheer relief when they go."

"I've just spent the last three months wishing my dad was dead, but then today, when I finally saw him, I was so happy to see him as well. It was so weird, Dan. I hate myself, but I guess I still love him in a weird way."

Dan took another large gulp of the homemade wine. The deep red brew was syrupy and extremely potent. He could feel it warming his whole body. "This plum wine really grows on you."

"Well don't hog it all then." Fiona reached across Dan to grab the half empty bottle from by the fireplace, her hand brushing Dan's leg in the process.

Dan watched the logs in the fire crackle and spit, orange flames flickering and jumping, tiny plumes of sweet smelling smoke occasionally breaking free and escaping into the room. "I'm really grateful for what you have done for me today. I can't imagine how difficult it has been for you."

"Thanks, it's not just for you. If there is any chance I can do even the smallest part to save the Queen, then I have to give it a go. No matter how hard." Fiona smiled. "God, that sounds so weird. Me, helping the Queen?"

"You know Fiona, the more I think about what your pop said about Shakespeare and his plays, the more I think he might be right."

"My father can be pretty convincing, can't he? But if

you think about it, there's no way that some country actor who didn't even go to school could translate ancient stories or know about the detail of life in Venice or the Royal Court. Let alone come up with all that poetry. However, Sir Francis Bacon, well that's different. His entire life was focused around royalty, education, philosophy, literature. Even now, hundreds of years later, he has a massive reputation."

"But if Bacon did write Shakespeare's plays, why didn't he just own up to it? You would have thought he would be proud of them."

"I could guess. A lot of the plays are really critical of royalty. Maybe he had to keep his views a secret, especially if he worked in the Royal Court. The Royal Family was seen as divine in those days, so if someone like Bacon who was so close to them had seemed to be treasonous, that would have been it for him, straight down to the Tower and executed."

"Maybe, anyway it's the best lead we have at the moment."

"It's the only lead." Fiona leaned forward and placed another small log on the fire. Dan watched her. The light from the fire softened her features and emphasised her cheekbones and lips.

"You look so different from when we first met."

"Meaning?"

"Don't take it the wrong way, but you seem prettier, more alive, as if you've come out of a cocoon, you're a butterfly drying its wings in the sparkling sun, ready to take off." Dan paused and put his hand onto Fiona's, she shifted to meet it, wrapping her fingers into his. "Or maybe, on a night like this with this fire, a better analogy is the phoenix, rising from the ashes."

Fiona turned her body to face Dan, the skin of her thigh grazed his hand as she did so. "That's really very sweet."

"But a bit much?"

She looked at him attentively. "Dan, what you said upstairs. About your dream. Is there more to all this than you're telling me?"

Dan's instinct was to lie, but he stopped himself. When he had spoken to Fiona in the café at the British Library he had needed to hold back. But now, something had changed between them. "The room I've been dreaming about is real. I was in the room a few days ago. With the Queen."

"You mean the Rosicrucians had you both together? You actually saw the Queen?"

"Yes. I had been kidnapped and put into this room. It was hot and dark and when they turned the light on I could see I wasn't alone. There was an old woman tied up opposite me. It took me a few minutes to work it all out. But it was the Queen."

"What's the full story? You have to tell me, Dan."

"The Rosicrucians kidnapped me, they told me if I didn't find something they called 'Shakespeare's Truth', they will kill me and the Queen on New Year's Day."

"Oh my God! Dan! You're trying to save your own life too? What on earth is Shakespeare's Truth? Why did they kidnap you?" The words came out in a flood.

"I have no idea," said Dan. "All I know is they mean every word. They'll kill me and the Queen if I don't work it out."

"You have to go to the soldiers now!"

"No, I can't. If I go to them, I'll be killed instantly by the Rosicrucians. I'm on my own."

"You're not on your own, Dan."

"I didn't mean to burden you with my problems, you've got enough on your plate just dealing with your parents. I'm sorry, it's just the wine, I'm talking too much. About everything. I should leave you in peace."

Dan moved as if he was about to get up and leave but Fiona suddenly leaned forward, kissing him softly on the mouth. He pulled away in surprise. There was a brief moment then Dan lifted his hand and ran his fingers through her hair. He bent forward and kissed her. He leaned into her, her body pushing back against his. He pulled his mouth away from her. "Aren't we supposed to be discussing Sir Francis Bacon?"

"Bollocks to Bacon." Fiona grabbed his shirt and pulled him down onto the rug.

Act 6: Scene One

*"Alas, poor world, what treasure hast thou
lost!"*

Venus & Adonis

23rd December

Fiona woke up not knowing where she was. Then in a flash it all came back to her. She was lying in a cramped single bed, the same one she had slept in as a little girl. It was still early and as her eyes adjusted to the low light she felt like she had been transported back twenty years. Her eyes fell on a dog-eared poster of George Michael, still Blue-Tacked to the side of a large wooden wardrobe that dominated the room. She smiled and then heaved herself up from the tiny bed. She walked to the window and looked out. The faintest wisps of morning sun were creeping up over the hill, bouncing off the sheen of frost covering the garden and apple orchard, creating tiny sparkles of light in the ice drenched landscape. The sky was a profound, almost startling blue.

Fiona found her dressing gown, discarded on the floor. She bent down, feeling her head jolt. She sighed. She knew she was going to have to put up with a hangover. The events of the night before were hazy, but she remembered what had happened between her and

Dan. She had shocked herself, it had been an explosion of passion and lust, and she had been the instigator, something extremely rare for her. She was angry with herself, convincing herself already that it was a disaster. He would think she was a slut.

She opened her door and moved across the landing towards the stairs. The old floorboards creaked under her feet and she held her breath as she stepped towards Dan's room. But the door to the spare room was open. Through the gap she could see the bed had already been made. He had already gone. Could she really have expected anything else? She walked downstairs and pushed open the kitchen door.

Fiona was greeted by a wave of welcoming heat. Dan sat in her mother's rocking chair. He looked at her and smiled. She smiled back and then looked away quickly. He was already shaved and showered, sitting by the kitchen window with a cup of tea and two slices of slightly burnt toast. Imogen had her back to Fiona, her attention focused on the ancient toaster.

"Hi Dan."

"Morning, Professor."

"I see you've made yourself at home. I'm surprised you're not wearing slippers."

"Ah, hello darling," said Imogen. "Come on in sleepy head, I've just made the tea. Although this dratted tin can with wires still seems to burn whatever I put in it."

"Some things never change, do they mum?" Fiona felt her headache getting worse and made her way over to the kitchen cupboard to fish out some painkillers.

"What time is it?"

Her mother glanced at the old clock hung above the Aga. "Half eight. Early for you."

"Whoever said the countryside was quiet was having some sort of laugh," said Dan. "I was woken up by some loud mouthed cockerel. It sounded like the broken starter motor on my uncle's old truck. I thought they were only supposed to start crowing when it was light, but this one started in the pitch black."

"Oh, that's Kenneth," Imogen replied.

Dan burst out laughing. "Kenneth the cockerel?"

"Oh yes," said Imogen. "And cock of the walk he is too. He's actually a bantam, so he's only a little chap, in fact he's dwarfed by the ladies he keeps his company with, but he makes up for it with his crow. That's quite a pair of lungs."

Fiona walked over and gave her mother a kiss on the cheek.

"Anyway, here we all are. How are you this morning darling?"

"A bit rough mum. It's your wine's fault. That stuff's lethal."

"What about you Dan, did you sleep well?"

"Yeah. For some unexpected reason I was really relaxed at the end of the evening." Dan smiled at Fiona.

"What are you two youngsters up to today?"

"I've got a couple of things I want to do here, if you don't mind me just leaping in and acting like I live here." Dan answered.

"Oh no, not at all. Make yourself at home. I'm off up the road to visit Sally. Her Neville's going into hospital today, so I thought I'd go with her. He's got a problem with his prostrate or his liver. I can't remember which."

It was another hour before Imogen left. As soon as they were alone Dan sprung to his feet and moved to sit next to Fiona. As he sat down he leaned over and kissed her quickly but firmly on the lips. "Last night was... fantastic."

"So we didn't mess things up?"

"No," replied Dan, "I don't think so. It feels, well, it feels right."

"Good." Fiona took hold of his hand and squeezed it.

"But did I mess it up?"

"Meaning?"

"I told you everything, you can see this isn't just a game anymore. It's real, my life is at stake."

"That's okay. I'm here for you. I'm in deep now."

He leant over and kissed her hard and quickly on the mouth. "That's so great to know."

"So, what do you want to do?"

"Fiona, I need to get into the barn."

"I knew that was coming. Do you really have to?"

"I need to see your pop's stuff. I've been thinking about it all morning. I'm hoping we'll find some kind of clue about what to do next."

"Mum would go mad."

"Your mom doesn't need to know. Come on, you know it's the obvious thing to do."

Fiona did her best to sound cheery, but the prospect made her want to run and hide. "If we're going to, I'd rather just get on with it now while she's out."

They walked out to the barn. Smoke damage had left black stains trailing up the outside of the crumbling walls. The two small windows were both smashed. Glass crunched underfoot as they walked up to the door. Dan looked up at the hole in the grey slate tiled roof created by the fire. Charred beams were exposed, several tiles had slid down and shattered on the ground in front of them. It was a sad sight. The old building seemed despondent, desperately in need of some love and attention. The door was made up of vertical strips of wood painted dark green. Something heavy had dented and splintered the wood, the frame was cracked.

"The firemen knocked it in when they showed up." Fiona pushed the door, it swung open with surprising ease. "They didn't need to, I just think they enjoyed doing it."

They walked in. Dan was hit by the same dark feeling of sadness as he had as a little boy at his grandmother's funeral. The inside of the barn was much colder than the garden, adding to the bleak atmosphere. Some natural light was filtering through the windows and roof but areas of the barn were in darkness. The air was filled with a smell of burnt wood mixed with mould.

"It's like a scene from Dante's inner circle of hell." Dan spoke as much to himself as to Fiona. In the centre of the barn sat a large hulk that had clearly once been a sofa, but it was now a burned shell. One small corner had been untouched by the flames where a deep brown leather was faintly visible under a layer of grime. Heavy piles of books and papers surrounded the sofa. Most were now just charred wreckages, foul smelling paper corpses, but some lay scattered around the stone floor, relatively unscathed by fire, but ruined by rain let in by the hole in the roof. Behind the sofa sat the remains of what Dan assumed was a photocopier; the heat had twisted its frame and plastic casing so it resembled a Dali sculpture.

"What happened here, Fiona?"

"You remember I said I was here for the weekend and had an argument with him? Well, mum told me later that the following week when I was back in London, he just got worse and worse. Then on the Saturday, he went into the kitchen to find her. He started screaming at her. She told me that he hit her and held her up against the wall by the throat, threatening to stab her, before running out into the garden. I'm so relieved she called me immediately. She was terrified, but even then she only told me he was getting angry and didn't say anything about hitting her. I got on my bike and started heading up here straight away. Then, about an hour later she called me again and told me that father had disappeared into here, and she had heard him screaming. She didn't want me to, but I called the police. I tried calling again but the phone went dead. Oh God, Dan, my heart stopped. I was so scared. Later, she told me he had grabbed her and dragged her into here, pulling out the phone. He was screaming at her, calling her the devil, all sorts of horrible things. During the struggle he hit her. Really hard. She was knocked unconscious." Fiona paused, her breath was sharp. "I'm sorry, it just makes me so…"

"You don't have to talk about it if you don't want to."

"No, I do need to tell you. When mum came to, the sofa was on fire. Dad had stacked books and papers against it. Mum remembers smelling petrol. The room was full of smoke. She was lucky. Another couple of minutes and she would have been dead."

Dan wrapped his arms around her. He felt her breath on his neck as she kept talking. "He'd shut the door to the barn from the outside. When mum tried to open it, she couldn't. She panicked and started screaming. She swears she could hear him moving on the other side of the door. She's convinced he was holding the door shut. The room was filling with smoke so mum smashed a window to let in some air."

"What happened? How did she survive?"

"The police. It took them about forty minutes to get here, but they made it in time. Just."

Fiona was tempted to tell Dan everything, but it was still too much. In truth, she had made it back minutes before the police had arrived. Her father's face as he was pulling at the barn door was burnt into her memory, the manic energy and hatred in his eyes, the things he had screamed, the smoke pouring out of the windows. She could still see him picking up that plank of wood with the nails in it, the pain as the nails went into her shoulder. Then her mum had come screaming out of the barn, grabbing Elwood to protect her daughter. Then finally the police had turned up, followed by the fire service.

"Are you sure you're okay?"

Fiona nodded. "We should start on his desk." She walked over to a large oak desk up against a wall at the other end of the barn. It was almost hidden in the shadows. The desk was relatively untouched by the fire. A sooty residue clung to the surface of the wood, grey slime making it feel and look malevolent. On its top were at least twenty pencils of varying lengths, some neatly lined up, some strewn randomly across the surface. All were sharpened to such a point that they reminded Dan of tiny spears. Above the desk was a maze of home-made shelves, seemingly constructed from any spare wood that had been lying around. Stuffed onto the shelves were dozens of books. It looked like a small library. Most of the books were old, leather bound. As his eyes adjusted Dan could pick out the gold leaf letters embossed on some of the spines.

"What's with all the pencils?"

"I'm not sure. He always had two or three at least when I was a kid, he used to sharpen them and line them up like soldiers on the desk."

"Looks like he was making a private army of them here."

Fiona pulled one of the books from the shelf. She looked at the cover, caressing it gently and then flipping it onto its side so she could gently wipe the soot from the spine. The title of book emerged, *Tudor Spy Lord*.

"I read this when I was fourteen." She didn't look up as she read. "It's a biography of Sir Francis Walsingham, the Head of Queen Elizabeth's Secret Police." She opened the cover and the pages inside were wrinkled, soaked with rain water. "Most of these books are first editions worth thousands. I can hardly believe my father would destroy these. I often used to think he loved his books more than me. Look at this." She pointed at a book on the top shelf. "That's a re-print of the First Folio of Shakespeare's plays, the first time the plays were collated and published." The book was too high for her to reach. Dan stretched over her and pulled it from the shelf. It felt dry and it seemed to have escaped the worst of the smoke damage. He handed it to Fiona.

She opened the old book. On the inside of the cover was an engraving of Shakespeare, the peak of his bald head seeming too large, like a caricature. On the opposite leaf was a verse.

"It doesn't look right," said Dan.

"What, the picture?"

"Yeah, the perspective is all off. His neck and shoulders don't look right. It kind of looks like an old puppet, the angles are all wrong."

"It does look kind of lifeless. I suppose it was just the style at the time."

Dan took the book and stared at it. "Check this out, look at the edge of the face." He traced his finger down the edge of the picture, following the forehead and cheek down to the chin. "Can you see? There's a thick line drawn around the edge of his face."

She looked at it carefully. "You're right. It makes the face look like a mask."

"It does, doesn't it? Like the true author is hiding his face. Fascinating."

"Listen to this," he said reading the poem. "*'To the reader, this figure that thou seest put, it was for gentle*

Shakespeare cut.'" Dan paused. "At the end it says *'Reader look not on his picture, but on his book.'* Jesus Fiona, that's a clue if there ever was one, they're saying ignore the picture of the so-called author." Dan opened the book at random, at the first page of *The Tempest*. The first word was 'Boteswaine' and the letter B had been enlarged and decorated with an elaborate design. Written over the design in pencil were a number of scribbles.

"Your pop added his own bit here. Look."

"Oh yes, can you see? Each of the scribbles seems to form a letter."

"Francis Bacon. If you follow your dad's notes the curls and whirls around the B spell out Francis Bacon. But, it's so obvious when you see it. How did he get away with it?"

Fiona grabbed the book and examined the page. "My father had already figured out Francis Bacon was the true author. All we did was confirm his suspicions when we found the cipher in Westminster Abbey."

"Yes. I wonder what else he found out? Fiona, we've got to go and see him again."

"I knew you were thinking that." She smiled weakly.

Dan realised he had been tactless. "So how old do you think this book is?"

"This is a relatively modern reprint." She flipped back to the opening pages. "Originally printed in 1831 according to this."

"How much do you think it's worth?"

"Maybe ten thousand pounds?"

"Wow!"

"Hey, a real first edition is worth much more. There

was one auctioned in London in January 2007 for well over a million."

"How much are the original plays, the hand written manuscripts worth?"

Fiona shrugged. "Lots more?"

"Where are they anyway? I assume they're like locked away in the British Museum or something? I wonder how often they come up for auction?"

"They've never come up for auction as far as I know. In fact, nobody knows where the manuscripts are. They're not on display anywhere."

"What do you mean, nobody knows?"

"Nobody has ever seen an original manuscript."

"You're kidding. I just kind of assumed they were somewhere, on display maybe, you know, like the Crown Jewels are in the Tower of London." Dan snapped his fingers. "Maybe that's it."

"What?"

"That's Shakespeare's Truth. That's what the Rosicrucians want. Imagine, if they had the original plays they could sell them for a fortune."

"This is about money?"

"Why not? Doesn't everything boil down to money in the end? Think about it. If somebody can pay nearly a hundred and fifty million dollars for a painting by a modern artist like Jackson Pollock or a few hundred grand for some scrawled lyrics by John Lennon what would they pay for the original handwritten manuscript for *Hamlet*? Imagine if you had the entire collection; *Hamlet*, *Macbeth*, *Romeo and Juliet*, *Measure for Measure*, all of them, plus all the sonnets, that's got to be worth two or three billion dollars, at the very least. Probably much more. And if you could also prove that the true author was someone else, you'd turn the world of literature on its head."

"Slow down, Dan. If these manuscripts are out there, someone must know where they are, and that kind of information has a habit of not staying a secret for long."

"If Shakespeare had written the documents, then I would agree. But..."

"But, as we know, Shakespeare didn't write the plays. Bacon did."

"Yes, exactly. All these years people have been searching, but in the wrong places."

They both looked at each other.

"So all we have to do is find out where Bacon hid the manuscripts and wham, bam, thank-you ma'm, the Queen is free, I stay alive and we're national heroes."

Dan picked up the book and flipped it open again. "Fiona, look at this." The page he was looking at contained long rectangular spaces where sections had been neatly cut out. "Bits have been chopped out. Why would your father deliberately wreck such an expensive book?"

"It wouldn't be the strangest thing he's done."

Dan continued to flick through the book. Every ten pages or so he found more gaps, often clustered in groups on the same page. "This makes no sense," he said. "Is it just the final deluded acts of someone losing their mind?"

Fiona took the book and began to shuffle through the pages. Dan looked up at her. Just for a moment he was happy just to gaze at her, hair flowing over her shoulders, a look of concentration on her face. The change in her since they first met was extraordinary.

"No, this must be the last piece of his research. Dan, it's a bit scary. There must be a couple of hundred quotes cut out." She stopped turning the pages. "Look."

Dan moved next to her and glanced over her shoulder. He saw that lying between the pages of the open book was a photocopy of a page from another book, folded in half and nestling between the yellowed pages. It was a copy of a picture of a bust of Shakespeare holding a quill. The sculpture looked pretty basic to Dan and the smiling face looked almost comical. Someone had taken a pencil to the picture, leaving heavy grey circles around a panel of lettering that could be seen underneath the bust and some scratched patterned lines underneath that. Dan picked it up.

"If you look carefully you can see the book's title at the top of the page." Dan moved towards the broken window and adjusted the paper to catch the light. He could feel a chill breeze blowing into the barn and shivered slightly. "Let's see... Shakespeare's Stratford."

"I wonder," said Fiona. Dan waited as she looked along each shelf from left to right, touching the spine of each book as she read the title and moved on. Finally she leaned forward and extracted a brown book.

"Let's have a look at that picture again." Fiona opened the new book. In its centre were six or eight pages of photographs, including the original colour image the photocopy was taken from. In the book the Shakespeare bust was revealed to be painted in lurid colours. Dan looked at and knew it was the work of an amateur.

"According to the text," said Fiona, "the bust is at Shakespeare's grave at Holy Trinity Church in Stratford-upon-Avon."

"Far from here?"

"No Dan, it's near the hospital."

"I feel a visit to Stratford coming on."

She picked up the book once again and flicked through the rest of the text. Happy that the book contained nothing else of interest she stretched over the desk to push the brown book back into place.

"Let me do that, Fiona." The damp books either side had expanded into the space. Dan pushed his hand into the space in an effort to make more room. "That's bizarre. The wall behind, it feels metal." Dan pulled out a couple more books either side of the space. Despite the gloomy light he could see steel glinting on the wall. "There's something behind here. Quick give me a hand."

Fiona and Dan set about removing the remaining books from the shelf. Inset into the wall behind the books was a brushed steel door with a dial in the centre and a handle.

"It's a safe!" Fiona reached up and touched the cold metal. "It can't be very deep, these barn walls are big and old, maybe a foot thick."

"You obviously don't know the combination."

Fiona shook her head. She could see numbers ranging from zero to fifty around the dial. She span it around a few times, tried a few obvious number like family birthdays, but quickly gave up.

"We could be here forever trying to figure it out."

"What do you think is in there?"

"Who knows with the state he was in? It could be something, or maybe nothing."

"It's not going anywhere. Let's go have a look at that grave in Stratford. We can come back to this later."

Act 6: Scene Two

*"Look like the innocent flower, but be the
serpent under it."*

Macbeth

Sawyer had never liked sleeping on the sofa. Twenty years ago after a poker night with the boys, maybe. But now he was over fifty it left him feeling depressed. The circle of events had been the same as always. He had returned home tired, stressed, his mind more on the case than his family. His wife Jennifer had complained, he had picked a fight and before you could say *'You don't listen to me'* - night on the sofa.

Sawyer's marriage wasn't great. Then again Sawyer couldn't think of a single copper whose relationship with their wives, if they were still around, was great. With his missus, the arguments seemed to spring from nowhere and inexorably revolve back to the same repetitive issue; Jennifer was the only daughter of the big boss, Chief Inspector Edward de Vere. It made Sawyer annoyed just thinking about it. Twenty years, and plenty of tears ago he had probably seemed attractive to her, a bit of rough. At three in morning in the broom cupboard at the office party in 1988 she had certainly been attracted to him. For about ten minutes. Nine months later, he'd been greeting his son into the world and congratulating a wife he barely knew. Over the years that followed, instead of growing closer, she had, along with her father, spent her time undermining him and complaining they didn't have enough money.

The policeman heaved his body upright onto the sofa and rubbed his face hard with the palms of both hands. He looked around at his living room. He didn't like it. Jennifer had chosen the house, a new build with cream carpets and a kitchen pretending it was in a Victorian manor house. A cloying sweet smell floated through the air, making Sawyer nauseous. He hunted around for the culprit. Another stupid air freshener plugged into the wall. Jennifer was obsessed by the things. He pulled it out and dropped it behind the fawn coloured couch.

His life had taken a turn for the worse in recent weeks. He could cope with Jennifer, at least that was predictable. It was life at the Yard that had become impossible. Ever since the death of the Prince he had been in charge of a pointless investigation looking for a hit-and-run driver that he knew didn't exist.

It wasn't like the old days. The passion was gone. He remembered the excitement he had felt when he had first joined the force, those first days out of the academy. The naivety, the feeling that he was making a difference. He chuckled to think he actually missed the days as a beat cop. The face-to-face, the stroppy lads on a Saturday night, helping the odd old lady across the road, dealing with villains who actually spoke English and didn't have automatic weapons. The good old days.

Sawyer mustered his strength and stood up. It was then that his headache hit him, pain welling up from deep inside his skull. As he shuffled across the carpet he kicked an empty whisky bottle. He forced his brain to comprehend his watch. Ten o'clock. He was already an hour late for work. He plodded across the living room floor to the drinks cabinet. He fumbled the door open, grabbed a small tumbler and lifted the first bottle that came to hand. Without even looking, he sloshed the amber liquid into a glass and emptied it with a single gulp. He grimaced. It was Cointreau, not his favourite. It was the sort of sickly crap he knew Jennifer loved. He refilled and dropped another one down the hatch.

Grabbing the TV remote control, Sawyer flopped back onto the sofa. He pressed the red button on the remote and the TV burst into life. The morning news had just begun and as usual it was a story relating to the Royal Family. The Queen had refused to make a public appearance since the death of her grandson. Sawyer thought that she was stupid. She was pissing off a whole lot of people and the presenter of the news seemed to fall into that category. He was relaying an official statement from the Palace, disgust dripping from his delivery. Apparently, Her Majesty would not return to her duties until the New Year and her first public appearance would be at William's funeral.

The next item was a story about Prince William. Sawyer had seen these reports hundreds of times and he was just about to flick the TV to a new channel, when a familiar image caught his eye. The news presenter had introduced a video and as Sawyer watched, he saw the opening few minutes of the video of William's murder. He cranked up the volume.

"...video first appeared on a number of websites

round about the time of the Prince's accident. Though only available for a short amount of time, many online communities throughout the world have seen it as evidence that the Prince was murdered. Conspiracy theorists are having a field day, some even claiming it is connected to the death of his mother, blaming MI5, the Government, the Church, even saying the Queen herself sanctioned the murder." The video played, but no images of the dead Prince were shown. "In an unprecedented move today, MI5 have announced that the video was a clever and malicious fake. The perpetrators assembled the video using footage taken from a real but unrelated case currently under investigation by the Metropolitan Police. Emmanuel Firenza was an illegal immigrant who was part of a South American and Bosnian drug cartel involved in importing crack cocaine and heroin, working with Albanian prostitution rings and Pakistani heroin dealers in London and Birmingham. He had been known to the police for nearly three years before his murder. It is believed he was killed in a brutal and sadistic manner and the killing filmed and distributed to other gang members as a warning. MI5 say this video has been mixed with footage of the Prince."

Sawyer clapped his hands in mock applause at the Major's subterfuge.

The news continued and Sawyer slumped back on the sofa absorbed in thought. He flicked the channel until the TV rested at CNN. The video of the Prince flashed on the screen again, cutting back to three experts in the studio discussing it. Sawyer grabbed his mobile

Rex Richards

phone and dialled a number. It was picked up immediately.

"Patel. It's Sawyer. I need you to do me a favour."

Act 6: Scene Three

"Adieu, and take thy praise with thee to heaven."

Henry IV

As Fiona guided Dan through the busy street she wondered what other people thought of Stratford-upon-Avon. She could see the beauty of the town and understood the historical importance, but to her it was just her local town. The tourists were an annoyance and the medieval black and white houses were just that, black and white houses. She was convinced for years that all towns looked like Stratford and it was not until she was older that the disappointment of the banal sprawl of most English towns had hit home.

Dan and Fiona walked down the narrow high street, its ancient buildings with their black beamed walls leaning into the street, seeming to envelop the hectic crowds of last-minute Christmas shoppers.

"So this is Stratford-upon-Avon," Dan said. "Birthplace and home to the great William Shakespeare."

"Whatever gives you that idea?" replied Fiona. "Is it the Shakespeare Tandoori restaurant on the right, or possibly the Shakespeare hotel on the left? Or maybe it's the Shakespeare Tavern pub further down the street, the Shakespeare statue above the bank or the Shakespeare Museum? Surely not the Royal Shakespeare Theatre, the S-Hake-speare Fish shop, the Shakespeare Italian just round the corner or Shakespeare's Birthplace?"

I'm surprised the swans in the river don't have his face tattooed on their butts."

Dan smiled and Fiona took hold of his hand. In a strange way Fiona wanted Dan to like Stratford. However boring it was to her, it was her local town, part of her.

"It's incredible isn't it, Fiona? A whole, global industry has built up around Shakespeare and he could barely even write his own name." He laughed.

"Even here, some of it is fake."

"What do you mean?"

"Shakespeare's Birthplace is a modern building faked to look old. Nobody really knows where he was born so they made it up."

Dan laughed again. "The whole thing is so ridiculous it's surreal. So Fiona, can you tell me something new about the real author, Sir Francis Bacon?"

"Sure. What would you like to know?"

"What kind of a person was he?"

"Where do I start? He was a really extraordinary man. I think even now he is considered to be one of the greatest intellectuals ever. I have to say, you really should have heard of him, he's considered to be well up there in the list of the top one hundred most influential characters in history."

"Really? Who's number one? Britney Spears?"

"No, surprisingly not, smartarse. It's Muhammad the Islamic prophet."

"Not Jesus?"

"No, he comes in at number three." They walked a

little further, ducking past a gaggle of tourists, cameras in hand. "Sir Francis Bacon grew up in a very privileged environment at the same time as Shakespeare. He died ten years after him in fact. His family was very well connected; his father was Queen Elizabeth's advisor. They lived on a huge country estate although Bacon was born in central London. When he was a teenager he was sent by Queen Elizabeth to work in the Royal Courts of France. Then he came back and trained to be a lawyer. He spent most of that period of his life very poor and in debt but things got better when the Queen took him under her wing. He worked as a spy, became Royal Chancellor and was knighted. When that happened he went home to the country and by all accounts put on the most incredible parties whenever the Queen came to visit. He was a scientist and philosopher as well; he actually died trying to prove ice preserved food, which sounds obvious now, but it was a revelation back then. He came up with tons of revolutionary theories on mathematics, physics, lots of things."

"How did he find time to write the plays?"

"He was a prodigious writer. He wrote many books and essays. His book, *The New Atlantis,* is a total vision for a new way of life. He really thought he could unify the entire human race. He was very much a man of peace. When you read his books they are full of big, huge ideas that would have improved everybody's life. Although he was knighted, in his later life, after Queen Elizabeth died and King James took over, the Royal Family turned on him and he spent time in the Tower of London. He was allowed to go free, but from that point on, he became ill and died poor and almost alone in his country estate. In fact, it's possible that he only printed up the plays and published the First Folio towards the end of his life to try and pay off his debts. That would explain why so many new plays suddenly appeared."

They walked along, weaving in and out of the busy crowds, and down past the river where chilly swans with puffed up feathers glided serenely and silently along the water. A smell of hot dogs and frying onion drifted through the air, and Dan's stomach started to rumble.

"Okay," said Fiona, "if my memory is correct, the church should be down the High Street and on the right towards the river."

"How come there are no signs to Shakespeare's grave?" Dan asked, staring at a clump of brown tourist signs that sprouted from a black pole.

"What?" Fiona's eyes focused on a crowd of American tourists flooding in their direction, led by a guide with a small open pink umbrella thrust high above her head.

"There are signs to Shakespeare's Birthplace, Anne Hathaway's Cottage, the river, the theatre, everything you can think of, but there are no signs to Shakespeare's grave. How come? Surely if his bones are somewhere around, that's going to be a place of pilgrimage? If this was in the States you'd have to fight your way past burger concessions selling William Milk-Shakespeares and Big Willy hot dogs to get to it."

"You're right. I've never noticed that before." Fiona started walking and Dan caught her up. They left the main street and walked towards a more modern building. It was a square grey concrete construction, a large blue sign revealing it was a car park. They made their way around the back of the building and onto a residential street deserted of tourists. They were soon standing in front of a church, its spire reaching high above the rooftops.

The entrance to the church grounds was an ornate and imposing gate. A long straight path ran to the doors and was flanked by eerie, skeletal trees guarding the route. The church was beautiful. A tall gothic steeple, heavy stone walls, stained-glass windows and a gabled lead roof with a mezzanine level window that ran all the way around the building.

They walked down the path. By now the blue sky had long since disappeared and a low cold and damp cloud had descended. Rows of ancient tombstones on either side receded quietly into the gathering mist. A faint sour smell hit Fiona as she entered the Church, and she was momentarily transported back to her childhood. It was Sunday and she was sitting quietly in her local church, arms wrapped tight around her body, shaking in the draught. The vicar was talking, something about sin, her father sitting next to her, his head held high, piercing eyes staring at the vicar.

Dan's voice brought her back to reality. "Where do we go?"

Rows of ancient dark wooden pews lined either side of the church, a red carpet ran between them leading to the altar. In front of the altar was a thin metal fence with a gate across it and an old man with a grey threadbare suit sitting at the side on a wooden stool reading a book.

"Up here," Fiona said. As they approached, the old man stood up, his book spilling to the floor. Dan glanced at the cover, just catching the words *da Vinci Code* before the man recovered his book.

"Sorry about that." The man smiled, stuffing the book into the large side pocket of his blazer. Dan saw tiny thin red veins running across the bridge of his nose and some dark hair creeping out of his ears. "Have you come here to see Shakespeare's grave?"

"Yes, we have, is that possible?" Fiona asked.

"Of course it is my dear. But I'm afraid that we'd like a contribution to the church funds. Sixty pence please. Each." The old man held out his hand. His hair was white and barely covered his head. Fiona looked at his face. He had kind eyes. Dan pushed a hand into a back pocket and produced a crumpled £5 note.

"Oh, I'll have to go into the back for change."

"Keep it. Shakespeare's grave for a fiver. Bargain."

"Very kind young man, it's all towards the steeple fund in any case." The old man smiled and returned to his chair. Within seconds he was engrossed in his book. The two of them heard him *tut-tutting* as something in it annoyed him.

Dan and Fiona walked up the few steps that lead to the altar, which was framed by a golden crucifix. On the left was the church organ, hundreds of years old, with giant, gleaming pipes rising to the vaulted stone ceiling. On the right were intricately carved wooden benches where the choristers would sit.

"Look at this, Dan. It's where people kneel to take

communion. Look how bowed and worn the stone is, and the bench here, look, the patterns in the carving almost totally gone. Imagine that, every Sunday for hundreds of years people grabbing the same bit of wood for support and kneeling in the same place."

At the very front of the church, set into the wall was a bust. It was unmistakably the same as the one in the book.

"Look. Just as bad in real life," said Dan.

Fiona stepped forward but her eyes were focused on the floor. "Look at these plaques," she said, kneeling down to read the inscriptions. "It's the rest of his family, his wife, daughters, and son-in-law."

Dan was stunned at the poor quality of the workmanship of the bust. Shakespeare was wearing a bright red shirt, with a dark waistcoat over the top. In his right hand he held a white quill and his left rested on a parchment. His brown hair was thinning, though his famous beard was clear. Under the bust was a gray slab, on which gold letters and words had been inscribed.

"Fiona, can you read the inscription?"

"Just about. I'm going to write it down." She rummaged in her bag and produced her notepad and pen and started to write.

IVDICIO PYLIUM, GENIO SOCRATEM, ARTE MARONEM,
TERRA TEGIT, POPULUS MAERET, OLYMPUS HABET
STAY PASSENGER, WHY GOEST THOV BY SO FAST?
READ IF THOU CANST, WHOM ENVIOUS DEATH HATH PLAST
WITH IN THIS MONUMENT SHAKSPEARE: WITH WHOME,
QUICK NATURE DIDE: WHOSE NAME, DOTH DECK YS TOMBE,
FAR MORE, THEN COST: SIEH ALL, YT HE HATH WRITT, LEAVES
LIVING ART, BUT PAGE, TO SERVE HIS WITT.

"Are the first few lines in Latin?" Dan asked.

"It is. I'm guessing you didn't do Latin at school?"

"No, and I skipped gladiator training too."

"Good job you've got somebody with a brain here then isn't it? The English private school system is a bit more traditional than you lot get in America." Dan wasn't sure if Fiona was boasting or being sarcastic. "Loosely translated," she continued "it comes out as '*a Nestor in judgment, a Socrates in genius, a Virgil in art.*'"

"I know Socrates was a philosopher."

"Yes. I saw *Bill and Ted's Excellent Adventure* too. Nestor and Virgil are similar characters in history and myth. The second line translates as '*the earth buries him, the people mourn him, and Olympus possesses him.*'"

"Olympus, as in the home of the Greek gods? Not the cameras?"

"Oh ha ha. Yes. But there must be more to this than meets the eye. I'm assuming if my father was interested then there's probably another cipher hidden in it."

"Let's go and ask him."

Act 6: Scene Four

*"I'll never pause again, never stand still,
Till either death hath closed these eyes of
mine. Or fortune given me measure of
revenge."*

Henry VI

S awyer sat back in his chair and stared at the computer monitor. He had set up a makeshift office in his spare room about six months before. A cheap computer, broadband access, a bottle of Laphroaig whisky and he was up and running. The plan had been for him to spend more time at home, more time with his wife, but it had never worked out. Sawyer sighed deeply and pressed the mouse button to run the video of the Prince's death once again.

He had asked the boys in IT to record the CNN show and email him as much of the video as possible. It turned out that the footage shown was only the first few minutes of the video. The scenes involving the Prince and the words cut onto his chest had not been shown on the TV. There was nothing he could do apart from watch the limited footage he had. He put the player on super slow-motion and watched as the frames flicked by one at a time. Half an hour passed and Sawyer glanced at the clock on the video. During all that time he had only actually reviewed just over a minute of the thing. Sawyer was bored. He didn't know what he was looking for, but something made him stick with it. In the video, a taxi and limousine stuttered slowly by and a tall man in a long coat jerked on to the screen, slowly making his way across from left to right. Then, for just a few frames, the man seemed to turn to face the camera. Sawyer hit rewind button and after a few attempts paused on the face.

Sawyer picked up his mobile phone from the desk. "Patel? It's Sawyer."

"Yes Inspector, what is it?"

"You busy?"

"I was up most of the night matching data from the car number plates on the congestion charge computers with images on security cameras against biometric data on the HMG-ID system trying to help find this hit-and-run driver. So yes."

"This is more important. I need you to look at something on that video from CNN."

"Okay, okay what is it?"

"Have you got it to hand?" Sawyer listened to the sound of Patel clicking his mouse.

"Yep boss. Got it on screen now."

"Right. Fast forward in to..." Sawyer strained to look at the timer on his screen. "Two minutes and eleven point three seconds. You'll see an image of a guy walking along the street, it looks like security camera footage. It's about thirty seconds after a cab passes."

"Wait a minute... got it, right, just a minute. Okay, playing it, so what are you looking at?"

"Have you got the guy walking on the street? Long brown coat."

"Got him."

"You have to watch this on slo-mo, otherwise you'll miss it. Play it back one frame at a time. See that blur of movement? Take a screenshot, you'll see his face in it, looking up at the camera. Freeze-frame it and try and analyze it."

"Okay wait. Okay got it. I'll call you back in a bit boss. I'm grabbing it now." The phone went dead.

Sawyer got up and wandered into the kitchen to make a cup of coffee. His head still throbbed. He sat in the kitchen staring at the steam from the kettle as it condensed into water droplets onto the foul blue wall tiles. His mobile rang.

"Hi Patel. Any luck?"

"It's a fake. I don't mean just the whole video being a fake like they said on the news, this face is another little fake inside it. It's a fake within a fake. Someone has inserted the image of a face on top of somebody walking along the street."

"Shit."

"It's not at all obvious. Very impressive in fact. This isn't the work for some bored school kid. This is a pro job. When you zoom in and increase the resolution and spot pick the colours on it there's a fractionally different CMYK value on one of the blues that you wouldn't expect, plus it's one that's outside of the range of a typical CCTV camera. Then if you look at things right down to a pixel level and do a boolean vector analysis, you can see the face is a different resolution to the rest of the image initially. And you can see some slight anti-aliasing, but the big slip up is that the light source is wrong. There's a full light on the face that's been faded back and re-coloured but the light source in the rest of the frame is from behind the subject from the street-lights. The face should be in shadow."

"Patel, you really are a glorious geek. Can you isolate that face for me and email it over as a jpeg?"

"Yep, Sure. If you give me a bit of time I can smooth off the edges, run it through some enhancement software."

"Will I be able to identify the man from the image?"

"Maybe. That stuff in the movies where they take a blurry image and suddenly make it look amazing is bollocks, but I'll do what I can. It'll end up as a bit of a mosaic, I'll send you the picture in about an hour."

By the time the photo pinged into Sawyer's email inbox he had showered, shaved and put on clean clothes. A handful of aspirins were going some way to dulling his hangover, but the monotonous ache in his limbs and the tiredness in his bones remained. The policeman pulled his chair close to the desk and doubled clicked on the attachment. It took a few slow seconds then the screen was filled with a face like a patchwork quilt, with the eyes coming from one person, the nose from another and the mouth a third. Sawyer was instantly depressed. This face was like an old-school photo fit and not accurate enough for his liking. He took a slug of whisky and looked at it again. Maybe it wasn't so bad. It certainly gave an impression and to any eagle-eyed copper out there, it might just be what they needed. He was convinced whoever this image led them to had something to do with the Prince's killing. What, he had no idea, but there was no doubt at all they were involved. He composed an email to Scotland Yard, attached the image and addressed it to the duty officer on the hit-and-run investigations team. He hit send and sat back.

Within three hours every copper in London would have a copy of the image in his hands. He smiled as he imagined the look on the Major's face when the image of the fictional hit-and-run driver hit the news.

Act 6: Scene Five

*"A most fine figure, to prove you a
cipher!"*

Love's Labours Lost

For the second time in two days, Fiona and Dan
stood outside the double doors to the high
security ward that held Elwood captive. The first
time Fiona had been frightened, this time she amazed
herself as she was actually looking forward to seeing
him.

The door was opened by the same nurse that had
greeted them the day before, Helen. "Fiona!" Her lilting
Welsh accent swept them into the ward. "Lovely to see
you again. Elwood will be delighted, my loves. Your last
visit made such a difference. He's been out of bed today
and left his room for the first time in a month. He came
into the common room, watched some TV, he even had
a talk with one of the other patients. I don't know what
you did yesterday, but he's really coming back to life.
Your father's condition is a chronic disease, but like
many mental illnesses you can sometimes get
remarkable remissions."

The nurse strolled ahead of the couple, her words
drifting over her shoulder. They walked back past the
room of the living dead, as Dan was beginning to think
of the TV room. An old woman, tiny, in a heavy knit
green skirt and dark green top was sitting on a chair
with a smile on her face, mumbling into a cup and

laughing.

On the right, before they reached Elwood's room there was another private room and they could hear a voice moaning from inside of it. "Somebody help me, somebody help me, oh please, somebody help me." It was a loud, deep, woman's voice, repeating the same words over and over. The woman in the chair who had been mumbling into the cup looked up from her cup and screamed out "Shut up, you old bitch!" then went back to her cup. None of the other patients even batted an eyelid.

"Oh my God, Dan. This place really is a madhouse." Dan squeezed Fiona's hand.

Helen didn't even seem to notice. Within a few seconds they were outside the door to Elwood's room. "I'm only down the hall if you need anything, my loves," Helen spoke as she walked away. Dan looked at Fiona, wondering how she was feeling but she had already let go of his hand, opened the door and walked in.

Elwood was out of bed, sitting on a chair in front of a new table. A pile of paper lay scattered in front of him, covered in diagrams and notes. An old tea stained mug was resting precariously on the edge of the table, a wad of lethally sharpened yellow pencils sitting proudly in the mug, points facing upwards.

Elwood turned to the visitors, his face alive with a broad smile.

"Fee-Fee. How delightful to see you." He started to rise from his chair.

"Don't get up daddy."

"Hello Professor Fletcher. Do you remember me?"

"Yes Roger, of course I remember you. I was at your wedding, don't you remember? I seem to recall it was a quite lovely day, English summer at its best. Swans on the river, Pimms in my glass, waltzing 'til dawn. Super." Dan glanced over at Fiona, even she was smiling. "What can I get you two lovebirds to drink? Isn't it about time I was hearing the patter of tiny feet with you two?"

"Daddy, where did the table and papers come from?"

"Oh." Elwood looked down at his papers. "A present from Helen. You know the Welsh nurse." He smiled looking up at Dan. "I think she's sweet on me," he said in a mock whisper.

"Daddy!" Fiona laughed.

"I've been running over a few ideas, Fee-Fee. Your visit seems to have jolted free a few thoughts about Shakespeare and Bacon that had been floating around in my old brain."

"Do you mind if I take a look?" Dan asked.

"No, go ahead."

Elwood sat back in his chair. Fiona thought he looked pleased someone new was taking an interest in his work. Dan picked up the papers and started looking through them. They were a mass of symbols and scribbles. Dan tried to make sense of them but soon realized it was hopeless. Elwood's notes were nothing more than nonsense.

"Daddy, do you recognize this?" She pulled her battered notepad out of her bag and handed it to her father.

Elwood held it close to his face, straining to read the words. "Of course I do, it's the inscription from Sir Francis Bacon's tomb."

"Not quite daddy, it's from William Shakespeare's tomb in Stratford."

"Good Lord, of course it is. Silly me. That's an easy mistake to make isn't it." Elwood burst out laughing again, and began to cough violently; phlegm dripped from the corner of his mouth onto the table.

"Fiona and I think there might be a cipher in there, and we were wondering if you agreed?" said Dan.

Fiona grabbed his arm and whispered in his ear. "Don't you think you're pushing it a bit?"

Dan shook his head. "Look."

Elwood had found some space on his pile of paper and was writing the quote from the grave out into a grid. Dan stared at him transfixed. The room was completely silent apart from the sound of Elwood's pencil scratching on the paper. Within a couple of minutes he had finished, and without a pause, he started to make rapid marks, highlighting the letters on the grid. He leant back and looked at them, his face still warm and friendly.

"Come and sit down here on the bed my little code cracker, and you, Roger, you sit down here too." Elwood turned around so he was facing the two of them. He leant forward and grabbed Fiona's hand. "Do you know what your name means, Fletcher?" He said.

"Ummm, no daddy."

"It means arrow maker. Now then what about Shakespeare, what do you think that means."

"Errr, spear maker?"

"Nearly, Fee-Fee, it means, surprise surprise, spear shaker. Any idea what William means? No, I won't tease, it's a form of German for helmet. Bacon's muse, his Goddess who he followed, his divine inspiration, was Athena, the Goddess who shook her spear at ignorance and fought for knowledge amongst the stars. She's always pictured wearing a helmet you know, and holding her spear. That's what drew him initially to the country actor whose real name was Shaksper. It was a piece of divine luck he thought, to see such similar names. Bacon's plays are full of references to destiny and fate you know. *'Men at some time are masters of their fate'* that's from *Julius Caesar*, *'Things must be as they may'*, *Henry V*, *'Who can control his fate?'* Othello."

He paused and stared out of the window. "You really must look at the plays more often, Fee-Fee. I love them. It's what started me on this research all that time ago. Just because he lied about the author's name doesn't make them any less brilliant."

"How long have you been working on this daddy?"

"On Bacon, you know my love affair with that brilliant brain. Most of my working life. But the connections with Shakespeare, I think the first voices told me to begin maybe three years ago. It's a pity that only now you choose to actually ask me, my dear."

Three years. It made Fiona realise how long it had been since she was involved in her father's life. She knew in her heart she had been drawing further away from him for a lot longer than that.

"But don't listen to me, Fee-Fee, I know you had

your own life to lead." His tone brightened. "It's incredible how much of Bacon's own thoughts and philosophies are in those plays. Bacon kept a meticulous diary you know. A huge volume of notes he made about his life, many written years before the plays appeared. In it there are over nine thousand references to events which I later traced in the plays. This was what made me definitively realise Shakespeare was Bacon." Elwood paused. "Here's an anecdote to show you what I mean. Two of Bacon's plays were performed to his fellow students when he was studying to be a lawyer, at the precocious age of seventeen. These plays were *As You Like It* and *A Comedy of Errors*." Elwood laughed. "You know a little of his life, don't you, my little code cracker. You know Bacon studied to be a lawyer?"

"Yes, in London, at Grays Inn College. I knew that daddy, but what about the cipher, we..."

"And what do you know of his brother at that time?"

"His brother? Anthony? Didn't he go and live in Italy?"

"Yes, my dear girl, he did. He was writing to young Francis from Italy. Anthony wrote about his experiences around Italy, especially from his time in Venice. And as for Francis, he was returning letters to his brother from London, complaining of a particularly difficult Jewish moneylender who seemed to have remarkably little sympathy for our young lawyer's failures to make regular payments on his debt. When Anthony got home he mortgaged his house and borrowed money to get Francis out of debt." Elwood fixed his piercing eyes on Dan. "Now, what play do you think miraculously appeared just a very few months later, first performed from an anonymous author? I'll give you a clue, it features a mean Jewish moneylender who strikes a lethal bargain with a young hero."

"The Merchant of Venice?"

"Why yes, that's right. *'If you prick us, do we not bleed? If you tickle us, do we not laugh? If you poison us, do we not die?'* Shylock was based on a money lender who wanted his pound of flesh off Bacon himself. The beauty of that play, Portia, why, that was the *bellisima raggazza* who captured Anthony's heart in Italy. And of course the heroic father figure of the play, the generous Antonio was based on Anthony himself."

"That's amazing," said Dan.

"Oh yes, all of the plays mirror Bacon's life you know. *Romeo and Juliet* was based on the great unrequited love of Bacons own life. She was a French princess he met whilst working over there in the Royal Courts of France. But she was trapped in the middle of a bitter family rivalry. Bacon was not seen as suitable. In later years, when all the great tragedies appeared such as *Hamlet* and *Macbeth*, they all reflected events in his own life; his mother's madness, his brother's death. Of course the greatest tragedy of all was that Francis died poor and alone, and possibly gay, although I personally believe he had at least one son."

Elwood paused and turned a smile on to Fiona and his voice picked up. "Oh Fee-Fee, I'm so glad to see you smile. It's wonderful to see you again, happy and in love. Is it time for us to go home now? I'm so tired of this place. Where is your mother?" He lifted both his hands up and shouted loudly into the room. "'*Joy, gentle friends! Joy, and fresh days of love accompany your hearts!*' That's from *A Midsummer Night's Dream*."

Faintly, outside in the hallway they heard a reply "Shut up, you old bastard!"

Elwood laughed, and disintegrated into another coughing fit. "*O, spirit of love, how quick and fresh art thou!*" he gasped.

Dan was starting to get impatient. When Elwood's coughing had subsided, he pushed the cipher back in front of him. "So what is this, Elwood? You did it so quickly, what is it?"

Elwood paused and looked at Fiona. "You see my dear, this is one of the pieces I wanted to show you that weekend, when you cast me aside and refused to listen to me. Funny how things turn out, isn't it? That day you showed me no respect and interest at all, and here we are."

"Daddy, that's not fair."

"Yes, exactly as I said, you only call me daddy when you want something, you treacherous little..." Elwood's voice had suddenly risen and his head jerked forward, then as soon as the flash of anger had come it was gone and he carried on as if the outburst had never occurred. He looked back at Dan and pointed to the grid and the marked letters.

"I'll make this easy for you. Bacon invented a number of different codes. This variety of Bacon's cipher follows intensely specific mathematical formula, driven by ascribing number values to letters and a range of geometric patterns and shapes which must balance on the grid. The question then, assuming the mathematical set of letters and their numerical value is fixed, is which of the variable sets of objects are to be used and, of course, what is to be extrapolated. Being artistic as well as scientific, the great ciphers such as these would draw inspiration from what was around them."

Fiona was certainly her father's daughter, thought Dan with a faint smile.

"Something amusing you, Roger? Would you like to share with the whole class?"

"Sorry sir, go on."

"Fiona? Care to do the honours?" Elwood handed her the grid he had written out."

"The cross shape in the middle, that's an anagram, of Bacon. These letters at the top, they spell Francis, and that leaves u, a, t, o, r, h at the bottom. Which is an anagram for author. Francis Bacon, author."

Elwood clapped his hands, "Oh how marvellous, that was quick, my little code cracker."

"It's all very impressive," said Dan, "but we're looking for something new."

"Such as?"

"Do you know where the original manuscripts for Shakespeare's... sorry, I mean Bacon's plays can be found?"

"My word, you are very direct." Elwood looked at Dan, cocking his head. "Of course I have spent time on that subject. The voices were most insistent about that subject. The pot of gold at the end of the Rosicrucian rainbow. How could I not spend time on that great question? Oh yes, I know where they are. But why should I tell you? I wouldn't tell the voices anything about any of my research, no matter how much they cajoled and pleaded. Why should I tell you?"

A rush of emotion flooded over Dan and before he could stop himself he was confessing everything. "The Queen's life is at stake. You're right, it's the Rosicrucians. They want the manuscripts and they'll kill her unless we find them."

Elwood stood slowly from his chair and walked to the window. "Why should any of this matter to you? An American." The old man's black eyebrows were knitted, his eyes slits. He studied Dan with what could only be interpreted as contempt.

"This has nothing to do with national pride. My life is at risk." Dan stopped speaking, his eyes pleading as he stared at the old man. Elwood looked back, his face expressionless. "I need your help."

Elwood abruptly turned to face Fiona. "How is your mother, my dear? Why doesn't she come to visit me? I do miss her so." Elwood voice had taken on a lighter tone.

Fiona was confused. "She's very cross with you father."

"Yes, I have this feeling I've done something wrong." Elwood lifted his hands to his head in a theatrical gesture of remorse. "I can't remember what it is. I just want to see your mother. So I can apologise."

Dan turned to Fiona. "The safe in the barn. It has to be. Is that what is in there, sir? Please, you have to tell us. How do we get into the safe?"

Elwood said nothing.

Fiona glanced from Dan to her father. "Please, daddy."

"Fiona." Elwood spoke slowly. "Do you see how important this is to me, to see you mother? To mend our broken relationship?"

"You want me to bring mum here? Then you'll help? Is that what you're saying?"

"My dear dear girl, my darling little code cracker, my favorite one. If I can say sorry, I would be so very grateful my dear."

A look of horror flashed across Fiona's face. Her voice sounded weak. "Okay father. I'll do it."

Elwood leaned forward, long fingernails brushed his daughter's cheek. "Thank you," he breathed.

Act 6: Scene Six

"This is the very ecstasy of love."

Hamlet

Fiona, Dan and Imogen sat in the warm kitchen. The drive from the hospital had been tense.

"Man, it's so good to be back in this kitchen," said Dan, "I don't know what happened to the weather today. I do apologise, I feel like I'm kinda dumping on you being back here again."

"Any friend of my daughter is welcome." Imogen rested on the word friend. Dan smiled and took a sip of his tea, wondering if she knew that he had slept with her daughter.

"I appreciate it's whack, having a stranger turn up so close to Christmas."

Imogen was looking out of the window into the fading afternoon light where a constant stream of grey drizzle and low cloud made the view two dimensional and featureless.

"Fiona, have you fed the cats? Ginger Prince is out there looking like he's stalking one of the chickens. What is that silly creature up to?" Imogen turned to Dan. "To be honest, Dan it's a very strange Christmas for me. If I can be candid, I feel quite alone. Fiona's brother won't be back so I really don't mind the company."

"That's very kind of you. If I can be equally upfront with you, my plans have all been turned on their head.

A couple of weeks ago I was set on heading Stateside for Christmas. That's not going to happen now."

"I'm sorry."

"Hey, that's fine, it's just circumstance. We'll have a family catch-up next year."

"What about you Fiona? We haven't really talked that much about Christmas. What did you plan on doing?"

Fiona could see the hope in her mother's eyes. "Well mum, I was thinking I could spend it with you?"

"Oh, I'd love that, it's been years. Why don't you and your friend just both stay up here? It's hardly worth your while going back down to London now, is it? We wouldn't have much, but I could pop into Stratford and get a turkey and some veg?"

"That's so sweet of you mum."

"What have you two been up to today anyway?"

Fiona and Dan exchanged glances.

"We went to see father again."

"Oh."

"Please don't be too cross mum, but we went into the barn earlier as well. I told Dan a bit about what had happened."

Imogen stood up and paced over to the kettle. "Want some more tea?" she asked. "I'd better fill up the kettle. This brew is old now. It'll leave a bitter taste in your mouth."

Dan could see her hands were shaking. "I think I should explain something. Mrs Fletcher, this is all my fault. The project that me and Fiona have been working on involves research into Prince William's death."

Imogen's voice was cold. "Prince William's death? What on earth does that have to do with poking about in my husband's study and seeing him in hospital?"

"There's a lot more to William's death than we've seen on the television." Dan watched Imogen as he spoke. Her expression remained frozen. "His death was organized by a gang of extremists called the Rosicrucians."

"Oh no." Fear flashed across Imogen's face. "I'm sorry Dan, I don't want to hear all this. He's been filling your mind with his poison hasn't he? It got to the point about a year ago where just hearing the words Bacon or the Rosicrucians used to make me feel physically sick. He used to talk about it incessantly. But without warning, it all stopped. In a way the silence was worse. He retreated within himself. He would disappear into that barn for weeks at a time, just coming in for food. He kept taking my scissors from the drawer, then he would lose them, or I would find them in the fridge or something. It was frightening. He even slept out there some nights. Can you imagine it? What would the neighbours have said if they found out that he had slept in that old barn?" Imogen's hand shot to the work surface to steady herself. Dan sprung to his feet and guided her to one of the old wooden chairs surrounding the kitchen table.

For the first time in her life Fiona saw her mother as a weak and frail old woman. The independent woman who had been such dominant force throughout her childhood was gone. It scared her.

Dan hovered uncomfortably next to Imogen. "Can I

help you at all?"

"No." A strength was returning to Imogen's voice. "These things need to be said. For months before that weekend, Elwood and I led this strange, silent life. The two of us were barely talking. It was awful, but in a way I was glad. The silence was better than his ranting. I thought that he would get over it, that he would come to his senses and things would return to normal. That weekend when you came back was the first time he had said anything at all in months." She smiled wryly. "Your presence certainly opened the floodgates, didn't it? He wouldn't shut up that day."

"Oh mum; so this is my fault?"

"Don't be so silly. After you left that day he accused me of driving you away, trying to steal his work. I told myself it would pass." Imogen shifted in her seat and looked at Dan. "He was once a very kind man, courageous, dominant and brave. I just want you to know that. I loved him a great deal. I still do."

"That means a lot, Mrs Fletcher."

"What have you got to do with this, Dan? You said it's to do with Prince William's death? How are you involved?"

"I never set out to get caught up in all this."

"Look," said Imogen, "from what I can gather you and my daughter have got yourselves involved in something pretty serious. Now as far I am concerned I will do anything to protect my child. Do you understand?" Dan nodded. "So, I suggest you tell me it all."

Dan started at the beginning and explained each event as it had happened, leaving out no details. Imogen listened, absorbing the words. "And you are convinced the Rosicrucians are behind this?"

"Yes, I am."

"Father can help us, mum. In fact I am pretty sure he is just about the only person in the world who can help us. He's agreed, but there's a catch."

"What kind of catch?"

"He wants something. Something I can't give him."

"You're not being clear. What does your father want?"

"You." Fiona's words were followed by silence. "He wants to talk to you." Fiona looked down at the floor as she spoke.

"I understand it's asking a lot Mrs Fletcher," said Dan. "But we have no choice. If it's too much for you we understand. We'll find another way." Fiona rose and moved next to him, her hand slipping around his waist. The two of them looked at Imogen and waited for her decision. Dan could hear the clock ticking in the background and a faint hiss of escaping steam from the kettle.

Imogen's voice was barely more than a whisper. "I'll do it."

Later that night, Dan got into his wheezing creaking bed. What a week! So much had happened. He closed his eyes, feeling relaxed and positive about the future, believing for the first time in what seemed an age he could actually have a future, possibly even with Fiona. He turned the light off and fell asleep.

In his dreams, he was diving into a blood red ocean; the water was cold and he was swimming hard. There was a light ahead, the closer he came to it, the warmer the water around him became. In the crimson sea around him, other forms were swimming as well, a huge shark, its teeth glinting, flicked in and out of view. He felt arms slide around him, he turned to see a mermaid swimming beside him, it had Fiona's face and her long hair drifted in the current as they swam together towards the light. It was so peaceful, then the mermaid was digging her nails into his chest and his eyes shot open as he woke up; a warm body was behind him in bed.

"Shhhh, don't move too much, this bed is terribly noisy."

"Fiona?" he murmured.

"Who else? The tooth fairy?"

He twisted around in the bed, to face her. "You're naked."

"So are you. Don't get any ideas, I just wanted to feel warm and close to you."

"Why Miss Fletcher, underneath the academic, there's quite a little devil inside of you, isn't there?"

"I'm not a hard person to work out, really," she whispered, feeling her blood starting to rush through her body and her heart race. What did this man do to her? "Although talking of being hard…" she ran a hand up his back and pulled herself towards him, pushing her hips into his groin, enjoying the feeling of pressure of his manhood pushing against her pelvis. She breathed deeply, the heat of his body felt so good. Dan ran his fingers over the contours of her face, then back down, stopping on her shoulder.

"Fiona, I'm so sorry about the way you were forced into this business with your mom. I..."

"Don't worry about that now." There was something incredibly erotic about being with him in her parent's house. She'd never done that before.

"What is it with you Fiona? A moment ago I was exhausted, and now I feel like my whole body is on fire." Dan whispered. She responded by pushing him onto his back and rolling over on top of him. He looked up and could see her outlined in the half moonlight through the window. Her naked profile was stunning. For a second he thought he saw a flash of red light on her neck, but paid it no attention; with her hair cascading down in front of her breasts, she looked so beautiful. He lifted up his hands and let them rest gently on her breasts. He could feel goose bumps on her skin and her nipples were growing hard under the palms of his hands. She felt hot, heavy and full in his hands, incredibly feminine and beautiful. He was amazed he hadn't seen any hints of this voluptuous, sensual side of her earlier. Up until the last few days she had seemed like a pretty, but cold and distant academic.

"I need you, Dan," Fiona murmured, moving her hips slowly up and down. He reached a hand up, stroked her cheek, was that a tear he could feel on her cheek?

"What is it? Fiona, are you okay?"

"Don't stop," she said, plunging her mouth down onto his in a fierce kiss. "Just take me, Dan." She lifted her hips and adjusted her position, then lowered herself onto him, pushing him as deep inside as she could, shuddering with pleasure. She rocked backwards and forwards on top of him, digging her nails into his chest. She felt connected to him, as if they shared the same fate.

Outside at the far end of the garden, a man dressed in a long black coat and balaclava covering his face crouched in the cold, his breath steaming as he zoomed in the powerful telescopic laser sight on his rifle through the gap in the curtains, the infra red lens giving everything a green tint. Back in the room neither Dan nor Fiona saw the red dot of the laser site flicker across the wall behind them, slowly make its way up her naked spine and settle on the back of her head for a few seconds before blinking out.

Act 7: Scene One

"Tomorrow, and tomorrow, and tomorrow,

Creeps in this petty pace from day to day,
To the last syllable of recorded time."

Macbeth

Christmas Eve

Fiona woke early, the cold morning air seeping though the sheets. For a few moments her mind raced and then a brief smiled flicked across her lips. She had lain in Dan's bed for hours, but the space was too cramped for two people, so eventually she had reluctantly crept back to her own room.

She clambered out of bed; another chilly morning. She picked up her mobile. She'd been missing Nicky and decided to give her a call.

The phone was quickly picked up. "Hello stranger. How's tricks up in the boondocks?" To Fiona, Nicky sounded like she was forcing a happy voice.

"That's a good question. I feel brilliant in some ways, other ways, not so good. How are things with you?"

"Oh really, tell me the brilliant bit?"

"You know that guy I was talking about, the one who felt the same as us about the video?"

"Oh him, yes, the guy you met at Westminster Abbey. The gorgeous gay one."

"Stop it, he's not gay."

"And how might you be so sure about that, honey?"

"Well, we've spent the last few days together."

"Oh, really? You've..."

"Yes, things have definitely moved forward in every sense." Fiona tried not to laugh.

"Good for you honey. Dare I say it, it's probably just what you need. Even if it doesn't last long, you may as well enjoy it."

"I can't remember a week in my life like it. Not only all that with Dan, but seeing my father, and the Queen and..."

"The Queen? What do you mean?"

"Oh nothing. Anyway, do tell, how are you? You avoided it when I asked you a minute ago."

There was a sigh from the other end of the phone. "Oh I'm fine, you know me. I might not have my pulling partner with me but I've still got my books and a worn out DVD of Bridget Jones to keep me company."

"Come on, Nicks. This is me you're talking to."

"All right, you got me. It's just all this business with Prince William and now it's almost Christmas. I'm just bored I suppose and missing my dad. It'll be the first Christmas without him. I'm going up to see my mum later today, but after that I've got nothing to do, time is just dragging and I'm thinking about stuff too much."

"Why don't we get together after Christmas? There's a good chance I'll be here on Boxing Day and maybe a couple of days after that as well. In fact, I know this sounds fairly random, but me and Dan have been working really hard on the Shakespeare project."

"And what?"

"If you've got nothing to do and you feel like a bit of excitement and a challenge, why don't you get more involved? I remember mentioning you to Dan before and he seemed positive about it. He knows we discussed it when we were in London."

"That sounds brilliant!"

"Oh, it is. But it's kind of scary too."

"Wow!. If I can help I'd love to. It sounds way cooler than sitting in my flat in London waiting for term to begin. Thanks honey."

"Let's speak on Christmas Day or Boxing Day. At the very least you could come up here for a break. It's the first Christmas me and my mum are going to have without my father too, so if I'm still here mum would love to talk to someone who understands how she feels."

"I'd love to meet your family. Okay honey, sounds like a plan, I really want to see you. Let's speak in a day or so."

Act 7: Scene Two

"How beauteous mankind is! O brave new world."

The Tempest

Dan woke up feeling great. He had even slept through Kenneth the cockerel's wheezing attempts to wake the world. He felt so much better about everything; more alive, more in control, and slightly in love too. As he was tying his shoes he stopped and looked through the window as a thought struck him. It was a funny thing, but the threat on his life, the fact that he could be dead in a week didn't frighten him any more. He realised that he now saw it as a challenge to beat, not something to run away from. He laughed to himself. In a weird way he was living what his pop always talked about, the spirit of the American dream, but thousands of miles away from home.

The image of the Queen came into his mind again; her sitting on that chair, the look of anger and frustration in her eyes. Her reaction to her predicament had been to fight against it and he felt a fool for having taken so many days to reach the same conclusion a woman in her eighties came to instantly.

He went downstairs. Fiona and Imogen were in the kitchen. Imogen gave him a half smile. "I phoned the hospital, we're going to go in tomorrow on Christmas Day." Dan bit his tongue, for a second he was disappointed he had to wait another day. What was he thinking? "Mrs Fletcher," he said, "I wish I could say I knew how hard it was, but I don't really. I've never been in the sort of position you're in, but, I think what you're doing is wonderful."

Imogen blushed. "They're having a party on Christmas Day round about lunchtime. The nurses are coordinating the relatives to all come at once. A senior charge nurse who I spoke to seemed to think it would be good for the patients. So I'm thinking we'll leave here about half eleven, get there for midday."

"All the mad people in one room? Sounds like a crazy party."

Imogen's hand flew to her mouth, as she stifled a giggle. "Oh my, you do have a dark sense of humour, just like me. But, you've got to laugh about it haven't you? Otherwise you just spend the whole time crying."

"Yes, sorry about that. I know I have my naughty side. Is there anything I can do to help you out this morning, Imogen?"

"Oh, he is a charmer isn't he Fiona? Why don't you two go and let the chickens out? Then I'll make us some breakfast. Scrambled eggs?"

"I'd be delighted. And eggs sound awesome."

Fiona and Dan walked across the damp garden, the huge pine trees that bordered the property on the left were glistening and dripping with dew, but for the moment at least the clouds had risen high enough for patches of blue sky to appear. White winter sunlight cascaded through the gaps in the clouds, lighting up patches of the stunning landscape. In front of them the steep slope of the hill rose behind the orchard where the chicken house was. In the opposite direction, the sweeping fields of the Vale of Evesham were a sea of smoke, low mist creeping over earth, curling around trees and hedges, clinging on before the rising sun transformed them into just a memory.

When they were out of sight of the kitchen window, Fiona stood on her toes and gave Dan a kiss on his lips. He smiled.

"Fiona, I really feel that we're right on the edge of something here. This time tomorrow, I'm sure we're going to know where the manuscripts are. And then it's all over – finished."

"I hope so."

"Fiona, do you mind if I go back to the barn and have another look round? I've not given up on the safe yet, and there's got to be more information in there."

"I'll come with you. Let's just try and keep out of mum's way though."

Act 7: Scene Three

"Take him and cut him out in little stars."

Anthony and Cleopatra

Jackson stepped back from the table and flicked open a silver Zippo to light a cigarette that hung loosely from his mouth. He inhaled the smoke and slowly released it in an almost invisible vapour. The smell almost masked the stench of urine and blood. The soldier looked down at the naked man who lay on the table. Jackson though that the man's double chins and squashed nose gave him the look of a pig. A particularly stupid pink pig, ripe for slaughter. The man's wrinkled testicles had shrunken back up in his hips in fear, or possibly because of the electrodes attached to them. On the man's left cheek sat his eye, the optical nerve allowing it to dangle freely.

"Fucker," said Jackson.

The man was the first of the Rosicrucians Jackson's interviews with the aged members of the Atlantean Society had led him to. He thought he'd had a lucky break after this one had been stupid enough to use a fake ID registered by MI5. The man had refused to talk. Popping out his eye and the electrodes had proved pointless, if enjoyable.

The soldier picked up the phone attached to the interrogation room wall. Dried streaks of blood covered the handset, red fingerprints clearly visible. "Put me through to Andrews."

A voice crackled into life on the other end.

"Andrews here. Are you ready for me now?"

"Yes, I've had a crack at this little prick. Physical pain isn't getting through."

"Time to go directly to the brain. On my way."

Act 7: Scene Four

"There are more things on heaven and earth, Horatio, than are dreamed of in your philosophy."

Hamlet

D an and Fiona spent the rest of the morning digging through boxes, examining piles of burnt books and damp documents. Dan's attention kept returning to the safe on the wall. They both knew that it wouldn't be easy to crack. They had tried everything they could think of – Fiona's name in numerals, the family's dates of birth, backwards and forwards. Nothing worked.

It had been over two hours since they started and Fiona was tired. It was late morning and the sunlight was slowly slipping through the dirty broken windows. The smell of charred wood and mould made her feel sick. "I think Dad had to be the last academic in the world without a computer. I spend so long on my PC these days I'd forgotten just what a pain dealing with piles of paper actually is. Look at this lot. I can't believe I'm even contemplating going through it." She was struggling with a box and dropped it heavily onto the oak desk.

"Hold on a minute, do that again," said Dan.

"Do what again? Moan about my dad's archaic ideas about filing or drop this box?"

"The box, clever clogs."

Shrugging, Fiona picked up the box of paper again and dropped it back down on top of the desk.

"Did you hear that? It sounds hollow."

"So what? It's a desk. It's got three drawers in it."

"Yes, but they're full to the brim with random books and old receipts and stuff. But it still sounded hollow when you dropped that box on it."

He put his hands under the area of the desk where Elwood would have sat and knocked on the bottom. "There's some sort of hidden space under the top and above the drawers." Quickly, the two of them cleared the boxes and books off the top of the desk. Then Dan put his hands under the front lip of the desk and ran his fingers up and down. "It's my bet there's a hinge or something under here that keeps it locked. Yes! Here it is – hold on." There was a click as he found a lever and pulled. The whole top of the desk swung smoothly up on hinges from the front.

"Dan – it's got a secret compartment. Why doesn't that surprise me?"

Inside were three piles of paper, each with numbered cover sheets. Pile number one had a title at the top and notes under it as well. Dan pulled them all out and stacked them up in order. He flicked through a few. "Now we know where all the passages he cut out from his First Folio went." Each sheet was covered in phrases from the plays glued on to the pages. Above every one, Elwood had written the title of the play it was from as well as the act and scene.

"There are hundreds of them," said Fiona. "This must have taken him months. No wonder mum didn't see him for so long. This must be the focus of his research. It must be the stuff he wanted to talk to me about the day we argued."

She glanced at the top page, there were tiny neat notes and strange arrows and designs and a block of text in the middle.

"Do you think this includes information on where the manuscripts are?" said Dan. "Is this what he's going to tell us about tomorrow?"

"I suppose it's possible." Fiona flicked through the piles of paper. "Perhaps this is the answer in its rawest form; one step before he got to the final solution. If the answer to where the manuscripts are is in that safe, this is the intellectual path he took."

"Where's your mom?"

"I think she's gone out shopping to get some food for lunch tomorrow. You can't have Christmas in England without turkey. Why?"

"Short of me heading out and buying some plastic explosive we're not going to get into that safe. Even if I had some I'd probably take the whole building out and kill myself as well as Kenneth the cockerel. Let's get out of this room, it's starting to do my head in. I'll make us some coffee and we can chill out in the house, read through this and try and figure it out. What do you think?"

Fiona was relieved. Every moment she spent sur- rounded in the scene of her father's descent into madness made her feel deeply uncomfortable. And the smell, the rotten damp smell of the place; she hated it.

With the papers laid out in piles across the kitchen

table Dan was reading the cover sheet in more detail. "Check this out, what does it mean?" He passed it over to Fiona.

<u>Bacon s Secrets Deliberate mistakes in the plays</u>

Why did Hamlet attend a university that did not yet exist? Why did he write about cannons when they had not yet been invented? Why did he write about clocks when they had not yet been invented? Bacon was a historian, these are deliberate mistakes.
My conclusion they MUST be referencing what was then contemporary life through the ancient stories. The clues - Nonsense passages in all the plays why are they there? CIPHER! HIDDEN STORY!
Unnecessary repetition of words and themes?
Out of context. Different fonts and strange page layout so many spelling mistakes and errors in the first ever printing must be DELIBERATE SOLUTION: BACON S BILATERAL CIPHER

"Bilateral cipher?" said Fiona. "I know that one, it's one of Sir Francis Bacon's favourite ciphers. You find phrases based on common themes – it's a way of connecting hidden information together to make a single message. You'd take numerical values of words and similar grammar and phrasing in a line, then use it as a pattern to jump to the next hidden message later on in the document and then connect it all together."

"I won't pretend I followed that. But, it was a cipher that worked with huge documents? Like for example, the First Folio of the plays?"

Fiona turned over and looked at the first page. It was a lines cut out from the historical play *King John*.

Thus I begin, the letters scattered wider than the sky and earth;

"I think I know what this is," she said. "But if I'm right, it's incredible. Each one of these pages contains phrases from the plays all cut out and placed in an order determined by following the patterns revealed with the bilateral cipher."

"In English please, missy."

"I think, when you put them all together, they spell out Sir Francis Bacon's life story."

"Holy cow, so not only did he write the plays, he hid his own life story inside them, piece by piece? Man, he was a brainy guy."

"Yes, he was." Fiona was bursting with curiousity.

"And hats off to your pop for working it out."

Fiona couldn't help feeling a rush of pride. "Yes, this is easily his most innovative piece of research. No wonder he got so secretive about it." She scanned through the first few pages. "Oh my God, look."

She pointed to a section on the second page where Elwood had laid out the snippets.

And if care be taken
And these words be diligently
Cut and sifted
and rearranged
the tragic story of my life
is now pulled asunder from its lair
and these words together as a
band of brothers
are revealed to you, dear reader

Fiona was enthralled as she read on. "Look, Bacon was

giving instructions! Use his cipher as a guide to which bits of the plays to cut up and rearrange." A wave of sadness crashed through her. If only her father wasn't so sick, she could have shared this with him.

Dan felt triumphant. He leant over and kissed Fiona hard on the mouth. "Suddenly, I can't wait for Christmas. A few days ago, I was dreading it, it was just one step nearer to my death, but now, this is the icing on the Christmas cake. Look at it, it's dynamite. Fiona, your pop is a genius. I'm sure he knows where the manuscripts are. When we see him, he's going to tell us, then it's all going to be over."

Act 8: Scene One

"Double, double toil and trouble; fire burn, and cauldron bubble."

Macbeth

Christmas Day

Dan was disappointed to wake up on Christmas morning and not see snow. It had never snowed at home on Christmas Day, but when he had moved to England he had still kept the romantic notion in his mind of opening his bedroom curtains to a blanket of white. But instead, it was cold and grey. He forced himself out of bed and grabbed his mobile. He phoned his mother to wish her a happy Christmas, but had forgotten about the time difference. He left a message saying he'd call back later.

The morning flew by, Fiona feeling as if she was in a trance, her mind preoccupied with whether she had done the right thing acquiescing to her father's demands and Dan's pressure. She glanced at her mum. Imogen seemed in good spirits, but was that frozen smile real or forced?

The three of them had decided to wait until after they had visited Elwood in hospital before eating lunch, so Dan found himself scraping and peeling vegetables after enjoying a breakfast of scrambled eggs, smoked salmon and a glass of champagne to toast the holiday.

He too was utterly lost in thought. The week had been bewildering and frenetic, but now, now he was sure that not only was there light at the end of the tunnel, but fresh air and a peace and quiet. The constant feeling of fear that had gnawed away at him before was just a memory, his overriding feeling now was one of determination.

All too quickly they were on the way to the hospital. The roads were quiet and the pale low sun apologetically broke through the occasional cloud break for a few seconds before being swallowed up once more. The steady pounding of drizzle on the roof of the car had a hypnotic effect. Brooding clouds sat heavily on the horizon and although it was only late morning it felt as if the daylight was already dying.

As Dan guided the Jaguar through the Stratford traffic and up to the hospital, Fiona grabbed her mother's hand. Imogen was pale, a tight fixed smile was on her face, her other hand gripping a hastily wrapped gift of some CDs: Edward Elgar's Cello Concerto and Samuel Barber's Violin Concerto.

"How are you, mum?"

"Oh, I'll be fine, don't worry about me. A family Christmas will make your father happy."

"Lots of guilty consciences here today by the looks of it." Dan spoke his thoughts aloud as he pulled into the busy car park.

He was lucky and edged into a space almost immediately. It was still raining and the three of them hurried into the hospital and down the grey corridor towards the heavy secure doors to the ward in silence. They paused as Fiona pressed the buzzer. There was a brief wait before Helen opened the doors. As soon as the Welsh nurse saw Imogen she rushed forward.

"Oh, Mrs Fletcher, how lovely to see you and Merry Christmas, my love!" Helen flung her heavy arms around the old lady, almost knocking her off balance. "This will mean so much to Elwood, he's been so much better the last few days. His behaviour has been much improved. They're trying him out on weaker medicine, and the consultant even popped her head in to to see him as well." Helen leant in conspiratorially. "You know what these consultants are like, quite happy to prescribe medicine without bothering to actually see patients, but Doctor Manzarek was so interested in Elwood's case she even spoke to him. Can you credit it? We don't even need to supervise him taking his pills anymore. We used to have to force them down him, but now half the nurses just leave them with him. Anyway, Elwood's with everyone else in the common area. They're all a bit disappointed though. They were looking forward to the Queen's speech, but it turns out it's been cancelled. Apparently she's too ill, poor love. She is getting on in years though and with all the stuff going on I can't say I'm too surprised."

As Helen's chatter tailed off, they reached the common room. Dan, Fiona and Imogen stood looking into the room. A small plastic Christmas tree had appeared in the opposite corner and its artificial lights winked feebly in a desperate attempt to bring a sense of Christmas cheer. The room was very busy. Six or seven families had come to visit sick relatives and the tinny

Christmas carols playing in the background were drowned out by incessant chatter. Fiona felt her mother take her hand as she caught a glimpse of Elwood.

The old professor was walking towards them across the carpet, dressed in grey sweat pants and a blue t-shirt, his skeletal arms sticking out like the remains of a roast chicken after Sunday lunch. A pink party hat sat ridiculously on his head, straggling white wisps of hair escaping from under the thin paper. Someone had tossed multicoloured streamers around his neck and they hung limply as he shuffled forward.

"Fiona, you brought her!" Elwood smile seemed to stretch from ear to ear. He looked at his wife, arms outstretched. "Is that really you, Imogen?" He lunged forward grabbing at Imogen's arm. Imogen recoiled instinctively. "Let me kiss you, my precious darling." Elwood pushed his face forward. Imogen twisted her head away, but his cracked and weathered lips brushed her cheek.

"Hello again, father."

"Fee-Fee! Who is this with you? Why, how silly of me, that's not you is it Jason?"

"No, it's not Jason," said Imogen, "this is Dan. You know, Fiona's special friend."

"Who's Jason?" whispered Dan to Fiona.

"My brother."

"No, I don't suppose it would be Jason, would it." Elwood stared at Dan, his eyes clouded in confusion and then his mouth broke into a grin. "Yes, of course, Roger. How delightful to see you again."

"Professor Fletcher." Dan extended his hand. Elwood ignored the attempted handshake and Dan's hand floated aimlessly in the air before dropping back to his side. "Don't you remember, I was here the day before yesterday? We were talking about finding the Bacon manuscripts."

"Ah yes, the contents of my safe. The Spear Shaker, Bacon's muse, the great goddess herself." Elwood turned to Imogen. "Darling, it is simply lovely to see you here. Have you met my friends here?" Elwood grabbed Imogen's arm, waving at the crowd of patients.

Helen bustled up to the group holding a tray full of plastic cups. "Have a drink everyone. It's a bit early, but it's Christmas."

Dan looked into the cups. They contained a yellow liquid, presumably wine, though the insipid colour reminded Dan of urine.

"Don't you worry my love, this is Lidl's finest. Might not be what you are used to with your fancy ways, but it'll do the job."

Dan smiled and took a drink, the rest of the family followed suit. Elwood threw his head back, swallowing his in one rapid movement, some of it splashing over his mouth and dribbling down his neck. He dropped the plastic cup on the floor.

"Won't be a second, my darling," he said, suddenly turning away from them. "I've just got to pop into the kitchen, do something. Back in a tic." The old professor shuffled away from them, into the throng, Dan could see him step into the empty kitchen.

"Can we go somewhere more private, do you think?" asked Imogen.

"What about his room?" Fiona saw Helen walking past with more plastic cups. "Excuse me, Helen, do you think you could take my father down to his room shortly? We're just going to walk down."

"Party a bit much for you my loves?" said Helen. "I sympathise. Bit of a rowdy crowd, aren't they? Just wait until they try charades. It's a riot." She threw her head back and laughed, the peal of laughter high and musical. "I'll find him in a minute for you my loves; you leave it to Helen."

They thanked her and walked down the corridor to Elwood's room. On the table was the same pot of sharp pencils, and a pile of papers. Dan picked one up. Yet more gibberish. Fiona caught his eye as he did so. Dan just shrugged. Fiona and Dan perched on Elwood's immaculate bed whilst Imogen sat down on the wooden chair next to the table. After a few minutes Helen opened the door and led Elwood in.

"Here they are, Elwood. Your lovely family."

"My darling, sorry to keep you waiting. I just had to pop into the kitchen to do something. Now, what can I get you to drink?" Elwood was speaking in a singsong voice, his intense eyes flashed as he stared at his wife. Helen waved goodbye and left them alone.

"Oh, Elwood, I don't want a drink." Imogen sighed. Elwood walked up behind his wife and bent over her, putting his bony hands on her shoulders. She tried not to flinch at his touch.

"Oh my darling, it's so good to see you. My love is truly like a red, red rose." Elwood leaned over and spoke softly into her ear. "When are we going home, my petal? I don't know what I'm doing in this place, have you come to take me home?" He paused. "Do you know who these people are? What have I done?"

"No. I'm afraid you're staying here, Elwood."

The old man looked at her, his smile stuck but his eyes narrowed. Imogen sensed the hurt and her voice softened. "Here, I've got you a present." She put the CDs down on the table, but Elwood ignored them and walked over to the window and stared out at the wet lawn and car park.

"I've done something awfully wrong, haven't I? I don't know what it is, but darling, whatever it is, you know I love you so much. I would never do anything to hurt you."

"You did hurt her. And you hurt me too." Fiona spoke calmly. Elwood frowned, his bony grey face seemed confused and vulnerable.

"I don't know, Fee-Fee, you know I would never hurt either of you. I'm so sorry if I've hurt either of you. All I want to do is apologise for whatever I did."

Imogen was still staring at Elwood. She covered her eyes and sobbed silently into her hands, her shoulders heaving. Elwood moved to comfort her, his long nails touching the outside of her scarred hands.

"What is it my darling, you can tell me?" he purred. "I'm your husband, I swore an oath, remember? *'Til death do us part.'*"

Dan stood up and moved towards the closed door. "Can you smell that?" He turned to Fiona, a worried look on his face.

"Yes, it smells like something burning. A turkey

lunch gone wrong?" As Fiona spoke a bell started ringing, its noise crashing through the building.

Dan pulled the door open. He stepped into the corridor. Down the other end he could see smoke billowing out of the kitchen. The common room had erupted into chaos as family members tried to get confused and panicking old people away from the danger. A withered old lady stumbled down the corridor towards Dan, her hands outstretched and holding a cup.

Dan was relieved to see Helen striding down the corridor and grabbing the old woman and pulling her back the other way. She shouted to Dan above the din. "There's a fire in the kitchen, we've got to get everyone out. It's probably nothing, but better safe than sorry, my loves."

The bell was ringing painfully loudly, its insistent tone reverberating around the corridor. Dan rushed back into the room, Fiona and Imogen were staring at him. Elwood was still staring at Imogen.

"What's going on?" Fiona shouted.

"A fire started in the kitchen. We've got to get out while they deal with it."

"Come on mum, daddy – we've got to get out of here." Fiona began to panic. The smoke was filling the corridor and Dan could feel it sting his eyes.

He coughed. It was getting painful to breathe. "Hurry up. Whatever it is, it's getting worse."

Dan led Fiona, Imogen and Elwood into the corridor, bitter tasting smoke filling the air. Everyone except Elwood started to cough. Whatever was burning had a chemical, acidic taste. Dan rubbed his eyes to clear them and saw the fire exit. Screaming and panicking patients were being ushered out by the nurses and their relatives.

"God, what a terrible smell!" Fiona shouted. "What is it, burning plastic, oil?"

"It doesn't matter, let's get everyone out. Down this way." Dan pointed towards the way out. "Come on Elwood, what are you waiting for?"

"A fire." Elwood was staring into the smoke, and not moving. "A fire, that will keep it safe. They said it needed to be protected. They are evil. Unclean, hellspawn." Suddenly he whirled round and with quick steps crashed through the double doors back into his room.

"Daddy! Come back!" screamed Fiona.

"I'll get him!" shouted Dan, but Imogen put her hand up on his chest to stop him.

"No, I'll go. He'll listen to me. Wait here." Dan hesitated, but Imogen was already gone, following her husband into the room.

Dan didn't know what to do. He looked over at Fiona, then decided to go in after Imogen. But even as he pushed the door open a scream burst through from inside. He ran in and was frozen to the spot. Elwood had transformed into a wild animal. He was holding Imogen by the throat up against the wall.

"She's the evil one!" screamed Elwood, his neck twisting to look back at Dan. "She wants to steal my secrets. They told me I couldn't trust her." He stared at Dan. His face was bright red, veins standing out. "They told me before and I let her live. Now I'll destroy her. You're sent by them. He's watching me. I know you." Imogen looked over at Dan, her eyes filled with terror.

"Daddy! What are you doing?" Fiona was inside the room, she grabbed Dan's arm in panic.

"Evil bitch, I know her, I know you all!"

Dan sprang forward, but even as he moved a pencil appeared in Elwood's free hand. It was long, yellow and lethally sharp. His arm swung in an arc, stabbing the pencil hard into Imogen's throat. It entered cleanly and the whole length disappeared into the flesh. Imogen's mouth fell open, her face frozen in an expression of terror and surprise. Dan's momentum carried him forward and he fell onto Elwood, wrapping his arms around the old man. The collision sent the two men crashing to the ground, freeing Imogen who collapsed onto her knees and slumped back against the wall.

At that moment the fire alarm stopped ringing. A few seconds passed when the only noise was weak gasping breaths from Imogen. Then Elwood started screaming, a high keening wail like a hyena. Dan looked over at Imogen. Blood was pouring down her neck and pooling on the floor.

"Hurry, try and stop the bleeding!" Dan shouted.

Fiona ran over to her mother. Imogen's face was turning white, she couldn't breathe. A lot of the blood was pouring down her throat and into her lungs, choking her. "Oh God, mum, no, please God, no."

Fiona felt like she was underwater, surely this wasn't happening? Time had slowed down, she pulled her mother's hand away and saw the pencil jammed in her throat, it was almost completely in, there was only a stub to get hold of. She grabbed the end of it and tried to pull, it wouldn't come and her fingers slipped in the slick blood. The pencil was stuck in some cartilage. She pulled the sleeve of her blouse over her hand and used it to get a better grip, and twisted and pulled at it, all she could think of was to get it out. But as soon as the pencil was free, the blood just started to come out quicker.

"What are you doing?" shouted Dan. "Don't take it out. Get a towel, try and block the wound, but be quick, we need help."

Fiona stumbled to her feet, but Dan was ahead of her, he had abandoned Elwood for a few seconds and jumped up, grabbing a towel over by the sink.

"Here, use this. You've got to stem the flow of blood, try and find the ends of the artery." He saw something moving out of the corner of his eye and turned round as with a howl Elwood stood up and threw himself at Imogen. Dan swung his fist hard and fast and caught Elwood square in the face, crunching his nose and sending the old man flying back. Elwood staggered to his feet, blood pouring from his broken nose, a thin high scream issuing from his lips, as Dan stepped forward and hit him again as hard as he could on the chin. Elwood slid to the ground unconscious.

"Stay with her," Dan shouted to Fiona. He leant against the table, breathing deeply, the smoking air burning his lungs. He thought he was going to collapse. He had been forced to hit Elwood with his broken hand and the waves of pain up his arm were brutal. But he couldn't stop, he had to find a nurse. He ran out of the room.

"Dan? Where are you going?" Fiona felt like she was about to pass out at any moment, her legs were impossibly heavy, her breathing tight, a terrible feeling of nausea swept through her body as she desperately stuffed the towel into the wound, but it didn't seem to do any good, it was red and sopping in seconds.

"Mum, please…" But Imogen's face was now a deathly white, she was drowning in her own blood as it poured into her lungs. Imogen fixed Fiona with her gaze, and gripped her hand tightly.

Dan ran through the smoke and out of the fire exit into the garden. Where were the nurses? He saw one trying to calm down an old man who was jumping up and down in excitement and pulling his trousers down; brown stains on his baggy undershorts, a Christmas party hat on his head.

"Over here, quickly!" The nurse saw him and ran over. "You've got to get into Professor Elwood's room now, he's stabbed his wife, she's bleeding heavily and she can't breathe."

The nurse and Dan sprinted back to the room. Fiona was kneeling on the floor, holding her mother's head in her hands, the floor around them covered in blood. Imogen's eyes were closed.

Fiona looked up and saw Dan. "Get out." She spoke in a low voice.

"What, oh, Fiona, your mother, oh Christ." The nurse ran forward and Fiona stood up to let her examine Imogen. Fiona's arms and chest were soaked in blood, Dan stepped towards her, but she shrank away from him.

"Get out of here!" she screamed. "It's your fault. You made me do it, if it wasn't for you she'd still be alive." Fiona felt such a terrible anger inside her. "Get out! This is your fault, if it wasn't for you…" Tears began to fall uncontrollably from her, Dan stepped forward and tried to put his arms around her, desperate to comfort her, but she pushed him away as hard as she could. He stumbled and fell backwards across the table, the papers and pencils scattering and crashing to the floor.

"Just get out of here, Dan. Now. I never want to see you again. Don't call me, don't you dare ever come near me again. You're poison." She turned away from him and knelt down to be with her mother's body.

Act 8: Scene Two.

*"Parting is such sweet sorrow, That I shall
say good night till it be morrow."*

Romeo and Juliet

Hedges flashed by as the Jaguar jostled for
position on the uneven country roads, clipping
verges, stones spitting up as the greedy engine
demanded more speed, more madness. Dan saw
everything as a blur, clouded by the sting of tears in his
eyes and the lash of rain on the windshield. He pushed
down again on the accelerator, not caring if he crashed,
almost willing it. He screamed out loud, a meaningless,
desperate howl. Fiona's words echoed in his mind. All
he seemed to have achieved so far since this whole thing
started was to ruin her life.

Dan saw the speed camera too late. A sudden white
flash lit the car up as he raced by. Fiona's words of
blame echoed in his ears. She had been scared and
upset, but even in his rage Dan knew she was right. If he
had not pushed so hard for Imogen to meet with
Elwood, she would still be alive.

After another couple of miles he hit another speed
camera. The second flash brought him back to his senses
and he slowed down and pulled over, bumping up onto
the grass verge. He turned the engine off and sat there,
staring out into the drizzle, wondering what on earth to
do.

A shrill ringing from the passenger seat caught his

attention. It was his phone. It was an unknown number calling, and he decided to take it.

"Dan Knight."

"At last."

"Jonny? What on earth are you doing calling me on Christmas Day?"

"It's the only way to get hold of you. Anyway, you've been sacked. Heathrow Airport cut the contract after you failed to phone me back or respond to any emails this week, let alone bother your arse and come into work. You've cost us over two hundred grand in lost business."

"So that's it, I've lost my job?"

"Yes. You really are the Christmas turkey in our office. Don't bother coming in to clear your desk, we've done that for you. There's a bin bag on the street outside the office if you want it, next pickup by the council on the 27th. Oh, and make sure you return your laptop by the end of the Christmas break or we'll send you a bill for that. You'll be paid up until the end of last week."

The phone went dead.

"That's just perfect," said Dan.

He returned the phone to the passenger seat and was just about to move into the traffic when it rang again. Another unknown number. He picked it up. "What the hell do you want now, Jonny?"

"Merry Christmas to you. Who's Jonny? Not your boyfriend is it, Danny boy? I know you Yanks tend to be a bit more adventurous in the sack than us frustrated Brits, but really – I don't need to know the sordid details pal."

Dan's stomach tightened as he recognised the voice of the Rosicrucian. "Luther. What do you want?"

"Having a good day? A nice family day? We see you've overcooked the turkey a bit there though boy, back at the hospital. Plenty of tomato sauce and dripping. I hope that doesn't mean you're thinking about skipping out on pudding does it?"

"You've been watching me. You lowlife bastard."

"Now, now, Danny boy, mind your language. What would your mother say if she heard you cursing like that. There she is, back in San Diego, basting your father's turkey, and here you are shooting your filthy fucking mouth off. Now I know you're in a bad mood, but that's no excuse to take it out on us, you know. Of course we've been watching you. We're going to be keeping a very close eye on you until you deliver or die, don't you worry about that my son. Deliver or Die. I like that, sounds like a James Bond movie. There's nothing you do without our eyes on you, you know. What about that girl the other night then, eh? You were having a right old time of it. You really should learn to close your curtains, you don't want the neighbours peeking in and seeing your dirty little games, now do you?"

"You're sick."

"Not as sick as our dear old Queen's going to be if you don't find Shakespeare's Truth and quickly."

There was a noise down the phone and then another voice came on. It was a woman's voice Dan didn't recognise. "Whoever you are, don't let these vile people intimidate you, we... " Suddenly there was silence, then a scream.

"Ten green bottles, sitting on the wall," sang Luther. "Ten green toes, sitting on her feet. And if one green toe," he paused, then screamed down the phone, "should accidentally be fucking cut off because Danny boy's mind was wandering, then there'd be nine green toes left." His voice abruptly became calm. "Damascus came up with that one. Cut off her toes, one at a time, one a day until you sort yourself out. He's had plenty of experience in these sorts of things you know. You'd be amazed at how losing a toe can affect your sense of balance." Luther's voice became muffled and Dan could hear him taking to someone else, "Terry, just give her a push will you?" There was a second of silence then the sound of someone crashing to the ground accompanied by the sound of laughter.

"What the hell are you doing?"

"Now look, sonny," said Luther returning his attention to the phone call, "we know you're a bit upset, but let's not get things out of proportion. You can't do anything about that old lunatic Elwood. The bird will get over it; you're better off without them in your life anyway if you ask me. I'm not saying you should bat for the other side, ride the chocolate highway, be a sausage jockey, bowl from the pavilion end or anything, just get your priorities straight. You get back on the case, you keep looking, otherwise I'll cut your head off and shit down your neck. And this old lady here will get a right royal kicking. Merry Christmas, Danny boy."

There was a click and the phone went dead.

The engine idled and the car rocked slightly as a lorry rushed past. Dan knew he only had one possible next step. He had to open Elwood's safe.

He drove back to Imogen's house, relieved to see it looked deserted. He parked the car in the drive and ran over to the barn.

He shivered as he stepped into the musty gloom. Nothing had changed. Papers were still strewn about and the desk top was still wide open. Dan pulled out the books around the safe, and stared at the cold steel dial and handle.

He had no way of forcing the safe. Fiona had tried all the obvious combinations already and had got nowhere. His mind kept going back to the meeting with Elwood earlier in the day. What had the old man said when Dan had asked him about getting in the safe? The old professor had mumbled something – what was it? Something about the Spear Shaker? He picked up one of Elwood's pencils from the floor, its end cut into a perfect point. He grabbed one of the loose pieces of paper and wrote down:

SPEAR SHAKER

He remembered Fiona's earlier attempts to get into the safe. She had tried all sorts of complicated combinations and techniques. The only one he could remember was where she translated the alphabet into numbers, A – 1, B – 2, C – 3, and so on, and used that as a code. Using that theory, Spear Shaker gave him:

20 19 5 1 19 20 9 1 11 5 19

He dialled the numbers in. Nothing. The handle refused to budge.

What else was there to try? Dan felt instinctively that whatever code Elwood had used, it would be something to do with Bacon or Shakespeare, not something personal or esoteric like family names, birthdays. He clicked his fingers. What about the original spelling of Shakespeare? Had they tried that before? May as well give it a go.

SHAKSPUR

It worked out numerically as:

20 9 1 11 20 17 22 19

No joy. Was he looking at things too simplistically? Any more complicated and he knew he was out of his depth. He replayed his conversation with Elwood again and again, trying to remember all the detail. What was that final comment Elwood had made before the fire? He could hear the words in his mind, '...the Spear Shaker, Bacon's muse, the great goddess herself.' Dan frowned in concentration. Elwood had talked about Bacon's muse before, hadn't he? The name sprang into his head.

ATHENA

He raced through the letters, coming up with the

numbers:

1 21 9 5 15 1

He span the numbers through on the dial, feeling excited, it felt like it could work. But nothing happened. He punched the wall with his fist in frustration. He was all out of ideas. On a whim he dialled the numbers in again, but this time backwards. He expected nothing from it, but when he stopped on the last number, there was a soft click. Dan held his breath as he tried the handle. It moved easily and the safe door swung open.

He was not sure what he had been expecting to be in the safe, but it was more than what he found; a single sheet of paper with a single word written on it.

Verulam

He memorised it, then turned over the paper and scrawled a message on the back.

Fiona,

I opened the safe. This is what was in it. Nothing else. Right now I don't know what it means, but I've got to find out and hope it leads me to the manuscripts. I'm sorry for coming back here without asking you but I didn't have a choice. They were torturing her on the phone. I'm so sorry I can't offer you any support, even if you don't want it right now.

I know you have every reason to hate me, but I think I love you.

D xx

He ran back to the car. He ducked into the driver's seat. As he tried to think about what to do, his body shook as the events of the day began to overwhelm him.

His mobile phone beeped, he rummaged in his pocket. It was his voicemail. After a couple of seconds he heard his mother's voice wishing him Merry Christmas. He rang back.

"This is the Knight household. Jake speaking."

"Pop. Happy Christmas. It's great to hear your voice."

"At last. Mom's been trying not to make waves, but she's worried."

"What can I say? It's been hectic. I'm so sorry."

"Hey, son. It's your life. Listen, your mom's not here just now, she's out picking up your aunt from the station. Your sister's here though. She's just grabbing breakfast, I'll pass you over."

"Tell mom I'll try to call back in a couple of hours."

"Sure. Here's your sister." There was a pause.

"Dan. Where the heck are you? Mom's tried calling you on your cell twice already today. What's up with that? She's too old for you to be spinning her wheels like a stroppy teenager. She put up with enough of that shit when you really were a stroppy teenager."

"Merry Christmas to you, Tam."

"Yeah yeah, whatever. I hope you've got her a nice present, by the way. Nothing's pitched up here in the mail."

"I'm sorry, I forgot. I've been massively preoccupied. Something very important has happened."

"Oh yeah, you forgot Christmas? What's her name?

She better be worth it. Mind you I guess I should be thankful you're hooking up with anyone at all, does she know dealing with you is like herding cats?"

Dan started to get frustrated and angry. "No, I'm serious. It's hugely important."

"Auntie Kay is coming over you know, never mind the cousins. Everyone was really vibed up to see you. After waiting for over thirty years for you to do actually do something focused and adventurous with your life, the whole clan wanted to hear all about it and then in classic Dan style you bail at the last moment."

"I phoned up last week and told mom I couldn't get over."

His sister sighed. "Look, I don't mean to go on, we're just disappointed that's all."

"I get that, Tam."

"Even you have to admit Dan, even for you, your behaviour looks super lame. Anyway that's enough from me. What's up with you anyway? You sound wiped out."

"Thanks, sis. I'm just tooling around the English countryside at the moment. You know, taking care of business."

"Fine, evasive as ever then."

"It's the project I'm on."

"What, they got you working on Christmas Day? That blows."

"You know all about work culture, Tam, you're a New Yorker."

"Yeah yeah, I'll admit it, I've done a few holidays at work too. Like, almost every year."

"Actually, Tam, can you do me a favour? You near the internet? I need you to check something out for me quickly."

"So you're not going to ask me how I'm doing?"

"I'm sorry Tam, I'll call back later for a proper chat, but I'm right in the middle of something now."

"Yeah yeah, sure you will. Wait there, kid brother." Dan could hear footsteps echoing on a wooden floor and a door creak. "Right, let's crank up mom's old laptop. God look at it, stone age or what? I'm gonna buy that girl a Mac. So, what's this all about?"

"It's just some research. You're not an expert on Shakespeare are you, Tam? It's not a secret skill you got that I don't know about?"

"Does the Pope shit in the woods? Of course I'm not. The only secret skill I have these days is farting quietly in bed."

"I'm gonna spell something out for you. Stick it in Google and see if anything comes up."

"Wait a minute, we're still waiting for Windows to load. Jeez, it's like a pregnancy test. The anticipation, it's overpowering."

"Has it loaded yet?"

"Are you kidding? This is Microsoft we're talking about. It's got a while to go yet."

Eventually the laptop came out of its coma and stuttered into life, and Tam connected to the family's wireless network.

"Can you type this in please. V... E... R... U... L... A... M." Dan could hear the click of the laptop keys.

"Verulam. What's that then, some sort of organic

cheese or something? And what does it have to do with Shakespeare?"

"It's more likely something to do with Sir Francis Bacon. Just tell me what comes up."

"God Dan, you're so cryptic suddenly. What happened to my geeky brother? You've morphed into some sort of crap spy. Who the hell is Sir Francis... oh never mind. Right. A couple of company listings, not much use, wait – this looks better. We've got something here. A website link, some bunch of old dorks in England called the Atlantean Society. Let's check it out." There was a pause as she clicked through some pages. Then she started giggling to herself. "This is far out stuff. Get this, Baron Verulam was the name Sir Francis Bacon gave himself after he was knighted by Queen Elizabeth back in the day."

"That's awesome, sis." said Dan. "Does it say why he used that name?"

"Yeah. It says here Verulam House is the name of the Bacon family home. You know, like the Duke of Edinburgh, Prince of Wales, naming themselves after places, same sort of rough deal."

"Does it say where this place is?"

"Sure, a village called Gorhambury, near some place called St Albans."

"And where's that?"

"How the heck should I know? It sounds like some sort of herb for depressed pets to me."

"Come on sis, have a look on the page. There'll be a link called something like 'how to get here' or a Google map."

"Hang loose, squirt. Yup, here we go. A map. I can see St Albans, it's a big town. Roughly north of London. What's this all about, Dan? I'm almost forgiving you not being here now. This is way more interesting than hearing Aunty Kay talk about her stupid pet chihuahua and its bowel movements. It sounds like a pretty sick project."

"It's certainly that."

"So, when are we going to get an invite over there? You know I'd love to come and see London. Have tea with the Queen and all that."

"How about next year? Spring break maybe? Sorry to rush you sis, but is there any more detail on this place other than north of London?"

"You're really focused on this aren't you? How about you ask me how life in New York is going first?"

"Please, sis. Just help me out here."

"Yeah yeah, right – hold your horses. Got something. It looks like there's a major freeway around London – M25? Pick that up and head north and you'll see St Albans and you can get to the village of Gorhambury from there easily enough I'm sure."

"Thanks Tam. You're a star. Speak soon." Dan killed the call and sat back in the driver's seat. He scrolled through the numbers on his phone and dialled. He wasn't happy about having to make this call.

"Hello. Who is this?" asked a woman's voice.

"Hi. Is that Nicky Dudley? It's Fiona's friend, Dan Knight. We haven't spoken before, but she gave me your number a while back."

"Oh gosh, of course, Fiona's new... ummm, friend.

Merry Christmas Dan, how are you? You sound a bit flat."

"Yes, Merry Christmas to you too Nicky. I'm sorry to interrupt your day."

"Hey, that's okay, it's all a bit sad here to be honest, just me and mum and a dried out turkey draped in anaemic bacon. How's Fiona? I'm really looking forward to seeing you guys. I can't wait to find out more about this adventure you're on, it sounds very romantic. I'm especially looking forward to meeting you, seeing you in the flesh."

"I'm not too sure about that at the moment, Nicky."

"Maybe that's Fiona trying to keep me away from you, eh? Three's a crowd and all that. She's never been keen to have me around her men, and you do sound kind of hot."

Was she flirting with him? "Nicky, sorry to dump on you, but I've got something really serious to say. You're a good friend of Fiona's, right?"

"She's my best friend. What is it? Come on, don't keep me in suspenders. Get it out in the open. As the actress said to the bishop."

"It's Fiona's mother."

"Her mother? What is it? What's going on? I thought Fiona was with you?"

"No she isn't. I'm on my own now."

"Ooh so I've got you on your own. Lucky me. So, her mother, what's happened? I hope she's okay. I'm meeting her tomorrow."

"I'm afraid that won't be happening. There's no simple way of telling you Nicky, but Fiona's mother died this morning."

Nicky's voice instantly hardened up. "She died? On Christmas Day? Oh my God, poor Fiona. Why aren't you with her?"

"She won't want me to be."

"She won't want you to be? What are you talking about?"

"It was her father. He killed Imogen this morning. About an hour ago."

"What? Dan, what are you playing at? You should be with her. You have to face up to your responsibility."

"I know Nicky, I so wish I could, but for now, you've just got to trust me."

"Where did it happen?"

"At the hospital."

"She's there on her own, at the hospital? Don't tell me you drove her there and she hasn't even got a car?"

Dan's heart sank. "Yes, I'm…"

"I think that's pathetic. I'm going to call her, she needs somebody." The phone went dead.

Dan stared out into the faint drizzle. She was right of course. But what else could he do? He slipped the Jaguar into gear and drove off in the rough direction of Oxford, which he remembered would get him onto the M40 and then to London. After half an hour a sign flashed by telling Dan that he was entering Moreton-in-Marsh and that he should be driving carefully. Ahead of him was a BP garage and he eased the Jaguar in to buy a road atlas and some dry looking pastry masquerading as food.

Once back in the car Dan opened the map and traced

a route to St Albans. It was difficult to judge the distance, but he thought if he pushed it he might make it in between two or three hours. Once closer to London he would head north-west through the broad sweep of Hertfordshire. He turned on the engine. There was no time to waste.

In a lay by, three miles down the road, Police Constable Simon DeMontfort stared at his turkey sandwich. What sort of a way to spend Christmas was this, he wondered? A load of cobblers, that's what it was. It really wasn't his lucky day. Although he knew his wife Mary would be cursing his name as little Simon junior screamed, dribbled and pooped his way through lunch, she'd be smiling right enough when they were on that beach in May. He leaned back and scratched his crotch. Oh yes, he could see it now, those rum cocktails, pina whatsits, the creamy ones, some beautiful native woman in a flowery skirt bending over him smiling as she topped up his drink, pushing her ample brown boobs at him and grinning saucily as his wife frolicked in the sea. Lovely. He gave his crotch another scratch. He was bored. There had been something on the radio about the Stratford loony bin. That sounded fun, but no; here he was watching out for speeding grannies and drunken farmers out on their tractors, weaving their way to some relative for a roast turkey and a glass of cheap sherry. He fiddled with the car radio, he wasn't supposed to listen to music or anything when he was on traffic patrol, but what the hell. It was Christmas.

He could see a small convoy of traffic heading his way. Three cars stuck behind what looked suspiciously like a gypsy truck. Chances were the tax disc would be from the last century and the tyres would be balder than Bruce Willis. That might be worth the effort, liven up the day.

Suddenly a silver Jaguar flashed out from the back of the queue and accelerated past the cars and the truck, and then kept on speeding up as it raced past where he was parked.

DeMontfort sparked his supercharged BMW into life, the engine grumbling, then he hit the lights and siren and set off in pursuit. "Maybe this is my lucky day after all," he murmured.

Dan heard the siren before he saw the car. He looked back in the rear view mirror. He couldn't see anything yet. What would happen if he was caught by the cops? Would they just fine him? How much would he be delayed by? He had been through at least two speed cameras. Did the English system mean the cop following him would know about that? A chill struck him, maybe it was something to do with Imogen's murder, they wanted him as a witness. He'd be 'helping them with their enquiries' for at least the rest of the day.

Dan was approaching another small town, Burford-upon-Avon and could see traffic lights changing in front of a narrow Cotswold stone bridge that crossed a thin stream. Two cars were waiting on the other side. He made an instant decision. He couldn't afford to get stopped by the police, there was too much at stake.

He floored the Jag, and reached the bridge at high speed, just as the lights changed to red. The car left the ground as it hit the hump of the bridge then he was over, wildly slamming on the brakes and heading left into the side streets of the town. All the buildings were the same: small ancient sandy coloured cottages with dark slate roofs hemmed in by narrow roads, parked cars making it even more cramped. Left, right then left again, it was a one way system. He skidded round a corner, clipping the side of a parked van and cursed, he was back where he started. He span left and accelerated hard up the hill. Then the sirens again. He looked in his rearview mirror, there was the cop car back down the hill, just crossing over the bridge.

He was still ahead. The Jaguar soon sped up to 80mph, then 90. He soon cleared the outside of the town and was back onto the country roads. He screeched round a corner, he seemed to be leaving the police car behind. The siren was fainter. There was another sharp hill ahead, he felt his stomach lurch as he flew over it. He kept going, pushing the car as hard as he knew how. He saw a small road off to the left. He slammed on the brakes, yanked on the handbrake and spun the car around, it was a single lane, pitted and old. He glanced in the mirror, the police car was further back. He realised he was getting away.

Dan raced round more corners, onto a straight and took a sharp left. "What the hell!" he shouted out loud. There was a family in front of him. A couple with a child were walking a dog in the middle of the road. He hit the brakes and twisted the wheel. The car swerved violently, up and over the verge. In seconds two wheels were into the ditch in front of the hedge and the whole car started to tip and roll.

His head smashed into the window. Mud and grass churned up around the car, covering the windscreen, branches from the hedge whipping and snatching against the car, stones clattering and banging into the bodywork in a thunderous roar. Dan caught a glimpse of the horrified family as he slid past them, the child's mouth open, eyes wide. The seatbelt tightened as he was thrown forward. The airbag ballooned out, pushing him back into the seat. The Jaguar was still travelling fast, but slowing quickly, he glimpsed a heavy oak tree, its massive trunk cutting through the hedge, its highest branches curving out and over the road. With a terrifying crunch the Jaguar smashed into it. Dan's last image was of a huge low branch swinging into and through the windscreen.

DeMontfort slowly drove his car up to the crash, giving a friendly wave at the family who were standing there in shock, their golden labrador jumping up and down in excitement. He thought the driver had got away, but no, here he was, face first into a tree, the prat. DeMontfort had already radioed in, support was on its way but he didn't think he needed it. He guessed the driver was some local kid, it usually was with this sort of thing. Whoever it was, he intended to enjoy the arrest. He leisurely got out of the car and unclipped a pair of handcuffs and slipped out his truncheon, tapping it into the palm of his hand.

Behind them, on the crest of a hill, the black BMW pulled over at the side of the road. The driver stepped out and jumped lithely up onto the bonnet of his car. He could see the wreckage of the Jaguar and the top of

DeMontfort's head poking above the opposite hedge as he walked towards the scene. The man lifted up a pair of huge binoculars and focused them in on the scene.

DeMontfort approached the Jaguar, the back wheels were slowly turning, in their death throes. The driver's side of the Jag was badly damaged. Mud and scratches and dents ran all along side of the vehicle, DeMontfort guessed there was a good chance the axle was broken. But the front of the car, that really was a mess. Crushed metal twisted and wrapped around the base of the tree. The trunk of the old oak looked like it had taken some damage, but in the battle with the car, it was the easy winner. Steam was rising from the mangled bonnet, there was broken glass everywhere, a low branch from the tree had punched a massive hole through the windscreen. The car was a write off.

He walked up to the Jaguar and gingerly clambered down into the ditch to have a look through the driver's side window, swearing to himself as he nearly lost his balance. He wiped the mud off the window and peered in. Instantly his attention was much more focused. The driver wasn't moving. There was blood on one side of his head and while the branch had pierced the windscreen DeMontfort couldn't see if it had penetrated the driver's head. He stopped and tried the door handle. No joy. He peered in through the mud spattered windows. The driver's head was on an awkward angle; it looked as if his neck could have been broken. He looked again, the driver looked familiar.

He flipped open his PDA and got the suspect image up from London Met. He grunted in surprise. "This really is my lucky day," he said out loud.

He cranked up his police radio. "Possible London Met suspect, now apprehended after high speed chase." He paused. "Requesting fire services and paramedics, suspect unconscious, probably dead."

Act 9: Scene One

*"The slings and arrows of outrageous
fortune, Or to take arms against a sea of
troubles And by opposing end them?"*

Hamlet

26th December, Boxing Day

Jackson and Andrews were sitting in the examination room watching the second Rosicrucian sweat and jerk as the drugs ran their course through his system. The prisoner was a tall, slim man; a crop of short blond hair and a messy beard flecked with spittle and grey hairs. His face was gaunt, his muscles wiry. The man seemed to have no fat on him at all. Blood dribbled down over his pale hairless chest while one blue eye stared up at the ceiling. His breath was sharp and shallow. Jackson didn't need to take his pulse to know it was hammering away faster than a fat man being chased by a rabid lion.

Jackson was counting on this Rosicrucian to be more useful than the last one. He was hugely frustrated. Royal Security was just hitting dead ends with the case and time was running out. Vaughan had got nothing from following up on Manchester Nick's family and contacts; there had been no increase in network chatter or suspicious comms either online or via the satellites. The Major's covert inquiries into the Church of England

271

and the former leader of the Freemasons were taking too long to lead to anything. His suspect, Moseley, had apparently refused any attempts to interview him and was now 'on holiday' at an unknown location. Nothing additional was coming through from MI5, the CIA, Interpol or the other international intelligence agencies. The man strapped onto the interrogation table was all Jackson had to work with.

This new prisoner had been picked up after the first one finally broke and supplied them with a few new names. A picture was slowly coming to light of a network of Rosicrucian cells based in London, made up of low level members like this one who had been recruited from right wing groups and other disaffected English white men. These people were merely cannon fodder. There was also an elite group with money and power who were only known by code names. Above them was the leader of the whole Rosicrucian movement.

Like al Qaeda, the cells were independent, none of them knew any more than their own individual purpose. The key to it all was this mysterious leader. Somehow, Jackson had to use this idiot to find him.

The new prisoner had prison tattoos and was tougher and mentally sharper than the first one. Getting him to breaking point had been a challenge. Jackson had employed the eyeball technique again and also pulled out three toenails with pliers and a utilised few more colourful techniques before calling in Andrews for some chemicals.

"He can't take much more, I'm warning you," said

Andrews. "He's right on the edge of a fatal heart attack or stroke."

"He's about to crack." Jackson walked over to the intercom on the wall and glanced up at where the camera was recording them. "Get me a photo-fit system online immediately."

"Yes, sir," the voice came back. Jackson didn't have long to wait. A junior officer soon appeared with a laptop and Jackson put it on the steel table and launched the software. The junior officer left and Jackson spoke into the intercom again. "Turn monitoring systems off."

There was a pause. "Yes sir, recording systems disabled."

Jackson turned back to the prisoner. "Andrews, I don't care if his head explodes. Give him some more juice. He's got information and we're going to get it. If he dies, too bad. Just as long as we get what we need."

Andrews pulled out some new needles from his briefcase and loaded up a syringe and slid it into the prisoner's neck. "Sodium pentathol, six milligrams. That'll pull him round to consciousness and make him more lucid and suggestible."

"Good. Give him something to intensify the pain."

Andrews pulled another vial from his briefcase. "Hydozane and LSD and adrenaline compounded extract. That will cause massive pain and delusions, but it will increase the strain on his heart considerably. I'm warning you Sergeant, it may be fatal if you place him under excessive stress."

"Just do it."

For about a minute there was no reaction then the

prisoner's ragged breathing became more intense and his back arched as a massive muscular spasm ran down his body. His remaining eye opened wide, the man's jaw dropped and he let out a weak guttural moan.

"Where's the Queen?" shouted Jackson. "I can take the pain away. Tell me where she is."

The man screamed as the drugs flowed through him.

"Where is she? You can feel it getting worse can't you? Your blood is on fire, your whole body is ripping itself apart with the pain. Nobody knows you're here, I can keep a piece of scum like you as long as I want, I can make it worse and worse for you. If I don't find the Queen, you'll be down here for years, my stupid little torture toy. I'll keep you here until you melt, you hideous pink fucker."

"I don't know. Only a few people know, Damascus only tells the inner circle." The man's voice was almost unintelligible, words coming out between rough gasps for breath.

Jackson smiled. He slipped out a wicked looking knife from his belt and held it up to the man's other eye. "Who is Damascus?"

"Damascus, Grand Master of the fra rosi crosse."

"So he's your leader. Tell me who he is. Tell me or the knife goes straight through your other eye and you'll be blind. All you'll be left with in this room is darkness and pain until I finally let you die."

"I can feel the flames, oh God..." screamed the man. His whole body was shaking violently.

"Be quick," said Andrews. "His heart rate's spiking."

"Better be careful, very careful about what you say

next," hissed Jackson to the prisoner. "I'm reaching the point where I'm not sure I can control my anger. I'll ask you again, who is Damascus? Who is your Grand Master?" He moved the knife down below the man's eye and cut it into his cheek, making sure to trace the blade across the nerve ganglion.

The man screamed again. "Nobody knows his real name, we all have a codename, we don't use our real names, I told you that already."

"Not good enough." Jackson pushed the blade in slightly deeper. He looked up at Andrews. "Give him some more."

"I have to warn you Sergeant, any more increases the chance of fatality."

"Enough with the fucking broken record. Just do it. Do I look like I care? It's now or never with this turd."

Andrews shrugged and injected the prisoner again. "I'd give him another ten minutes maximum without treatment before he's either dead or in a constant vegetative state."

The man's face jerked with the fresh pain, his muscles twisted and veins stood out like knotted rope under his skin. His whole body was sheathed in sweat.

Jackson leant in close. "Come on, you fuck," he whispered. "You're going to die unless you talk now. Your only hope is to tell me everything. Just tell me all of it, I can take the pain away."

The man was shaking, coarse breath coming out in short spasms. "Damascus always appears with his ceremonial robes on. He's never addressed us without them, but…"

"Keep talking."

The man's voice was hoarse and weak. "I did see him once, we were in York House. I saw his face once, reflected in a mirror. I was looking into his private sanctum as he was preparing himself to commune with the deity, I saw him, just for a second." His voice began to rise in tempo, as he screamed. "Please, please stop the heat, my skin's blistering, I can feel the flames."

Jackson pulled the blade back and smiled in satisfaction. This guy had started out tough, but just like everyone else, when you reached the limit and crossed over to the other side, they were broken and that was that, no turning back. It was as if you had slid a knife into their soul.

Jackson turned to the laptop and swivelled the screen so the prisoner could see it. "Well done, boy. Now I want you to describe Damascus to me. We're going to go through every detail of his face, we're going to build up a picture of him here on this computer. Then after that, you'll be free to die in peace. Let's start with his hair."

The man's breath was getting shallower and sharper as the drugs flowed through him. His voice was so weak. "Yes, alright I'll tell you, his hair, yes, he doesn't really have any…"

"What do you mean? He's bald? Keep talking, scum."

"Yes… his hair… it's not hair… he has these two giant round black shapes on top of his head." The man slowly grinned and his final words were almost clear and calm. "Like enormous cartoon mouse ears. Oh and

I've remembered his name, it's Mickey." His back arched and the veins on his face and neck stood out in sharp relief as he gasped in pain, the smile twisting into shock.

"He's going into cardiac arrest." Andrews pushed Jackson out of the way. He smashed another needle through the man's ribcage, sending a bolt of pure adrenalin into his heart, but it was too late. He looked up at Jackson. "That's the end of him. He's dead."

Act 10: Scene One

"Death lies on her, like an untimely frost,
upon the sweetest flower of all the field"

Romeo & Juliet

27th December

The fat bereavements officer gave Fiona a professionally sympathetic smile from behind her inexpensive laminated desk. She looked at Fiona over the top of her large round blue-rimmed glasses and leaned forward slightly as she spoke. "And how many copies of the death certificate would you like, Miss Fletcher?"

The bereavements office was a soulless room in the main hospital tucked away behind a Starbucks coffee shop. The air was stale and smelled of violets. Fiona and Nicky stood in front of the officious desk.

"I don't know, how many do I need?"

"You definitely need one for the funeral home and another for your solicitor. Now, they may offer to handle the relationship with the banks or building societies for you, as you go through the probate process. Did your mother have a pension?"

Fiona wanted to scream at the woman, tell her how she didn't know about her mother's financial affairs, demand what the hell that had to do with her. But she didn't. "To be honest," she said calmly, "I'm not sure."

"I'm afraid your solicitor will definitely need to look into that because if she did have one the pension company will certainly need a copy."

"I suppose I'd better have four of them."

"That will be £28 please."

"I've got to pay?"

"Yes, it's an administrative charge."

"So my father is sectioned under the Mental Health Act, locked up in a secure hospital, given thousands of pounds worth of drugs that did nothing apart from drag out his illness, all paid for by the National Health Service, but I have to give you money for bits of paper showing he murdered my mum?"

"Yes, I am so very sorry for your loss, but as I said – it's just an administration charge."

Fiona wanted to scream 'administrate this, bitch!' and slap the woman. But she just stared in silence as the officer kept talking.

"You do need to check the main certificate, make sure the details are accurate, then you need to take it to the registrar. He's down one floor, down the corridor on the left, next to the canteen. He'll take the bottom copy off you, and you'll need to give the top copy to the undertaker."

"Okay, thanks very much Mrs Hilton." Nicky grasped Fiona's hand and gave it a squeeze. "Come on honey, let's get out of here."

Fiona was so thankful Nicky had turned up. Going back to the house alone had been the most miserable and wretched experience of her life. Everywhere were ghosts and memories of either her mother or that monster, her father. The smallest thing set her off in floods of tears, from the bowls of prepared vegetables they were supposed to cook for Christmas lunch through to the family holiday photo mum had kept on the kitchen windowsill.

Nicky's journey had taken about three hours and she had arrived late in the evening. Fiona had spent the time cleaning and trying to keep herself busy. She had tried to get in touch with her brother Jason but he hadn't answered his phone and each time she rang she ended up leaving yet another message.

"Come on Fiona, let's get you along to the registrar's office, and then we can escape."

Fiona let herself be led out of the room and as they stepped out they were immediately hit by the air conditioning in the huge open atrium at the front of the hospital. It was a testament to glass and chrome. They went down one floor to the registrar's office. It was a clone of the previous room, the only difference being that it was a slightly chubby man in a grey suit behind the desk. An hour later they were back in Nicky's small vintage BMW and heading back to the house.

They sat in silence as Nicky guided the car through the traffic. Fiona's phone rang. She didn't recognize the number and decided to ignore it. The last two days, the phone had just been ringing non-stop. Telling the same edited version of the story over and over again was just too draining.

"Who was that, honey?"

"I don't know. Probably some long lost relative who

suddenly decides they care."

Nicky snorted with barely concealed anger. "It was the same for me when dad died. People I didn't know or hadn't heard from for years were on the phone. These people just kept calling, and every time mum answered it was like her reserve of energy was just drained that bit more. I was so scared, I thought it was going to finish her off. Every hour or so she just started crying. And to make it worse, that would set us girls off too."

"And here you are watching over me."

"Hey, I just want my pulling partner back in one piece and out on the town again with me."

"How did you cope? I feel in bits."

"You'll be in a bad way for a while, but that doesn't mean you can't do anything about it. I know this sounds trite, but having things to do really helps, keeping yourself busy. It was when I sat there on my own, you know, with nothing to do but think, that I really lost it. You don't have to worry about that though honey, I'm not leaving you on your own until this is all over."

"Thanks Nicks, I can't tell you how much it means."

"Okay honey, the next stop is the funeral home. We've got to go and make arrangements. Are you up for it, honey? I was thinking, if it's all too much we could just head off somewhere for a few days, get a hotel or something away from the house."

"No, I thought of that too – how nice it would be to just run away. But I can't. I need to be at home. I've got to face this head on."

"What do you mean, honey?"

"I left mum to deal with my father on her own for

years. And now she's dead and I can't say sorry. I turned up with Dan, knowing it would cause trouble, and even then I just let her walk back in that room on her own. I hadn't learnt my lesson even then."

"Honey, you've got to stop this line of thought right now. It's not your fault. It's only natural to try and find a reason for it all, but it's so fresh in your mind. You can't. You just have to concentrate on accepting it and dealing with it."

"If I'd been around more, this would never have happened, would it? If I hadn't met Dan, mum would still be here. My father would have been put in hospital years ago if I hadn't just left mum to deal with it on her own. Now she's dead and there's so much I wish I could have said to her."

"Oh babe, I know how you feel. I blamed myself when dad died. I hated myself for not spending more time with him before he went. It's the worst feeling. Don't beat yourself up. It's just not worth it, I know, I've been there honey, believe me."

"I don't know, I really don't know what to think."

Nicky tried to change the subject. "Have you heard from Dan yet?"

Fiona tried not to snap at her friend. "No. And I don't want to."

"What happens if he calls? Will you talk to him?"

"No. Let's not talk about him, If I hadn't met him I would still have a chance with my mum. But I don't. I'm planning her funeral because of my own cowardice, and because I met Dan Knight."

Act 11: Scene One

"Having nothing, nothing can he lose."

Henry VI Part Two

28th December

Sawyer stared at himself in the small bathroom mirror. The heavy black bags under his bloodshot eyes looked big enough to smuggle drugs in. Grey stubble ran wild across his creased chin and his hair looked like a dead mop. The three-day-old shirt he was wearing was starting to reek and looked more grey than white around the collar. The policemen reached for a pill bottle on the side of the sink and tipped out two of the chunky white painkillers. He was about to replace the lid but changed his mind and tipped out two more. He threw the dry pills into his mouth and swallowed.

He lay on the bed replaying the events of the past day in his head. He knew that his sudden departure halfway through the family party last night had not been too clever. The day after Boxing Day was an annual post Christmas tradition with his wife's over-privileged and overpaid friends. All of them tolerated him for the sake of Jennifer. As for him, he loathed them all and wanted to give each and every one of the sanctimonious snobs a hard kick up the arse.

He would usually tolerate the party as a marital

duty, but this time it was too much. So when news came through of a suspect arrested after a road crash who had also been identified as a foreign national, he used it as an excuse to go and see for himself. Jennifer's instant response had been ridicule. He could hear her whine now. If the man was already under arrest, why did he have to go? Couldn't the country bumpkin coppers deal with it? It was, he knew, a fair question. It ended up in yet another slanging match and him storming out in front of her appalled friends. He had ended up drunk in a cheap hotel room gazing vacantly at pay-per-view pornography that was about as erotic as getting a filling at the dentist.

Sawyer decided to skip breakfast and headed straight to the hospital. Within the hour he found himself looking down at the unconscious body of a crash victim that had already been identified as Daniel Knight. He was lying with a drip into his arm and a machine monitoring his heartbeat, blood pressure and other vital statistics. Sawyer pulled out the crumpled photofit image Patel had put together from the video and compared it to the unconscious man. The local plod had been on his game. There was a strong resemblance. He started to get excited. Maybe this was the break-through he needed to investigate the real case and show that prick the Major what he was made of.

"There was a very real danger he could have died, but we think he's over the worst of it now, his condition is stable." The young Indian doctor had entered the room without Sawyer noticing. He turned to face her, pushing the photo back into his jacket pocket. She was short, slim and in her late twenties. Her hair had been cut into a functional bob and her square rimmed glasses gave her a thoughtful air. Sawyer could see a moustache of fine but very dark hair above her top lip and tried to stop staring at it.

"What's his status, doc?"

"Mr Knight has technically been in a stage six coma for two days now, but his heart rate and blood pressure have normalised over the last twenty four hours and we've taken him off the ventilator."

"A coma? Bollocks. I need him back in London."

"He was administered a blood transfusion when he was admitted, but he responded well. He suffered a serious head wound, a blow to the left temporal which needed immediate attention." The doctor indicated the side of Dan's head. It had been shaved around a large cut which had been stitched neatly up. "The main problem aside from a couple of cracked ribs and suspected whiplash is concussion and internal bruising, which is why we had to induce the coma."

Sawyer couldn't believe it. "What? You put him into a coma? What the hell are you people playing at?"

"Yes. It's a fairly common practise when there is a risk of severe neurological trauma. It's the best way to allow recovery. He was very agitated. He tried to get out of bed, we had no choice except to heavily sedate him. Plus there was internal bruising and some minor bleeding which had to be stopped."

"He's been out of it the whole time since? Lying here like a bloody vegetable?"

"No, not exactly. There are differing levels of coma,

from completely vegetative to constant physical movement and also responding to verbal stimuli. The patient has been exhibiting stage three verbal responses."

"He's been talking?"

"Rambling is more apposite. Something about the Queen? I wasn't on duty, so it's just hearsay, none of it appeared to make much sense to the night nurses. Maybe you should have a word with them."

Sawyer smiled. This was all extremely promising. "I will."

"There was also a period last night when he was very disturbed. He was in a highly emotional state. His movement almost caused another major bleed so we had to increase the level of sedation considerably and restrain him temporarily. All I can say is he's a very lucky chap. He could easily have died in the crash."

That settled it for Sawyer. The man had obviously been trying to escape. "When can we move him? I want him back in London. It's very important."

"We're looking to bring him back round in about two to three days. I expect he will be safe for transfer a day or two after that. So, I would say maybe New Years Day." The doctor was examining Dan's chart and avoiding his eyes. "Inspector, is it true, is he a suspect in the hit-and-run on Prince William?"

"Where did you get that from?"

"Everyone knows it's something serious with your goons on the door." The doctor pointed to the two uniformed officers that stood guard at the door of the private room.

"Standard procedure. This guy is a suspect in an ongoing police investigation. Why does that matter to you?"

"It doesn't to me personally, I'm not much of a Royalist, and a patient is a patient, but I'm worried from a professional care point of view. There's a lot of resentment building up at the idea of treating him. Everyone's talking about it. He might be at risk sooner or later from, um, what you might call 'negligence'."

"You can tell your team this man definitely did not run Prince William over in a car. You treat him like any other patient. He's wanted for interview alongside another dozen men. He may be involved, he may not. Either way, he's categorically not a hit-and-run driver."

"Oh, that's a relief."

"But your timings are simply not acceptable."

"But..."

"I want that man back in London. You just get him ready, he's coming back with me tomorrow morning."

"That's impossible Inspector Sawyer. He shouldn't be moved for at least a week. You move him tomorrow, you just delay his recovery."

Sawyer was about to force his demands again, but stopped. A little compromise on his part would do no harm. "The day after tomorrow, but that's it. I'm not leaving it any later."

"But he may not have regained consciousness. How can..."

"These beds have wheels don't they?" interrupted Sawyer. "I'm not asking your permission. You just make sure your team gets him ready. Sleeping Beauty's coming with me back to Scotland Yard for questioning on the thirtieth either on his feet or in his bed."

Act 12: Scene One

*"Pray, sit; more welcome are ye to my
fortunes Than my fortunes to me."*

Timon of Athens

29th December

The evenings were the hardest to bear. The darkness in the living room had seemed romantic and intimate on that night with Dan, but now, Fiona just found it oppressive. She looked at the cold fireplace, ash had settled all around and the remnants of a few burnt logs sat in the grate. Nicky was in the kitchen cooking and Fiona hoped she wasn't going to be long. She started to feel alone every time her friend was out of the room. Fiona knew the food would be pretty basic, Nicky had murmured something about pasta. Fiona didn't care.

The door opened and Nicky emerged but instead of holding two bowls of pasta, she was holding a pile of papers.

"Brrr, what are you doing sitting in here, honey? It's freezing compared to that lovely warm kitchen. Supper's just boiling away in the background but I saw this lot stacked up on the windowsill. Bacon's Secrets? It looks like some sort of giant scrapbook. Made up of what looks like loads of bits from Shakespeare's plays?"

"That's pretty much exactly what it is," replied Fiona. "I think it was my father's big secret project. I've no idea how long it took him to do, but yeah, it's an autobiography put together by Sir Francis Bacon hidden piece by piece in the plays."

"An autobiography? That's a bit of a mind-boggler, honey. Have you read it yet?"

"Not really. I read through the first page or two before Christmas, but then everything happened and I've not touched it since then."

"This was part of your research with Dan into this Shakespeare's Truth business?" She paused. "Sorry to bring him up."

Fiona smiled wryly. "Who, Shakespeare - or Dan?"

"Honey, a little smile!"

"I'd really rather not talk about Dan."

"Fair enough. I just mentioned it because in my experience keeping busy keeps your mind off other things. Let's talk about it later. Right now we need a glass of wine. There's half a bottle of home-made plum wine next to the bread bin in the kitchen. It's got a rubber vacuum stopper thingy on it."

"Tell you what, you go and get us some wine. I'll build us a fire, warm the place up a bit." There was a pile of newspaper over by the fireplace, so Fiona started taking sheets and screwing them up into balls and putting them on the grate.

"Sounds good, honey. Anyway, off I go, back to the kitchen like a good little wifey, supper's almost ready. Is there a tin opener in that cutlery drawer?"

Fiona nodded. Basic food it was then. She squatted

down again and put some kindling, a couple of tin split logs and a sprinkling of small coal lumps around the balls of paper and lit the fire. It started off weak and she sat there with a pair of old bellows, encouraging it with puffs of air. It wasn't long before she had it blazing, and a few minutes later Nicky returned with the wine and some classic student food, tuna pasta.

They chatted for a while about Nicky's Christmas then Nicky put down her fork. "So honey, that pile of papers in the kitchen you said was Sir Francis Bacon's autobiography. Do you mind talking about it? Did you find it with Dan?"

"I thought we weren't going to talk about him."

"Okay honey. Sorry for being nosey. Don't forget I'm a historian too. I can't help being curious."

"Nicks. I don't want to fight with you. Everything around me reminds me of my parents. I can't deal with thinking about Dan too. I still feel so furious with him."

"Maybe you can look for positive things to think about, you know, remember good times. Even Dan's not all bad is he?"

"No, no of course he isn't. But I just can't face any of that. It's just way too much. There's only a certain amount of shit anyone can deal with at any one time, know what I mean?"

"Only too well."

"Of course I think about him. But all that stuff I was doing with him, it's too much, it's like a wall in my head at the moment. I just feel… " She paused.

"Full up? Just so full of grief, you've got no extra capacity for life's complications?"

"Yes, Nicks, that's it."

Nicky sighed. "I know how you feel, honey."

"Of course you do. I don't mean to remind you of your own tragedy."

"Dad died. That's life. You never get over it, but you deal with it. In time." She pointed at the pile of papers. "At least you have something great to remember your dad by as well as all the horrible stuff. My dad left nothing but unpaid bills."

"Yes, you're right as usual. I'll have a look at it soon. It'll remind me there's more to my father than the monster."

"That's a brave way of looking at it, honey."

"Thanks."

"How did Bacon manage to hide his life story inside Shakespeare's plays? Didn't Shakespeare have something to say about that?" asked Nicky.

"Please Nicks. I'll tell you all about it soon. Just not now. Is that okay?"

"Sure, honey. Whenever you're ready."

After they had enjoyed a glass of wine or three, the conversation started to flow more. Once she started, Fiona found it almost impossible to stop; the whole black story of her dad's illness and her guilt came out in a flood of bitter tears, anger and grief. Once the terrible tale had all been told, she needed a break.

"Would you like a cup of tea or anything Nicky?"

"Have you got any herbal?"

"Probably, mum was an old hippy… " Fiona felt a catch in her throat.

"Do you mind if I go watch a bit of TV? I should be

knackered, but I don't think I'll be able to sleep for hours after what you've told me. Maybe some late night junk will send me off. I wouldn't mind seeing if the news is on quickly, maybe check out CNN or BBC News 24."

"Sure, there's a TV next door. Just go through that door there, you'll see a big old box in the corner. It's probably older than you and the remote control looks like it's made out of Lego, but it still works."

Nicky got up and went into the other room whilst Fiona headed to the kitchen. After locating a packet of camomile tea at the back of a cupboard, Fiona returned to the fire with the drinks. She could hear the sound of the TV next door. For a moment she thought about joining Nicky but instead picked up Bacon's Secrets.

Fiona had read just two pages when Nicky burst into the room.

"Quickly, you've got to come and see this, hurry!" Fiona jumped up and ran into the room with the TV, just in time to see the end of the piece. The newsreader was talking over the top of some video footage. A silver Jaguar had smashed into a tree, police were all around it.

"...the man is believed to be American. Police will be taking him back to Scotland Yard once he has regained consciousness. He was apprehended on Christmas Day heading south towards Oxford after police picked up his trail in the small town of Burford-upon-Avon."

"Did you hear that?" said Nicky. "It's got to be Dan. He's hurt and he's been arrested."

A harassed looking Inspector Sawyer appeared on

the screen as the presenter's voiceover continued.

"... no comment from the police, but the American, believed to be working in London before being apprehended near Stratford-upon-Avon, was arrested after a high speed car chase. He lost control during the pursuit, careering off the road and nearly killing a local family. Our sources say he's been arrested on suspicion of being the hit-and-run driver who killed Prince William."

"Fiona, they think Dan killed Prince William!"

Act 13: Scene One

"Hell is empty, and all the devils are here"

The Tempest

30th December

Sawyer eyed the buffet breakfast with suspicion. The large metal tureens of bacon and sausages were drowned in oil, the grilled tomatoes were either raw, or shrivelled and burned, whilst the lump of scrambled egg looked like a dead Sponge Bob Squarepants. Eventually he plucked out some anaemic sausages and rashers of bacon from their metal grave, piling them haphazardly on his plate. He ignored the radioactive looking fruit juice, poured a large mug of black, over-boiled coffee that looked like a mix of coal dust and gravy, and sat back down at his table.

He forced the food down and cleared a space on the small brown table, pushing aside the fussy paper pink napkins and a pointless plastic flower. He reached down and grabbed his briefcase from under the table, pulling out a brown folder and a clear plastic bag. Sawyer opened the folder. It contained Daniel Knight's profile. He flipped through the file. Nothing interesting. Knight was American, mid-30s. He had been arrested after a traffic crash once before and spent a night in jail, but seeing as the misdemeanour was being drunk in charge of a shopping trolley, it wasn't exactly in the same league as this latest incident. In truth, Sawyer was relieved. A totally spotless record would have worried him more. But there was nothing in his past at all to suggest Knight would suddenly turn into a murderer.

The plastic bag contained Daniel Knight's personal belongings: a mobile phone, some cash and his wallet. Sawyer saw the mobile had been left on and the battery was low. He scrolled through the list of recent calls.

Work
Nicky
Mom cell
Fiona F

He made a note of the numbers. There were also a few withheld numbers, something else for the boys to check into later. He turned the phone off, checked his watch. 7:30 am. Time to go and get Knight from the hospital and escort him down to London. Sawyer had done enough waiting. He didn't care if Knight was still unconscious. A flicker of thought crossed his mind that he was actually up here and obsessing over this case in order to get away from his wife.

Sawyer looked up. A waiter was hovering at his table. "Excuse me Inspector, but there are two police officers waiting for you in the hotel lobby." Sawyer stood up. "Off to work we go."

Act 13: Scene Two

"Help me! do thy best To pluck this crawling serpent from my breast!"

A Midsummer Night's Dream

Nicky had already prepared tea and toast and was sitting at the kitchen table with a worried expression on her face when Fiona finally got out of bed and struggled downstairs. Fiona looked at her friend. "What is it? You've obviously got something on your mind."

"Actually, yes. But we don't have to talk about it."

"It's about last night, isn't it? On the news. You're thinking about Dan. You want to know what we were up to and how come he ended up like that. I don't want to talk about it."

"It is that partly," replied Nicky, "but it's not what you think. I don't want to ask you about any of the stuff that happened between you two."

"What is it then?"

"I'm wondering if I can check something with you. On TV they said Dan had been in a chase between Burford and Oxford."

"So what?"

"Burford's not on the way to Oxford from Stratford, is it?"

"But it is from here," said Fiona.

"So... "

"Dan must have come back here after mum died and

before they caught him."

"Yes, that's what I thought. I thought I was going mad. What was he doing back here?"

"I think I know." Fiona felt a flash of anger. How dare Dan come back here after what had happened!

The friends walked out of the warm kitchen and into the barn. Fiona paused briefly as she walked back in, suddenly filled with a sense of foreboding. Even though the light was low, she immediately saw the safe door was open.

"He did it."

"Did what, honey?"

"He opened the safe. He cracked the code."

"He broke into the safe? How?"

"I have no idea."

Nicky walked over to the desk that sat in front of the safe. She looked into the safe for a second and then bent down to pick up the only thing that remained on the desk - a single piece of paper.

"Look at this?" Nicky handed the paper to Fiona. "It says 'Verulam' on the top. Mean anything?"

"Vaguely. Let me think." Fiona found her eyes pulled to the note written by Dan. She couldn't resist reading it. As she read the last line where Dan said he loved her, her stomach lurched and she felt herself collapsing onto the ground.

Act 13: Scene Three

"Out of the jaws of death!"

Twelfth Night

S awyer groaned as he saw the photographers, TV cameramen and members of the public gathered behind a quickly erected police barricade in front of the hospital entrance.

"Look at them," said Sawyer, pointing though the window of the police car. "It's just pathetic. Some nurse blabs to her boyfriend at the local rag and next thing it's fucking chaos and they're all out here barking and yapping like a bunch of royal corgis with some of Prince Charles' organic carrots up their arses. I don't know what they think they're trying to achieve. Best thing they can do is piss off back home and watch it on TV instead."

Sawyer ordered the car to pull up in front of the hospital. As it drew to a halt all of the eyes and lenses in the crowd turned in his direction. Sawyer swung open the car door and strode towards the hospital entrance. A microphone was jammed in his face and questions thrown at him from eager journalists. It took all of his self control to not just tell them all to fuck off.

"Kill the murderer!" screamed a voice.

"Lock him up! String him up! Lock him up!" It turned into a chant from the crowd.

"Fucking bumpkins," Sawyer muttered to himself and walked in with his officers, the giant hospital doors muting the crowd. Inside, a worried looking young doctor was surrounded by two nurses and an immaculately suited man who Sawyer suspected was the hospital's press officer.

"Inspector Sawyer," said the doctor, "I really have to protest. The patient should not be moved."

"Doctor Khiroya. Nice to see you again too. You're looking frazzled. Is he awake?"

"No, he's still unconscious, He's in a much better condition than yesterday, we're very pleased with his progress. No more risk of any internal damage, but under normal circumstances he would have been kept under observation and certainly not discharged for another day or two and..."

"Is he in the ambulance?" interrupted Sawyer.

"Yes. He's in the ambulance with one of your armed officers and a junior nurse monitoring him."

"Good. In that case, I'll be on my way." Sawyer turned to the officers who had followed him out of the car. "You two are in the support car with me. We'll be driving in front of the ambulance containing the prisoner. Two of our men will be in the ambulance. I've organised a motorbike escort when we get near London to make sure the roads are clear into town."

Half an hour later they were on the move. Sawyer sat in the back seat of the lead car. In front were two officers. Sawyer swivelled round in his seat and looked at the ambulance behind them. He could see a paramedic driving and one of the two other officers sitting alongside him. Sawyer knew the other officer was in the back along with the nurse and unconscious prisoner.

In less than ten minutes they were out on the country roads and Sawyer ordered the driver to turn off the sirens. The ambulance behind followed their lead. The roads were quiet and the tarmac had an effervescent black sheen from the early morning showers and low winter sun that intermittently broke through the scattered grey clouds. Although the trees were bare in the winter countryside, the colours were still vibrant and intense. It was all a bit green for Sawyer and the air was much too clean. He glanced at his sergeant driving the car. Middle aged, a bit fat, but focused on the job in hand. The man in the front passenger seat looked similar. He could see a damp patch of sweat under the man's armpits and a few beads of sweat on his forehead. They were both armed and Sawyer wondered if either of them had ever shot anyone. He doubted it, but could imagine the fat one out at the weekend shooting rabbits for his tea.

Sawyer felt exhausted. The previous late night, hotel whisky, crap porn and over efficient air conditioning were all combining to knacker him out. He closed his eyes and leant back in the car's soft back seat. His mind started wandering. His wife, what was he going to do about her? There was a part of him that didn't really expect her to be there when he got home this time. There was something about that last argument. It had a finality, a coldness to it. It felt like something had finally been broken. Maybe he should call her. Okay, she was a nightmare, but she was still the wife and he knew it wouldn't hurt him to make a bit more effort. He felt the car slowing down and opened his eyes.

"What's going on?"

His driver looked back over his shoulder at him. He had a broad west country accent. "It looks like road works, boss. It shouldn't take a minute to clear."

Up ahead was a set of temporary traffic lights and a line of traffic cones blocking off half the road for about eighty metres. Inside the cones, on the closed-off lane, two large grey vans were parked. A team of three of four men in hard hats and yellow workmen's jackets were milling around the back of the rear van.

As Sawyer's car approached, the lights flicked to red. Two cars ahead of Sawyer ducked through as the light changed, but his driver was forced to halt. They waited as a couple of cars went past in the other direction, then the traffic lights changed to green. Sawyer's driver put the car into first gear and started down the free lane, checking in the mirror to see that the ambulance was following.

"What the bloody hell?" shouted the driver, his eyes wild with fear. Sawyer looked up. Ahead of them a huge truck was heading straight towards them at high speed.

"Get out!" Sawyer shouted, opening the rear door and throwing himself out and into the road. He landed heavily on his shoulder and hip and rolled over on the tarmac, his momentum carrying him into a low ditch on the other side of the road away from the crash site. A wave of pain rushed through his shoulder and hip, but he ignored it, lifting his head up to look out of the ditch. There was a massive explosion of metal and glass as the heavy truck ploughed into the BMW police car. The truck's high wheels hit the front of the car, folding and crunching the metal before hammering up and through the windshield at head height. Sawyer winced as he saw the driver's head and chest being hit by the heavy tyres. The police car's back wheels left the ground as the massive weight of the truck rolled over the top of it and crushed it. The ambulance behind skidded to a halt, sliding sideways and hitting the back of the police car.

In the confusion Sawyer saw the workmen running away from the back of the second parked van towards the crashed vehicles. He was stunned to see they were carrying small black submachine guns. Two of the workmen ran up to the driver's door of the car and fired a controlled burst into the car. Sawyer could see the driver, who he assumed was already dead, being hit by bullets. The other officer scrambled out of the window on the other side of the car as the bullets exploded around him. The officer managed to get clear but then he panicked. He started running back down the road. Sawyer was expecting the two gunmen to set off in pursuit, but they ignored him.

Smoke briefly drifted across his view and Sawyer lost sight of what was happening. When the smoke cleared he could see the officer was running down the road, about to disappear from sight over the brow of a hill. Sawyer could see a new figure had appeared. A man dressed completely in black had climbed out of the cab of the rear parked van. He was holding a high-powered rifle on which was mounted an outsized telescopic sight. In one fluid movement he lifted the gun up and fired. The bullet struck the fleeing police officer between his shoulder blades. Sawyer knew the man was dead before he hit the ground.

Sawyer lay down as low as he could, cold mud at the bottom of the ditch soaking him. He prayed he hadn't been seen. He checked his pockets for his mobile and swore violently. It was sitting on the back seat of the car.

The ambulance driver had reacted quickly to the collision but still had no way to avoid hitting the back of the police car in front. He slipped the ambulance into reverse gear and tried to get clear. But the gunmen were quickly on him, shooting out the tyres. The driver gunned the engine hard, but the ambulance didn't respond, it had become sluggish and almost immobile.

The officer next to the driver removed his pistol from its holster and opened the door, using it as a shield. He leant out and fired quick shots in the direction of the nearest attacker. They slammed into the man's chest, killing him instantly. But a stream of automatic fire from the other gunman sprayed the door, punched through the thin metal, ripping into the policeman's stomach, chest and thighs. He screamed in agony, lost his grip and rolled out into the road, into a hail of bullets that tore him to pieces.

A new attacker sprinted out from the back of the parked vans towards the ambulance. He was greeted by a young police officer, who looked no more than twenty, still covered in acne, stumbling out of the back door, gun in hands. The policeman lifted his pistol, a look of fear on his face, his hand shaking as he raised the pistol.

"Stop. You're under arrest." The policeman's voice

was thin and terrified.

The gunman smiled and squeezed the trigger on his machine gun, instantly pulverising the policeman's face into a mess of bone and blood.

As the gunman opened the back door of the ambulance he was joined by his accomplice. A nurse sat cowering in the corner of the van, her legs pulled up to her chest. The first gunman levelled his gun at her but didn't fire. Instead he helped the other man pull out the stretcher trolley with the unconscious Dan on it. The nurse inched her way out of the van and ran for her life. The gunmen watched her leave.

The attackers wheeled Dan's stretcher to the first of the two parked grey vans, and with the man in black watching, lifted it inside. They dragged the body of their dead comrade to the same van, and slung it inside. Soon all the attackers had climbed in, and within seconds it was disappearing over the hill.

Sawyer climbed up and out of the ditch. His heart was pounding. He knew he was lucky to be alive. The whole attack had taken about two minutes in total, and apart from missing him, they had been ruthlessly efficient. He walked over to the scene and looked down at one of the dead officers, a black rage building up inside him. He heard a car horn behind him. A blue Toyota Prius had pulled up at the traffic lights set up by the workmen. He strode up to it and tapped on the driver's side window. A furious looking bespectacled Chinese man was sitting behind the wheel.

"What the bloody hell is going on?" The man opened the window, revealing a face almost purple with anger. "First of all we get flagged down a mile back and held up by some fool and now this. I'm supposed to be in a sales meeting."

Sawyer looked at the road ahead. The man was right, there was no way through. The remaining van blocked one side of the road, the crash blocked the other. Whoever had organised this had thought it through impeccably. "I'm taking this car."

"What the hell! Who do you think you are?"

Sawyer flashed his badge. "Don't fuck with me, sonny. You can either get in the passenger seat or you can stay here and bleat to the sheep in the field and see if they listen."

"Yes, yes, I'll do what you say." The frightened man shuffled over into the passenger seat. Sawyer opened the driver's door and got in.

"Give me your phone," said Sawyer.

Act 13: Scene Four

"Oh I am fortunes fool!"

Romeo and Juliet

Dan woke up shaking with cold. He was lying in a low, simple wooden bed covered by a coarse woollen blanket, in the middle of a large square room. On each stone wall he could see narrow vertical slits of windows letting in thin beams of weak light that highlighted swirling motes of dust. A fierce wind buffeted the building. He could see a stone stairway hugging the walls heading up to a high stone ceiling criss-crossed with wooden beams, leading to what he assumed was the next floor up. He tried to sit up. A sharp pain flashed through his head with the effort of moving. He raised his hand and gingerly touched the stitching around the bald skin.

He rested for a couple of minutes and tried sitting up again, this time with more success. He frowned when he saw he was dressed in a hospital gown. The last thing he could remember was driving the Jaguar, trying to get away from the police. Other jumbled images fell into his mind - nurses, lights. He had been in hospital, obviously from the car crash. But for how long? What had happened exactly?

Dan swung his legs off the bed and tried to stand up. The grey slate slabs were shockingly cold on his bare feet. The room seemed to be some sort of cell. He rubbed his chin and felt stubble. It felt like it was a couple of day's growth and he began to worry.

Opposite the staircase was a hefty wooden door set into the grey stone walls. Dan slowly hobbled over to the door, his muscles slowly waking up, pins and needles flickering through his tired limbs. The door had intricate carved metal hinges, a cumbersome but solid iron handle and an old-fashioned lock. He tried the door. It was locked.

The stairs were the only option. A wooden banister ran along the wall and Dan kept one hand on it for support as he made his way upwards. His heart was racing by the time he reached the top and he was breathing heavily. The stairs led up to a wooden trapdoor in the stone ceiling which he pushed open, and with a final burst of energy, lifted himself through.

The wind was so unexpectedly strong that for a second Dan almost lost his balance. He looked around and realised that he was standing in the open air on top of a flat roof of a small, high tower. In front of him he could see stone parapets rising up at the edge of the roof and far beyond that a huge boiling red sun was beginning to dip over the horizon. Above the dying sun he could see ominous bruised storm clouds gathering. The countryside stretched away for miles in front of him, woodlands and fields laid out like a patchwork quilt. A silver river weaved its way subtly through the rolling landscape. He counted four villages nestled along its banks. Directly in front of the tower a jagged rock outcrop reared up from the edge of the hill.

"The tower's called the Colonel's Folly." The loud voice came from behind, half snatched away by the wind.

Dan span round. "Luther. I should have known. What am I doing here?"

The Rosicrucian was hunched against the rear parapet of the tower, his head lowered and jutting forward, like a black vulture; his long black coat flapping in the wind, a balaclava covering his face, eyes glittering in the low light. He was holding a pistol which he casually pointed at Dan. In front of him was a small suitcase.

"The hill is only nine hundred and thirty one feet high. About a hundred years ago a stalwart true English gentleman, one of our group, a certain Colonel decided he wanted to turn this hill into a mountain, so he built this tower on top to get it up to a thousand feet. Unfortunately he came in four feet short, but if you stand up here, your shoulders are high enough to make it a mountain. The planning went awry, but there was a human element at the end of it to make it a success."

"What happened? Was I arrested? Why aren't I in jail?"

"That's thanks indeed for sparing you a lifetime of being buggered in Brixton jail by big horny black men who want you as their skinny bitch. You're a lucky lad to be alive you know. Yes, of course the cops got you after your stupid crash. But we got you out. There was a debate of course. Three members of the High Temple believed that you had shown weakness allowing yourself to be arrested and that perhaps you weren't the one we seek after all. But Damascus came to your defence again. So it was decided to give you another chance."

"Who is Damascus? Why does he care about me?"

"See that strange rock outcrop in front of you, does it remind you of anything?"

"What are you talking about?"

"Just humour me will you. Go on, have a look."

Dan looked at the rocky outcrop in front of the tower. "Yes, it looks like some kind of animal, an elephant. The rock at the front looks like a trunk."

"That's it Danny boy, it's called the Elephant Stone. Legend has it, every fifty years on Michaelmas, it comes to life and walks the hill."

"Why should I care about that? Why the hell am I in a hospital gown?"

"You really should pay attention to legend you know, Danny boy. The great myths and legend of this world are the texture of modern life. What are we here for if we don't wish our own stories to become legendary? And that is where you stand, Danny boy, on the edge of legend."

"From what I can see, I'm on the edge of a hill. What's happened to me? Why am I dressed in a hospital gown?"

"Yes, you do look like an escaped lunatic dressed like that. You must be cold. You're shaking like a leaf." Luther paused. "You know what, Danny boy? I'm not sure where that phrase comes from, are you? Shaking like a leaf? I've never really seen a leaf shake. Maybe I should change it to something else. How about this – you're shaking like an old lady with only five toes left."

Dan remembered Luther's threat to cut one toe off the Queen's feet every day and he paled. "What day is it?"

"Haven't you been keeping track of time Danny boy? No I don't suppose you have. You've overslept a bit, it's the thirtieth."

"The thirtieth? That's impossible."

"All too possible, Danny boy. You were in hospital for quite some time."

Dan put his hand up to this head and felt the wound and the stitching. He could feel the wound had already partly healed over. Luther was telling the truth.

"You've got to give me more time!"

Luther raised the pistol higher and pointed it at Dan's face. "Listen you dumb fuck, you're lucky you're not dead. You don't have any more time. Find Shakespeare's Truth by the end of tomorrow night or you die and she dies. That's right Danny boy, nothing's changed, I've still got my money on you failing and when you do it'll be my pleasure to skin you alive and spit on your corpse. Now, I've spent quite enough time with you. I'm only under orders to check you actually woke up out of the coma. We had to jack you up with some pretty serious chemicals. Don't worry though, Danny boy, everything you need is in here." He pushed the suitcase towards Dan with his foot. "Pick it up." Dan walked over warily.

Luther leant back against the parapet and kept the gun trained on Dan as he leant down to pick the suitcase up.

"Personally, Danny boy, I think it's more than you deserve to be still alive, but what can I say, you've got friends in high places." He laughed. "You know what, when you fail, I think, just for good measure I'm going to kill your woman too. Oh yes, I'll take personal care of her. I'm sure she'll get a kick out of my weaponry. It will make a change for her to experience a real man with a decent gun on him instead of your limp little Californian barrel."

Dan could put up with Luther taunting him, but now he was talking about Fiona. It was too much, he lost his self control. He grabbed the suitcase with both hands and swung it up and forwards, knocking the gun out of Luther's hand, sending it skidding across the rooftop. Luther swore violently and lifted a leg, aiming a hard kick at Dan's ribs, but the blow hit the suitcase first, sending it into Dan's stomach, knocking the breath out of him.

Dan fell to his knees. An image flashed into his mind. The attack back in his apartment in Shepherd's Bush that had started all this. That must have been Luther too. In which case, he knew what was coming next. Back then, he had been kicked low, then the next blow had been to the head...

Even as the second kick swung over aiming at the side of Dan's face, he lifted the case up, Luther's boot thudded into it. The Rosicrucian grunted in surprise and pain. In the same movement Dan held the case up above his head, and using it like a battering ram he jumped up, hitting Luther as hard and fast as he could in the chest before Luther got both legs back solidly on the ground.

There was a moment where their eyes locked and the Rosicrucian's arm uselessly reached out to grab at Dan, but the momentum was too great and Luther lost his balance. He fell backwards over the parapet and off the top of the tower. A thin scream was whipped away in the wind as he fell.

Dan was frozen to the spot, the realisation he had just killed a man overwhelming him. He leaned over the parapet. The Rosicrucian's body was visible far below, arms and legs splayed grotesquely, a broken doll.

Dan sank to his knees and breathed deeply. His whole body was shaking; he felt light-headed and dizzy. His blood felt as if it was boiling, his heart was hammering so fast he thought he was about to have a cardiac arrest. As the adrenalin charged brutally through his system, he forced himself to breathe slowly and deeply. After a while, he felt strong enough to stand up. He tried to work out how he felt about what had happened. He had crossed a line. It wasn't that he felt guilty or even sad, Luther had deserved it.

It was as if a gear had changed in his mind. It had been a moment of pure fury when he charged at Luther and knocked him off the roof, but even in the middle of it, he had known what he was doing. He wanted to kill Luther, and he had done it. He wondered what else he was capable of. The days of sitting in an office dreaming up advertising campaigns for airport parking seemed a lifetime ago. He picked up the suitcase and headed towards the steps. He was just about to head back through the trapdoor when he remembered the gun. He walked over to the other side of the roof and found it. He'd never held a pistol before, it was heavier than he expected, but the feeling of it in his hand was frighteningly natural. He headed down the stairs.

Back in the room at the base of the tower, Dan sat back down on the bed and opened the suitcase up. At the top were some newspapers from yesterday and today. Dan glanced at them and groaned. On the front page of each newspaper was the photo of him used on the Big Fish agency intranet, smiling in a black designer suit. Where had they got it from? He realised it was probably Jonny. He scanned through the stories, there was plenty of wild speculation about who was behind the attack to rescue him and his role in the events. Dan noticed that one name kept coming up, an Inspector Brian Sawyer. He seemed to be the officer in charge of the investigation.

Under the newspapers were the clothes he had been wearing on Christmas Day. They had been washed and folded neatly, presumably by the hospital. He took off the gown and put the clothes on gratefully, feeling better instantly. He slipped the pistol into a jacket pocket. Underneath his clothes was a smaller bag containing his wallet, watch and mobile phone. He opened his wallet and frowned to see that though his credit cards were untouched, he had just ten pounds in cash. Had someone been light fingered? Dan slipped the watch on, checking the time. It was half past five in the afternoon, but already the sky outside was almost black.

He turned on his phone and waited for it to kick into life. It didn't take long to find a signal and instantly sent him a text message telling him there were thirty seven voicemails and a huge list of text messages. The phone let out a loud beep to tell him the battery was low. He dialled up his voicemail, hoping against hope to hear something from Fiona. The first message was from about an hour ago. It was the editor of the *News of the World* newspaper. Dan wondered idly how the woman had managed to get hold of his mobile phone number. It must have been through work. Jonny probably gave out the number in exchange for some sort of favour for one of their crappy clients.

The next message was from another journalist, then another one, then one from his mother. Dan stomach lurched at the realisation of the worry she must be feeling on finding out her son was the prime suspect in the most notorious murder of the century. The battery beeped again. He skipped to the next message.

"Daniel Knight, this is Inspector Brian Sawyer of Scotland Yard. My advice to you is to surrender yourself immediately to the authorities, go to any police station. The only possible chance you have is to turn yourself in, otherwise I'm going to hunt you down and when I catch up with you, you'll..." Then abruptly the phone turned off as the battery ran out. Dan cursed. Maybe there had been something from Fiona, but he wouldn't hear it now. He started to worry. Could the police track him from his phone? He had seen enough movies and TV shows to think it might be possible, but he doubted it was going to happen so quickly. He had only been on the phone for about two minutes. Still, it was probably better it was turned off.

He had more important issues to deal with. He walked up to the locked door, pulled out the pistol, aimed it at the lock and pulled at the trigger. Nothing. He examined the gun, found the safety catch and flicked it to OFF. Dan aimed at the lock once again and slowly squeezed the trigger. This time the gun fired, flame and smoke belching from it and it kicked in his hand.

He had missed the lock completely, instead punching a useless hole in the wooden door. He tried again, this time the bullet crashed into the ancient lock, splintering the metal. He took two more shots, turning the front of the old brittle lock into a mangled lump. He grabbed hold of the handle, but it was jammed. He started to panic. Was that all he had done? Jammed the lock entirely? Dan took a deep breath and pulled the handle down with all his strength. At last he felt it move slightly. He increased the pressure, then suddenly something broke inside the mechanism and he had the door open.

The bitter wind rushed into the tower as Dan walked outside. He walked around the tower until he found Luther's mangled body. Dan crouched down next to it and pulled the balaclava off and put it in his pocket, it was mercifully clear of blood.

The man now revealed was hard-faced even in death. A strong jaw line and acne scars dominated his features. His black hair had been kept short in a military cut. His green eyes stared glassily up at nothing. Dan realised that when he had seen him on the London Eye, the grey hair and moustache had been a disguise.

Dan put a hand down to close the eyes. The hackles on the back of his neck went up as he touched Luther's face. The body was still warm. He searched Luther, finding a spare clip of bullets and some car keys. There was no wallet or ID.

Dan stood up and started scanning the surrounding landscape. He noticed a track leading away from the tower that disappeared over the brow of the hill via a small copse of trees. That seemed as good a place as any to hide a car. He walked over and clicked on the remote control key fob. Sure enough, hidden in between some holly bushes and some fern trees he caught a glimpse of orange flash of indicator lights as the car unlocked.

Dan walked over to the BMW and swung open the driver's door. It was a big car, squat and brutish, an M5, much more suited to life on the autobahn than up a hill. He lowered himself into the driver's seat and scanned the controls. It looked pretty straight forward. He adjusted the rear view mirror, turned on the ignition and started the car up. The low rumble reassured him and he put the heating on full. The fuel tank was full. He sat there for a few minutes, impatiently waiting for the car to warm up. Eventually it did and he sighed with pleasure, slowly feeling sensation returning to his frozen body.

He leaned forward and opened the glove compartment. Inside he found sandwiches and fruit juice, water, a road atlas and a Sudoku puzzle book. He opened up the book to have a look. Luther hadn't done too well on the puzzles, but he'd done enough to suggest he had been on the road for some time. Dan wolfed the food down and felt better immediately. He climbed out and walked to the back of the car and opened the boot. Inside was a case closed by two clips and another long coat, this one an expensive dark woollen overcoat, like something a city banker would wear. He picked up the coat and slung it over his shoulder. He flicked open the case to reveal an evil looking hunting rifle and infrared telescopic sights, Dan left out low whistle. He knew very little about guns, but this was obviously a serious weapon. He closed the gun case up, picked it up and threw it into the bushes. He got back into the car and tossed the coat and balaclava onto the back seat.

He opened up the road atlas and looked at it but his eyes couldn't focus on the small print. He knew he needed to get moving, but now he was sitting in the car, and the adrenalin rush of the fight had left him, he was hit by a crushing wave of exhaustion. He reached down and found a control that tipped the seat back, and closed his eyes. He would just sleep for an hour or two, then set off.

Act 14: Scene One

"That it should come to this!"

Hamlet

New Year's Eve

The morning sun flooded through the windshield, waking him up, and for a moment Dan had no idea where he was. Slowly the events of the previous day filtered into his memory and he searched the car dashboard for a clock. It was 8.04 am.

For a few seconds the old feeling of panic started to well up inside him, alongside furious anger that he had already managed to waste precious hours of what was potentially his last day alive. He forced himself to stay calm. He was going to fight with everything he had.

The BMW started easily and he nosed the car out of the copse and onto the track. The dirt road led away from the tower and sloped steeply down the hill, meandering in and out of broad swathes of dark green woodland. A layer of low mist clung to the fields, floating delicately above the grass. The track was no more than a couple of ruts carved by tractors over the years, and was strewn with loose stones and holes. The fastest he dared go was around five mph. Any faster, and when the low slung sports saloon hit a pothole or stone, there was a terrifying groan or crash, making him worried he was in danger of crippling the car.

It took an hour of frustration before the steep track began to flatten out as it reached the bottom of the hill. It ended with an ancient cattle grid and on the other side was tarmac. Dan edged the car over the grid and then onto the road, a joy spreading through his body as he accelerated, at last he could make some progress.

The steep and twisting road led down into a village. Ancient thatched cottages started to sprout up either side of the road as he raced down, then an estate of modern redbrick houses and the road started to widen out as finally he reached the junction with the main village street.

He stopped the car. He had no idea where he was or which way to go. He guessed left, and drove down the tree-lined village street. The buildings on either side were far more grandiose than those on the outskirts, perfectly groomed trees adorned the grass and pavement verge. As Dan drove past an ancient weathered church surrounded by gnarled trees that hung protectively over the wall, he saw a sign - Elmley Castle. He pulled over and looked at the road atlas index and soon located the village. He worked out he had been on top of Bredon Hill, and could see a marking on the map for the tower at its summit. With the hill behind him Dan swivelled the map and made a note of the next few villages he had to get through, Netherton, Hinton on the Green, Broadway, before reaching the main road which would take him to Oxford. He guessed it would take him about three hours driving to get to Verulam House.

Another hour and a half passed as Dan struggled to reach the road to Oxford. Traffic was slower than he anticipated. The road seemed to be full of doddering old people crawling along at half the speed he wanted to go. By the time he had pushed through Oxford and down the M40 to the M25 it was past lunchtime. The low winter sun was already starting to slide down towards the horizon.

Dan slowly made his way up the west of London and approached St Albans. He headed into the town centre and soon found signs directing him onwards to Gorhambury. After hours of mind numbing travel, his destination was suddenly upon him.

The village of Gorhambury was very beautiful and very old, but totally different from the Cotswold stone villages he had become used to seeing. He cruised past a church and then he saw a sign to Verulam House. Soon Dan found himself in front of a majestic white mansion. He drove up to it and parked. The house was breath-taking and made Dan think of a smaller version of Buckingham Palace. It was a vast building with dozens of windows and two huge pillars at the front, framing the regal front doors.

He felt anticipation and fear in equal measure. Before stepping our of the car he looked at himself in the rear-view mirror. He almost laughed. His stubble and stitches made him think of the zombies in *Night of the Living Dead*. He rolled up Luther's balaclava so it resembled a beanie hat and put it on to cover the wounds.

He climbed out of the car. Somewhere in the building in front of him were the manuscripts. They had to be there. Finding them seemed impossible, but failure simply wasn't an option. As he walked towards the front door of the mansion he was surprised to see an elderly smiling woman wearing a fifties style grey dress suit sitting inside a green wooden ticket booth.

"Would you like to go on the tour?" she said brightly. "You're lucky, I'm about to take the last one in. We close up an hour early today, being New Year's Eve and everything. Funny thing really, one kind of expects today to be a holiday too, but it isn't, it's merely a half holiday. Still I won't complain, keeps me on my toes."

"Definitely," said Dan. "Can I ask you what areas of the house the tour covers?"

"You get to see the West Wing, and of course the library."

"What's so special about the library?" Dan's spirits rose. Surely the library was as good a place as any for manuscripts to be hidden.

"It's where Sir Francis Bacon's books are of course. A really wonderful old collection and very much the heart of the house." She raised heavy eyebrows covered in mascara and eye pencil makeup. "Do you know who Sir Francis Bacon was, young man?"

"Oh yes." smiled Dan. "I'm getting to know quite a lot about Sir Francis Bacon."

The old lady clapped her hands. "Isn't that simply marvellous. In that case you jolly well have to come along. That'll be six pounds please." Dan warily handed over his last ten pound note.

The old lady gave him his change and briskly hopped off her seat, opened the door to the ticket booth and walked outside. "Come on then," she said. "Let's join the others."

Dan smiled wonderingly and followed her through the front doors into a cavernous atrium. High walls were decorated with diamond patterned wallpaper in gold and black. The ceiling was dominated by grandiose curling rosette designs bordering a large central scene of cherubs and dancing angels. There were three other people in the tour group, two Japanese businessmen and another old lady. Dan tried to keep his face away from them, wondering if they would recognise him, but catching his own reflection in one of the large gilt mirrors lining the hallway, he realised he barely recognised himself.

"So you're the tour leader as well?"

"Oh yes, it seemed a bit of a shame to ask any of the other girls to come in today. I don't mind popping in. Alright everybody, let's go and have jolly good look round."

Dan checked his watch. The first few rooms were full of opulent antique furniture. He was impatient to get through them. Then they entered the library. On one wall hung a row of large family portraits, their expressions aloof and disinterested. Under the pictures sat a glass case. Along two other walls climbed imposing oak bookcases. At the far end, huge lead lined windows framed the room, letting natural light pour in.

Dan detached himself from the group and started to examine the immense book collection looking for clues. He was stopped in his tracks when he saw one ancient book, *The Macbeths of Scotland*.

"What's this book?" he asked the guide.

"Oh, that's what is so remarkable about the collection," she said. "The wonderful old history books. This one is a history of the Macbeths, an ancient royal Scottish family. And yes, before you ask, it is the same family as in the Shakespeare play, although by all accounts it's a far more severe and academic history of the family and not anywhere near as colourful a story."

"But it could have given somebody the inspiration and factual background they needed to write the play?" For a few moments Dan forgot about the manuscripts and imagined Bacon sitting in his library, reading this book and dreaming up the tragic story of Macbeth from the history it contained.

"Oh yes, it's one of the prized possessions here alongside the Quartos."

"What on earth is a Quarto?" said Dan. "I remember some dodgy fizzy drink from the nineteen eighties with a name a bit like that."

One of the two Japanese businessmen perked up. "Quattro. Disgusting," he said with a satisfied smile. Dan goggled at him.

The guide giggled. "A Quarto is how plays were printed in the Elizabethan period. To save money, they would be printed on both sides of the paper in quarters, then the paper folded four times so that a single sheet of paper could contain eight pages of a play." There was a tremendous amount of pride in her voice as she led the group over to the glass case under the portraits. "We believe there are no more than a handful left in the country from the Elizabethan period, yet we have eight here, all of them Shakespeare's plays."

The Quartos were laid out in the case. Dan noticed something immediately. "They don't all have the name of the author on them."

"That's right, it's a bit of a mystery," said the guide. "But we know they're Shakespeare's plays. We've read them." She burst out laughing.

Dan looked up at the portraits hanging on the wall and his eyes widened with surprise. "Excuse me," he said to the tour guide. "What are these pictures on the wall? I thought this was the ancestral home of the Bacon family? These pictures seem to have a different name on them. Radcliffe?"

"Oh no," smiled the old lady. "The original Verulam House which Sir Francis Bacon built fell into ruin after he died. This is a new building," she tittered. "It was built in the eighteenth century by the Radcliffe family. If you look out there," she pointed through the large lead lined windows, "you'll see all that is left of Sir Francis Bacon's home, the original Verulam House."

Outside was a ruined wall sinking into long grass. It stretched along the edge of an immaculately kept lawn. Climbing roses and ivy had engulfed it. The only real feature indicating what the building once might have been was a broken arch at one end.

"That's it? That's all that's left of Sir Francis Bacon's home?" Dan's heart sank.

"Yes, that's it. But that archway that you're looking at, that's where the original library that housed this magnificent collection of ancient history books once was." Dan looked out at the ruins. He was close to total despair. There were no manuscripts hidden here.

Act 14: Scene Two

"Now is the winter of our discontent."

Richard III

"So that's it," said Dan. "The only memory of Sir Francis Bacon is this old ruin."

"Of course not, young man," said the guide. "That would be jolly silly if that were the case. There's his monument where he was buried in St Michael's church."

Dan stared at her. Of course, why the hell didn't he think of that before? He excused himself and left, running out. It made total sense. The manuscripts would be buried with their true author. All he needed to do was find Bacon's tomb. He had passed the church on the way in, looking for Verulam House. He jumped back into the BMW and drove back, retracing his steps.

He soon found St Michael's church and parked up outside on a grass verge. He sprinted through the immaculate graveyard to the church. As he approached it he could see it was made of a mixture of flint and brick, but there was no time to appreciate it. He tried the wooden door, it was open.

He stepped into the empty church. It had an open design with an unusually high roof held up by four central pillars. He stopped in his tracks. On a long wall opposite the font was a large white marble statue of a man sitting on a large chair, resting his head on his hand. The statue was dressed in Elizabethan clothes and sitting languidly on a high backed chair, resting its bearded chin on one elbow. The other hand was drooping and hanging down in a disconsolate, bored, almost resigned manner. The statue was set against a deep red background inside an alcove. The overall effect was of a man who looked distracted and lost in thought.

Dan sat down on a pew in front of the monument and looked closely at it. Underneath the main statue were two Latin inscriptions. On the first was Francis Bacon's name.

FRANCISVS BACON

BARON VERULAM

SEV NOTIORIBVS TITVISSCIENTIARVM LVMEN
FACVNDIAE LEX SIC SEDEBAT

QUI POSTQUAM OMNIA NATURALIS SAPIENTIAEET
CIVILIS ARCANA EVOLVISSET NATURAE
DECRETUM EXPLEVIT COMPOSITA SOLUANTUR
AN DNI MDCXXVIAETAT LXVI

Dan saw the word Verulam immediately. He put his head in his hands. If Bacon was buried under there, he may as well give up now. What was he going to do?

"Can I help you?" Dan span round to see a vicar standing behind him. The man had sandy brown receding hair, freckles and a wispy ginger beard. He was smiling warily.

"That was a surprise," said Dan. "I was completely lost in thought."

The vicar looked relieved. "Oh my word, I do apologise. You're American. I didn't mean to disturb you, but when I saw you from behind, now I hope you don't think I'm being too judgemental, but when I saw you from behind in that hat I thought you were one of our local tramps. We get them in here you know; they sneak in and go to sleep on the pews, which is all very well and good, and one has to show Christian charity and all that, unless of course they have a little accident with bowel control. But on New Year's Eve we have a fairly packed programme of services from evensong through to midnight, as I am sure you can imagine, so we really can't have people snoozing."

"I'm not a tramp," said Dan. "Although I realise I probably look like one with this stubble. I've had a long night."

"Anyway, jolly glad to meet you, and season's greetings to you old chap. I'm Piers Connolly, the vicar." The vicar held out his hand and Dan shook it.

Dan was already thinking how he could make the most of this new arrival and rescue the situation. "Same to you, my name's, um, Jack."

"I see you're looking at the monument to our most famous son, Sir Francis Bacon. He really was quite a character you know."

"I was admiring the monument. It's impressive. So, is Sir Francis Bacon buried under it?"

"Good Lord, no. The Bacon vault was at the back of the church."

Dan felt hope. "Vault? Sorry for being dumb, but do you mind telling me what you mean?"

The vicar laughed. "Yes, not everybody ends up six feet under the earth or turned into a jar of ashes when they go. Some have a rather more exalted resting place. I always think of a vault as like a giant safe for the deceased. More akin to a cellar, if you like."

"So access to the coffins would be possible in a vault?"

"Yes, they would have to be, to allow other family members to be buried alongside." The vicar frowned. "Those are rather peculiar questions. May I ask your interest? And I must say, you look strangely familiar, Jack," he said. "But I can't place you. Have you been round here before?"

Dan had an idea. It seemed utterly outrageous, but anything was worth trying. He leant forward conspiratorially. "You may have seen me here before, but I'm telling you this in confidence. I'm in advertising. I'm doing some research here for a big TV campaign for a product. I came by here last week for an initial scouting expedition and I'm pleased to say you've moved to the next stage of approval."

Dan saw the vicar's eyes light up with excitement. "Gosh how exciting. Do tell, what are you working on? It's not Kellogg's Crunchy Nut Corn Flakes is it? They're my favourite."

"Don't take this the wrong way Piers, but it's all quite high profile and a bit of a secret; we haven't actually decided if we're going to use your church or not for a location shoot yet. I'm really not supposed to be telling anyone what we're up to."

The vicar looked crushed. "Oh, I'm sorry, I didn't

mean to intrude."

"Unless…"

Piers brightened up instantly. "Unless what, Jack?"

"Unless of course you were the kind of guy who could help us out. What we really need is some local colour, somebody with a sense of history, someone who has access to some of the more private areas in the church."

"Well, Jack, I think you'll find history is pretty much an Englishman's favourite conversational idiom, apart from the weather of course." The vicar rubbed his hands. "Every vicar in the country knows something of the history of his church. And of course as vicar I have keys to every nook and cranny here. Now, how can I help, old chap?"

"Piers, the story behind the advertising campaign is buried treasure."

"It probably isn't Crunchy Nut Corn Flakes is it?"

"I'm afraid not. It's much more upmarket. And I don't mean muesli. Now Piers, one of the producers thinks that churches have a credible brand as a place to find hidden treasure, but I'm not so sure. What do you think?"

"Of course they do, old chap. The first thing the Vikings did when they came to England was dig up the gold hidden in graves in the abbeys and steal it after they killed the monks and raped the nuns, naturally. There's plenty of tall tales of buried treasure in tombs and vaults in English churches. It's not just the Egyptians who were buried with their valuables. If, God forbid, you were to exhume some of the more venerated inhabitants of my church, Lord knows what you could find."

Dan felt a wave of excitement. "So Piers, you were talking about a vault Sir Francis Bacon was buried in?"

"Yes, the site of the old apse vault, it's out the back."

"Could you possibly show it to me? Would it be a good location for a photo shoot?

"It would, after a fashion I suppose, but I can think of much better ones. It's really not very thrilling to look at in comparison to some of the other areas of the church."

"Do you mind showing me?"

"No, not all old chap. Follow me." The vicar started to walk towards the front of the church and Dan followed. After feeling utter defeat just minutes ago, he now started to believe the end truly was in sight. They walked past the altar and turned right heading through a narrow side door between the choir's pews and the font.

"Mind your head." The vicar opened the door and ducked down to go through it. Dan followed, feeling a huge sense of exhilaration. They stepped outside and were hit by the cold winter sunlight.

Dan was puzzled. All he could see in front of him was a large mound, overgrown with grass. At one end a huge ornate headstone to an ancient grave stood, surrounded by flowers and cut grass. "Why are we outside? Where's the vault?"

So this is where the apse vault was," explained Piers. "I told you it wasn't much to look at."

Dan stopped in his tracks. "Where it was? What do

you mean?"

"Well, the apse of a church is a hemispherical extension to the main building. It's usually constructed at the eastern end. Many centuries ago we had a beautiful apse which as I mentioned contained a vault built for Sir Francis Bacon. Now, after the apse fell into ruin we now have this rather grand headstone to the first Earl Radcliffe in its place."

Dan's heart sank. "What do you mean? The apse was destroyed? You mean there's no easy way to get into the vault?"

"Oh no, you misunderstand me. The vault no longer exists. After Sir Francis died, the Bacon family fell on really rather hard times. They certainly didn't stay round here. The Radcliffe family took over the ruins of Verulam House and built their own property. When that happened they became the local nobility and *de facto* sponsors of the church. The Earl of Radcliffe took this spot after Bacon's body was moved. Now I would imagine you can see why I say there are some much more dramatic locations around the church for your photo shoot."

Dan was plunged into total despair again. "Sir Francis Bacon's body was moved. You mean he's not buried here now? Is he somewhere else in the graveyard?"

"Oh no," said the vicar cheerily. "He's not in my church, old chap. This all happened a long time ago. 1740 is our best guess."

"And what about Sir Francis's body? Where did it get moved to?" said Dan. He felt a deep sense of dread.

"I have absolutely no idea," the vicar smiled. "Nobody knows where the body went. It's just one of life's little mysteries."

Act 14: Scene Three

"But never doubt I love."

Hamlet

New Year's Eve. It was turning into another long drawn out day for Fiona. It had been exhausting. She put the finishing touches to the fire she was building and struck a match and threw it on. Every bit of newspaper she had used to lay the fire had Dan's face on it. The fury she had felt towards him was slowly cooling from a white heat to a more contained anger. Dan and the Queen could both die today.

She sat down and watched as the hungry flame licked against the kindling. Her first meeting of the day had been with the police investigating her mother's murder. The fire at the ward when her mother had died had been caused by a stack of aluminium foil trays in the microwave oven. It had been turned on full power for ten minutes. The oven had burst into flames and the fire had spread. Although the damage was minimal the amount of smoke had been colossal. The police were treating it as arson. Elwood was the obvious suspect.

She knew it had to be him. It was a twisted re-enactment of the original attack. She was filled with a black and impossible rage against her father and found herself wishing him dead.

To make matters worse, after seeing the police she had to sit through two doctors arguing in front of her about Elwood's treatment. The debate was whether electro-convulsive therapy would help. She couldn't understand their attitude. They were turning it into an intellectual medical game between themselves. In her view the most effective treatment would have been to take him off all medication, then hopefully the disease would take him over and he would just die.

The phone had been ringing constantly all week from friends and acquaintances, but yesterday some of the calls had taken an ugly turn. Some enterprising journalists had worked out the connection between her and Dan. Two had even turned up on her doorstep.

Nicky poked her head around the door. "Fancy a cup of afternoon tea or anything? I'm going to have one of those funny powdered cappuccino things."

"Not for me thanks."

"Well, give me a shout if you need anything honey. I'll be in the kitchen."

It was amazing how well Nicky had settled in. Fiona had hardly lifted a finger around the house for days. Nicky had fed the cats, collected the eggs and shut the chickens in, and now she was making what she called her special pizza for tea. As far as Fiona could tell, this was a margarita pizza from the supermarket with mushrooms, tomatoes, onions and anything else Nicky could think of piled on top.

Fiona was slowly starting to come to terms with what had happened. The funny plates, that crazy old set of encyclopaedias, the myriad of personal objects her mother had left scattered all over the house were things Fiona was beginning to cherish, as opposed to triggers to restart the flood.

The fire had caught so she settled back in her seat and picked up Bacon's Secrets again. It was her antidote to the hate. Whenever she was most angry with her father she read a few pages and its genius reminded her of what her father had once been.

The story had reached a point where Bacon was starting to talk about his childhood. As she read on she furrowed her brow. Bacon had just written something about his parents she found bewildering. She sat back, genuinely shocked. The implications were huge.

Her mobile on the table next to her rang. Irritated to be disturbed she glanced at it briefly. It was a weird looking number, not local. It went through to voicemail. Whoever it was simply put the phone down and redialled. She sighed with annoyance and picked it up, determined to give the caller a mouthful.

"Fiona?"

"Dan!" She nearly dropped the phone in shock.

"Fiona, I'm so sorry about what happened. Please don't put the phone down."

"I probably should do, but I've seen the papers. And today is New Year's Eve. Of course I've been thinking about you today. Where are you?" Her heart was in her mouth, even after everything it was breathtaking to hear his voice.

"I'm in a phone booth in Gorhambury village where Bacon's memorial is. My cell's gone flat but I just got your number off it before it died forever."

"Have you found the manuscripts, is that why you're calling?"

"No, I haven't found anything."

"Why are you calling? I told you I didn't want to hear from you."

The words came out in a torrent. "I know you don't want to hear from me, but I've failed. It's all over. I'm going to die, and so is the Queen and Prince William's killers will get away with it. I've needed you so much. I know you don't want to hear from me. I know you blame me for everything. But I just had to speak to you. Just to hear your voice. To say goodbye."

Say goodbye? "Dan, I know it wasn't totally your fault what happened with mum."

"Hell, Fiona. It was my fault. If I wasn't there you'd never have got involved in the first place." His voice sounded so flat. "I'm just so sorry it worked out this way. You're a special girl, Fiona. I just wish I could have met you in other circumstances."

A big part of her wanted to scream at him as a flood of memories returned from that day at the hospital. But her heart was still beating like a drum, just talking to him. "So that's it? You've surrendered?"

"I've done everything I can. You saw what was in the safe?"

"Yes."

"It led me here, I worked out the manuscripts were originally buried with Bacon in his grave. But it doesn't matter. The body's been moved. Nothing's here. It's over. I'm dead."

"Dan, I can't believe you're giving up. The manuscripts wouldn't get moved without a clue being left behind. There must be something, there has to be. You said you were at Bacon's monument?" Fiona was shocked to hear the defeat in his voice.

"Yes."

"Well what about the inscription on the monument? Maybe there's something there? Some kind of clue?"

"The body was moved a hundred years after his death. There can't be a connection."

"Have you got a better idea?"

He paused. "No. But anyway, it's no use. Even if there is something in the inscription on the monument I'll never work it out."

"So you've phoned me up to wallow in self pity and tell me you're about to die? You blame yourself for what happened with mum, but this is just as selfish." Fiona started to get really angry. "How dare you phone me up just to tell me you've given up? I don't want to hear that from you. You want me to feel guilty about you too?"

"God no, Fiona, you can't think that. I'm sorry, I just wanted to say…"

"Yes, yes, you've already told me. You want to say goodbye. Well tough shit. I won't accept that. You're not even trying any more. But maybe I can. I'm not going to let you just die, even if you don't care enough to help yourself."

She heard his voice lift. "You'd help? After everything?"

"To be honest, part of me just wants to put the phone down. But I can't. So this inscription. What does it say? Did you write it down?"

"No. But I can do. I've got something I can use as a notebook, a Sudoku puzzle book in the car."

"So, go and do it."

His voice faltered. "Before I go, did you read the note I left you?"

"Yes I did."

"I know it probably sounded stupid to you, we don't know each other that well, or anything. But you've been the best thing to happen to me in an age."

She felt a lump in her throat. "Thanks, Dan. It was a bit of a surprise. But I'm just trying to help you. It doesn't mean anything else."

"I meant it. When I said I loved you."

Her heart skipped a beat. "Look just go and get that inscription and call me back. We can talk about this later, if we get through the day." She put the phone down.

Act 14: Scene Four

"This thing of darkness I acknowledge mine."

The Tempest

Fiona scanned the Latin she had written down.

Francisvs bacon

Baron verulam

Sev notioribvs titvisscientiarvm lvmen facvndiae lexsic sedebat
qui postquam omnia naturalis sapientiaeet civilis arcana
evolvisset naturae decretum explevit composita soluantur an dni
mdcxxviaetat lxvi

"That's it, nothing else, Dan?"

"That's it, Fiona."

Fiona was finding it hard to concentrate with him on the phone again. Why couldn't she just hate him? He said he loved her. She made herself focus.

"What do you think?" said Dan. "Does it mean anything to you? Is there a cipher in it?"

Fiona realised there must be a cipher in the inscription that pointed to the manuscripts being buried with Bacon's body in its original resting place in the vault at the back of the church. Her father must have worked it out, which is why he left the word 'Verulam' in the safe. But that was of no use now. The body and the manuscripts hadn't been in the vault for hundreds of years.

"Yes, Dan, I'm sure there's a cipher, but it would probably only point to where the manuscripts were originally buried, not where they are now."

"So what are we looking for then?"

"Give me a chance to think will you? One thing I can do easily enough is translate it into English. That could help. Hold on." She grabbed the pencil again and started working through the Latin.

After a few minutes she looked back at the results.

Francis Bacon, Baron Verulam, also known by the more remarkable titles: Lord of Science and Light and Master of Eloquence in Law, Sat thus. Who after he had revealed all the knowledge of nature and secrets of civil life, fulfilled nature's final law. Let everything dissolve. In the year of our Lord 1626, aged 66

She read the translation out to Dan.

"Does that mean anything to you?"

"No."

Fiona circled the words *Let everything dissolve* with her pen.

"What's going on Fiona? Say something will you?"

"Shhh. I'm thinking." Why did that line jump out at her? She couldn't work it out.

She looked back at the Latin line *Let everything dissolve* translated from.

composita soluantur

Was it significant? She looked at it hard, utterly absorbed. Then she clicked her fingers. It contained an anagram of 'manuscripts' in a perfect pattern.

composita soluantur

She could hear Dan's breathing on the phone as he put another coin in the phone box. "Fiona I don't have much money left. You've gone all silent like when I met you at Westminster Abbey."

Then it hit her. Of course. Westminster Abbey.

"Dan, do you have any idea what year Bacon's body was moved?"

Dan heard the excitement in her voice. "The vicar said it was 1740."

"Dan, Shakespeare's monument in Westminster Abbey was built in 1740 through to 1741."

"So?"

"Dan, the key line on Bacon's monument translates as 'Let everything dissolve.'" She felt incredible, it was suddenly making sense. The roses down Shakespeare's legs, the pictures of Bacon carved into the monument... and that huge secret revealed in Bacon's Secrets...

"And?"

"Don't you see it? The cipher key we used to find the name Francis Bacon at the Shakespeare monument back at Westminster Abbey was 'shall dissolve'. The key line in Bacon's monument where you are is: 'Let everything dissolve'. It's a bilateral cipher. It's linking the two together."

"You mean Bacon's monument here and the Shakespeare monument in Westminster Abbey are connected?"

"Yes. Dan, Sir Francis Bacon's body was moved out of his grave in the same year as the Shakespeare monument was built in Westminster Abbey."

Dan was beginning to see. "And the Westminster Abbey monument was built by Rosicrucians."

"More than that, it was commissioned and designed by Sir Christopher Wren along with another senior Rosicrucian Alexander Pope."

"So what are you saying?"

"Wren secretly buried Bacon's body and the manuscripts underneath the Shakespeare monument in Westminster Abbey."

Dan's defeated tone had disappeared. "He chose the quote from *The Tempest* for Shakespeare's monument at Westminster Abbey on purpose."

"Yes, it was a signpost, a clue pointing out where Bacon's body and the manuscripts had been taken from, and where they were secretly reburied. Dan, you remember when we first solved the cipher at Westminster Abbey and it revealed the name Francis Bacon, we didn't know what it meant?"

"No, we didn't have a clue. But your pop told us it revealed the name of the true author of Shakespeare's plays."

"He was wrong. What the cipher was actually doing was showing where Bacon's body and the manuscripts are buried."

"Fiona you're amazing! I've got to get to Westminster Abbey!"

"Wait Dan, There's more, I found something else out, reading Bacon's Secrets, I…"

The door to the sitting room creaked open and Nicky poked her head round the corner. She looked scared and worried.

"Fiona."

"What is it? I really can't talk now."

"Fiona, you've got to get off the phone. Now."

"I can't, I'm talking to Dan."

"Please! Put it down now."

Fiona realised she was serious. "Dan, wait there." Fiona put her mobile down, keeping the connection live with Dan. "What is it Nicks?"

"We've got unexpected visitors. It's the …"

But Nicky didn't get time to finish the sentence. Inspector Sawyer impatiently pushed her out of the way and strode into the room, his eyes blazing with anger. "Fiona Fletcher," he said, "I want a word with you."

Act 14: Scene Five

"Give thy thoughts no tongue."

Hamlet

Dan heard the policeman's arrival and slammed the phone down, left the phone box and sprinted back to Luther's black BMW and fired it up. He looked at the clock. 7.14 pm. He had five hours left.

He kept to the legal speed limits as he negotiated the ring road around St Albans. The traffic was mercifully free flowing and he was soon on the M25 motorway and heading south towards London. Signposts for the centre of London began to appear and he left the motorway, his heart racing. With every mile he drove closer to the heart of the city, the more sluggish the traffic became. Time was flying by. Dan turned on the radio and tuned into a local station hoping for local traffic news. He didn't have long to wait.

"It looks like being a record turnout in central London this evening for the New Year's Eve festivities." The presenter's voice was excited, clearly reporting directly from the streets of London. "Hundreds of thousands of people are expected to congregate in Trafalgar Square and along the river to watch the fireworks display on the London Eye; it's going to be an explosive and exciting night. The Metropolitan and Transport police are advising everyone to allow plenty of time to get in and out of town. The Tube will be running until 5 am but the huge crowds along the river will make the journey a challenge, even for you seasoned commuters. The show itself is going to be live on BBC TV and this year's special music soundtrack composed by Sir Paul McCartney and Duffy will be broadcast on BBC Radio Two. Now, over to the weather centre where it looks like the rain's going to hold off, Trish?"

Dan turned the radio off and pulled over to the side of the road. Luckily there was a London Tube map at the back of the road atlas. He knew driving all the way in was a waste of time. The subway was his best bet. He peered up through the dark and saw some signs to a London district called Queensbury; he traced the map and found its tube station. It was on the Jubilee line, and would take him to Westminster. It was perfect.

It took Dan thirty minutes to drive into Queensbury and find somewhere to dump the car. He didn't care about a parking space, and ended up just shoving it in a bus stop. He jumped out of the BMW, still wearing the balaclava rolled up as a hat. He grabbed the long overcoat from the back seat, and slipped it on. He dropped the pistol into the coat pocket and ran towards the High Street, where he could see the red sign for the Tube station beckoning him with a stained red glow.

Dan walked into the station and paused for a moment to locate the ticket machine. He stepped up to the machine, punched up a single adult fare to Westminster and slid in his credit card. There was a delay before the card was spat back out. It was rejected. He realised the police must have frozen his bank account. He checked his pockets, there was a bit of change, but not enough for an adult ticket. He only had one option, to buy a child's ticket.

The Tube was busy. Sixty or so revellers milled around, injecting life and energy into the normally faded and soulless platform. Dan threaded through the groups and made his way to the end, up near the soot stained tunnel the trains came rumbling out of. He stared down at his shoes and prayed the coat and balaclava made him look inconspicuous. He started to worry. Had the police traced his credit card? Were they on their way right now? After an interminably long wait a train wheezed into view. The doors grunted open and he stepped on board.

The tattered carriage was bursting at the seams. Everyone was laughing and smiling. Random snatches of song drifted through the busy chatter. Dan felt it was ironic that people were actually looking at each other and talking, the exact opposite of how they would normally be in rush hour on this same train.

Luck was with him. A young guy rose to get off the train as Dan entered. It left a seat that he managed to slide into. He turned away from his neighbour, looking out of the window, gazing at the cables and crumbling stained brickwork of the tunnel.

The journey seemed to take forever. At every stop the doors sputtered open and wildly drunken revellers poured onto the carriages. More and more people squeezed into every space. Dan felt himself shrinking into his seat. He prayed he looked invisible.

After well over an hour he arrived at Westminster. The Tube doors opened, disgorging their contents into the steel and glass station. The mass of people headed to the towering steel escalators that slid them to the surface. Dan merged into the crowd, carried along by the crushing exodus. At last he reached the ticket turnstiles at the exit. Too many people were trying to get through too few gates. Finally it was his turn. He pushed his ticket into the machine. It beeped and a red light signalled a child's fare. He heard a voice behind him comment on him being a 'miserable tightfisted sod,' but Dan kept his head down and stayed with the noisy laughing crowd as it flowed out onto the street. A couple of policemen were outside on the street at the entrance to the Tube, but they just seemed interested in whether the crowds were getting out of the station safely.

The London night was alive with lights and noise. There was already a vast crowd building up on the Victoria Embankment, the road running alongside the River Thames opposite to the London Eye. Dan began to walk towards Big Ben, away from the London Eye. He was going against the flow. Everyone seemed to be heading to the river to be closer to the fireworks. It was a journey that would normally take five minutes, now he felt like he was wading through treacle. But once he passed Westminster Bridge the crowds began to thin and by the time he reached Parliament Square, it was far quieter.

Dan walked quickly through the Square until he was in front of Westminster Abbey. The huge doors were firmly shut. It had not occurred to him that the Abbey would be closed and he stood looking up at them hopelessly as he tried to figure out just how he was going to get into the building. If Dan's brief visit to the Abbey before had taught him anything, it was that the building was very large. There must be any number of doors and windows.

He remembered his meeting in the café and an idea formed. He glanced around to check he wasn't being watched and then clambered over the low wall dividing the pavement and the front section of the Abbey. The main lighting was fixed about twenty feet up on soaring pillars. They extended away from the upper main walls like stone ribs. Much of the ground level of the Abbey was unlit. Dan crouched down and ran through the pools of darkness, using them to make his way towards the back of the building.

At the rear of the building Dan found himself in front of a familiar circular wall with tall stained windows. It was the back of the cafeteria where he had sat down with Fiona and solved the first cipher. He was betting there was an entrance for catering supplies and staff. He located a small grey anonymous door but his heart sank when he saw a security camera perched above it. He shrank back against the wall and prayed it had not spotted him.

"You lied to me."

The voice came out of nowhere. Dan span round, one hand fumbling in his coat pocket for Luther's pistol.

Act 14: Scene Six

*"Friends, Romans, countrymen, lend me
your ears."*

Julius Caeser

S tanding in front of Dan, dressed in full combat gear, was Major Barnes-Jones. "Put your hand on the back of your neck," he said. Puzzled, Dan did as he was told. "Now using your fingers, push under the skin." Dan moved his fingers around. "Can you feel anything on the right-hand side of your spine?"

"I'm not sure. A tiny bump?"

"It's a micro receiver. It sends out a strong radio signal. You came back on my radar after you were in the car chase and our friend Inspector Sawyer started spitting your picture out to the police. I had the receiver implanted when you were comatose in hospital."

"You've been tracking me since then?"

"What do you expect? You're a wanted man. First of all, we thought you were nothing, but then all our other leads dried up. And here you are, in the very heart of it."

Dan dropped his hands back to his side and looked at the Major. "So, what next?"

"You lied to me. You told me when the Rosicrucians kidnapped you it was all a big mistake. You lied to me. That's unforgivable. You've put the Queen's life at risk, when you could have been honest with me and we could have resolved this a long time ago. She only has hours to live. The only way out is to tell me the truth. Starting now."

"I'm sorry Major, but I can't tell you. It risks both my life and the Queen's."

The Major drew his pistol. "If you're not prepared to work with me now, even at this crucial stage, then you leave me with no choice. I'm placing you under military arrest."

Dan made a snap decision. "Okay, okay, take it easy. I did lie to you before. But you can't arrest me. I know how to save the Queen."

For a second the Major looked totally stunned. Then the emotion disappeared. "Dan, this could have been so much easier if you'd confided in me from the start. But I'm assuming you had your reasons."

"Yes, you better believe it. It's the Rosicrucians. They made me do this. We can still fix everything, but you've got to promise me you'll stay out of their way when they contact me. If they know you're involved, it's all over."

The Major stared intently at Dan then lowered the gun slightly. "You have to trust me, just as you're expecting me to trust you. This is the second time I've gone against protocol. There will be no further leeway. Now tell me, what's going on?"

"Under one of the monuments inside the Abbey, something's hidden that will save the Queen's life. But I've got to get it before midnight."

"So you know what they want? And if we can get inside Westminster Abbey and find this object, there's a chance of saving the Queen?"

"Yes."

"Before midnight." The Major checked his watch. "Dan, it's nearly twenty two hundred hours. That gives us two hours. This isn't going to be easy. I assume you've seen the security camera. Also, the door is alarmed."

"Yes, I've kept out of the way of the camera."

The Major smiled. "I'm tempted to ask you exactly how you thought you could possibly get in and do what you want to without help from someone like me. But I think we both know the answer. Right, wait here. I shall be as quick as is humanly possible, but I need to return to HQ for equipment."

Then he was gone into the darkness.

Dan sat propped up against the wall, out of sight of the security camera and waited for the Major to return. Big Ben chimed 10.30 pm, the sound echoing through Parliament Square. The minutes dragged interminably by; all Dan could hear was the distant noise of the huge crowd, occasional bursts of music and the muffled sounds of taxis and buses on the road the other side of the great Abbey. It was another twenty minutes before the Major appeared again, weighed down by a large black rucksack.

"Right, first step is to get inside." The Major swung the rucksack off his back, undid the top and pulled out a device that looked like a small black pistol with a silver blade projecting out of the front.

"What's that? A miniature harpoon gun?"

"You're not a million miles away. You know what a TASER gun is? It fires darts into people and gives them

50,000 volts of low level direct current electricity. The police use it to incapacitate people. This little baby does something similar except it's about fifty times as powerful and sends an alternating current into a device and back down its power cable. We're going to use it to short circuit the camera."

"But won't that draw attention to us?"

"Unlikely. The security system here at Westminster Abbey was installed twenty years ago. This won't be the first time it's malfunctioned. The local network comprises over forty cameras on the Abbey, all hardwired and monitored by three guards inside the building. That's a lot of hardware wired up to some very old power circuits. There are plenty of ways it can go wrong without raising too many suspicions."

"How do you know all that?"

The Major let out short laugh. "The coronation of virtually every English and British monarch since 1066 has been held in Westminster Abbey, never mind all the burials. We're holding Prince William's funeral in less than two weeks. It's absolutely my business to know the security of this building. With these cameras there's only short circuit and overload protection up to the standard supply level. When we fry this one, it'll go back down the line and they'll need to reboot the system. That will, knowing the quality of the staff employed here on a public holiday, take them at least fifteen minutes. That easily gives me time to get us into the building and take care of the guards."

Dan hadn't been following everything the Major said. He could hear the giant bells of Big Ben tolling the hour. A huge cheer came from the direction of the river.

"What was that about?" he asked.

"It's an hour to go until midnight. They'll be cheering the big countdown clock. It's a huge projection of the face of Big Ben onto the Shell building next to the London Eye."

"Why can't you just phone somebody up and get them to let us in? I'm running out of time."

"Certainly, if you care to wait a couple of months for permission from the Dean of Westminster after he's come back from his skiing holiday in Switzerland. I'm still waiting for him to get back to me on another urgent matter from over a month ago. What do you suggest I tell him anyway? 'Let us in right now so I can damage your property otherwise the Queen's going to be killed?' They all think she's in bed with a cold. This is the only choice. It's going to be messy in more ways than one, but I'll tidy it up afterwards. Now, why don't you just let me get on with it?"

The Major lifted up the gun, took aim and fired it at the camera. The silver dart flew up into the air, trailing a gossamer thin filament wire. It struck the outer casing of the camera and stayed in place. The Major looked at Dan, smiled and pushed a button on the gun. There was a barely audible high-pitched buzz that lasted no more than five seconds.

"Are you sure it's worked?"

The Major ignored Dan and yanked hard on the gun. The dart came free and fell at the Major's feet. He pushed a button and the wire scrolled back inside the pistol. The Major dropped the gun on the floor and turned his attention to the door, kneeling down to look closely at the lock. He stood up, leant over the rucksack, pulling out a device that looked like a miniature flat screen TV. Dan moved forward to stand next to the soldier as he placed the screen against the door beneath the handle. The screen flickered into life, revealing an x-ray image of the lock.

"That's cool. Very James Bond."

"Oh yes, we've got a pretty good toy chest back at the office." The Major swept the device around the door. "You'd be amazed at how backwards the Establishment is when it comes to security. You wouldn't believe how many intruders we get at Buckingham Palace. The ones that make it into the papers are just the tip of the iceberg. I've been trying to get a budget for wireless motion sensors and ground based pressure plates in the Palace for over two years. It always takes a disaster before they sit up and take notice." He grunted in satisfaction. "Excellent, the alarm is connected to the same power relay system as the camera, so this alarm won't be active while they reboot the servers."

"What does that mean, Major?"

The Major stepped back, lifted a leg and kicked the door hard. There was a sharp crack, the lock splintered and the Major pushed the door open.

"That's what it means."

Dan was about to walk through the open door but the Major put a hand on his chest.

"Not yet. There are two guards who will be busy with the server and one on foot patrol inside. He may have heard the noise. I need to secure the situation."

With this the Major slipped through the door into the Abbey. Once again Dan found himself standing alone, wondering how exactly the Major was going to 'secure the situation'. He decided not to ask.

Another fifteen minutes went by before the Major returned. "Okay, Dan, what's our destination?"

"Shakespeare's monument in Poet's Corner. There's something buried underneath it."

"What's buried there? Come on man, I need to know everything now."

Dan paused. "William Shakespeare didn't write any plays or sonnets. They were all written by Sir Francis Bacon."

"The Rosicrucian founder?"

"Yes. The Shakespeare monument was paid for and built by senior Rosicrucians. They buried all the original manuscripts for the plays along with Sir Francis Bacon's body, right here under this monument. That's what the Rosicrucians are after."

"That's extraordinary. And you're sure about this?"

"Yes."

"That's good enough for me. Let's go. You can carry the rucksack."

Dan heaved the pack onto his back, feeling the massive weight bite into his shoulders. What on earth was in it? He looked around him as they walked into and through the empty Abbey. The marble statues loomed out of the dark. Fractured beams of light seeped through the windows from the lights flooding the outside walls. The Abbey felt even more cavernous at night. All Dan could hear was his own breath and footsteps on the stone floor. The Major walked silently, like a ghost. They soon reached Shakespeare's monument. The marble figure stared blindly out, the white stone ethereal in the low light.

"Okay, leave this to me. Put the rucksack down here. We won't need it much more after this." Dan obediently put the rucksack down and the Major opened it up. Inside Dan could see large pale coloured packs of what looked like clay.

"Are those plastic explosives? You're planning to blow it up?"

"That's the idea. Unless you've got a better way to crack open the base of huge stone monuments?"

Dan shook his head. In the distance he heard Big Ben striking. "Half an hour left."

"This is going to take a little while. We've got to be careful. If there's something under there, the explosives need to be positioned in such a way that when we destroy the wrapping, we don't damage the gift. Here," the Major produced a telescopic shovel and threw it to Dan. "Open that up. You might need it in a minute."

Dan stepped back and watched the Major. He was moulding the explosives into the monument, placing them on the base and the surrounding stone flooring. Fuses were gently slid into each lump of explosive and after a few minutes the Major stood up.

"We need to take cover."

The two of them ran back into the main body of the Abbey and crouched down behind a huge pillar.

"Want to do the honours?" The Major handed Dan a small black remote control with a single switch on it covered with a safety cover. Dan flipped the safety cover up. Big Ben tolled out quarter to the hour.

"Wait. Belay that order."

"What is it?"

"We're going to have to wait until midnight."

"Why?" Dan's heart jumped. What now?

"The fireworks on the river will provide the perfect cover. If we fire the Semtex now we could have the police in here in minutes. We need to wait."

"Okay, alright, damn it I can see the logic of that. But what about the Rosicrucians?"

"Don't worry about them. Just stick with the plan. I'll keep an eye out." The Major tapped his pistol.

Dan slumped against the stone pillar and looked at his watch. He had no choice. Finally, in the background a huge chant began to swell from the enormous crowd outside.

"We're into the final minute," said the Major.

Dan felt his heart beat rising as the countdown reached ten, then five, then zero.

Enormous crashes and booms rolled through the empty Abbey. Glittering fireworks raced into the sky and detonated in a celestial shower of colour and noise above the wildly cheering crowds. Bursts of red, blue and green light flashed through the Abbey's highest windows.

"What are you waiting for, Dan?"

Dan looked at the remote control, flipped open the protective cover and pushed the button.

A titanic sonic wave ripped through the Abbey. Even though he was crouched behind a pillar, Dan could feel a hurricane of hot air swirl past him. The explosion ripped and echoed around him. Dust and smoke followed the sound. At last the noise subsided and Dan and the Major stepped out.

Shakespeare's monument was gone. The huge arch the statue had been set in lay split into three jagged chunks. Legs, arms and pieces of the statue lay scattered around. Other monuments in the vicinity showed signs of damage, hit by shrapnel from the blast.

"Come on," said the Major, "let's see what's there."

They ran over. Broken bits of rubble and split stones lay randomly on the marble floor. Dan stared at a chunk of stone, and realised he was staring at the statue's decapitated head. Cracks in the stone floor zigzagged out from the centre of the blast area. In the middle, where the monument had been, a large patch of earth was revealed. It looked like a grave.

"This isn't natural earth. Somebody's filled this in," said the Major. "The foundations of the Abbey are far deeper. Get the shovel."

Dan ran back to the pillar and grabbed the shovel. He walked up to the edge of the pit and took Luther's coat off, throwing it to one side. He started digging feverishly at the earth. It was hard work, the earth had been there for hundreds of years and was solidly set.

After about ten minutes the Major stepped in and grabbed the shovel off Dan. He started digging purposefully and efficiently. Gasping for breath and sweating from the effort, Dan climbed out from the deepening hole and sat down on a large chunk of the broken monument. Outside, the explosions and screams of excitement continued. Eerie coloured flashes lit the Major as he dug.

They kept swapping over, kept on hacking at the dry soil. Slowly the hole deepened, the Major doing the lion's share of the work. Eventually, the Major stopped digging and looked coldly up at Dan. "This hole must be over three feet deep now. We've been at it over half an hour. There's nothing here." He clambered out and sat down next to Dan on the broken arch. "Nothing but dead earth."

"There has to be something." Dan snatched the shovel off the Major and jumped back in the hole and started digging again.

"Give it up Dan. You made a mistake. You look like you're digging your own grave down there." The Major's voice was flat and monotone.

Dan could feel tears of anger and frustration rolling down his cheeks as he chopped the shovel blindly and savagely into the earth. He had never felt so desperate and afraid in his life. He could feel his will to keep fighting draining away with every futile blow.

Then the shovel hit something. His heart jumped as he bent down and tried to grab it but it was just a rock.

"That's the end Dan. You're starting to hit the foundations now. It's over. Come on back up."

The Major was right. It was finally over. After everything he had been through, it was all for nothing. Fiona's mother had died for nothing, and now he was going to die too. In rage and frustration Dan slammed the shovel into the earth with all his strength.

There was a metallic clang.

Dan got down on his knees again and frantically started scrabbling away at the earth with his hands. The Major was standing above the hole, staring down at him impassively.

"Major! Get down here!"

The Major's expression changed and he jumped down and started clearing the earth away with Dan. The two of them quickly revealed the shape of a large chest. It was about four foot long and two feet wide. The two of them dragged it out of the earth and heaved it up onto Abbey floor. The chest was ancient, made of a mix of iron and what Dan guessed was oak. Carved on its wooden top was the Rosicrucian's symbol, a rose inside a cross. It was secured with a padlock.

"Stand back." The Major pulled out the pistol and expertly shot the lock away, the sound of the gun like a sharp echo to the crash of the fireworks. The Major stepped forward and opened the chest. They both looked inside. On the top was a velvet sack covered in ornately stitched red roses. The Major leaned in and gingerly lifted it out of the chest. He pulled loose the knot tying the sack's neck. Once it was opened he put one hand inside.

"My God." He said in an awed voice. He slowly removed the contents of the bag and turned to show Dan the remains of a crumbling skull. "Dan, meet Sir Francis Bacon. Baron Verulam himself."

The Major placed the skull back into the sack and gingerly placed it on the ground. It had been covering the chest's much heavier and bulkier contents. Dan could hardly believe what he was seeing. Pile upon pile of immaculately bound hand written documents. He pulled the first one out.

"This is it," he breathed. "We really found it." Although the writing on the binding was ancient and grandiose, there was no mistaking what it said:

The Most Excellent and Lamentable Tragedie of Romeo and Juliet

By Sir Francis Bacon

He looked in astonishment at another one:

The Tragicall Historie of Hamlet, Prince of Denmarke.

By Sir Francis Bacon,

Dan turned to the Major. "Look. Hamlet, Romeo and Juliet, the original manuscripts. We've found them. This is what the Rosicrucians want. We can save the Queen."

But the Major wasn't listening. He was unpacking the chest, still searching for something.

"Major? What's wrong?"

Act 14: Scene Seven

*"There is a tide in the affairs of men which,
taken at the flood, leads on to fortune;
omitted, all the voyage of their life is bound
in shallows and in miseries."*

Julius Caeser

The Major pulled out the manuscripts one by one, throwing each carelessly onto the floor. His blue eyes shone with anger. Then he stopped. A look of triumph flashed onto his face as he glanced at Dan. As he stood up Dan saw he was holding a rolled up parchment. It was secured with a wax seal.

"At last. Shakespeare's Truth."

Dan stared at the Major. "How do you know about Shakespeare's Truth? I didn't tell you that."

The two men locked eyes. Dan was the first to move, diving for the coat and reaching inside for Luther's pistol. But the Major was too fast. Even as Dan pulled the gun out, the Major stepped towards him and swung his leg across in an expert kick. It knocked the gun out of Dan's hand and sent it spinning through the air and skidding into the hole the chest had been buried in. The Major pulled his own pistol and trained it on Dan.

"You're behind all this aren't you? You're the Rosicrucian leader. You're Damascus." Dan kept his eyes on the Major's gun and took a pace backwards. "What is that?" Dan pointed at the parchment in the Major's other hand. "I thought Shakespeare's Truth was the manuscripts. I thought you wanted to sell them."

"Don't be naïve Dan. We don't need the money. The manuscripts aren't Shakespeare's Truth. This is Shakespeare's Truth."

The Major slipped the gun back into its holster, clearly believing Dan was no threat. He snapped the wax seal on the parchment and the ancient paper slowly unrolled. Dan could see dense handwritten text and at the bottom two signatures, one of them florid and eloquent, somehow familiar.

"This is justification. The beacon we can hold aloft to prove our cause is just and true. It is proof of the royal blood in Sir Francis Bacon's veins, proof of his birthright. Of course the manuscripts are a majestic discovery, and you are to be applauded. But Shakespeare's Truth is more. It is proof that Sir Francis Bacon was denied the greatest treasure of all. The English throne."

"But, that's impossible. Queen Elizabeth was on the throne around the time Bacon was born. She was famous for being the Virgin Queen. She didn't have any children. They've made two movies about her."

"You're wrong, Dan. Queen Elizabeth had a child in secret. That child was Francis Bacon. He was born just a short while before she became Queen. Go to Hampton Court Palace, there is a painting there of her clearly pregnant. This document is Shakespeare's Truth. It is the birth certificate signed in secret by the father Lord Robert Dudley, and by Elizabeth herself."

"Sir Francis Bacon was Queen Elizabeth's son?" Dan's mind span.

The Major placed the parchment reverently on the

ground on top of the sack containing Bacon's bones. He stepped towards Dan and grabbed him by the shoulders and stared fiercely into his eyes.

"Don't you see? Sir Francis Bacon's real name is His Royal Highness Francis Tudor. He lived his whole life with his true destiny stolen from him. He was born out of wedlock, given up for adoption to Lord Nicholas Bacon and his academic wife. Elizabeth could never admit in public who he was, but Francis knew. He realised his destiny. If his mother had admitted his existence, he would have become King of England."

"But what's that got to do with the Royal Family today? Why attack them now?"

"Elizabeth was the last great English Queen. She was the end of the Tudor line, the last pure English family to hold the throne. The current family that pretend to rule are the biggest charlatans of them all. Never mind not being English, they're not even British. They're German."

"So what? You can't bring Bacon back to life."

"Of course not. We can't bring him back, but we can bring his bloodline back. We can reclaim the throne for the Tudors. We can use this as proof of Bacon's heritage. We can restore England to the English."

"But what will that achieve?"

"Restoring the true bloodline is only the tip of the iceberg. Bacon was so much more than just a denied king and secret playwright. He was the greatest strategic mind in history. He created a great vision, a blueprint for how to run the perfect society. The Rosicrucian brotherhood was reborn under my control to make Bacon's vision a reality. To reshape England into the greatest country in the world."

"So, you're what… " Dan was trying to take it in. "You're planning some sort of social revolution? By murdering the heir to the throne and kidnapping the Queen? That's just…"

"Every great change in the world has needed a spark to set it in motion - the Russian Revolution, the Third Reich, the American Revolution, the end of Apartheid, the fall of the Berlin Wall. They have all come from a time of economic recession, of negative thought, of people losing their jobs and being unhappy, exactly like today. At times of crisis there have always been acts of courage and violence that woke the people, pulled them out of their slumber. Made them realise great change was possible. With every single revolution in history, the first few blows seemed madness, but once the fever of change swept over the people, a momentum was created that reshaped history."

"You mean the idea of order from chaos?"

"Exactly. When we destroy the rest of the Royal Family and replace them with true English blood the seed will be planted. The people will rise up and support us. The silent majority, the middle classes who have lost their jobs thanks to greedy bankers in this idiotic credit crunch; the working class who are taxed and bullied, crushed and humiliated by a system designed to break their souls and drive them to a grey unfulfilled and anonymous death in the rain. They will unchain themselves, join the revolution and rediscover the Spirit of England."

Dan pushed the Major away from him in disgust.

"You killed Prince William. You admit it."

"Yes I did it. I killed him myself. It was easy. I cut him with my knife, I watched him die. I marked him with the message that would set you on the path to your destiny, Dan. Then I left him to die alone. It was pathetically simple. All I had to do was replace his driver and two of his security team over time with my own men. Then after another of their gluttonous parasitical free nights on the town, when the rich privileged youth play at the working man's expense, I simply spirited William away to his doom with no-one the wiser. It was a sacrifice that needed to be made." He smiled grimly. "A shame really. I quite liked the lad."

"And the Queen? You kidnapped and tortured the Queen of England. Why do that? Your men tortured her on the phone. I heard them!" The two men began to circle each other, Dan trying to keep out of the Major's reach, only too aware he would stand no chance in a fair fight.

"That was all just play-acting to spur you on. I won't say she's been entirely comfortable but I wouldn't risk hurting her before tonight. She's an old woman. I wouldn't be surprised if she died before the London Olympics anyway."

"You're mad."

"Can't you see where this is leading, Dan? Haven't you worked it out yet? You're standing at the edge of fulfilling your destiny. You solved challenges none of us could."

"You keep talking about my destiny, but all that

happens is people around me die. And for what? Your twisted ideas? Your mad idea of some bloody way to pull England out of a recession?"

"Your destiny is calling you. What's the big question remaining in your mind? The one thing left in all of this merry dance you don't know the answer to?"

Dan paused. "Why you picked me in the first place."

"Exactly. Why you. The answer is in your blood. What do you know about your family?"

"I was born in America, my parents are American and my grandparents too, before that, they came from Europe, my great grandparents were English." He stopped. The Major smiled.

"You understand now don't you? I'll save you four hundred more years of family history. I've researched all that for you. You're Sir Francis Bacon's only true direct descendant. Do you know what that means? It means the blood in your veins is that of royalty, you're the true heir to the English throne. Why do you think we chose you? Why do you think I spent fifteen years of my life planning this and hunting you down? I was amazed when you came to England of your own free will. It was divine proof that I was on the right course. Then the economy started to go to wrack and ruin. The omens were perfect."

"I came here for work. That was just a fluke."

"No, it was the universe bringing you to me. Your destiny is to be with me, to take your place as our spiritual leader. Killing Prince William was just the first step, there's so much more to come." The coloured lights of the fireworks reflected on the Major's face as the huge barrage of explosions continued outside. "I know it's hard to accept, but it's true. You have more right to the throne than the people who sit there now. Let me tell you about them. The Royal Family we have, their real name is not Windsor, it's Saxe-Coburg-Gotha. Queen Victoria was a German princess who took the English throne and married her cousin, another German, Alfred. In any other family, people would gossip and call it incest. Queen Elizabeth who is on the throne now married a cousin too. She made sure it was another German Prince. The Queen and the Duke of Edinburgh are related by birth as well as marriage and neither is English. That means all the rest of them, the whole Windsor family, Charles, Andrew, Edward, none of them are English. They're inbred Germans. They made up the name Windsor. It's not a real name. It's another lie. They changed their name at the end of the First World War when Germany was at war with England. They were scared of being kicked out by the English so they brushed their German ancestry under the carpet. And in World War Two, it didn't even stop then, Edward VIII, you know the one who left the Royal Family to marry your American woman, Mrs Simpson?" Dan nodded. "He was accused of supporting Hitler. He was thrown out because of it. He was stupid enough to show his German heritage at the wrong moment. Churchill tried to save him, in meetings at Whitehall Court, but to no avail."

"But that's no excuse for murder."

"Ah yes, William. He had to go. An English mother. And popular. A sacrifice."

"But Harry will just take his place. People like him too."

The Major laughed again. "Of course. But he isn't Charles's son is he? Just compare him to James Hewitt, one of Princess Diana's old boyfriends. He's the spitting image of him. Without William, the Windsor family is already dead. William was the only real obstacle. This isn't a pipedream Dan, there are plenty of us, powerful people with money and influence and we want to restore the throne to Tudor blood. To you. Do you think I could have done this on my own? This operation has required vast resources, weaponry, property, technology, people in high places turning a blind eye. People who will welcome you with open arms. People who can make your destiny a reality. People who have faith in you."

"You planned all this."

"Of course, every step of the way."

"Did you know that Bacon wrote Shakespeare's plays before this started?"

"No. Dan, the fact that you discovered that is for me one of the greatest signs that you are of royal blood, that Bacon's genius flows in your veins."

"I didn't work that out on my own. I had help. You must know that."

"Yes."

"But the quote cut into the Prince's chest. The thing that started all this. Where did that come from?"

"The legend that Bacon was of royal birth had long been prevalent in the *fra rosi crosse* brotherhood. We always believed one day, Bacon's prophecy of the *New*

Atlantis would become a reality, and the catalyst would be the installation of Bacon's bloodline as King. But we had no proof that Bacon's mother was Elizabeth Tudor. It wasn't until a hundred years after Bacon's death that Sir Christopher Wren, a senior Rosicrucian, told the brotherhood that proof existed. But Wren was a clever man. He made the discovery of that truth difficult, to make sure only the most dedicated Rosicrucian could discover it, someone worthy of instigating the revolution. He left a clue, something that until now has never been solved even by the greatest Rosicrucian scholars."

"And the clue Wren left," Dan was thinking it through, "was the quote you cut onto the Prince's chest? Those two words. *Shall dissolve*."

"Yes. Placing you in that video and using the quote was for you. My plan was to shock you into action, to force you to wake up and see your destiny. Kidnapping you was the second step."

"But you threatened to kill me!"

"That was no idle threat, Dan. If you had failed you would have been killed. But facing the knowledge you could die ripped away the soft weakling you were. Look at yourself, look at how much stronger you are. You've stared death in the face and it's turned you into a man. Through your own efforts, every piece of the picture has been slowly revealed and now you stand at the apex of your own brilliance."

"But you killed two Rosicrucians when you rescued me. Your own men!"

"They were willing martyrs to help gain your trust. I allowed them to escape with the Queen. I didn't put that tracer in you at the hospital. We put it in when we kidnapped you. Every step you have taken has been monitored. When you needed help, we supplied it."

"What do you mean?"

"Professor Elwood Fletcher. As the world's foremost expert on Bacon and the Rosicrucians, we prepared him for you years ago. His madness made him malleable. We brought you to him via his daughter."

Dan was stunned. "When he was talking about hearing voices, he really had been?"

"Yes, but we hadn't realised how useful his daughter would be."

"You've been manipulating Fiona as well?" Dan was furious.

A shrill beeping sound cut through the air. The Major unclipped a cellphone from his belt. He flipped it open and spoke into it.

"Yes, now is the time." He cut the call off and slipped the phone back into its holster.

"Time for what?"

"It's my men, Dan. With the Queen. This is your final initiation."

"What are you talking about? My initiation?"

"My men will be here in an hour. A King only becomes a King by destroying his rivals. To take your place as the spiritual leader of England, a sacrifice is needed. You must kill the Queen."

Act 14: Scene Eight

*"Is this a dagger which I see before me, the
handle toward my hand?"*

Macbeth

D an swung his fist forward as hard and fast as he could. The blow hit the Major on the cheek, sending him spinning backwards. Yet even before Dan had recovered his balance the Major launched a kick at him. Dan met the kick with his arm, parrying the blow. But the kick still landed heavily and Dan gasped as pain shot up his arm. Dan swung another wild fist. This time the Major was ready and stepped back, calmly letting it fly past his face. Dan scrambled backwards trying to get out of the Major's range. Booms and crashes from the fireworks echoed through the Abbey as the Major strode purposefully after him, his clear blue eyes fixed on Dan.

"Accept your destiny, Dan. When they arrive, you must execute her, finish your transformation."

"I won't be the figurehead for your sick games." An idea was forming in Dan's mind. He began backing up, clambering over pews, drawing the Major after him. "Sir Francis Bacon would never have murdered people. You're so consumed with your own screwed up ideas you've lost sight of what he would have wanted. Sure, he was a visionary, but he was a man of peace. He died because he caught a cold trying to work out how to preserve food for God's sake. He wasn't a killer." Dan began circling back around towards the pit the chest had been buried in.

"But he never saw modern England, or what's left of it. England is dying on its feet, The Empire is gone. We're sending ill-equipped innocents to fight in wars designed to help American Presidents get elected, and to secure oil supplies. Our native sons are pushed out of their own homes by so-called asylum seekers looking for handouts. Foreign criminals dominate the streets of every city, politicians only make the news for their thievery, public services are collapsing, an immigrant family is on the throne. The entire economy is ruined by a handful of greedy bankers, belief in the system is at an all-time low, industry is ruined and we have to import our food and electricity. The country is poised for revolt. The English people have had enough. We will stage manage their revolution, and you'll be our figurehead, the icon. Can't you see the glory in that?"

"It's not glorious, it's moronic. You're one act short of a play, buddy." Dan had made his way back to the ruins of the Shakespeare monument. He was standing next to the pit he had dug with the Major. It was now or never. He took a deep breath and rushed screaming at the Major. Dan saw the Major jump and spin, another high kick flashing round aimed at Dan's head. Dan ducked, feeling the Major's boot brush the top of his head. He crashed into the Major, grabbing him round the waist, and attempted to knock him to the ground. But the Major used the momentum to twist them in mid-air. Dan hit the ground heavily on his back. The Major landed on top of him and thrust a knee into Dan's throat, pinioning him. Dan took a swing at the Major from the ground but it was easily parried. The Major pulled out his pistol and stood up, training the gun at Dan's head.

"Dan, you're starting to disappoint me. You have to pass this final test. Don't think I won't kill you, I will. This is your last chance. How many people do you think are given this chance in life? To be part of something that will shake the very foundations of history? Embrace your destiny, join me."

"I'll never be your puppet. You're a clever and dangerous sonovabitch, but you're also a total wacko. I don't know what made you so nuts, but it sure works."

The Major looked down at Dan lying on the ground. "Dan, I really hate to do this. But you leave me no choice. You do realise if you're not with me, if you truly will not accept your destiny, then I can't possibly let you leave here alive."

"You'll have to kill me then."

The Major sighed and raised the gun.

Act 14: Scene Nine

"Fortune brings in some boats that are not steer'd."

Cymbeline

The sharp retort of the gun echoed through the Abbey. The Major span round in surprise as bullets chipped the stone wall above his head.

"You're under arrest!" Sawyer roared. The Major was stunned to hear the Police Inspector's voice coming from the other end of the Abbey. He crouched down and took aim with his pistol. He could just make out Sawyer and five uniformed armed police running towards him in the low light. Behind them were two female figures. Dan saw the gun jerk as the Major fired three shots.

Dan's plan had gone wrong, but now unexpectedly, it had another chance. While the Major was distracted he grabbed a small chunk of masonry from off the ground. One of the police screamed and span to the ground, hit even from this distance by the Major's accurate shots. As the rest of the police ducked for cover, the Major turned back to face Dan.

"You think you've escaped your destiny, Daniel Knight. I told you, if you're not with me, I'll kill you." He raised the pistol and pointed it at Dan. Dan threw the chunk of stone hard at the Major's face. Instinct took over and the soldier threw up his arm to protect himself just as he fired the pistol. Dan felt a sharp tugging sensation in his shoulder. He rolled over on the ground and fell back into the pit they had dug earlier.

Another shot came in from the police. The Major ignored it. He looked down at Dan. "How suitable, this truly shall be the grave for Baron Verulam and his failed bloodline."

More bullets flew in from the police, and the Major growled in anger and turned and shot back at them, loosing off four or five shots, flashes of flame from the barrel lighting up his blue eyes and snarling face.

Dan had gambled everything on this moment; to find a way back into the pit where he had seen Luther's gun fall. He scrabbled in the dirt, and his hand closed around the familiar cold steel. He lifted the gun up and while the Major was shooting back at the police, Dan pulled the trigger. The gun kicked as Dan fired it, once, twice, three times. The Major was knocked back by the force of the bullets. His knees buckled and he dropped to the floor.

Dan lay on his back, staring at the high vaulted ceiling of the Abbey. There was a massive roll of thunder from the fireworks outside on the river and then silence. A smell of cordite drifted in the air, along with smoke from the gun. A final huge cheer erupted from the massed spectators outside on the riverbank. A blazing pain in Dan's shoulder started to grow. He could see blood beginning to spread on his shirt.

Suddenly two faces appeared over the lip of the hole. Dan looked up to see Fiona alongside a face he recognised from the newspapers. It was Inspector Brian Sawyer of Scotland Yard.

"You're alive." Fiona looked close to tears.

"Give me your hand, son." The policeman leaned over and offered an outstretched arm. Dan accepted the help with his uninjured arm and was easily pulled out.

"You've led us a merry dance haven't you, Knight."

"So, I'm not under arrest? I thought if I ever met you it would be on the way to a police cell."

Sawyer laughed. "You've got quite a rap sheet by now; breaking and entering, evading arrest, speeding, reckless driving, quite a lot more. But your young lady here convinced me we're on the same side. So you might get off with a caution."

Dan turned to Fiona and slowly moved towards her. She hesitated, but then she opened her arms and he rushed into them, ignoring the pain in his shoulder.

"Oh God Fiona, I've missed you so much, I'm sorry about your mom, I wish I could have come to you but…"

"I know, I'm sorry Dan. I couldn't help it, I know I lashed out. But you're here. I can't believe it's over and you're safe."

"It's all thanks to you. I'm safe and now you're here, it's more than I ever deserved. You saved my life. How did you do it?"

"Oh Dan, I showed the Inspector Bacon's Secrets, I found more stuff in there. Bacon talked about how he was Queen Elizabeth's son and for me that was it. It all clicked, all those Tudor roses on the monument. It was a sign of his royal blood. I realised there was more to it than just the manuscripts. There had to be a more fundamental connection with the Royal Family. A reason the Rosicrucians killed Prince William. I realised why the Royal Family was so important in all this."

"I know all about that too now. Believe me, I've had a firsthand education on Elizabethan bloodlines and royalty."

"I've got to say it took a bit of convincing, but she's a persuasive girl." Sawyer put a hand on Fiona's shoulder, wry admiration in his eyes. "But after she'd shown me everything you two discovered and she told me you were on your way here I knew I had get down here. And Little Miss Obstinate and her mate here insisted on coming too. Boy did she give me an ear bashing en route. By the time we got here I was ready to give you a bloody medal not arrest you." Sawyer looked down at the Major's dead body. "But finding out Major bloody Barnes-Jones was the culprit after all... well pal, to be quite honest that's a bloody good result for me. My wife would have loved him, but I never liked the sod. He was a right arrogant piece of work. But enough of the mutual admiration society. What about the Queen?"

"Inspector, you can still rescue her. The Rosicrucians are on their way here with her. They're expecting me to execute her." Dan saw Sawyer's face stiffen and laughed. "It's a long story. You've probably got no more than half an hour to get your men ready for them."

Sawyer allowed himself a malicious grin. "Oh yes, we'll be ready. Don't you worry about that. Those bastards are going to taste some British steel."

Dan watched Sawyer as he started gathering his officers around him and issuing orders. Fiona walked over and picked up one of the plays. "Dan, I can't believe you found the manuscripts. Look at them, they're so beautiful. The writing, it's so ornate, so precise."

"Open one up."

"No! I can't. That needs to be done properly, in a controlled environment."

Dan laughed. "Dear Fiona, ever the academic. It's a pity Bacon couldn't be around to see all this. He'd probably have turned it into another play."

"Yes," said Fiona looking at the cover of Hamlet. "What would he have called it? *The Tragical History of Dan, Prince of America?*"

"*A Midwinter's Night Nightmare?*"

Fiona squeezed Dan tightly in a hug. Her heart leapt with joy.

"Dan, there's someone I really want you to meet. This is Nicky. She's been just fantastic to me, a real lifesaver. She wouldn't even let me come down here on my own."

Nicky had been hanging back but now she walked forward smiling.

"Nicky! Wow it's so cool to meet you after all this. You went up to Fiona's place. You've been looking after her?"

"Yes. I've been keeping an eye on her." Nicky ran up to Dan and hugged him. The embrace was tight and Dan felt the young woman's firm body pushing into his. Then she suddenly pulled back away from him, a look of hatred etched onto her face. A sharp knife had appeared in her hand and she slashed at his throat in one ruthless movement. Dan stepped back from her in horror. He put his hand up to his throat, it came away wet with blood.

Nicky turned round and hit Fiona hard across her face, sending her spinning onto the floor, then she turned back to Dan, her voice dripping with venom. "You ruined everything. I played my role, getting close to Fiona, encouraging her to help you, bringing her back to you when you messed it all up. I even encouraged the bitch to make love to you. Damascus spent his life hunting you down and preparing the ground for your ascension. And you thank him by killing him. Now I'll watch you die."

Dan collapsed onto his knees, blood starting to soak his shirt. He was getting weaker by the second. He looked up at Nicky, her deep blue eyes stared back.

"Your eyes. You're the Major's daughter."

Nicky stepped forward with the knife raised, but in a whirl of movement Sawyer appeared from behind her, grabbing her arm and twisting it violently behind her back.

"Yes." Nicky spat in Dan's face as she struggled in the policeman's grip. "The greatest Englishman since Baron Verulam was my father. And you, the one person he cared so much about, the one he put all his faith in, the one who was supposed to be King, you betrayed him. And to think he had promised I was going to be your Queen."

Epilogue

*"In order for the light to shine so brightly,
the darkness must be present."*

Sir Francis Bacon

Late August

Sawyer sat on the sofa watching TV, a drink in his hand. The news was showing Queen Elizabeth waving to the crowds and smiling at the unveiling of the public display in the British Museum for the manuscripts of Sir Francis Bacon's plays. He glanced down at his mobile phone.

"Look Brian, darling. They'll call as soon as there's any news. Staring at it won't help."

Sawyer looked over at his wife who was nestled in under his shoulder and kissed her on the forehead. The shock of feeling love for this woman still caught him by surprise.

"I suppose so honey, but I can't help being anxious."

"I know, I know," she murmured. "I'm thinking of her too. She doesn't have many people around her anymore, does she?"

"No."

Fifty miles away in Westminster Hospital Fiona crouched sweating and screaming. Two members of staff were fussing over her. Her body filled with pain once more as the contractions intensified, coming closer and closer together. She had refused the epidural and didn't want a Caesarean. She wanted the birth to be as natural as possible. She wanted to feel everything, to be close to the moment.

Dan sat next to his wife, stroking her arm as she lay on the bed, his heart in his mouth as she struggled through the final stages of the delivery. The scar on his throat still throbbed but as the baby arrived any pain was washed away. An intense wave of emotion, of such happiness swept through him, he thought he was going to explode with joy.

"It's a boy." The midwife smiled as she bundled the tiny infant into Fiona's arms. "Congratulations."

Dan stood up in a daze and leant over to kiss Fiona. Pulling him close, she whispered in his ear. "Come and say hello to our son Francis."

The End.

Author's Notes

Hi, I hope you enjoyed my book! The Queen and Prince William are both hopefully doing well, and regardless of who wrote them, Shakespeare's plays are incredible. This book is dedicated to my own father, who, before he died, spent many years, writing about the Shakespeare Authorship Question, alongside great talents such as the academic Thomas Bokenham who discovered the ciphers. However that most cruel of diseases, Alzheimer's, claimed dad's mind and the work was never completed.

I decided to take elements of their story, simplify it all and turn it into a thriller. It's a mix of fact, speculation, rumour and my imagination.

Calling all treasure hunters! I reckon Shakespeare's Truth *does exist – I've hidden a cipher in the chapter involving the London Eye that, if you are smart enough, reveals where I think it really is. Imagine if you found it!*

Rex

rex@rexrichards.com

PS If you like the book – tell your friends. There is no big publisher supporting me, so if you can help – it won't be forgotten. If the book does well, I will give what I can to the Alzheimer's charity which gave my mum such support when things were so very hard for her at home.